MARTYN J. PASS
TIM MASON

Martyn J. Pass is the author of many bestselling books including 'Project - 16, 'The Wolf and the Bear' and 'The Unfinished Tale of Sophie Anderson'. He lives in the United Kingdom.

martynjpass@outlook.com.

ALSO BY MARTYN J. PASS

AT THE DAWN OF THE RUINED SUN
WAITING FOR RED (With Dani Pass)
SOUL AT WAR
HAGGART'S DAWN

THE UNFINISHED TALE OF SOPHIE
ANDERSON

THE TRIDENT SERIES
TRIDENT: DEAD SIEGE
TRIDENT: COLD VENGEANCE
TRIDENT: RAW JUSTICE

TALES FROM THE BRINK SERIES

PROJECT - 16
SHEPHERD
PROJECT - 17
THE BRINK
BEYOND HOPE
THE WOLF AND THE BEAR

TRIDENT

RAW JUSTICE

MARTYN J. PASS
TIM MASON

TRIDENT

RAW JUSTICE

GLOSSARY OF TERMS

HUD: Head-up-display – the screen that is overlaid upon the inside of the operator's helmet. It displays target information, health and armor status, and communication data.

DZ: The drop zone in any operation involving aerial deployment.

LZ: The landing zone in any operation involving aerial deployment and refers to the intended landing site for aircraft.

OVERWATCH: The independent action of a Sniper deployed to a stationary position 'watching over' a particular target or structure, ready to engage at his or her own discretion.

FARGO: The FARGO Company, responsible for the manufacture of high-end combat suits and technology to both Earth military and non-military organizations. Originally founded by former Earth Government Contractors, FARGO led the way in top of the range military equipment such as armor, weapons and fighting vehicles but more recently moved into the commercial sector, developing civilian tech as well.

ETA: Estimated time of arrival.

JAG: The Judge Advocate General's Corps, a branch of the military specializing in military law and justice.

PRT: Private response team. The name given to companies formed after the Mars War to fill the vacuum left by severe Earth Military downsizing. PRT companies can be hired to deal with domestic armed conflicts but are forbidden to take part in Earth Government military action unless specifically called upon to do so. All PRT companies must be registered and are ranked annually on a public table based on performance and casualty rates.

RosCO: The leading producer of robotic construction equipment and tools, a subsidiary of CHERICA-AUTO.

CHERICA-AUTO: One of the earliest manufacturers and suppliers of affordable exo-shells to Earth Government during the Mars War.

UNITED GALACTIC COMMONWEALTH: The UGC was founded after the first colonists began to leave Earth's solar system and a unified form of government was needed that allowed fair representation from all parties involved.

PROTECTORAT: The Protectorat is a Police Force that maintains jurisdiction across all of Earth Gov. space and has the power to act on its behalf in nearly all legal matters, sometimes overruling even local government laws and verdicts.

AO: Area of Operation.

DEATH SQUADS: Highly illegal synthetic humanoid units manufactured and made available for hire somewhere within the Commonwealth. Despite efforts to find and destroy the manufacturing base, these artificial 'hit-men' are rarely seen and are only affordable to the very elite.

PROLOGUE

NOCTIS LABYRINTHUS
16 MONTHS BEFORE THE MARTIAN SURRENDER

The dropship fell from the sky with little grace but demonstrating an enormous amount of skill on behalf of the pilot. Negotiating the jagged valleys of Mars was no small thing, especially when maintaining a safe distance below the scanner range could make the difference between life and death. Anyone observing the hulking shape might have mistaken it for a damaged vessel, fighting desperately to minimize the impact of an incoming crash. What they would have seen was a sudden pull of the stick, a brief jet of exhaust and a smooth return to a normal flight plan.

On this occasion, the pilot had been handpicked for just such skill. No rookie could ever have been trusted with a mission of this nature and especially not one who might have gone on to blab about what, or more precisely *who* was on board. The girl with the purple-streaked hair had come as the first recommendation from the Air Marshal. As General Alexander Bourmont sat watching her from the back, he realized that the choice had been a good one. From the moment he and his bodyguard of Special Forces agents had strapped in, the pilot had said nothing. Taking all her cues from the NavCom which the General altered from where he sat, she never asked a single question or turned around once to view her cargo. Instead she seemed to laser-focus on the displays before her, right up until the moment she settled the craft on the jutting outcrop of stone which Bourmont had chosen specifically for their meeting.

"We won't be long," he said to her as his team disembarked. The dust and the whipping air from the engines made speech almost impossible. "Wait here."

"Aye, sir," she replied – the only two words she would ever speak to him that day. Then the General was gone, and his team led the way ahead of him into the mouth of an abandoned mine shaft.

Twenty minutes passed before the Special Forces team reappeared with the General between them. They climbed on board and strapped in. The NavCom laid out the directions for Operation Headquarters and the pilot took the dropship back into the darkening skies above the mining facility of Noctis Labyrinthus and turned for friendly territory.

A week later and Chief of Staff Robert Wash advised the President of Earth Government to send forces to capture those very same mines – a force of several divisions that had expected their enemy to be very few and very surprised. The Intel had been good; Noctis Labyrinthus was a weak spot in the Martian defenses and would provide such a victory that would propel Wash into the Governor seat of Alaska back on Earth with a view to the Presidency once the war was over. Instead, it became one of the bloodiest defeats in the entire campaign with the loss of nearly all forces in the attack, either through death, capture or missing in action. The Martians had been ready and had funneled all their available reserves into the tightly built mine shafts of the facility. What had once been a footstone to power had become a slippery slope into obscurity. Wash was relieved of his position and vanished behind a desk on the lunar colony to see out the last months of the war.

What few noticed was the sudden rise to fame of a certain General Alexander Bourmont in the wake of the disaster…

2

1

Alice's luxury speeder didn't slow for any of the space lanes between the platform and TRIDENT's new headquarters in the heart of the business district of Setti, Titan 5's hub city. I was grateful for that and as the vast sprawling network of commerce and wealth below pulsed with neon and halogen, I began to realize that Angel was in more trouble than I could ever realize. Taken from us the moment we set foot on the planet on charges of treason, we'd had no time to think and no chance to question the whole thing until it was too late.

"I don't care if he's on a cruise, call him back," cried Alice into her comms unit. "This isn't an unpaid parking ticket – this is high treason against one of our staff!"

My sister was flushed red with anger and yet still managed to maintain some semblance of dignity that came from years of waging war in boardrooms and meeting halls. I, on the other hand, had slipped into silence, settling back in the vast leather seats of the TRIDENT speeder with a third vodka in my hand, ice cubes and all.

"Treason," said Mason from the chair next to me. "Like she's even capable of that." He scratched the scar tissue that ran down his sternum without realizing that it'd become a new habit of his.

"She's not," I said flatly. "Period."

"Baz didn't seem so sure."

"Fuck Baz," I spat, draining my glass and reaching for another. "I can't believe he even opened his mouth after what happened. He looked *glad*."

"Is that why you left him behind?"

"Partly," I admitted. I added more ice just for something to do.

3

"Also, because Alice is right – wheels have been set in motion and the next one will be to impound the *Helios* as evidence. They'll want to turn her inside out if they think there'll be anything incriminating on board. All our security protocols are revoked on an accusation of treason."

"Kind of makes you glad for Argo's cleansing then."

"Kind of makes me think he's in this somewhere too."

"Seriously?" said Mason. I shook my head.

"Not like that. Maybe he's stirred up some hornet's nest and now we're the ones being bitten. I mean, where could they have dug up a charge of treason for a war that's been over for years?"

"You know Earth Gov.," he grinned. "You owe them something; they'll come for it eventually – even if you're dead."

"Especially if you're dead."

"True."

Alice swiped across her comms unit and sat back with a loud sigh, kicking both of her shoes into the other compartment like an angry child. She suddenly reminded me of her younger self, throwing a tantrum for losing a game.

"Got one of those for me?" she asked, pointing to my drink. Mason mixed a gin and tonic and passed it to her. "Thanks – you're a gent. Unlike my brother of course."

"He's only after a pay rise," I said.

"He can have it. You both can. But that won't help Angel, will it?"

"Tell me what you know so far," I said. She sighed, took a long pull from the glass and wiped her lips with a napkin.

"It's treason – all bets are off. Any other crime listed in the Galactic Law and Civil Rights Handbook, circa 1254BC, and we'd have heard about it. Treason though? Nothing. Nada. Zip. The paperwork from the Protectorat is valid. Of course, it would be, and it says nothing. The Earth Gov. Center for civil disputes here in Setti is saying nothing. Our own lawyers are in the dark. It's to be expected, my dear brother."

4

"So, she's screwed?" said Mason. Alice threw up a hand and shrugged.

"I couldn't say one way or the other. Treason is a big word. Back in the day, you could be charged with treason for leaving rations behind on Mars for the enemy to use. Treason included information exchange on social media. Treason also covered collusion with known informants even if you didn't realize that Mr. Jones next door to you was a Martian sympathizer. It was a terrible time for freedom even though the irony was that that was exactly what Mars was fighting for in the first place."

"So, what now?" I asked.

"You fight wars on the ground and in space with guns and zappy lasers, I fight in the courts. This is *my* thing so you're going to have to play this particular game my way if you want to see Angel alive again."

"Okay," I agreed. "So, what do Mason and I do then?"

"For now, nothing. I mean that! Don't even think about some crazy escape plan to rescue the damsel in distress from the evil witch's castle."

"Why would we?"

"I know you, Carter. Your first port of call was probably an all-out assault on where ever it was that they were keeping her, and I have no doubt whatsoever that you'd have managed it too."

"But?"

"But you'd have doomed her to a life in exile and TRIDENT INC. would have been shut down. You know this."

I nodded and grinned.

"Can't blame me for thinking about it," I said.

"I don't." She smiled and finished her drink. Mason reached for the glass, but she shook her head. "Thanks, but I need to keep a clear head. It's going to be a long night for all of us."

"And what about our ship?" I asked.

"Which one? The *Helios* will be impounded. Aleksei has warned us

5

of that, which means that he already has the paperwork on his desk as we speak. The sale of the *Aurelius* shouldn't be affected because the transaction was already underway before she docked. We have many friends and many favors outstanding which I plan to call in especially now we've got a hefty wad of credits coming our way and the prestige of bringing home a valuable relic."

"All this for Angel?" asked Mason.

"*Especially* for Angel," she said, turning pale as she spoke. "She was my choice and I hired her without your consent. I feel she's my responsibility."

"She's *our* responsibility," said Mason. She smiled and handed him the glass this time.

"Maybe I will have that second drink after all."

The new headquarters of TRIDENT INC. on Titan 5 was a modest tower block built from sleek looking stone the color of obsidian and it shimmered as the rain ran down its sides in great sheets. The speeder landed on the roof in Alice's personal parking zone and a weather shield was already in place before the doors even opened.

Walking beside us, Alice led the way to the elevator and, once inside, pushed the thumbprint reader for her own office level.

"Nice," said Mason.

"It's not," she smirked. "We bought it with the view to struggling financially for the next few years. When the prize money was agreed upon, I put it up for auction and picked out something more *appropriate*."

"You don't hang around," I said.

"Hanging around doesn't get you the top spot on the PRT Gold Standard lists, little brother."

"Capturing ancient vessels does though," I laughed.

"That it does, and TRIDENT INC. thank you both for that. You don't realize yet the impact that money is going to have on the business, on those who work for us and even for yourselves."

"Right now, I'd prefer to have Angel here reaping those rewards too," I said. Alice nodded.

"You're right," she said. "I can't switch off from the job. Sorry. There's just so much to do and at least paying for it all is no longer a burden."

We stepped out onto a luxury-carpeted hallway decorated with lavish but tasteful art arranged on the walls and on plinths all the way to her office. Most depicted great military leaders or images taken from decisive victories like the fall of Mars Prime or the burning of the *Acheron* during the Battle of Mars. There was even a painting of Admiral Argo, the hero of the same battle who also happened to be Captain Argo's father.

Mason stopped by the scorched data-map of one Colonel Edmond Aposa, framed in gold, and leaned closer to see the minute detail.

"A gift," said Alice without stopping. "From his daughter who fought in the same battle."

"Olympus Mons," he said.

"The very same."

"Seems like a strong Martian theme," I said. "Were we involved in any other wars?"

"Many, but our customers want to be reminded of victory, of a time when Earth Gov. fought back from the brink. You know the spiel."

"No point letting the truth get in the way of a good story," I said.

"This way," said Alice and we followed her through two enormous glass doors which parted at a wave of her hand. Then we were inside the beating heart of the company and we found it to be decorated in cats.

"Seriously?" I cried, taking in the feline obsession. "How is this professional?"

"I can't help it, I love them!" she laughed. "Aren't they cute?"

"They're hideous!" I said and Mason's face agreed but he didn't say it aloud. "How did you end up with so much crap?"

"Gifts from happy customers. It started years ago when I put up a

7

couple of pictures of them on Ajax. It spiraled from there. Have a seat."

"I don't think I want to," I said. "It feels creepy."

Her desk, an ornately carved thing from some distant planet, was crawling with the ceramic monsters, all looking directly at me and grinning. Mason and I took the big leather seats in front of them and she sat in her own chair.

"Try to look past the cats and let's get some work done, okay? It's going to be a long night as it is. We should order food."

"Now I'm listening," said Mason.

Alice called up for supper from the diner across the street and it was delivered to her office less than twenty minutes later. I dragged a coffee table towards us and laid out the food, piling up a plateful while we caught up on some trivial news. Then, when we'd begun to eat, Alice looked at us both and pressed a button on her desk.

"Okay, might as well get this done while we're here. Full debrief for the board, omitting anything of a level 1 classified nature, of course. Just audio so keep eating."

And so, we did. From all that happened on Golan IV to some of Captain Argo's involvement and our crash landing in pirate territory. Between us, Mason and I managed to cover the salient details in as brief an account as possible and Alice listened to it all. The food vanished and the clock turned. As I got up to pour us some more drinks from the world's largest liquor cabinet, Mason finished with his account of the taking of the *Aurelius* even though he failed to add that he was off his head on combat meds at the time.

"That's all?" asked Alice, reaching to turn off the recorder. We nodded and I passed her another gin. "The files will fill in the gaps I guess."

"They should," I added.

She turned off the device and let out a long low whistle. Then she examined her drink and found it to her satisfaction, gingerly sipping at it.

"Some of it I knew," she said. "Some I didn't. You've been through the wringer. Poor Jack though. I'll have many letters to send tomorrow. Families. Other organizations. You took some serious losses."

"We did," said Mason. "But a lot of lives were saved too."

"Yes, they were."

Outside the wind was blowing hard, sending sheets of driving rain across the glass that ran in strange curving streams. I could see my reflection in it, and I turned away.

"Formalities aside," I said. "Let's talk about Angel."

"Okay."

"What happens now?"

Alice opened a drawer and took out a manila envelope, casting it onto her desk so that it slid towards me.

"Officially you're all supposed to be on a three-week psyche evaluation at the company retreat in the hills. As we're new here I took the liberty of buying up some prime real estate for just this reason. Nice place, overlooking the most beautiful pine forests you've ever seen."

"You don't expect us to go now, do you?" cried Mason.

"On paper, you're legally obliged to."

"And off paper?" I asked.

"Three weeks, that's all I can give you. After that, you'll be expected to report for duty following a full physical. In that time, you'd be exempt from any kind of interrogation or surveillance because of medical grounds. It's the only leg we have to stand on given that treason trumps every other protocol we ever bought. At least your mental wellbeing buys us some time."

"To prove her innocence," I said. Alice nodded. "You don't think it can be done through the courts?" She gave me a sardonic 'what do you think?' kind of smile and drank some more. "I guess not."

"Look at it this way – the case is so cold it's frozen. How many

9

years since the war? And her accuser has sat on it for this long? I don't buy it, and neither will Aleksei. I can already hear him saying 'who have you pissed off this time?'."

"What about Carter's theory that Argo might have something to do with it?"

"Directly?" she asked. Mason shook his head. "Stirring up the pot, so to speak? It's possible and he might be the first place to start given that his fleet has just reported in from some backwater galaxy in the middle of nowhere."

"Intact?" I asked, remembering his date with the alien ships.

"Apparently according to the morning news feeds but don't expect a full report from the Admiralty any time soon. Short of announcing world peace the Navy would never discuss matters of that nature with the civilian population."

"We might have to ask him ourselves," said Mason, turning to me. I grinned.

"Hold your horses," said Alice, her cheeks rosy with alcohol. "You're officially at the retreat."

"What can you do about that?" I asked.

"I can do what all good big sisters can – get their little brother out of the house without Mom and Dad knowing."

"I like it," said Mason.

"You will. But it'll only be for three weeks. If you can't find good hard evidence we can use, then I wouldn't expect to see Angel alive again. Do we understand each other?"

"Perfectly," I said. "About that…" She shook her head.

"No chance. In the eyes of the Protectorat, you could be just as guilty as she is. For treason cases, only her assigned legal representative will be allowed access and I'll be paying a lot of credits to have Aleksei be that person."

My heart sank a little. I'd have preferred to see her myself before leaving the planet, even if it was just to reassure her that we were working on her behalf. Alice, ever the perceptive sister, looked at me

10

with sympathetic eyes.

"I know," she said. "I'd have liked to have seen her too but for now she's out of our reach. Don't worry, she'll be looked after. We've got friends in the penal system. If there's any hint of trouble, we'll probably hear about it before it happens."

"We should probably worry more about whoever is stupid enough to try and hurt *her*," said Mason, laughing.

2

Not long before dawn, we separated; Alice to her own apartment where no doubt a certain ex-Martian soldier was waiting for her and we to a higher floor reserved for guests as a kind of in-house hotel. It was pure luxury with more of that lavish décor we'd already witnessed but certainly no cats in sight. Outside my room, Mason stopped.

"Set your alarm for eleven," he said. "I noticed the sign for the gym on our way up here. Things will look better after we've made some gains."

"I've yet to see you bench with that contraption," I grinned, pointing to his chest. He scratched it again and shook his head.

"Even without it, I'd still lift heavier than you, pal. Get some sleep and you might be more in tune with reality by eleven."

He turned to go but I stopped him. Something was bothering me.

"What is it?" he asked.

"Angel was a sniper, right? On Mars?"

"Yeah. So?"

"Hardly the best gig for an espionage trick."

"Doesn't rule out assassination though."

"True, but she was also a pilot."

"For a spell. What are you getting at?"

"Honestly? I don't know. Something's niggling at me though, something I'm trying to recall but it just won't come."

"Sleep on it. Like I said some gym time won't hurt the old brain functions will it?"

"Only if you drop your ass again."

"We had Titan food for supper – we should be okay."

"We better. Goodnight, man."

I went into my room and barely noticed how well stocked it was until I'd showered and sat in a towel to dry on the edge of the bed. Alice had intended for us to stop here all along and some of my usual stuff, toiletries, drinks etc. were in ample supply. I made the most of it, pouring myself a generous glass of vodka and adding ice from the mini-fridge built into the wall near the door. Then, sitting back down, I let out the breath I was holding and tried to think it all through. The alcohol I'd already had since leaving the *Helios* was now taking effect and I felt my mind drifting towards images of Angel. There were feelings that hung on the edge of reason that willed me to ignore all that I knew in favor of their serpent-charms.

I emptied the glass and changed into t-shirt and shorts, lying out on the bed to think even less about Angel and more about the next few days and what we were going to do about a charge of treason against one of our own. The exact opposite happened and as sleep washed over me, I thought I could just detect the faint scent of lemon tea and that natural perfume she sometimes wore on her days off.

"Real helpful," I said to myself. "You'd have made a great detective, Carter."

At eleven I was ready for the knock on my door, or perhaps the cannon blast that struck it; Mason liked to make sure the occupant of anywhere heard him when he knocked.

"You ready?" he said, already in his gym gear.

"Yeah, I guess."

"You look like shit," he laughed.

"Struggled to sleep. Let's get this over with and have some breakfast, okay?"

"Sure."

Down we went, taking the elevator to the third floor where an

13

empty gym of machines and free weights waited for us.

"Makes a change," said Mason, starting up a treadmill and beginning to warm up. "Apart from our ship most places are rammed at this time of the morning."

"I have a suspicion that it's no accident it's empty just when we needed a workout," I said. "My dear sister will have engineered this I suspect."

"She did," said a voice behind us and, strolling up to the empty machine next to Mason, she started a brisk jog in tight-fitting workout pants and a loose tee. I caught him looking at her side-on and made a mental note to play the 'that's my sister!' card the next chance I got.

"Is this normal for you?" I asked her.

"No," she replied. "I usually come here before going home, maybe around seven-thirty or eight. I figured you'd want to go early so I closed the place until after lunch."

"Considerate," I said. "Fancy benching with us?" She snorted a laugh and increased her pace.

"Other than the obvious fact that I'd out-lift either of you in a heartbeat-"

"Go on then," said Mason with a wry grin on his face. "Put your credits on the table and let's see what you've got."

Alice smirked and rolled her eyes. There was something between the two of them that made me anxious. They'd never been that flirty before.

"I don't do weights if I can help it," she fired back. "Not good for the company image to have a muscle-bound woman in charge. Our clients might mistake us for liberal feminists or something."

"*In charge*?" I laughed.

"Because you didn't want to be, oh my little brother!" she cried. "Don't make out I forced you into it."

"I'll let you have that one."

"And you'll let me have the next one too – Aleksei has been to see Angel. He'll be here at 12.30 to brief us. Don't be late. My office."

"Come on then," said Mason. "Let's get on with it."

True to his word, he smashed his personal best on the bench and made me look like a pussy. For all the years I'd known him this was nothing new, but I rather hoped he'd have at least one bad day after his extensive surgery. I was destined to be forever second best and as he grunted approval at his own performance, he wasted no time in mocking mine.

"FARGO spine my arse!" he laughed. "Is that all you've got?"

I half-rolled half-fell from the bench and got up, flexing my arms about until the pain eased off.

"Come on," I protested. "We stayed away from weights on the *Helios* until we landed. I'm rusty."

"That's what you'd call it, is it?" he grinned. "Come on, let's finish the workout and get ready for this brief. I'm eager to find out what this guy knows."

We knocked out the rest of the upper body push sets and dashed back upstairs to get cleaned up. Then, throwing on a hoodie and jeans with my TRIDENT INC. cap to hide the knotted mess of hair on my head, I met Mason on Alice's floor just as Aleksei arrived. A quick glance at myself in a mirror just outside the elevator reminded me that my beard was out of control and I was long overdue a trim. At that point personal grooming was just about bottom of my priority list.

Aleksei Rokossovsky was a name I only knew from company paperwork. He was one of, if not *the* best, legal co-ordinator outside of Earth Gov.'s own cadre and Alice had not exaggerated when she talked about spending a lot of money to have him working on our behalf. He was Martian born but had been a strong opponent of the war, arguing that Mars' long history with Earth and its cultural and commercial links, forged over many years, should not easily be broken. Alice had known him in part from her days in logistics and when we'd begun the company, a large amount of our start-up funds had gone into having his name on our books.

When we entered her office, Alice was pouring coffee from a porcelain pot into delicate white cups on saucers. She looked up as we entered and Aleksei turned from the window he was staring out of and smiled. Tall, thin and dressed in a perfectly fitting grey suit, the legal backbone of Angel's defense looked formidable. His jawline appeared to have been carved out of granite yet a glint in his deep jade eyes softened those hard edges. He wore his salt and pepper hair swept back, revealing a sharply defined widow's peak on the top of a weathered brow.

He came towards us and extended his hand. We shook. Fingers of steel cords gripped me, and I returned the pressure.

"Aleksei Rokossovsky," he smiled. "You must be Carter. I'm assuming there's a first name to go with that."

"Don't ask," laughed Alice. "He's made me call him by our last name since he was six."

"A pleasure," I said. "This is Mason." They shook and Alice began handing out the cups before we all sat down.

"The kitchen will send up a late breakfast shortly," she explained. "In the meanwhile, we should make a start – I know you have a busy day ahead, Aleksei." He tilted his head in a graceful gesture. He was smooth; every twitch of muscle fiber seemed perfectly used. He reminded me of a performer, an actor who knows that every single action he makes is being assessed and marked.

"Tell me first, how is Angel?"

"She's being held at a high-security detention center, isolated of course, but it has a good reputation. Although I still do not have access to the entire case yet, what I do know tells me that we're dealing with something much bigger than Angel or even TRIDENT INC." He took up a tablet and began tapping at the screen, rattling out dates, times and co-ordinates for key locations on Mars during the war that he showed were within Angel's AO at the time.

"So far, she's not been formally charged, which is good news. But they're building a case and this is just the beginning. They had enough to arrest her with but that does buy us some time."

"What exactly is she accused of?" I asked.

"Treason," he said. "Vague, isn't it? But that's all they're offering right now. They have her at several key locations where alleged incidents of collusion with the enemy took place. They have a number of names that they're keeping to themselves, names of Martian informants and a few Earth Gov. brass that I suspect may be behind the accusations in the first place."

"All this for Angel? Is no one else implicated?"

"Angel is the start. She admits that she was the pilot for several 'dark' missions but claims she knew nothing about their intentions, which is to be expected from a pilot; it's not her job to ask, just to fly. Others are involved but I haven't been privy to their names yet."

"So, what's the next step?" asked Alice.

"Once the information is given to me, I can begin formulating a defense. Until then we'll just have to sit tight."

I looked at Mason who shook his head. Sitting tight wasn't a phrase we used often.

"Did Angel say anything else?" I asked. Aleksei sipped his coffee with such gentleness that he barely seemed to take any.

"Would you like my honest answer or the rhetoric of a qualified representative of the law?"

"Both."

"The law first then. In my opinion proving her innocence is what your credits are paying for but in cases like this with such far-reaching effects for those involved, success is a remote possibility. She's at the bottom of the proverbial hill, deliberately, and as we all know excrement is subject to the laws of gravity."

"But?"

"As a friend of TRIDENT, and of Alice, my belief is that she's holding back. I believe that from her expression and choice of words she's protecting someone or something and she's willing to suffer in

17

order to continue that protection. Even, perhaps to death. This may not appear to be, but is in fact, good news."

"So what should we do?" asked Alice, looking grave.

"I can only buy you time. I have the ability to string out the case, take my time so to speak, but in the end without knowing what really happened on Mars and Angel's true involvement, eventually, the Prosecution will succeed, and she will be executed."

"You're that sure the case will go against her?" asked Mason. He nodded and barely a hair moved on his head.

"Do you believe that Earth Government would be willing to try and convict say, a General or an Admiral of the Fleet over a lowly pilot who works for a private response team?"

"I take your point."

"Indeed. Right now, public opinion of the Martian war has changed and history will soon rewrite itself with Earth as the villain. The last thing the President will want is another scandal about a war she's trying to put behind her administration. I'd even go as far to say that if word got out that somehow Earth Government, through negligence or intention, passed over a chance to end the bloodshed earlier than it did, it would shake the very foundations of power."

"Which might actually be a reason to do so," I said. Aleksei grinned and suddenly I felt like both his best friend and his worst enemy. I hoped I'd never find myself sat in court with him on the prosecuting side.

"Generally speaking, most 'crimes' have a trail to follow. Either money or power or lust. We can rule out a sexual element, perhaps, but money and power coupled with two warring Governments? I know where I would begin to look." Aleksei glanced at his comms unit and sighed. "My apologies, Alice. I will have to pass on the meal."

"Perhaps dinner then?" she offered, rising to her feet.

"Tonight?" Another look at the sleek and elegant unit on his arm. "Yes, that would be possible."

"Salvatore's at eight."

"Wonderful. I would very much like to see your partner again. We didn't finish our discussion on the ruins beneath Olympus Mons."

"I'm sure he'd be glad to do so tonight."

Turning to us his face became stern.

"Alice has shared a little of what has occurred between yourselves and Captain Argo. You may not know this but very recently that man has become a thorn in many sides. Perhaps there is a link. I do not know."

He reached into his suit pocket and barely creased the fabric before pulling out a slender rectangle of metal.

"My card. The number is secure and is capable of receiving subspace transmissions with little degradation. I do not wish to know the details of what you intend to do but any information, no matter how trivial it may seem to you, *must* be passed on to me as soon as possible. It may gain us further time. Bear in mind that the nature in which you acquire this should also be taken into account."

He stood up. Then, shaking Alice's hand, he turned to go.

"Anything, Carter. I mean it. And if I were you I would consider paying your old friend a visit. Good day."

With that, he left and as the door closed behind him it opened again to allow two floating trays of food to enter. Behind them, two members of the kitchen staff carried jugs of fruit juice and a rack of plates, knives, and forks. As it passed him by, the granite-featured man reached out, snatched a pastry and grinned. He was human after all.

"More for us I guess," said Mason helping himself.

"I'd hate for you to go hungry."

"We need to keep up our strength. Besides, free food always tastes better."

"It's hardly free!" cried Alice. "But I reckon you've earned it."

We ate in silence and I stared down at the card Aleksei had given me between mouthfuls of toast and sausage. I didn't like the feeling I

19

was getting. Angel's case was looking less and less hopeful and here we were, laughing over a meal she might never be able to enjoy again.

I put down my plate, wiped my hands and coughed.

"Right, let's get on with it," I snapped, perhaps more at myself than the others. "We've wasted enough time."

"Wasted?" asked Alice with a flare of anger tipping the edge of her words.

"What did he tell us we didn't already know? That Angel is screwed unless we can get to the bottom of what exactly happened? That although he's one of the best lawyers we can find he can basically do nothing with what he has?"

Alice didn't reply. She stared at me from across the desk and folded her hands neatly in her lap.

"All this is true. Go on," she said.

"And we're sitting here, laughing and joking, while she's rotting in a cell. Time is running out and-" She held up her hand.

"We're not sitting here idle, Carter," she said very softly. "You almost died out there on Golan IV and again on the way home. Don't you think we both have a right to a few hours together before you rush off again? Do you not think that perhaps we needed to stop being heroes for five minutes so I can see the little brother I thought I'd lost twice over? Is that so selfish a thing to ask?"

Burning hot with shame I let out a sigh and sat back down. I wanted to sulk, just like old times, but she wouldn't even let me have that. She continued.

"For us, there aren't going to be downtimes very often. So you go out there and rescue Angel and all is well – what then? Do you think for one minute that you're going to sit down and take a year out? No, I thought not. Neither am I. It's who we are, it's what we do. So in answer to the question you didn't ask – no, I don't feel ashamed to have a handful of minutes with you before you leave. So eat your bloody food and grant me this time."

"You're a dick to sisters trying to be sisters, pal," snorted Mason and the tension broke.

"You know," I said, "I think I preferred you on the combat meds. Where did that Mason go?"

"Disco-dancing Mason? I never heard of that guy."

So we laughed and we joked and we ate some more and I realized she was right. In all the carnage and flying around I'd forgotten what mattered most to me.

When the trays were taken away and we'd settled down with some more coffee, Alice nodded to me and smiled.

"Now you may start. Let's get to work. What's the plan?"

"A ship," said Mason. "Something fast. Light. Ready to set sail now."

"That can get us to Argo?" I asked. "How far away is he?"

Alice tapped on her desk and brought up the Naval dispatch page.

"If you were to set off tomorrow morning you could intercept him at his current speed the same day."

"What about credits?" I asked her.

"Not a problem. I've already put the wheels in motion. New identities, cards, and comms units which I insist you wear this time."

"Weapons?" I said, turning to Mason.

"We go shopping."

"How do we get them through customs without our PRT credentials?"

"I've managed to secure you..." Here she paused and made a mock shudder of her shoulders. "Employment with another firm. I know, I know, it pained me but Alan over at Hasker & Finn owed me one. You'll be working on his behalf so to speak."

"Wow," I laughed. "That must have hurt."

"It did. Caplan's team will be waking up to new orders that I'm sure will result in a nasty communique by around noon. He drew the short straw and will be on loan to Alan for the next six weeks. Let's move

21

on."

"What do we have that can send subspace messages to Aleksei?" asked Mason. I shrugged.

"Damned if I know," I said. "Ideas?"

"If we rigged him up, Thor could be kitted out with a transmitter. He can generate the power needed I guess."

"You'd take Thor with us?" I laughed. "That'd be a hoot. Probably get us killed or arrested or both."

"It would handle a problem I have," explained Alice. "The *Helios* will be scoured for evidence and that includes any robotic units. Baz called me last night and expressed his concerns for him. I planned to have him taken off the ship. As it turns out Jack hadn't declared him on the official cargo manifest in the first place."

"Oh shit," I said to myself. "You're both serious aren't you?"

"Deadly," said Mason. "I could stow all kinds of kit inside him and customs couldn't touch him."

"I want it on the books that I said it's a bad idea."

"You haven't said it yet," laughed Alice.

"It's a bad idea. There. Make a note in the log."

"Done. But he saved your life. Twice in fact."

"That doesn't make us friends. It means he's an efficient jack-hammer, that's all. I'm not taking my plasma-wrench with us, am I?"

"You need to make your mind up, pal," said Mason. "One minute you like him, the next you don't."

"I like my robots at a safe distance, that's all. And you know that as soon as we tell him what the plan is he's going to go loopy again and dress up like it's cosplay."

"What?" cried Alice. "What's that about?"

"Don't ask," said Mason. "It's a long story."

"Speaking of Baz..." she said.

"I hate to say it but we'll need him. He pissed me off after Angel was taken and I'll have some words with him, but for now, it's best to keep him with the ship. When we're ready to leave can you arrange for the two of them to meet us without alerting the Protectorat?"

"I can do my best. I'll have Jo begin work on the ship the moment they release it. I've signed off on the modifications you requested and I'll use the time to have her fully serviced."

"Thanks," I said. "I mean it."

"I know you do," she grinned. "But there'll be a price to pay once you return."

Mason looked at me and shrugged.

"I really don't like the sounds of that."

3

We left TRIDENT INC. in the mid-afternoon, taking a cab across the city towards the commercial district. The rain began to fall almost as soon as we got outside and as the driverless vehicle deftly negotiated the busy ground traffic, our view of the streets blurred in the driving sheets of the stuff. I could see strange shapes through the glass, shimmering forms of people going to and fro, shopping, eating, living. After months in deep space, the feeling was strange. It felt more alien than what we'd seen on Mars or even on Golan IV and I sat back, staring at the NavCom as it worked its calculations.

"Too long," said Mason, reading my thoughts. "Alice was right. We go from one job to the next and we've stopped caring for the very thing we signed up to protect. *Them*." He gestured to the people out there, on the streets, just doing their day-to-day stuff.

"What are you saying?" I asked.

"I'm saying that once we've helped Angel then perhaps we should take that trip to the hills. A few weeks of doing nothing and a chat with an attractive psycho-analyst might do us some good."

"Or maybe you'd prefer more time with my sister?" I laughed. He grinned. "But yeah, maybe you're on to something there. I'm staring out of this window and I don't recognize what I see. That can't be good."

"No, it's not."

"I look and I start to feel fear. Like arriving someplace we're not welcome."

"Like homecoming day after Mars?"

"Kind of. More subtle though, like a faint memory of a feeling.

24

Shit, what am I saying? I sound like I've cracked already."

"For a minute there, back at the Magnus Gate when we faced the pirate horde, I thought you had."

I turned in my seat to look at him. He didn't move though. He just stared out of the window.

"Explain."

"Things you said. The risks you took. Alarm bells were ringing. For a split second, I thought we were done, that we'd lost our edge. Then, later, when I came out from the op with a new chest, it dawned on me that we weren't indestructible anymore. You with your spine, now me with this-" He scratched it again. "And I'm thinking 'do we carry on or call it a day?'"

I said nothing. He was only voicing something I heard in my mind more and more often now. It was the drip-drip of confidence being eroded away. It was the first step of many on the road to retirement. It was terrifying to hear him say it out loud. I was just about to say something when he spoke again and that moment, though I wouldn't realize it until many years later, defined everything that came after it. I sometimes try to think what might have happened had I managed to speak first and I shudder at the thought.

"But then I saw you crawling out of that pit when they fried your spine. I didn't say it at the time, but I could just see you clawing your way up and I thought to myself 'there's our edge'. Where others gave up, we were willing to crawl on, to keep going, to fight on. My chest caved in and I fought on. You had your spine turned to mulch and you fought on. Angel right now is fighting on. I know she's waiting for us to help her, but she's fighting too. She didn't give up when they took her. We've never given up. Not on the mission and not on each other. That's why we'll still be doing this work until the very end. That's our edge."

I said nothing. The streets passed us by and blur turned to sharply defined edges and colors. People. Lives. Coming and going and us, setting out again, still fighting, still refusing to surrender.

25

He had a point and it was a bloody good one.

We pulled up outside Vertigo Flyers & Light Craft just as the rain decided to dial it up a notch. Adjusting the cap and the collar of my jacket, I ran into the reception area of the large open court and almost collided with the glass door coming back at me.

"Sorry!" cried the young man on the desk. "It's playing up. It won't close when the rain starts coming in."

"But it will when paying customers do?" replied Mason, shaking off his long leather coat. The man flushed scarlet.

"How c-c-can I help you today?" he stammered.

"We'd like to look at your high-end craft, something inter-galactic but favoring speed over payload," I explained. The young man smiled and revealed a mouthful of shiny white teeth.

"I'll have one of our staff come and show you around immediately. Would you like to take a seat?"

We didn't. Instead, we stood looking at some of the speeders parked in the window display. Sleek, colorful things that would no doubt crumple in a collision especially given that they were manually controlled and not guided by NavCom. Mason gave his attention to some of the bigger models, the Ford Galactica, a bulky tank-like thing, and I ran my fingertips over the hood of a Tri-Star Rover, the kind only built on Earth these days, but neither of us were buying.

"Hi!" came a sugary-sweet voice from behind us and we turned. I almost collapsed there and then for, standing in the archway to the outer forecourt, stood O'Shea – or his ghost. "My name is Patrick. What are you fellas in the market for today?"

"Are you seeing this?" whispered Mason.

"I'm glad both of us are. It's him, right?"

"It can't be. It has to be a relation or something."

"Or a clone!"

They were identical. In spite of the poorly fitted suit he wore, that

26

shock of red hair framing that distinctive face was something I would never forget. He came closer, his hand outstretched and a wide toothy grin on his lips.

"And you boys are?" he said. Even the voice was the same, that annoying Irish lilt.

"Wes," I said. "And this is my business partner, Tom."

"A pleasure," he replied and shook both our hands. He had feeble, clammy fingers and it felt like I was shaking a dead squid. "My colleague over there says you're in the market for space travel, am I right?"

"Yeah," I managed to say, steadying myself by grasping the rails of the Tri-Star Rover. "High speed over payload."

"Looking to cover some ground eh?" he laughed – if a noise like that could be considered 'laughter'. It sounded more like a dozen grinding gears. "Come this way."

He set off through the arch and, reluctantly, we followed. Outside a shimmering forcefield crackled against the rain overhead, forming a massive dome over the entire forecourt. The size of vessel we were looking for would never have fitted inside that space, large as it was, so I assumed he had something else in mind.

"Here we are," he said, reaching the middle and standing still. "If you'd care to step inside the circle we can begin looking at what we have to offer."

We did so and noted that there was a glassy blue ring set into the concrete floor about ten meters in diameter. Once inside O'Shea's ghost touched his wrist and the forecourt vanished into darkness.

"Fancy, eh?" he chuckled. "Fools everyone. It's the latest in holographic imaging. Best on the market."

"You'd better hope that your product lives up to it then," growled Mason. If he was shaken by this, Patrick didn't show it.

"Oh, it will. Don't worry."

He touched his wrist again and suddenly we were standing on a metal platform that floated in the deep dark void of space. Even the

27

air went cool, almost too cool, and there was nothing but eerie music far off, almost imperceptible.

"Let's start with some basic models and refine just what it is we can sell you today," he began. "Here at Vertigo Flyers & Light Craft, we hope that it's the brilliant investments that will make you dizzy and not our prices."

"Nice pitch," I said.

"You think so? I made it up myself." He pressed some more on his wrist and there was a brilliant flash of light. A ship sped into view, turning at the last minute to float before us displaying its port side.

"Here we have the *Darkstar*, a class D light craft capable of inter-galactic travel up to twelve pargams. It can hold a class E and F payload or below and requires a crew of twelve persons of rank 6B or higher. We also offer to outfit any of our ships with NavCom guidance units and auto-crew consoles should you wish to sail with less of a compliment."

It was nice and Mason seemed to agree but twelve pargams was slow and limited between jumps. We needed at least sixteen or higher given that our time frame was only three weeks.

"Something faster," said Mason. "Sixteen to twenty pargams."

"And the payload?"

"E and F are fine. We'll have a limited crew so factor in the guidance units if you please."

"Sure," he grinned, no doubt hearing the cash box rattling already. "I've got just the thing."

He tapped again and the *Darkstar* shot off into outer space. From where it went came another ship, long and elegant with bluff bows and a fine line. It almost slid into view, turned sharply and drew up before us.

"This, my friends, is the *Hikane*. Beautiful, isn't she? I can see you boys aren't messing around here so I've jumped right to a class A light craft. She boasts no less than twenty pargams of travel and a B rated payload. A crew of thirty-five is needed but we can offer you two

FARGO control consoles which would reduce that to just three operating pilots of rank 4A or higher. How does that sound?"

I looked at Mason and he was grinning. It was a fine ship, there was no doubt about that but we would be parting with a serious amount of credits. What the hell would Alice say?

"Go on," I said. "Hit me with the figures."

"Wouldn't you like to take a look around her first?" He smiled again and I felt a cold shiver run down my FARGO spine. For a split second, I was back in that tunnel, running again.

"Sure," said Mason.

"Be my guest," said Patrick and the *Hikane* was suddenly closer now with its port cargo door beginning to slide open. The next thing we knew we were inside, staring at glossy bulkheads and standing on a plush carpeted floor. It looked more like a pleasure yacht than a starship.

"All that you see can be changed," he explained. "But this is our most popular theme. We call it the *modern adventurer*."

"We're looking for a quick sale," I said. "We expect to leave in her tomorrow. Is that going to be a problem?"

"Well, I..." Patrick blanched and tried to regain his composure. "If you were able to hold off on your trip until, say, next week we could be sure to have her in ship-shape condition and to our Vertigo high standard – get it? Vertigo?"

"That won't be possible," I said. I turned to Mason. "Maybe we should try Franko's?"

"Now hold on," cried Patrick. "I never said we couldn't come to an arrangement of some sort. No need to go to the competition, eh guys? I can see you want this ship but-"

"How much is it going to cost to have her ready by tomorrow?" said Mason.

"Cost isn't the issue, fellas, it-"

"How much?"

He was sweating now and I felt a sudden pleasure. If he was a member of the O'Shea family then his suffering might go a small way towards paying off their debt to my dead spine. He began working his wrist control, sending messages back and forth to what I assumed would be the space yard above us. Some engineer was probably being chewed out right about now.

"I've spoken to the team," he stammered. "But he's saying that it would take several work crews to pull this off."

"How much?" I said again.

"On top of the quote I'm about to give you..." He paused. Looked down. "Two-fifty."

I laughed and so did Mason. Patrick laughed, albeit with a nervous tremor.

"Too high, right?" he said, probably seeing his commission vanishing down the drain. I looked at my own wrist unit and saw Alice's message waiting for me.

YOU'LL BE THE DEATH OF ME. JUST BUY IT.

"Looks like you've got yourself a deal," I said and held out my hand. "Now let's talk 'extras'."

We left Vertigo Flyers & Light Craft just as the rain stopped and we hailed a cab to take us westward to our next destination. When we got in, Mason turned and held up his own wrist unit for me to see.

"My new friend Sharky is going to the space-yard to fit the weapon systems," he said. "Look at those specs."

I did. Forward plasma lances and several broadside cannon – nowhere near the output of the *Helios* but sharp enough teeth in case we came under attack.

"He says he will have to wire them into the FARGO units because at the speeds we'll be traveling no human could calculate the firing patterns in time."

"Do it," I said. "I hope we won't need them but I'll be happier having them on board. After what we've been through it's taking all my willpower not to buy a battlecruiser. But I do find it amazing how quickly people will move when you throw money at them."

"Ain't that the truth? I've known Sharky for all of ten minutes and he's already behaving like we're old friends. Money really does have a language of its own."

We sat there in silence for a time and watched the city of Setti pass us by. I tried not to think about Angel but it was becoming increasingly more difficult. Would I have felt that way about Baz had the roles been different? Maybe. He was like a son to me in one way or another. A downright irritating disappointment of a son. A child I kind of wished hadn't made it to the egg over all those other-

"Look at that," said Mason, breaking and entering my train of thought. I turned to look out of his window and at first, I couldn't quite understand what he was seeing. Maybe I didn't *want* to see it. But I did and the moment understanding dawned on me I pressed the STOP paddle on the control panel of the taxi and climbed out.

"I'm not seeing things, am I?" I said to Mason. He shook his head. "It's him."

"How the hell did he get here? And why is he trying to thumb a ride?

From where he stood on the corner of the street, Thor, the robot on board the *Helios* with questionable self-awareness, held out one of his enormous robotic limbs, the one that gave him his name – a gigantic construction hammer. It pointed upwards the way a hitch-hiker's thumb might, and he glared at passers-by with bright vision slits. He looked different somehow, less bulky in his overall frame, but no shorter. He towered above the crowds who made a wide arc to avoid him.

"How did he escape Baz?" I asked.

"Who said he escaped? Knowing Baz, he probably let him go of his own accord."

I waited for a break in the traffic and then crossed the road towards

31

him. He hadn't seen us and so he continued to try and hail any one of the small, lightweight craft that zoomed by, all equally unable to carry someone, or something, of his size.

"Thor?" I said once we'd gotten closer. The robot turned on his waist axis, hammer still raised, and looked at us.

"Mr. Carter, sir?" he said in that awful Cockney accent we'd kind of gotten used to during our service together. "And Mr. Mason? The very people I've been lookin' for."

"What in the name of all that is good are you doing wandering the streets? Where's Baz? Why aren't you on the ship where we left you?"

"Baz dropped me off, sirs, told me to go lookin' for ya. He says you're goin' on your 'olidays and that I was to join you, sirs. If you'd be so kind as to 'ave me," he replied.

"He what?" cried Mason.

"Well sirs, beggin' your pardon, but I work for TRIDENT, right?"

"Well I-" I began but he cut me short.

"Well as an employee of one Alice Carter of TRIDENT INCORPORATED LIMITED-"

"But you're a-" I stopped myself short of finishing the sentence and thought again. Somehow acknowledging the origins of this... *machine*? Didn't sit well with me. On the other hand, saying that he was something more didn't seem appropriate either.

"Damn you, Jack," I said to myself. "What the hell have you created?"

"What?" said Mason. I shook my head.

"Nothing."

"Sir?" said Thor.

"Yeah?"

"Please don't speak about 'im like that."

"Who?"

"Jack, sir. Please don't speak badly about me mate, sir. He was good to me. Sir."

I looked at the bot and felt even worse. If Jack had been stood there,

I'd have throttled him myself. *How dare you mess with life, Jack?*

"Sorry, Thor. But we can't leave you to wander the streets, buddy. Where were you going before we showed up?"

"On a holiday, sir."

"To where?" I asked.

He looked puzzled if a bot could actually look puzzled. He turned his head to look up and down the street but he still had no answer when he returned to staring at me.

"I don't rightly know, sir."

I sighed and wondered if the Fates of life had chosen me to be made an example of.

"How about you come with Mason and I while we arrange some things?" The bot lit up with excitement.

"Really, sirs? I wouldn't be no bother, promise."

"I'm sure you won't," said Mason. "Come on, we're going this way."

"On our feet, sir?" he said.

"It looks like it."

How Mason found these places was a mystery to me. As far as I knew neither of us had been to Titan 5 before, we knew no one on the planet besides the staff of TRIDENT who'd come here recently and yet already he'd managed to source a Craft Weapon's firm of questionable repute and a small arms dealer. Sharky was already outfitting the *Hikane* with what I was sure would be the best kit for the job (Mason knew his weapons, it was that simple) and no doubt he'd referred him to the compound of plain white concrete walls and prefab storage units that formed Alan's used arms and armor. A garish neon sign hung over a wide gated archway that simply said ALAN'S. Beneath it, cast in a cold blue glow, were two towering defense bots that reminded me faintly of our encounter with the drones on Capus Nova. These were painted military green and sported twin Hydra cannons. They moved back and forth before the archway on clanking

33

tracks, digging great ruts into the tarmac beneath them.

"Wow," I said. "You've got to appreciate a good brand."

"It does what it says on the tin," said Mason. Then, to Thor, he said, "Friends of yours?"

"Model 8 Faradays, sirs. Not to be trifled wiv'"

We stepped closer to a glowing white arc that began and ended on either side of the arch. It didn't take the message stencilled on the floor to communicate what it meant. Step inside that arc without permission and you'd probably have enough time to realize your mistake before being turned into mulch.

"What's the protocol?" I asked. Mason shrugged.

"Maybe they're open to reason," he replied. Then, stepping closer to the white line, he called to the bots. "Alan's expecting us."

They stopped patrolling and turned on their waist axis. Not a sound came from them and the nearest began rolling towards us. Well oiled, well maintained. It boded well for the product.

"Sanders?" said a voice from the machine that now loomed over us, maybe twelve feet high, maybe more. It was Alan himself, speaking through the bot.

"Yeah, Sharky sent me," said Mason. I looked at him and mouthed the word 'Sanders'. He grinned.

"Yeah yeah, he warned me you'd be coming. Didn't say anything about your bodyguard robot though. He'll have to wait outside."

"No deal," I said, jumping in. "He's with us."

"Look, pal, I don't know you from shit. You ditch the bot, or we don't transact. It's that simple." I turned to Thor.

"Let's go, buddy. We're not welcome here."

"But sir-" he began but I waved him away.

"Let's go. I'm not wasting credits on this goon. I'm sure his competition will welcome us."

Mason looked at me and smiled. Then, turning back to the bot, he raised his hand and saluted.

"Kindly go and self-replicate."

We began walking away and the bots began to roll towards us, Hydra cannons raised. We kept on walking.

"Okay, okay," said Alan. "He can come. In fact, I have a few bits he might be interested in. Not seen his type for some time. All got replaced a while back with CHERICA-AUTO units, the new ZES4 enviro types."

Something like a snort of derision came from Thor but he fell in beside us as the two defense bots parted and made for the archway. We followed.

4

The compound opened up before us just as the reinforced doors
closed shut behind us. There were many buildings, each tall and wide
and made from the same blast-crete that old military surface
installations had once been quickly and cheaply constructed from.
Each one was blazoned with a stencilled number and each one had its
own bot guarding the entrance, equally armed with the same twin
Hydra cannons as the gate guards. The road was well cared for,
lacking any kind of weathering and it appeared to be reinforced,
probably against damage from heavy vehicles.

"Reminds me of the Pargon conflict," said Mason.

"That's something I'm trying to forget, okay?" I laughed. "Which
way?"

"I guess we follow that," he said and pointed to a glowing arrow
that appeared out of nowhere on the floor before us. When we took a
step forward, the image moved with us, directing us to the left of unit
235.

Around the next building the compound opened up a little and we
saw many tanks, APCs and other assault vehicles lined up in a way
similar to the light craft showroom, as if for just the right amount of
credits you too could drive away in any one of these fine machines of
war. One even had a price sign that hung down from the elongated
barrel of its rail cannon. I looked at Mason whose eyes seemed to
glow with pleasure. I shook my head and walked on, following the
arrow all the way to a more aesthetically appealing building nestled in
an out-of-the-way corner of the place.

We approached the door and the dark oak-effect portal slid to one side, sending out a jet of warm air infused with cinnamon and fried eggs. It wasn't a pleasant combination.

"Come in," said a voice from within. I stepped inside and Mason followed. Thor waited outside.

It was a bare room, nothing much in the way of décor other than a coffee table made from an upturned ammo box, a battered looking couch of green leather that had been patched with duct tape and the man who now sat on it. I wouldn't have been risking a lot by betting he was Alan. He wore faded DPM pants and an old, tired looking shirt with the top three buttons missing. He had both his combat boots on the ammo box and was leafing through a printed edition of the Sports News Weekly. He looked at us, smiled and stood up.

"Sanders? And you must be McDonald. I'm Alan." We shook and he offered us a seat on the couch. I declined but Mason flopped down causing the thing to groan in agony. "Sharky says you're the type of customers I'm interested in selling to. That right?"

"Sharky says you're the kind of dealer we should be buying from. Is he right on that score?" said Mason.

"I've run your names, you're clean. I'm assuming you've done the same for me so let's drop the bullshit. What do you need?"

Mason looked at me and I shrugged.

"We can do business," he said. "I need a bit of everything. Specifically, this list."

He took a folded piece of paper from inside his coat and passed it to Alan who began reading it aloud.

"Phos shields, 50-watt output... Two H and K laser pistols, extended cells... Two HARG rifles with twin ports and refocussed lenses..."

He went on, reading the entire list that even I hadn't read. I wondered if Alice would still be happy with the idea of us spending those credits a little early with Mason holding the card.

"Any of that a problem?" he asked as Alan folded the paper back up.

37

"Not if you've got the dough."

"We do."

"Then let's scribble a little figure here..." He took a pencil from his shirt pocket and wrote on the top of the last fold, then handed it back to him. Mason read it and laughed.

"Change the six to a four and you've got a deal."

"How about a five? Looks less like I cheated on my homework."

"That'll do." Mason stood up. Negotiations were over. "Can you deliver by tomorrow morning?"

"Sharky mentioned the rush you guys are in. Sure, as long as one of you is there to sign for it."

"Like UPS?"

"Just like UPS. Brown suits and all."

Mason shook his hand. "You mentioned our bot before."

"Oh yeah, sure." He scratched his beer belly. "Go over to unit 626 and take a look. Most of it was heading to the furnace but you can take what you want. My son will give you a price, he's down there breaking shit up."

"Thanks," I said.

"Nice doing business with you, as they say."

We followed the arrow again and it led us away from Alan's not-so-plush office to the only building that had its rolling shutter door wide open. Sparks from a cutting torch lit up the place and as we came closer the hiss of a plasma set slithered towards us.

"Well Thor," I said as we looked into the unit. "What do you think to all that?"

The place was full of stinking piles of robotic parts including entire models heavily worn and falling to pieces. The smell of oil, of burned metal and leaking servos assaulted us as we stood in the pale light coming from overhead lamps. Thor, clearly delighted by the finds, stomped in and scanned everything he saw, turning his head this way and that.

"Like a kid at Christmas," said Mason. "He should be careful that boy doesn't mistake him for the next victim of that torch."

"I'm more concerned that he'll want to take it all."

Thor came back to us a few minutes later dragging a crate behind him loaded with various indescribable bits. Then he turned to go back but I called to him.

"More?"

"Yes sir, much more sir. It's a find and no mistake!"

Mason began laughing as the bot appeared to be skipping away, back into the unit. I shook my head which, if things carried on as they were, was going to result in whiplash.

"I'd best go speak to the boy and find out how much this is going to cost."

From the look on Alice's face, it cost a lot more than we realized. We'd arranged to meet her for lunch at a big open market she knew that sold burgers on an open grill and somewhere big enough for Thor's bulk to fit in. He didn't draw much attention; it wasn't unusual to see bots his size moving around that part of the city given that a vast amount of it was still under construction where the old districts made way for the new. It was, however, strange for people to hear him speak so I asked him to keep quiet for a while, at least until we were out of public view. He seemed happy to comply, perhaps still thrilled by his purchases which were also on their way to the *Hikane*, having no way of sending them to the *Helios* without blowing our cover.

"I can't recommend the steak burger enough," she said, sipping bubbly water from the neck of the bottle. "Ask for the hot sauce if you dare."

Mason and I got up and went over to the grill, placing our orders and coming back with two heaped plates and several bottles of soda. She wasn't kidding. The sauce was hot. I felt tears pricking my eyes as I bit into it.

39

"You like?" she laughed. I dabbed my face with a napkin.

"It's mild enough," I lied. "Is everything ready?"

"Just about," she said. "Baz will meet you at the platform first thing tomorrow. He's done a pretty good job of keeping the *Helios* in order."

"Just not Thor," added Mason.

"Yes, he did spin me some line about rules and regulations. I warned him that there were also rules and regulations about staff relations and caring for company property. He got the message."

"Good. Us three will take the next shuttle up there and oversee the final stages. Our friend at Vertigo flyers says the living quarters are done so we'll catch a nap on board the *Hikane*."

"It's going too well," said Mason. "I don't like it. Something should have gone wrong by now."

"Just wait until we're flying. I'm sure there'll be some hiccups the moment we leave Titan 5."

"Just be careful," said Alice. "You're moving into a world of shadow and lies. Guns and explosives won't always get you what you want."

"You'd be surprised," laughed Mason.

"Yeah, we've found them pretty effective so far."

We ate and the time seemed to go nowhere. The next thing we knew we were all standing and saying our goodbyes. A taxi pulled up alongside Alice's limo and she wiped away a tear from her eye after we embraced.

"Be careful. *All of you*," she said. "Come home safe – and preferably without any more replacement parts, okay?"

"That's something we just can't promise these days."

5

The shuttle was swift enough once we'd waited for an hour and a half. The queue to the boarding desk snaked well beyond the entrance and it seemed like the entire planet suddenly wanted to be someplace else. It might have had something to do with the interstellar cruise liner which had arrived yesterday and was set to take 4,500 holidaymakers on a one-year tour of the galaxy. How it could be done in that little time was anyone's guess.

By the time we'd made it to the business desk, Mason had demolished three burgers from the kiosk, two brownies and a large bottle of soda. I couldn't blame him – I was starving myself, but I settled for a coffee and a ham sandwich instead.

"Dirty bulking," he explained when I frowned at his food. "I lost muscle mass during the op."

"Bullshit. You were back on your feet in under 24 hours."

"Are you a doctor?"

"No, but neither are you."

"I've taken medical advice and I was told to regain my strength. I'm doing it right now."

"You're regaining your waistline, that's all."

Once we'd cleared customs and they'd searched Thor with every conceivable device they could find, we made our way onto the shuttle and took seats in the business suite. Thor was ushered into the loading bay because that was the only place he would fit into. He was happy enough; the flight was only thirty minutes and as we disembarked, he came tramping towards us, narrowly missing a group of school kids on a field-trip.

41

"Makes a change, sir," he said. "Travellin' like you boys. Felt like a true gent on that barky."

"Wait until you see the ship," I said. "I was told it was in dock 32. This way."

Thor took our cases and followed behind as we crossed the busy platform to the entrance of docks 30-40. The cruise liner was beyond that and most of the passengers sped past us, dragging behind them their floating luggage racks. The whole place felt like some mad game show, some desperate chase to win the prize of having arrived at your ship in the fastest time. Despite our size and the hulking shape of Thor we still found ourselves being buffeted and knocked by frantic herds of people dressed in cheap suits or bright summer clothing. As we moved out of the firing lines, I felt a wave of relief as the only people in our hallway were us and, just up ahead, the grinning face of Baz.

"You're early," I said. "We didn't expect you until tomorrow."

"Alice explained things and I headed straight over. Jo has the ship covered. I'm not giving you a chance to leave me behind."

"The thought had crossed my mind," I laughed. I didn't mean it though – right there and then I felt that we were starting out on something deep, something new and I won't lie, it scared me. Right then I wanted Baz with us. It was only right. We'd been through a lot together.

We moved along, Thor now carrying all our luggage and whistling to himself as he did so. Beyond the next gate was the *Hikane* and its name flashed in bright lights on the digital display above our heads.

"What does she look like?" asked Baz. "Alice didn't have an image for me when I asked."

"You'll see," said Mason.

We rounded the corner and there she was. The loading bay opened up into an enormous chamber, perhaps the size of several football fields and there, suspended on its dry dock, was the *Hikane*. In person, she looked even finer than the image back at the dealership.

42

She was no *Helios*, but she sported a much sleeker hull, curving lines on her prow and a sweet humming engine core. There was none of the bulk or bristling firepower of a warship. Instead, the firing ports were discretely worked into the shape of the craft and the finery of interstellar travel was given top priority.

"Wow," said Baz. "That's a ship."

"A fine vessel, sirs, if I may say so," added Thor.

"Let's just hope she's space-worthy," said Mason.

"We're about to find out."

Coming towards us at a jog was a short, squat man in stained coveralls and an oil streak across his brow. He was carrying some component with wires trailing from it and he held it up as he panted to a stop before us.

"Have you come for the *Hikane*?"

"Yeah," I replied. "I'm the guy who parted with a lot of credits to have this ship ready for tomorrow morning. Tell me that you're on schedule."

"Well sir, the problem is this-"

"Problem? That's the last word I want to hear."

He held up the component in both hands almost like a supplication. I looked at it.

"It's the nebulus buffer," he said. "We can't get it to align properly but my best team is on it. We just need a little more time."

"How much time?" I asked.

"Another day, maybe two. Then she'll be ready to sail. You have my word on it. Believe me, sir, my crews have been working all day long and plan to go on through the night, barely stopping even for a mouthful of tea."

I looked at Mason who was shaking his head. Baz and Thor were still staring at the *Hikane*, now dead in the water without a nebulus buffer. I assumed it was unable to sail – I didn't really know what a nebulus buffer actually was. It sounded like something I wouldn't want to sail without. But there was someone who did.

43

"Jo?" I offered. Mason shrugged.

"Why not?"

I brought up my comms unit and got hold of our engineer who appeared on the display with her hair in a messy bun and the same oil streak as our friend with the nebulus drive.

"Go," she said. "But bear in mind I'm busy, boss."

"I've got a guy here says he can't align the-" I looked at him and he mouthed the name of the thing to me. "-the nebulus buffer."

"Why the hell not?" she barked.

"I don't know," I replied. "Here, you speak to him."

I pressed the reverse icon and Jo's image spun to face the engineer. Words were exchanged, terms and instructions I had no hope of understanding, but it seemed like our friend did. By the time Jo had finished the man's skin had turned a bright pink and he bounced on the balls of his feet, eager to leave.

"Carter?" said Jo. I spun her back round.

"Yeah?"

"It should be okay now. Two hours tops. Anything else, boss?"

"No, that'll be all, thanks." I laughed.

"It's tough being the best. *Laters*."

Before arriving at Titan 5, Jo's staff had handed in their resignations. It was a great loss; Ali and Jana had been with us for a long time and they were some of the best technicians we'd had the pleasure of working with. It was a heavy blow to lose them, but if I'd found Jo's resignation in that pile of paperwork, I might have thrown my own towel in. When you had someone, who was the best at what they did, you looked after them. Period. I only hoped that in our absence she'd be able to rebuild what we'd lost.

We followed the blazing trail of the engineer towards the *Hikane* and skirted around a fork truck that sped across the open space straight into the loading bay of the ship.

"Might as well start there," said Mason. We followed. There were cries from within, cuss words and the general racket of people at work. It had a faint aroma of our days in the service when life was organized around the bell and the yelling drill sergeant only this time no one would tell us what to do or how badly we were doing it.

We climbed up the ramp and found ourselves in a narrow loading bay already stocked with sealed pallets arranged in long neat rows. Some of it was Thor's parts horde, some an advance delivery of Mason's weapons from Alan. The rest would come during the night.

"You think they'll tidy up before they finish?" asked Baz, kicking at a pile of refuse.

"I'm sure they will," I laughed. "For these credits I expect it to be spotless.

We went deeper into the ship, leaving the loading bay through the rear door. Here the halls were decked in steel all the way to the stairwell and the elevator pad. At my request, the walkways and steps had been widened and reinforced to allow Thor more access to the ship though I left the living quarters as they were. Flashes of our previous bot still played in my mind and having him turn up in my room one night was a possibility I didn't relish.

Up we went, having found the engineering decks sealed from unauthorized personnel. We passed the living quarters and carried on to the bridge where several crewmen were just replacing the bulkhead panels.

"Is it okay to go in?" I asked as we stood outside.

"Sure," said the woman with a ratchet in her hand. "We're all finished here."

The doors parted and the sweeping vista of the bridge appeared before us. Elegant was a good word to describe it. Ornate? Bespoke? After years on the bridge of the *Helios* which looked more like a gamer's bedroom than the nerve center of a vessel of the line, the *Hikane's* center of command blew us away.

"Is that real wood?" said Mason as he ran his fingers over the consoles. They curved round in a great arc, ending in the Captain's seat which looked more like a leather recliner than the helm. The

FARGO drives had been seated within the walls and made to look like part of the design and not simply stuffed into the most convenient gap.

"Best tell Angel there'll be no feet put up on these beauties," said Baz.

"I feel like I should be wearing slippers," I said. "Look at the floor! Look at the ceiling!"

We spent a few minutes walking around touching stuff. It seemed the right thing to do. The air was full of newness like we'd bought a high-end speeder and not an expensive spaceship. Even Thor seemed mesmerized by it and was reluctant to walk around on the new flooring.

"You're free to go where you like," I told him once we'd finished fondling the ship. "We'll head to our quarters and settle in. You can leave the cases there."

"Thankee, sir," he said and turned to go. "I've got a few things to tend to meself before we depart. Good-evenin' gents. Sleep well an' all."

With that he strode away, ducking as he passed through archways even though they were high enough to accommodate him. When he was gone, we grabbed our cases and headed back down, closing the bridge doors behind us.

"Quite a ship, isn't she?" said Mason.

"Let's see how she sails first," I replied. "Then I'll make my judgment."

On the living deck, we separated. All of the rooms were identical so there was no real need to fight over them. I took the one nearest to the stairs and thus the bridge. Mason took the one opposite. Baz vanished around the corner just because he could. No doubt he'd pick a random room and claim it was better than all the rest.

No less impressive were the living quarters. Decorated in the same design as the bridge, the lavish surfaces, the ornate flooring, and the very soft looking bed made me feel a little less anxious about the coming departure. I threw my case on the desk near the 'window' – a digital display of whatever I wanted to see and began to unpack. I found storage for my clothes and my personal items but kept my rail pistol – a gift from a customer long ago, in its holster near my bedside. It was a relic from before Mars when wars had been fought on Earth herself, but it still fired better than most plasma pistols and with a 13 round magazine capable of punching holes in most armor types it made for a comforting bedside weapon.

I laid back on the bed and took a deep breath. I set my alarm for two hours, closed my eyes and tried not to imagine Angel doing the same thing somewhere else in some forgotten cell. Cold. Damp. Friendless.

Maybe my breakout plan was still a better option.

6

The cell wasn't quite as damp as I'd pictured. In fact, it turned out to be quite the opposite. Situated some 300 miles south-west of Setti, the Avalon Center for Criminal Correction and Rehabilitation sat alone in the baking sun where temperatures beyond the forcefield that surrounded it sometimes peaked at 62 degrees centigrade. Angel, after being read her rights but not formally charged at that time, was swiftly admitted into the towering, hulking mass of plascrete and molanium without a word.

At the desk, she hadn't waited for the administrator to ask her to strip. Rather than give them the satisfaction of seeing her blush, she'd gone through the drill like she'd written the book herself and the whole procedure took no less than eight minutes to complete. At the end, wearing her prison-issue coveralls and boots, she'd marched ahead of the guards and straight into the cell that waited for her. They said nothing to her. She hadn't been on the news. She wasn't a mass murderer. People's interest in the Martian war had long since faded and a 'traitor' could mean many things to many people. All that mattered was that she was isolated, that she didn't try to escape and that she received her allowance of three meals a day plus access to her lawyer and the exercise yard.

Many the guards were former Earth Gov. veterans and once word mysteriously got out about what crime she'd been accused of; they began to take a serious interest in her.

On the night that the *Hikane* was reaching readiness, as I lay on my bed thinking just what kind of cell Angel was in, her door opened.

48

She heard the lock turn and the chime sound somewhere far off. Instinctively she stood up from the bed and turned to face it. Nothing happened. She waited. Her breathing slowed and her stance became combative. If they knew anything about her, they'd try to rush her, not give her chance to strike. She had to be ready.

The door suddenly flew sideways, and the lights went out. Anticipating this, Angel had closed one eye to the light above her and now, by opening it, she retained some of her night-vision.

The first attacker crumpled as her open hand struck a throat in the darkness. The next grabbed her other arm but already Angel was bringing her right arm back around and up, hitting an elbow and forcing it towards the ceiling with an audible crunch. The third managed to tackle her legs and she went down, grazing her brow on the steel toilet seat and narrowly missing a direct impact. The attacker scrambled on top of her and she could smell the rancid breath of a habitual Spatz popper. Thin bony hands found her throat and began to close around her windpipe, but this didn't unnerve her. With her own two hands, she grabbed the head of the addict, found the eye sockets and drove the knuckles of her thumbs deep into them. There was a high-pitched squeal and Angel found her throat released from the vice grip but she didn't let go. She felt the eyes beneath her hands pop and run with hot gummy fluid and still, she didn't let go. It was only when the lights came back on and the guards came rushing in that Angel, panting with furious anger, finally released her. The bleeding woman, a prisoner, now blind, rolled on the floor with her hands covering her face. Blood poured from between her fingertips.

"What the-?" said one of the guards. "Who-"

"Be quiet!" said the other. "You didn't see this. Right?"

"What the hell are you-?"

"You didn't see this. Do you understand? This never happened."

Turning to Angel, the second guard gestured to the door. She stood up, wiped the blood from her thumbs on the shirt of the prisoner, and did as she was directed.

"I've never seen anything like it," said the first guard in a kind of dazed whisper.

"You still haven't," said the other. "Now take this one to the shower block and clean her up. When she comes back these three will be in the medical bay. Make sure you say nothing to anyone. Understand?"

"No, I don't, but I'll do it. Anything to not be here."

7

The alarm woke me from a fitful doze. For a moment I was lost. I couldn't remember where I was or what ceiling was above my head. I found myself staring at the intricate design of diamonds and squares until my memory kicked in. Then I was up and looking for my boots.

On my way down to engineering, I passed no one. The corridors were spotless and any of the debris from before was gone. The work crews weren't messing around. The air filters were pumping out cool new-speeder smells and it was pleasant to breathe.

When I reached the stairwell the NO UNAUTHORIZED PERSONEL sign was still in place but as I technically owned the ship, I decided it no longer applied to me. After 'authorizing' myself down to the lower decks, I saw our friend from before talking to one of his team.

"Is it done?" he asked.

"It's done," said the other. "The nebulus buffer is working fine now. I don't know what you did but-"

"I need to find out who that woman was. I've never met anyone who could explain it so well. She needs to be on this crew."

"Haven't you asked?"

"The owner? Hell, he doesn't look like the type of guy who-"

I stepped into the room and they both turned to look at me.

"Who what?" I asked.

"Nothing. Nothing at all, sir," he mumbled. Then, to his teammate. "Run along and make sure we don't leave any kit behind this time. Alright?"

"Aye, boss."

51

The man vanished and we were left alone. The hum of the drive engines was louder down here but it sounded smooth and in good working order.

"Well? Do we have a space-worthy craft or what?" I asked. The engineer grinned.

"We do, sir. All functions are now within the green. I've just got my crew to finish up and remove our muck and she's all yours."

I looked around. The drive room bore a close resemblance to the *Helios* but was, perhaps, slightly smaller. Two enormous chambers, each glowing a dull green, throbbed with power while various pipes and relays snaked in and out of them to run off in all directions. The control consoles and workstations were exactly where they were on the *Helios*. I felt better about taking her out for having seen it.

"About that... woman, sir. I was thinking-"

"She's not for hire," I said. "Is there anything else?"

"No sir," he replied. "I'll be off."

He turned to go but I called him back.

"You've done a good job. Expect a bonus."

The man brightened and rubbed the oil streak on his brow.

"Why thank you, sir. It's been a pleasure."

Then he was gone, and I was left alone with the pulsing heart of the *Hikane*. I walked up and down the gantry, inspected the readouts on the command console and put my hand on one of the chambers.

"It's not a hard life," I said. "Just get the job done and it'll go easy. Deal?"

The ship didn't reply. They never did.

An hour passed before our cargo arrived and, true to his word, it was delivered by guys in brown suits. They met Mason and I at the loading bay and quickly began shunting pallet after pallet into the hold. Some of it was more of Thor's stock parts, the rest were simply plain-looking crates with no markings save a single stencilled number.

"Am I missing something?" I asked Mason as he signed for it all. "What the hell is this?"

"I haven't wasted a minute of our time here," he began. "As you know, the ship has weapons and so do we. Sharky gave our name to Alan and, in turn, he passed ours on to a start-up company west of Setti, located in the Urloc mountains. After all the trouble we've been having with FARGO-"

"What trouble?" I cried. "A glitch with my spine and some issues with the suits in the extreme cold? That hardly calls for brand betrayal, does it?"

"I think we can go deeper than that, pal," he said.

"How deep?"

"FARGO has been slipping. Everyone knows this."

"Who's this 'everyone' and when can I ask him some questions? FARGO had a setback, it isn't the end of the world."

"It could've been the end of *our* world, don't forget. We had to wear our old kit, well beyond its safe working limits thanks to them."

"So, you're telling me that these crates are basically CHERICA-AUTO suits? You've gone over to the other side after one saved your life, is that it?"

Mason laughed and shook his head.

"Alan told me to look at the online specs for a new company that's just begun producing its first line of exo-shells. He suggested we think about trying their product."

"A new company? How new are we talking?"

"Six months actual production time but they've been designing for years now. Remember the old GAMMA vests we had last year for that Toi job?"

"Yeah."

"That was their patent."

I sighed and shook my head.

"So, these crates...?"

"Three suits made to order. I took the specifications from the

FARGO sheet."

"Have you seen one of them in action?"

"That's why I'm down here. Time is running out. Let's crack one open and see what we've got."

Feeling like I could already hear Alice shouting at me when the invoice landed on her desk, I reluctantly agreed. Thor joined us with Baz and together we moved the three largest containers into a clear space and let the bot do his work.

"I'll just pop these open in a jiffy, sirs," he said and spun the tool holder on his back, selecting a pneumatic chisel. The first crate shook with the carnage he wrought on one side and splinters of metal and wood flew into the air. He moved around to attack the other side, but we got there first before there was nothing left.

Together Mason and I tore off the panels and unveiled the suit rack and the unit suspended in its curving arms of molanium. Baz whistled his appreciation and even Mason began to smirk.

"They sure look attractive," I said. "Doesn't mean they're going to work."

"Ye of little faith," he replied.

"Where's the instruction book?" I asked.

"It came with a sim disc. We just upload it and climb inside."

"How?" asked Baz.

"How what?"

"How do we get in?"

The suit was indeed something else. Much lighter in construction with much less bulk, these exo-shells were a fraction of the material but boasted a stopping power beyond that of the FARGO suits we'd just worn to help take the *Aurelius*. The plating was smooth and rounded, more like something an athlete might wear and certainly not something that looked able to withstand the trauma we'd put it through. Unlike the FARGO suits, these hugged the physique of the wearer and still managed to make him or her look massive.

"They're nice – I'll grant you that one," I said. Then, seeing a red ribbon hanging around the back, I yanked on it and the suit gave a three-chime alarm. We took a step back. The exo-shell was lowered to floor height and its back parted, separating at the spine and all the way around to the side.

"You first, Baz," said Mason.

"Why me?" he cried but was already moving into position. When his whole body was inside, the plates slid back, and the suit became alive with static.

"You still breathing?" I asked.

"Yeah," came back an almost identical voice. "Can you hear me?"

"Loud and clear," I replied. "What's it like?"

Without warning the helmet slid apart and Baz' head was there, gaping at us.

"That's cool!" he laughed. "I hope it's shielded though."

"Walk about," I said. "Give us a Waldo check."

Baz turned to his left and, passing around Thor, took several steps towards the loading bay ramp. He seemed to move normally like he wasn't even wearing the thing.

"Well?" said Mason.

"It's weird," he replied. "It doesn't feel like anything. No loss of sensation, no delays in response time. Nada. Zip."

"And the controls?"

"The same as FARGO. All but a few icons I don't recognize."

"We should check the disc," said Mason. "There was talk of some special features somewhere."

Baz went through the Waldo's and they passed just fine. Then, heading to the far end of the bay, he turned and sprinted towards us, stopping inches from my boots.

"I can't fault the responders. There's almost zero drag."

"What about internals?" I asked. Baz nodded and activated the helmet again, sending overlapping plates of dark metal speeding across his face. In a split second, he was gone, safe behind a smooth, glassy window of darkest jet.

"HUD is online. Again, just like FARGO. The direction markers are out but that might be because we're disconnected from the mainframe."

"What about comfort?" asked Mason.

"All soft in here and relatively cool. There are controls for that on the HUD. Strange for a suit like this but I guess that's just their way."

I looked at the other two crates and signalled for Thor to open them. If they were going to be trusted, then I'd have to see for myself.

"We've got a few hours to spare once we're underway. I suggest drills and weapon acclimatization as soon as the autopilot takes over. Agreed?" Baz and Mason nodded. "Good call, pal. Looks like they might turn out okay."

"As I said – things are going too well. Something has to give."

"Maybe not today. Maybe."

The night passed and I felt every hour of it. Up and down the ship we went, the three of us, checking over every room, every cabinet and every button that could be pushed. We met the Instructor for an hour, and he took us through the NavCom, courtesy of Vertigo Flyers, before telling us that the *Hikane* was a dream ship, one he'd had the honor of sailing out of the shipyards above Mars. Then he'd gone, leaving us with only an hour to wait before we could take her out of dry dock and into the infinite vastness of space.

"So, we have Argo's flight plan, enough gear to start a small war and parts to build a dozen more Thor bots. What are we waiting for?" asked Mason as we sat on the bridge watching the crews clear away through the viewer.

"Other than the harbour master to okay us, nothing," I replied. "Is there a coffee machine here?"

"By the door."

"Good."

The docking bay began to empty as the last of the technicians pushed their floating tool chests away. On the console, before me, the readouts began to move into the green. The harbourmaster changed our status from DOCKED to PREPARING TO LEAVE. I tapped the confirm icon and returned to propping up my chin with my fist.

Then, coming into the docking bay, I saw two great chests blazoned with the FARGO brand come scooting towards the camera. I sat upright and stared at the person hurrying behind them with a suitcase at her side.

"I can't say I'm surprised," I said aloud, and Mason turned to look.

"She'll have played that conversation over in her mind once you'd signed off. Then she would've called Alice and demanded to know what was going on."

"What about the *Helios* though?" I asked. "Who the hell is keeping an eye on her?"

"I guess we'll just have to trust her to Alice."

Jo, waving at us from below, gestured that we should open the loading bay doors. She was in her usual green overalls, stained with oil and burned in places. She had her hair in a messy bun and it was held together with an elastic bobble on the crown of her head.

"I can't say I'm not happy to see her," I said, thumbing the controls. The doors opened and the camera followed her inside along with her tools. In five minutes she was at the door to the bridge and we both turned in our seats to grin at her.

"How dare you!" she cried. "Are you mad?"

"Hey there, Jo," I said, beaming. "What brings you here?"

"A nebulus buffer, that's what. Sailing a ship without an engineer is suicide, Carter. Why didn't you ask me to come?"

"Has Alice filled you in?" asked Mason.

"No. She said you would. Then she gave me a set of false papers and ID and sent me on my way. Said you'd need me. Is that right?"

"If Alice said it then I guess so."

"Right." She sat down in one of the empty chairs and sighed. "Start at the top."

So the *Hikane*, floating gracefully out of dry dock an hour later, had a crew. Of sorts. Her mission? To find the evidence needed to clear the name of one of our own, one very dear to all of us. As we left the platform behind and saw the cruise liner begin its long voyage, I felt a strange kind of peace settle on me. It wasn't going to last – I knew that. But as the ship asked for confirmation to gain speed, I pressed the icon with a smile playing faintly on my lips.

The *Hikane* lived up to the praise. Once we'd become familiar with our stations and inputted the data into the NavCom, we gathered speed. Under the careful supervision of Jo, we were able to push her almost to her limits and keep the readouts in the green.

When we found ourselves at a safe distance from any other ships Mason ran some firing drills, giving a few broadsides to empty space and blasting debris with the forward plasma lances.

"Happy?" I asked.

"Very," he replied. "There's a slight issue with the targeting array but I think I should be able to recalibrate that."

I turned to Baz who was sat at the comms and scanner console. He had a knotted brow and was leaning quite close to the display, squinting – the universal sign for confusion.

"Well?" I said. "Mastered it yet?"

"I was a grunt back on Mars," he replied. "Not a signalman. Give me some time with the manual."

"You handled it well enough on the *Helios*," cried Mason. "What's the problem?"

"It's broken."

"I doubt that," I laughed.

"It is. I'm doing what it tells me to do but I'm getting nothing."

I got up and went to look over his shoulder. On one side of the display was a long set of user notes and on the other nothing but a blank screen.

"Have you turned it on?" I asked.

"Of course I have, you dick!"

"Where?"

"There, on the side. The rectangle icon."

"And what happened when you did?"

"Nothing – that's what I'm trying to tell you. It's faulty."

"That's the internal comms icon, buddy. THAT is the standby icon."

I pressed the lightning bolt image and the console came to life.

"We've been sailing blind since we left dry dock," said Mason. "Nice going, buddy."

"Piss off!" he responded and flushed red. "I'm sure I must have pressed that before, I'm sure."

I looked at the display and saw a flashing icon in the top right-hand corner. I tapped it and the audio nearly deafened me.

"TO ANY SHIPS, THIS IS THE EARTH GOVERNMENT VESSEL, *THE PEARL*, PLEASE RESPOND. WE ARE UNDER ATTACK. PLEASE RESPOND. THIS IS THE EARTH-"

I swore under my breath and hit the wrong icon, sending a blast of static all around the ship. Then I hit the correct one.

"Call up the star chart and show me where she is," I said. Baz nodded and went to work on the controls with more success than before. Soon I was looking at a stretch of empty space not far from our rendezvous point with the *Agamemnon*. "*Pearl*, this is the *Hikane*. We will assist. Please stand by."

"Action?" said Mason, grinning. I wasn't as happy as he was – maybe this would be the start of things going wrong.

"What are the odds of the *Pearl* being one of Argo's ships?" I asked.

"I might be able to tell you," said Baz. The screen changed. A single blue dot appeared, surrounded by at least a dozen red ones. They buzzed around like flies, having no real pattern. An opportunistic strike on a weakened vessel by some rogue element maybe?

"Well?"

60

"She's surrounded by a level 2 classified protocol. All I know is that she's called the *Pearl*."

"Mason?"

"I've been idle long enough. Let's go help her out. It's maritime law to get involved anyway."

I took another look at the screen and sighed. Without a deeper scan, we wouldn't know what we were up against until it was too late to withdraw. Risky at best.

"Okay, let's do this," I said. Then, to Jo in engineering, "Are you seeing this?"

"Yeah, got the same feed down here. You thinking of getting stuck in?"

"If you and Thor can handle damage control, then yes. ETA to the *Pearl*, six minutes."

"Gotcha. We'll be ready."

"Suit up?" said Mason. I nodded. "Let's do this."

Without the drills, I had to wing my first time in the exo-shell and I quickly felt like a child who'd just learned to walk. Years spent in models that offered at least some lag between action and deed had made me adapt without realizing it and when I stepped into a new lag-free world I found myself struggling. That was until the first shot struck our starboard shields and nearly sent me reeling drunkenly sideways.

"According to the comms that was their way of welcoming us," laughed Baz.

"It would be rude not to respond. Mason, if you please."

"I'll send them our calling card."

I looked at the viewer which now gave us a good idea of what we were up against. The *Pearl*, a Legion-class ship of some 800 crewmen, sat dead in the water, barely able to fire off its few remaining plasma batteries. Swarming around it were a dozen Corvettes and, according to the scanner, they were being supported by a larger Corsair, the *Wayward*, two points off our port side.

"ID puts it under the jurisdiction of Athens 6. We're legally allowed to engage," said Baz.

"Always good to know," I grinned. "Any ideas, Mason?"

"I'm not a sailor," he said. "But one did say that you should 'forget tactics and sail straight at 'em'."

"Sound advice. If we hit the Corvettes, what's the *Wayward* going to do?"

"Move to engage I guess."

"Do we just hit it first and go for the serpent's head?"

"That would be my preferred choice."

"What's it putting out?" I asked.

"Only 25 cannon on its broadside," said Baz. "No lancers. It's a Corsair, they generally don't carry much firepower. They're support vessels."

I tapped the comms.

"*Pearl*, this is the *Hikane*. Your pests are being supported by a Corsair in the region. I suggest we take it out of the battle first. Can you hold out against the Corvettes while we do this?"

"*Hikane*, this is Captain Sole. That'd be mighty nice of you. Our shields can take a bit more of their stings yet."

"Captain, we'd be happy to oblige. Moving to engage."

I plotted our intercept course into the NavCom and confirmed it. The ship banked to port, fired its main engines and shot like an arrow towards the *Wayward*.

"Cripple and board?" I asked.

"Maybe just cripple," said Mason. "That should be enough to put them off any further action."

"I hope your shooting is up to scratch then."

"I'll leave that to the computer."

We were approaching the *Wayward* from her starboard side and a little beneath her, exposing her underbelly without directly flying into her cannon. Of course, no ship would let this happen so she began to turn down and to port, bringing her full weight of broadside to bear on us.

"Increase speed to 12.6," said Mason and I did so. "That should outrun those guns."

"Done."

"Firing pattern is locked. Going for a sweep across her starboard batteries. Plasma lances should strike her engines as we pass."

"Sounds easy," I said.

"Time to find out. Hit the AUTO icon when it lights up, pal."

I watched the console on my right, letting my armored digit hover over it. Then, when the icon appeared, I pressed.

"Right, she's all yours," I said.

"Well, not mine. We're going too fast for me to control the weapons. NavCom will do the rest. Hopefully."

"I admire your confidence," I grinned.

"When we pass, move to re-engage as soon as possible."

There was no point watching the viewer now. All we'd have seen was space and a fraction of a blur. Instead, I put the star chart up on the screen and we all watched the dots move about. Each one was now named and there, in green, was the *Hikane* as she drew closer and closer to the *Wayward* in red.

"Thirty seconds," said Mason.

"I'd have felt better boarding them," offered Baz. "This feels like a bad video game."

"On this rare occasion I'm actually going to agree with you," I said. "It's not how I like to fight either."

"Here we go."

The dots passed each other in a flash. The only thing we felt was a rumble on the aft shield as we caught the tail-end of the *Wayward's* broadside. Then we parted and the viewer switched back to a visual image.

"Well?" I asked.

"Direct hits from all but three of our batteries. Plasma lances have taken out two of her four engines. Fires on multiple decks and six minor hull breaches. Looks like she hasn't seen a dry dock in a while."

"Where were her shields?"

"Our shot went straight through them. Remind me to send a thank you note to Sharky."

The *Wayward* had stopped dead and was spewing great clouds of superheated plasma from its sides. It began to list to port, unable to check its movement and there were now tiny specks firing off in all directions.

"Escape pods," said Baz. "They're bailing."

"Didn't we agree to *cripple* the ship?"

"I underestimated the yield of the cannon. My bad."

I brought the *Hikane* back around and gave the wreck of the *Wayward* a wide berth. Then, facing the *Pearl*, I hailed on all frequencies.

"To the attackers of the *Pearl* – discontinue your attack and power down your ships immediately. This is over. Comply and you will receive fair treatment."

I tapped the comms again.

"Jo – damage report."

"Nothing, Carter. Two shield emitters went down but Jimmy is already on that. Aft compensators nearly burned out but we've got spares and-"

"Wait," I said. "Jimmy?"

"Yeah, little Jimmy. He's in the service shaft and he's already-"

"Who the hell is Jimmy?"

I looked at Mason who shrugged.

"It's Thor's apprentice."

To facepalm whilst wearing an armored suit was never a good idea but I gave it my best shot. For no reason I could fathom, I noticed that the small plates that made up the surface of the exo-shell were warm on my skin, like living flesh. It bothered me, but not as much as the explanation for Thor having an apprentice that I knew was coming my way.

"Please explain. No, in fact, don't. I'm on my way." I turned to Mason. "Take the big chair and get us to the *Pearl*."

I left the bridge and picked up my HARG rifle that was held in magna locks by the coffee machine. It was a bull-pup design and it fitted the gauntlets of the new suits perfectly – another eerie coincidence on behalf of Mason. It wouldn't be the last. Then I strode along the corridor, heading to the stairwell.

When I arrived in engineering Jo was stood by the mouth of the service shaft with a tool bag in one hand and her overalls tied by the sleeves around her waist. She wore a simple vest, exposing her heavily tattooed arms to the warm air of the engineering bay. One of the designs was a build completion plate normally found on the engine core of a craft. Instead of a ship's name being engraved on it, the inked letters read JOSEPHINE ASH and had a birth date stamped where the completion date would have been.

"Explain what it is," I said. "Before I destroy it."

Jo snorted a laugh and turned to look at me.

"Just wait until you see him," she said. "He's cute."

"Where's Thor?"

From around the other side of the engines, he appeared looking sheepish, if a bot could look sheepish.

"Hullo, sir," he said, coming towards me. "Please don't-"

"Where is he?" I asked. "Tell me now before I space the entire deck."

I saw something move in the opening and I raised the rifle but the shape retreated into the shadows.

"You've scared him!" she cried.

"Scared? I'll show him scared. Thor – get it down here NOW."

The bot, great blocky shoulders slumped, called to the thing.

"Oy, Jimmy, get yer arse down 'ere me little friend. He won't 'urt

65

you, I promise."

In the darkness of the service shaft I saw two small beads of light appear and hover for a moment. Then a head appeared, if it could be called a head. It looked like it'd fallen down a hundred flights of stairs and bore the scratches and dents of a seasoned stock-car. It had a small square opening for a mouth and its cheek plates were missing, exposing the servos and wiring beneath. By no accident were the eyes bigger than they should be – a human weakness associating it with cuteness. I would go to my grave never admitting it but as its little legs kicked out over the side and struggled to find the ladder, I found the guy heartbreakingly cute.

When it was stood beside Jo, barely tall enough to reach her waist, it lifted one of its odd arms and held on to her hand. The poor thing was a mishmash of spare parts and exposed internal systems but worst of all this, most heinous of crimes against my senses, was the downright manipulation of my feelings by Thor's delicate little arm as it reached out and put a cloth flat-cap on its little head.

"Jimmy," he said in a fatherly tone. "This is the boss I was telling you about. This is Carter."

"He-he-hello, sir," he managed to squeak. "Pleased to meet you, sir. I'm terribly sorry if I've done anyfink wrong. Sir."

"Thor. A word."

I stepped out of earshot of Jo and Jimmy and the bot followed.

"Yes sir?" he said.

"Explain. Now."

"Well sir, you see, it woz those bits and bobs from the gun dealer. I found him in amongst them, sir. All by hisself. He was just a CPU at that point, but when I fired 'im up I realized what I'd found and I had to give him a body like me own, sir. I hope you don't mind."

"What machine has a CPU like that?"

"I don't rightly know, sir, if I'm honest, like."

"So you found a suspect CPU and thought 'hey, I'll give it legs and arms and let it roam the ship'? Seriously, Thor – what were you

66

thinking?"

"But look at 'im!" he said and gestured back to the little guy. "He's just a young boy, sir. He just needs a bit of care and he can do all kind of fings. He's maintained stuff in places we can't get to and he's no bovva."

I looked at the bot and stared for a moment. He didn't move. All his functions seemed paused somehow.

"You're lying to me," I said, now turning stern. "I can see it."

"I don't know what-"

"Thor. Right now, the next words you speak will determine whether or not I throw both of you out into space. Up until today, I've let Jack's work wander unsupervised about my ship, trusted it with the lives of my team and given leeway to something I don't understand or, quite frankly, want to. Honestly? You disturb me. In hundreds of years, no human has managed to successfully build an AI unit capable of self-replicating. Now, listen closely and listen well." I pressed the safety release on the HARG rifle and adjusted my stance. "Your life hangs on the next words you speak. Tell me the truth. *All of it*."

If this was going to happen, there was a pretty good chance I'd lose. Against Thor in the confines of the engine bay, I'd be turned into mulch. HARG rifles used magnetic drives to launch plasma shot and as powerful as they were I wasn't sure it would do enough damage in the split second I'd have to shoot him. I'd taken a huge risk on this bot already and if I was wrong then I was about to meet my maker very soon.

"I made him," he confessed.

Those words hit me like a thunderbolt. My heart threatened to beat itself out of my chest.

"Why?" I said.

"I don't know. I found the CPU and I noticed it was a similar construction to my own. I was able to replicate some of my hardware and install it onto the quantum board. When I interfaced, it became self-aware."

No accent. I was talking directly to the mind inside the shell that was our friend, the one who'd fought pirates and zombies, the one who'd saved my life on Golan IV. I was talking to *someone*, not something.

"Do you realize what you've done?" I asked without condemnation. It was a straight-up question. "The implications are astronomical."

"Yes."

"What action do you think I should take?"

He didn't reply immediately. His head turned and he looked at Jimmy who was beckoning to him from Jo's side. The engineer looked pale and terrified and was stepping back very slowly.

"You should deactivate us both and submit us to Earth Government for disassembly and investigation."

"Is that what you want?" I said.

"My wishes are irrelevant."

"*Your wishes are irrelevant?* Do you hear what you're saying, Thor? A construction bot doesn't have 'wishes' – it does the job it was designed to do or it gets broken down for spare parts. It doesn't have opinions or loyalty or the desire to save lives and make new ones. It doesn't have anything you have. So I ask again – what do you *want* me to do?"

The robot didn't reply. I felt my hand tightening around the grip of the HARG, applying that first amounts of pressure to the trigger.

"Let us live, sir," he said after an eternity of silence.

I felt my body sag inside the exo-shell. This was too much. I had enough on my mind; Angel, the new ship, our future at TRIDENT. But this had been long overdue and now I had a decision to make. One that might doom many, many lives or create many new ones. Once more I cursed Jack and then, in turn, cursed myself.

"From this moment on," I began. "You are an official employee of TRIDENT INC. You work for Alice and I, understand?"

"Yes."

"That means you'll read the contract and sign it. You'll obey it the same way we do."

"Yes."

"There are rules to being alive, Thor. You'd best start familiarising yourself with them."

"And Jimmy?" he asked.

"He stays on as your 'apprentice' until I decide whether or not he can be a part of the crew. If he steps out of line-"

"He won't sir,"

"If he steps out of line I'll hold YOU responsible. Understand?"

"Yes, sir."

I stepped closer this time so that I had to look almost directly up at him.

"And should either of you cause harm to any one of your teammates I'll end you myself. Are we clear?"

Thor stood upright, his great servos whirring and grinding into place. For a moment I thought he was going to attack, but instead, he brought his construction hammer up to his head and saluted me.

"Thankee, sir," he cried, returning to his familiar cockney accent. "You won't be sorry you hired us, sir."

"Make sure I won't," I replied.

"Jimmy!" he bellowed. "The boss says we can stay!"

The little bot skipped from one foot to the other and made a kind of joyful squealing sound. Jo looked relieved. I went over to her, barely able to stop my legs from trembling.

"Holy shit," she whispered. "I thought-"

"A word. Now."

She followed me out of engineering and we climbed the stairs to the living quarters. Then I stopped, turned and looked at her.

"Did you hear that by any chance?" I asked. She nodded. "And?"

"I've had my suspicions all along though advanced robotics isn't really my field."

"I know I've heaped enough on you since we got back but I want you to make it your field."

"Carter I-"

"When this is over, I'm going to hire you all the staff you need and rip the engine room apart. You'll rebuild it the way *you* want it and dedicate most of your time to finding out just what we're dealing with here." She beamed but looked troubled.

"Thank you, but as I said, it isn't-"

"Alice will see to your training. Anything you need, it's yours and you can ask for any wage you like."

"Carter, you're scaring me."

"Jo – I'm scared myself. Jack somehow managed to do what millions of people haven't and now, to make matters even more serious, the bot has gone and self-replicated. If this were to get out I don't think I could stop Earth Gov. from marching down here and seizing both of them. By the end of the year they'd be dissected, taken apart piece by piece and used to recreate Jack's work in millions of AI slaves. Can you begin to imagine what this kind of knowledge would mean for humanity?"

"I can, actually."

"Right now, I need to focus on saving Angel from the executioner's block, I can't deal with this now as well. Will you help me?"

"You know I will," she said and put her hand on mine. I flinched. "Sorry," she said and withdrew.

"No, it's not that," I said. "I felt it."

"What? Through the armour?" I nodded. "Wow."

"Like I don't have enough to think about?"

"Okay," she continued. "It's a big deal for me, but if you're willing to pay for it all as you say, I'll take on the challenge. And you have my-"

I raised my hand.

"Don't ever say that," I said. "Your loyalty and trust are without question, I don't need to hear you say it."

"Maybe I need to say it," she replied. "Maybe I need to hear myself commit to this. We're having this conversation because we all believe Thor is one of us, he's a member of the team. If it weren't the case you'd have shipped them both to the lunar colony the moment we got to Titan 5. I'll be quiet, Carter. I'll take their secret to the grave if I must in order to save this new life Jack made. Only the future will show if we've made the right choice or not."

"That's what really scares me, Jo."

Then, to my surprise, the hardened engineer stepped forward and put her arms around the suit and hugged me. I felt all of it pass through the plating and transfer to my nerve endings. It was the strangest, nicest thing I'd felt in a long time.

"You're a good man, Carter. Don't let the universe change you."

I felt my eyes pricking with emotion and my throat clench. I returned the embrace – gently.

"I couldn't be who I am without my friends," I said. "Now get back to work before I dock your pay."

"Aye, sir," she laughed and walked away. I flicked the safety back on the HARG rifle, noticing that the chambered round had been set to maximum yield.

Captain Sole greeted us personally on docking bay 2 as we passed through his safety shield and settled on the platform. The attackers had all powered down their ships and were holding position at a safe distance from the *Pearl*. The *Wayward* had vanished in a flash, her engines overloading, causing a massive explosion to rip the vessel apart. The survivors had steered their pods towards us and now, with limited life support, waited just beyond Captain Sole's weapons systems for mercy.

"I owe you a debt," said the tall, dark-skinned man who held out his hand to me as we disembarked. "I don't know where you came from, but it was perfectly timed. A little longer and we'd be either dead or imprisoned on that Corsair."

"What happened?"

"I can't give you too many details but suffice it to say Captain Argo sent us to scout ahead. We have many damaged vessels in the fleet and we knew there'd been sightings of marauders in this part of the galaxy. When we arrived here, we had a major systems failure. As repairs began, we were attacked. We were barely able to hold them off."

"Where is the Captain now?" I asked.

"We expect him to arrive shortly. They weren't that far away but I don't believe that we could have lasted long enough for help to arrive had you not shown up. May I ask – what is your business here?"

"The same as yours," I grinned. "To meet the Captain."

"Are you from the admiralty? Your ship is not on the system."

"No, we have business with him of a... *sensitive* nature."

"There's a lot of that going around," he laughed. "In the meantime, perhaps I can show you some of our hospitality in way of gratitude?"

"I'd like that," I smiled. Then, looking about the docking bay, I asked, "What will you do about the survivors of the *Wayward*?"

"If I had my way, leave them to die. But that's not how the Navy does things, you know. Crews are gathering them up and securing them in the brig as we speak. They'll face an Earth Government court by the end of the month."

"Anything we can help with?" He shook his head.

"You've done enough. How about you shed the armor and join me in my lounge in, say, one hour?"

"Agreed."

We returned to the ship and changed into fresh clothes and I instructed Jo to join us. She looked abashed by the idea but quickly cleaned up and put on her best slacks and a loose-fitting shirt. She still wore her engineering boots, but she'd let her hair down and sprayed on a little perfume.

"You don't normally ask me," she whispered as we were escorted down the corridor to the Captain's lounge. "I didn't know what to wear."

"You look fine," I said. "Calm down."

"Calm down? Have you seen this ship? It's a beauty. I wonder who their chief engineer is?"

Sole met us at the door to his private lounge. He was wearing his full-dress uniform and several aides stood behind a long table of darkest mahogany, eager to serve. The smells that greeted us were beyond exquisite.

"Come, sit," he said, smiling from ear to ear. "Drinks?"

Another aide appeared just as the door closed behind us and as we were shown to our chairs, he took our requests. We all ordered vodka but Baz had to be awkward and asked for whiskey, neat. Captain Sole asked for Karuizawa, a strong, clear liqueur that was rarely seen these

73

days after the sinking of Tokyo; only a few bottles were known to exist.

"I'm officially off duty," he grinned. "My number one now has the bridge – and the hard work."

"This is very kind of you, Captain," I said. "Though I feel we didn't really earn it. The *Wayward* was outmatched, it wasn't quite a fair fight."

"I'll grant you that, but the gesture is valid. We've been out in the depths of space for quite some time and I won't lie – I will enjoy the company of fresh faces."

Once we were seated the drinks arrived. Condensation glistened on the crystal cut glass and the measure was more than generous. Sole raised his drink to us, tilted his head and smiled.

"To coincidence and good fortune – the most welcome companions on any voyage."

We toasted and the meal began. I was grateful that, unlike most dinners hosted by those with ample means, the food wasn't pretentious. To start, Sole offered us a smooth orange and duck pate served with delicate slices of crisp, fresh bread or mushrooms bathed in garlic and chili. For mains, a section of roasted meats was placed in the center of the table and a man dressed all in white, who I assumed was the Captain's personal Chef, carved off great slices to Mason's delight. Steaming vessels of vegetables were brought in and ladled out in enormous portions along with rich beef gravy and other assorted sauces. Desert was no less sumptuous. Three cakes tiered several times were placed where the roasted meat had been and slabs were cut off each, chocolate, vanilla, and a heady rum concoction. Custard in the style of the English came in long boats along with melted chocolate sauce and fresh cream.

Throughout the meal, the conversation remained light while our stomachs grew heavy. Our engineer surprised us all by putting away great platefuls of food and helping herself to no less than three bowls of the rum cake which soon became my favorite.

74

"A family recipe," explained Sole as he helped himself to another slice. "Passed down for over 200 years. The sponge is soaked in the liqueur overnight and fresh cream is then whipped and added on the top. Delightful."

As the last of the dishes were cleared away and the coffee arrived, my mind was swimming. The vodka hadn't stopped coming and one of my great weaknesses, when company and food were good, was an inclination to drink to my own good health. Even Mason looked well oiled as we each took a cup of coffee and leaned back in our seats.

At that moment an officer was admitted into the lounge and she strode towards Sole at the head of the table. Words were exchanged and the woman was dismissed.

"The *Agamemnon* has just entered scanner range," said the Captain. "She should be with us in a few hours."

"That's good news," I said.

"It is. Repairs will go much faster with the help of the fleet, diminished as it is."

"Diminished, Captain?" asked Mason. Glassy-eyed, Sole leaned forward and put his elbows on the table, almost knocking over his empty glass. One eye seemed to grow larger as he took on a conspiratorial expression and began to whisper. I realized then that we'd all been 'well oiled' by that point.

"I shouldn't be saying this," he began. "But we're all good friends here..."

We nodded and smiled like fools. Baz even winked as he leaned in.

"That little ruckus with the 'enemy fleet'," He even managed to do little scare-quotes with his fingers. "Argo would never admit it, but we fair got our asses handed to us if you understand my meaning."

"We do," said Mason.

"Never seen anything like it before," he whispered. "Ships twice the size of ours. Ugly things, blocky, bulky, like something made from children's bricks but I'll be damned if they can't fight like the devil. Shields virtually unbreakable. I saw our finest shot just soaked

75

up by them."

"Where are they from?" I asked.

"Who knows? Scanners could barely get through the interference being put out by those defenses."

"Are they... *alien*?" asked Baz. Sole snorted a laugh and flecks of spit showered onto the table.

"No, my boy, they aren't. Humans at the helm, like you and me."

"How do you know?" he retorted.

"I saw 'em, that's how. If it hadn't been for the Captain, we'd never have lived to tell the tale."

"Argo?" I put in.

"That's the one," he grinned. "Surly bastard, to be sure, but got generations of Admiral's blood in his veins. No sooner had the battle begun than-" Here he stopped and with one sweep of his arm, cleared the space before him so that the cups and saucers and spoons nearly toppled onto the floor. An aide quickly ran to clear them away as he snatched for the remains of the bread basket.

"Here's how things lay," he said and began arranging the bread rolls according to their formations. "The ones with a bit torn off represent the fleet. The ones without, those bastard ships."

He recreated the scene for us, granted, in only one plane which wasn't unusual for large space-faring craft to do in fleet-to-fleet engagements. It made life simpler for both sides and appeared to be a kind of unspoken agreement. It was 'good form', one famous Admiral had said.

"This one with the coffee stain," He sloshed a generous amount from his own cup onto the roll at the front. "Represents the Captain."

Thus began a baked recreation of the battle with the enemy fleet. Sole had a great passion for recounting the event and he flooded the table with facts and figures, weight of shot and the effect upon each ship. It was clear from the beginning that although Argo had had the greater number of craft, the enemy had bested him in firepower and defensive capability right from the start.

"Fucking ships just kept coming," said Sole towards the end. "Lancer. Broadside. Plasma. All nothing to those shields."

"So how did you survive?" asked Jo.

"Ah," he grinned. "Here's the pinch. The Captain, seeing that we'd already lost three heavy cruisers with all hands, knew that withdrawal was the final option. Don't forget – these creepy ships weren't responding to any hails and offered none themselves. They simply saw us and engaged. There was no hope of parley or mercy here and attempting boarding actions were out of the question."

Sole began to shift the bread rolls on the table and re-arrange them as he remembered.

"One of their ships, a big one, looked different to the others. It stood out, not just because of its shape or design, but something about the way the shields refracted starlight caught the Captain's attention. He has an excellent science officer on board and, according to a meeting held after the engagement was over, he put him on that disturbance immediately.

"What do you know? Whenever the ship fired its broadsides, there was a split second opening, a fraction of the power needed to keep them going was diverted to the cannon."

"That's a hell of a weakness," said Jo.

"You're damn right," he laughed. "And it saved our skins. The Captain, when he realized this, gave orders to follow his flight plan as he ran down the port side of the craft, within pistol shot as we say here in the Navy. It seemed like madness – he'd have to take every single hit from their cannon as he passed them."

"But it gave you the chance you needed," said Mason.

"Exactly!" Sole slammed his fist down onto the table and the bread rolls went flying. "I'll never forget it as long as I live. As the *Agamemnon* began to move we drew up aft of her, priming every weapon we could bring to bear. She let loose everything she had into the side of that craft just as they did. You should have seen the exchange, like two titanic fighters trading blows, fist for fist, punch for punch. I thought the Captain was done for."

"And?" said Baz on the edge of his chair now.

"That's when we saw our chance. We had to fire blind. The NavCom wouldn't accept our firing patterns and so the other Captains and I had to guess when to let loose our shot. It was touch and go, believe me. As the *Agamemnon* soaked up the hits, we gave that ship everything we had. You've never seen so much plasma, so many streaks of lancer or cannon. Space was lit up from here to Earth, I'm sure of it.

"As the Captain, crippled and barely holding a course, passed the aft of the ship, we knew that our doom or our victory was at hand. We were committed to follow and if none of our shot had struck during that one window, we'd face the full weight of the enemy broadside. Let me tell you, the *Pearl* is a fine ship but there was no way we'd survive half of what this craft was putting out."

Silence fell in the lounge and even the stoic aides who had kept rigid discipline against the far wall had turned their heads as the story reached its climax. If Sole noticed he didn't mind – I was sure he was enjoying the captive audience at that point.

"As we made our run, I turned the viewer on the ship. I will never forget the moment when those shields came down and the enemy vessel shuddered with internal explosions up and down that ugly, hulking shape."

Sole fell silent then and his eyes lost some of the light that had been in them from the beginning of the account.

"And that's when I saw them..." he said, hushed now, his face grave. "Hundreds of them. Men. Women. Children. The hull had split into several places on her port side like a tin can and bodies were being sucked out into space. Have you ever seen such a thing?" he asked. I didn't reply. It was the booze that asked that question for no serviceman ever spoke of the horrors of war openly. It was an unwritten rule, common courtesy and something for the quiet places of friendship or a lover's arms. Not for the dinner table.

"What happened next?" I asked feeling somewhat sobered by the telling.

"The Captain believed that this had been their flagship. Its destruction caused a full withdrawal of the enemy fleet without another shot fired. No one knew why. Perhaps the loss to them was beyond our understanding. Maybe they respected what we'd done. I guess we'll never know."

"And the *Agamemnon*?" asked Mason.

"She came to within an inch of her total destruction. The engine cores had been breached and were on the verge of a meltdown. Only luck and skill managed to stop her from imploding. Hence the delay in our return; repairs have been going on ever since the battle ended."

The coffee had gone and the room fell silent. Captain Sole, straightening his uniform, stood and we joined him. I guessed that the meal was over.

"I thank you for being such considerate listeners," he said with a faltering smile. "But I will bid you a good night, such as it is. I find that good food and even better company makes me a little fatigued. Please feel free to remain docked for as long as you wish but you have my permission to leave whenever you will. Good night."

"Thank you, sir," said Jo as he turned to leave. "That was one of the best meals I've had in a very long time. And one of the finest accounts of a heroic engagement I've had the pleasure of listening to."

"Thank you, ma'am," he said. Then he was gone and we left the room by another door. An aide led us down the corridor, back towards our ship.

"They won't make that mistake again," said Mason.

"No," I replied. "They certainly won't."

10

We decided to leave the *Pearl* and stand off from her as the rest of the fleet arrived. Being a ship unfamiliar to Naval systems at that time, I wanted to appear open-handed and not a threat when the battered ships saw us.

Once my stomach had settled and I'd drunk some more coffee to sober up, I sat on the bridge and watched the feed relay the arrival of the *Agamemnon*. I felt exhausted and with only two hours sleep and far too much food, I craved a good, long nap. The others had gone for a rest while I took the first shift – something I always regretted offering to do, and I was alone.

"Computer, alert me when the Agamemnon is within range," I said. There was a chime of response and I fumbled around for the mechanism that would recline my seat. Then, sitting skewed, I was able to put my boots up on the corner of the console and rest my head against the edge of the seat. I remembered to deactivate it too after a rather embarrassing incident the first time we took the *Helios* out. Then, tilting my cap over my eyes, I nodded off. I dreamt, that much I remember. Maybe it was other ship battles, maybe not, but on waking I thought that I could see that enemy ship destroyed, see those same bodies floating out into space and feel the same revulsion any normal human being would have felt. To die in battle was one thing, but to be a civilian killed simply for being on the wrong ship at the wrong time never sat well with anyone.

But I had no time to dwell upon that because the next thing I knew the console was chiming and a few hours had slipped past me while I dozed. The fleet had entered the area and was bee-lining for the *Pearl*.

Twenty-two ships in a loose formation came out of hyper speed and it was clear from the scans that they'd taken a battering.

"When I see an unidentified ship standing off from one of my fleet I tend to shoot first and ask questions later," said an all too familiar voice over the comms. I wasn't prepared to give him that much credit – no doubt details of our involvement with the *Pearl* had already been passed on to the *Agamemnon*.

"Captain Argo, we meet again," I said. "It's been too long."

"Indeed. I do not believe that you and your team are here on some kind of mercy mission so I suggest you come up alongside and discuss the matter in person."

"So our friendship hasn't warranted the privilege of docking?"

"That's a luxury beyond my power to extend," he said. "You may be aware of a little ruckus we've just had with some nasty elements. They've rendered our docking bay rather untidy for the moment. Surely that pretentious craft of yours has an umbilical?"

"I'm sure it does," I lied, convinced that I didn't have a clue whether it did or not. "I'll be with you shortly."

"Indeed. *Agamemnon* out."

It didn't. Mason and I met in the loading bay, suited up and unhappy with the idea of what we would have to do to board. After scouring the buyer's guide several times it seemed that the engineering team had neglected to fit the relevant umbilical pairings, wiring and socket attachments given that we'd rushed the sale to leave the following morning. On this rare occasion, I took the blame for that, having never expected to connect to another ship in such a primitive and highly dangerous fashion.

"Classic Carter," said Mason as we stood in the loading bay, watching the horrifically damaged port side dock of the *Agamemnon* appear before us. "You didn't read the small print."

"It was hardly small print," I said. "The engineers thought we wouldn't need it and, if I'm honest, neither did I. Plus it would've added to the prep time."

"We paid for it, we should get it," he replied. "Ever heard of a HARG inverter compensator?"

"No."

"It's an optional extra for the HARG rifle, right?"

"If you say so."

"It stops the projectile from overcharging and taking tiny fragments off the inside of the barrel. Fire it a hundred times, you might never notice the scoring it makes. Fire a thousand times and you might find yourself wondering why your shots are slightly off. Fire a hundred thousand times and the thing explodes in your face, probably taking your arms with it."

"What's your point?"

"I made sure the HARG rifles were fitted with inverter compensators. That's the kind of small print I'm talking about."

The *Hikane* was almost touching the *Agamemnon* at this point and I stepped closer to the forcefield that stood between us and deep space.

"How about the small print on these suits?" I asked. "Did you check those out too?"

"More than you know, mate. Now shall I go first or you?"

"What kind of question is that?" I cried. "You know the drill. Never let someone do something you aren't prepared to do yourself."

"Well stop talking about it and do it, okay?"

"I'm going. Keep your suit on."

I stepped towards the forcefield and hesitated. The distance wasn't an issue because gravity wasn't a factor. The problem was what waited on the other side. The platform I was aiming for was a tattered mess of broken steel and scorched plating and watching from the edge of the devastation was Argo himself with his arms folded behind his back. He was wearing that twisted smile, the one no doubt caused by nerve damage and beside him, like bookends, were his two lieutenants.

"Well?" said Mason.

I shook my head. Then, taking a few steps back, I sprinted for the opening and felt the suit rumble as it passed beyond the forcefield and into deep space for all of three seconds. Another tremor ran up my body and the artificial gravity of the *Agamemnon* yanked me down onto the crumbling platform.

"Welcome aboard, Carter," said the Captain as I stumbled to a halt before him. "I'm sorry for the inconvenience."

"Not as sorry as I am, sir," I replied and stood upright. "But needs must, I suppose."

"Indeed."

Mason landed beside me, elegantly and without the need to steady himself. He nodded to the Captain who gestured that we should follow.

"You'll find my hospitality lacking of late," he explained as we left the docking bay. "My ship has taken quite a beating."

He wasn't kidding either. The damage was extensive and every corridor we walked down was thronged with engineers and technicians desperately trying to repair and rebuild. Sparking conduits and venting gasses followed our steps and on one floor we found ourselves assaulted by the stench of burning plastic and a wailing klaxon.

"Is she going to hold?" I asked as we neared the bridge.

"Of course!" he roared over the deafening sounds of workmen cutting away a collapsed roof beam. "She's a tough old girl. She's seen worse."

Mason gave me a skeptical look but we followed after him, taking a left at the entrance to the bridge and passed through a wide doorway. It was another lounge, this one far more spacious and lavish than that of the *Pearl*. The door closed behind us and the silence was almost deafening.

"My quarters took a fair brunt of the damage," he explained, seating himself at the head of a curving metal table ornately decorated with carvings of old sea-fairing vessels. "I'm afraid we'll have to speak in here. Please, take a seat."

Both Mason and I deactivated our suits and stepped out of them, leaving them standing against a far wall whilst we took chairs near to the Captain. His two lieutenants joined us though one now bore a great scar down one cheek, ending at her left shoulder. It looked recently healed.

"I extend my thanks to you," he began, adjusting his uniform as he sat bolt-upright. "I've looked at Captain Sole's report on the encounter with those pirate scum. Looks like you showed up in the nick of time."

"You're welcome," I replied. "He's a good man and a fine host."

"Ah, so you've had the pleasure of his table, eh?" he grinned, slightly lopsided and the empty socket of his right eye seemed to glare at me. "I do enjoy it when we Captains dine on the *Pearl*, I'll fair admit that."

Turning to an aide standing at the back of the room, he gestured for him to come forward. His head bore a bandage across one eye and his left arm was in a sling.

"I cannot match Sole's hospitality but I can at least offer you something to drink." Then, to the aide, "Bring in the refreshments."

The aide vanished through a door and Argo, looking slightly embarrassed by this, shuffled uncomfortably in his seat until he returned.

"Here we are!" he cried and got up to pour us all a triple measure of vodka. There was no ice. When this was done, he toasted the Navy and the Lord Admiral and we drank. "To business then," he said. "What brings you here, Carter? Had we not concluded our 'arrangement' by the time you returned to Titan 5?"

"We did but this is of a different nature," I explained. "It concerns one of my team."

"Ah," he said and relaxed a little. "The woman with the purple hair."

I could have happily stood up and punched him then but that

wouldn't have been in Angel's best interests. Instead, I ground my teeth together and pressed on.

"Her name is Angel," I said.

"That's *one* of her names, yes."

If a cat who grew up on water all its life was suddenly whisked off the streets, given the rank of Captain in Earth Gov. Navy and handed a bowl of the finest fresh cream, it wouldn't have looked half as smug as Argo did at that moment. With steepled fingers resting on the table beside his glass and the book-end lieutenants as stony-faced as ever, the urge to kill was foremost in my mind.

"Is there any chance we can bypass the bullshit and skip to the part where you explain to me exactly how this happened?" I asked through gritted teeth.

"Certainly," he replied. "But I'm not sure you'll like the truth."

"Try us."

Argo adjusted his posture and emptied his glass, pouring himself another. Then he passed the bottle to me. I did the same.

"The battle at Noctis Labyrinthus. I've no doubt that you're both aware of it." We nodded. "On the surface, it was a tragic defeat. All the pieces were in place, all the hard intelligence work done, it was a perfect mission which came on the heels of the fall of Mars Prime. Then Chief of Staff, Robert Wash, was the first to propose the full-scale attack on the mines to the President at the time.

"History has always laid the blame for the loss at Wash's feet despite all the evidence in favour of it being a sound tactical move. I saw the intelligence reports myself first hand, read the same graphs, the same spectroanalysis and heard the testimony of our own agents in Martian Command. No one could say that they would have acted differently."

"You sound invested," I pointed out. Argo smirked and took a sip of his drink.

"You could say that I am. Robert is a good friend of my family, particularly my Father. His sudden and very public shaming after the

85

defeat was a heavy blow to us and, until recently, a cause for argument at the family table."

I looked at Mason who was thinking the same thing – what did the Argo family table look like? Was Admiral Argo seated at the head or his wife?

"But it failed miserably because the Intel was wrong," said Mason. "Are you going to tell us differently?"

"Yes, though I admit that I felt the same way until I received a visit from Wash before leaving to engage the enemy fleet. He seemed excited, happier than he had been in decades. He couldn't speak fast enough to tell me that he'd come across some new information that would, in his own words, 'shake the very foundations of Earth Gov.' Then he handed me a data cube before leaving, saying that it would explain everything."

"And did it?" I asked.

"Not really, I admit. Upon returning into Earth Gov. space we received our normal coded message packet which always includes the news feeds. When I heard of several arrests from the admiralty made by JAG officials and saw the suspects, I was able to fill in the gaps. No doubt Robert had come upon evidence of collusion with the enemy, the kinds of which named names. Big names and little names – of which Angel was one and, unfortunately for you, the most important one to Wash."

"Why?" asked Mason.

"The Martians knew we were coming," said Argo. "Someone told them. In order to have told them, the informant needed to have been flown in – our signal jammers were in operation for the entire war. That requires a pilot of skill and silence. Only one was recommended to anyone of significance around that time and that was Angel."

"And who was the person of significance?"

"One General Alexander Bourmont who we cannot hope to implicate without proof and, preferably, an eyewitness. Say, a pilot who flew him and his bodyguard into those mines. We can build a case against him but without Angel's confession, we don't have much else to nail him on. You see our dilemma?"

"Again, why are you taking such an interest? Why did Wash come to you in the first place? Because you had Sunday dinner together?"

Argo waved an arm about him, gesturing to the heavily damaged ship all about us.

"This is why. This is just a taste of what's to come. There are a people out there who've managed to slide into a dark corner of the galaxy and be forgotten. Out of sight of Earth Government, they've built a fleet crewed by experienced and skilled sailors. They have questionable degrees of advanced technology. And we know nothing about them, perhaps only that they're coming and that they aren't friendly.

"Earth Government, and more acutely, the Navy, isn't ready. Cutbacks by peacetime cowards who've never fired a shot in anger have weakened Earth's defenses. Liberals have robbed fighting men and women of their pride and their desire to protect the weak. Right now, our people back home are probably celebrating the winner of some TV game show instead of remembering real heroes who fought and died in the voids of deep space, defending their homes. Bottom line – our leaders aren't who Earth Government need and we and a few others have a very limited window of opportunity to change that."

"You're talking about a coup," said Mason. Argo shook his head.

"No. I love our way of life too much to take such drastic action. To so dramatically overthrow our own government would be a wound so grievous that Earth would take a long time to recover from it. But I'm willing to use the system to help rid us of the corrupt and the traitorous and help those who have earned the right to defend Earth and her interests."

"And you believe Wash is just such a person?"

"With him in line for Presidency, we'll have a trustworthy combat veteran at the helm with the moral fiber to boot. It'll be the first step in preparing us for the war that's coming. Don't misunderstand me, gentleman – you've seen the evidence for yourself. We've taken a damn good thrashing off what I believe was only ever an advanced scouting party, not even a full-strength fleet. What horrors are lying in wait for us when the time comes? Should I stand back and let weak men and women lead us to our doom?"

"Even if it means offering our friend on the altar?" I asked. Argo stared at me and held my gaze. It was as if he was weighing up two equally dangerous options and, after his impressive speech, deciding upon which course of action would further his cause. He made his decision because he broke away first and looked down at his hands.

"I sent a coded message to Robert last night. I wanted to know where he'd gotten this new evidence from and if it could be trusted. He seemed hurt by my question but eventually, he did reveal its source. Suffice it to say I wasn't much comforted.

"He claims that Aaron Hurt was one of the bodyguards who flew in with Bourmont on the day he handed over the battle plans to the Martians. In exchange for something he wouldn't reveal, Robert was given most of what he needed to start proceedings and begin a thorough investigation. Since then Hurt has vanished, according to Robert, and he can no longer get in touch with him."

"And?" said Mason.

"And I looked into it with far more vigor and resources that even the former Chief of Staff has access to and learned that no such man ever existed."

"Officially?" I asked.

"Both officially and unofficially. Which means that this man is either hiding his identity or working on behalf of some other party."

"So, it's a dead end?"

"Not necessarily. He knew too much, according to what Robert told me and a little more digging revealed to me the actual names of his entire personal security team, all of whom are currently on the planet Sargon in the Solaria system, maybe two days from here."

"Why are you telling us this?" asked Mason, clearly frustrated.

"Because one of them, alive, would have more to say than a stone-faced pilot who might just slip from the eyes of JAG with a bigger prize in sight."

He let this sink in and I finished my drink, pouring a third. Here we were again, having our strings pulled by the same man who'd been pulling them since Golan IV. Maybe he did have a valid point about Earth's weakened Navy, but did we really want to help put his Cadre into power? Alice had always warned me about getting involved in politics, in planetary disputes, but this was an entire galaxy and the stakes had never been higher. And for what? Angel? One person? How would history tell this story when it all boiled down to it?

I looked at Mason who, in turn, looked at me. His expression said it all – what choice did we have? It was one of our own and what was history if not a tale of many, many individual lives?

"Okay," I said. "Tell us what we need to know."

I was dead on my feet by the time I reached my room. The revelations from Captain Argo had been too much to take in all at once and I was glad that Mason had shown the proper initiative and recorded the whole thing using the new suits.

Other than what was said, it was also strange to notice that Argo made no attempt at secrecy and that the eerie looking Intelligence officer I remembered from our last encounter was nowhere to be seen. I had no question about his lieutenants; apart from being carved out of granite I had little doubt about their unwavering loyalty and to even be in those positions aboard the *Agamemnon* told me a great deal about their worth and their character.

But Argo, rather than appear clandestine, was wide open about his involvement in Wash's plans to climb to the seat of Earth Government's power. Did he really believe that the enemy fleet, now having suffered a major blow at his own hand, posed the greatest threat to a galactic superpower such as Earth Gov.? So much so that he was willing and able to supplant democracy in order to install his own people in the key positions of power in order to safeguard it?

My head swam. I was tired and I needed to sleep. At the end of the day, I was a soldier and soldiers didn't involve themselves in the machinations of their superiors. But I *had* involved myself, that was undeniable. First, by accepting the D122 and not safeguarding myself and the others against the very manipulation we'd suffered both at the hands of Earth Gov. and Captain Argo. Then, by taking up the cause of Angel's innocence I'd dragged us all back in again only to bind ourselves to this Captain's crusade. How much blood might be spilled because of these actions? But on the flip side, how much might be saved?

I didn't think any more about it. Instead, I threw off my clothes and crawled under the covers, leaving the thinking to Mason. The Solaria system was a full 32 hours away which gave me plenty of time to dream of something other than work.

11

Whatever I'd been dreaming of didn't get chance to linger once the comms unit began wailing at me to get up. With a dry mouth and a numb arm, I dragged myself out, padding over to the bathroom half-dazed. The lights came on and as I leaned over the sink to spit out a mouthful of cleanser, I caught a glimpse of something in the mirror behind me. I spun around like a fountain, spraying the walls with blue liquid.

"JIMMY!" I cried, sending flecks straight at the bot. "What the hell?"

There, his little hands neatly folded in front of him, was the bot. He was still wearing the flat cap but his eyes wouldn't look directly at me.

"I'm sorry, sir," he whispered. "I didn't mean to frighten you."

"Well you did, Jimmy," I said, trying to calm my erratic heartbeat. "How did you get in?"

"The door wasn't locked, sir."

Of course. Why would I lock the door on my own ship?

"Well, you should know that we... *people* normally press the button on the outside of the door to let the person inside know you're there, right? Does that make sense?"

"Yes, sir. I fink me old man said somfink about that."

"Okay. Remember that for next time."

"I will, sir."

Then we both stood there, looking at each other in silence. Jimmy shifted weight from foot to foot, still avoiding direct eye contact.

"Well?" I asked. "What can I do for you?"

"Oh!" he cried. "Yes, I remember now. Miss Jo asks for you to visit

91

her in the engine room, like. When you're ready."

"Okay, I'll do that." Another moment of silence. Then, "You can go now, Jimmy. I'll be down shortly. Thanks for the message."

"Aye, sir. I'll be running along then."

The bot turned, waved goodbye and left through the door. Just as I was about to let out a long-held breath, the door chimed. I went and opened it.

"Like that, sir?" said Jimmy, pressing the button again for good measure.

"Yeah, exactly like that."

"Gotcha!" He beamed and then began to whistle as he walked down the corridor. I closed and locked the door behind him. Then, getting changed while the coffee machine in my room did its thing, I took the drink and myself down to engineering.

"Something wrong with the comms?" I asked as Jo appeared from under a length of ducting with a wrench in her hands.

"No. I was starting the... *work* you gave me to do," she replied. "That for me?" She pointed at my cup. "Milk with no sugar?"

"It isn't and yes, it is," I laughed. "I'll grab you one though."

While she gathered up her tools I went and got her a drink and together we headed beyond the thrumming engine cores and into a separate workshop that was already looking like her own spot on the *Helios*. She walked over to the bench and moved some pieces away from a part that looked like it should be inside the ship and doing something, not sitting there.

"Well?" I asked.

"It's the nebulus buffer," she said. "Look familiar?"

"No."

"It shouldn't – this is the nebulus buffer from a P675 control unit, most often seen on those junkers they use to ferry scrap metal to and from the forge moons. Basically, ships that don't leave the safe network of orbital platforms."

"And you're going to tell me that it doesn't belong on this very expensive yacht we're sailing in, right?" She nodded. "He screwed us over, didn't he?" Another nod. "Okay. We're still alive and the ship is moving. Would it be a stretch to say that we don't need the buffer?"

"Yes, it would; we need the buffer. Period."

"Okay. That one doesn't look healthy, Jo."

"It's dead."

"Options?"

"We're heading for Sargon, yes?"

"That's the plan."

"There's bound to be a maintenance platform. We need to dock there so I can make repairs without the dock officials getting involved. If they saw us flying around without a nebulus buffer we'd be impounded on the spot."

"Can you repair it?" She snorted her derision. Clearly, I'd said the wrong thing.

"It's not a case of 'can I' it's a case of having something to repair. This thing is beyond the grave and even if it was working, I would never install it into a ship of this size. It'd be suicide."

"Tell me what you need."

"A new one," she said. "We'd better hope they sell one where we're going or we can't leave Sargon for the foreseeable."

"I think I'm actually happy about this."

"Happy?"

"Yeah. It's the first thing to go wrong and I'm still alive. I was wondering when things were going to go south and now it's begun. Thanks, Jo."

"Don't mention it."

"You'd better do a full system sweep too, just to make sure there aren't any other gremlins standing by to pounce."

"It's already being done."

I made my way to the bridge, carrying the dead component in one

93

hand and a second coffee in the other. When I entered, Baz was in the command chair, snoring.

"Didn't you get some sleep?" I asked, setting the nebulus buffer on an empty console. He jolted awake.

"Kind of. Then Mason came and woke me up for my shift. What time is it?"

"Not a clue," I said. "How far from Sargon are we?"

"Another 22 hours maybe."

"Okay, go and get your head down. No point us both being up here while the ship does its thing."

"Nice one."

He vanished through the door and I took his place, checking the log for the previous 8 hours. Nothing much had happened. All the readouts were in the green despite running without the buffer, and the scanners hadn't detected anything more than the usual traffic on the space lanes heading in the same direction as us. All we had to do now was wait.

An hour or so later and Mason, dressed in his gym gear, appeared on the bridge. I was reading a book with my feet up when he arrived, finishing a third coffee.

"How long to go?" he asked.

"Just over 20 hours."

"Good. Suit drills in 30 minutes. We'll use the loading bay. I got Thor to clear some space for us. Baz will meet us down there." He finally noticed the lump of metal on the console. "What's that?"

"The nebulus buffer," I replied. "Or our 'ex' nebulus buffer."

"It's broken?"

"It's dead. Jo discovered it earlier."

"How are we still moving then?" he asked.

"Damned if I know. While we go looking around Sargon for a bunch of soldiers, Jo and Baz will have to locate and install a new one or this will be where our journey ends."

94

He looked the thing over and shook his head before turning to go. I got up, set the bridge controls to alert me to anything serious, and followed him out.

"I've been reading up on the exo-shells," he said as we walked. "There's some pretty serious hardware in them."

"Such as?"

"Well you can see the plating material – that's some high-end armor. Light, flexible but able to withstand far more than even the FARGO units."

"So they claim."

"So I know," he laughed. "I fired a HARG rifle at one. Didn't even scuff the finish."

"You fired it at your own suit?" I cried.

"No, you idiot. That would be stupid."

"Good. That means you fired it at Baz's."

"Exactly."

"No damage?"

"Nothing. I did 10 controlled shots, high yield. Same result."

We descended the staircase and found the air was cooler on the lower decks – an odd phenomenon.

"What else?"

"It has some clever features. The right or left gauntlet can be charged to deliver a high-frequency burst on impact. It will seriously deplete the cells each time but they say they're working on improving the power core for the next model."

"What about jump capability?"

"Not included with ours but they're designing a lightweight booster that should replicate the FARGO jump pack. Again, early days I guess."

"So you're serious about investing in the company then?" I asked.

"Deadly. I think this is the way forward, I really do. We'll have a majority share in the business which means we'll be able to push for our own designs and ideas. It'll be a damn good investment for us and

95

TRIDENT. They got excited when I showed them the pilosite swords. They're looking into other melee options."

"Having a less bulky version would be a blessing."

We reached the loading bay and found Baz was already suited up and running through the basic exo-shell warm-up rituals. Now, with time to watch, I realized how impressive they looked. Their smooth operation and elegant design made FARGO look blocky and clunky. With the HARG rifles, they looked positively dangerous. I went to suit up myself.

"Time to work up a sweat," said Mason, grinning. "Wouldn't want to get rusty now, would we?"

12

Captain Argo's assessment of Sargon hadn't been exaggerated. As we docked it was clear from the masses of grey cloud that swamped our view of the planet that we were in for a soaking. Human beings are known for their ability to capitalize on unfortunate situations and orbital platform 'Theta Sanderson' was by no means exempt from this. We docked in the maintenance side of the rotating structure, left Baz and Jo to look for a new buffer and made our way to the sprawling shopping district that made two circuits of the platform. Our clothing wasn't designed for anything like the weather predicted inside Sargon City and we needed to change that.

Mason and I strolled up and down, checking out the stalls and storefronts, looking firstly for anything in our size, and secondly for anything that wasn't overtly designed. The latter wasn't much of a challenge; it seemed like most of the planet's population wore long ankle-length coats made of synthetic leather and water-tight boots that came up to the knee. The temperature was known to vary throughout the year offering a rather unpleasant mix of high humidity one day and extreme cold the next. This leaned fashion towards a polymer that kept the body insulated but cool. How that worked was beyond me but it felt pretty good against the skin.

We took our purchases back to the ship, changed and noticed that Baz and Jo hadn't returned yet. Thor and Jimmy were in the loading bay, sifting through the junk from Titan 5.

"We're heading out now, Thor. Get ready," I said. I wanted the bot with us. He would serve two important purposes, three if you thought about it. One, to provide a direct link to Angel's defense. Two, to hide

97

light weapons inside while we passed through customs, and a third was physical protection. Nothing put off an attacker like a half-crazy construction bot with a hammer.

"I'll be wiv you shortly," he beamed. "I'll meet you on the platform. Got to get ready, you see."

"Okay but don't hang around. Each day that passes puts Angel at risk in that prison."

"I understand, sir."

The coat was a good fit and warm with a fur lining and a deep hood that almost hid my entire face from view. I adjusted it as Mason handed me a portable shield generator, clipping one to his own belt before we left the ship.

"Same as always, four strikes and you're out," he explained. "Though in this weather I expect it might only manage three."

"What are you stashing in the bot?" I asked.

"Two of the Calimar-six plasma pistols. I've downgraded their output in favor of rapid fire. If we do get into a firefight I don't expect anyone will be shooting straight in the downpour. Accuracy through volume on this one."

"That's a habit we need to break."

"Blame Golan IV."

"I blame the fact that we haven't had a break since we got slammed with a D122."

"Maybe today we'll get that break."

"From a handful of 'advisors'? I doubt it, pal. More likely we'll be left with some corpses and a whole bunch of unanswered questions."

"That's the story of our lives."

"Ain't that the truth?"

We left the *Hikane* and stepped onto the platform, our new boots creaking as we broke them in. The maintenance platform was busy, frantically busy to be more accurate but there was less people traffic which worked in our favor. After a few minutes, the loading bay door opened and Thor finally appeared. Mason stifled his mirth.

"I told you," I said once I'd seen him. "Didn't I tell you this back on Titan 5?"

"Yes, I'll give you that. You said this would happen."

"I'm not even surprised," I laughed. "That's how bad things have got. I'm not shocked by him now. It's just the norm."

Thor, coming down the platform, greeted us with a kind of courteous, conspiratorial nod. He was much smaller, having shed most of his bulk using the body he'd begun building on our journey home. Now he only stood two feet above Mason and perhaps twice as wide. But that wasn't what struck us first. What failed to surprise us was the trench coat, the trilby and the newspaper under his mechanical arm.

"Good-evenin', gentlemen," he whispered. "Is the game afoot, as they say?" I sighed.

"I see you're dressed for the part."

"Of course," he said without a single atom of humor. "We're investigating the setup, sir. The fix. The frame-up of one of our own, sir. We need to be on the low, the QT, the-"

"Okay, we understand," I said, cutting him short. "Let's go."

"Aye sir," he said, trying to doff his hat. "Let's go."

We took the shuttle down to Sargon City West, the nearest landing pad to where Argo told us that a contact of his would meet us. I couldn't say that I was overjoyed with the idea; contacts were for spooks and Earth Government 'advisors' and I had a deep loathing for all things clandestine. Perhaps there was a role for it to play in the exercising of power for the sake of democracy, but beneath that, I wondered if the means didn't justify the ends. No good could come of lying to both yourself and everyone else.

When we landed, we walked out onto the street, keenly aware that even so late in the day, the streets were tightly packed with people and business. Street pedlars and hawkers of gaudy gifts roamed up and down the wide pavements, speaking in strange and often hypnotic languages. The towering skyscrapers acted like great walls, hemming everyone in at their feet but casting a mystical neon glow all about. The air stank of ozone, of sweat and of misery. People shopped and people came and went to work, but no one could be mistaken in believing that the people of Sargon City were actually happy. A funk of dark mood pervaded every corner, every side alley and even down to the cracks in the slate grey paving slabs and once it took hold it was hard to shake off. Three streets later and the rain began, coming down in a great wash that beat us down, sending us deeper into our hooded coats.

"This is nice," said Mason, lacing the comment with sarcasm the same way a cheated wife might murder her wayward husband. "Why do people live here again?"

"Two reasons," I replied. "Molanium and soft-core midget porn."

"Eh?" said Thor. "Midgets, sir?"

"That's right. Just above the planet's core are rich deposits of molanium, the most used metal in prosthetics. That keeps the mines outside of the city running night and day but molanium miners are prone to exposure to fumes that cause them to be attracted to the smaller person."

"Really?" laughed Mason but Thor was genuinely interested.

"Yeah. It's said that if you receive a molanium part it'll bleed the same chemical into your bloodstream and the next thing you know, you're getting hard-ons for people of a vertically challenged nature."

"That's incredible, sir," remarked Thor. "I never knew this."

"Neither did Mason but I've seen the way he's been looking at Baz recently."

The next thing I knew Mason's hand was coming straight at me, open palmed and directly at my chest. I felt it hit with full force and I barely remained standing.

"That's for being a dick," he said as I stumbled upright again. I tried to suck air back into my lungs but it refused.

"What kind of attack was that Mr. Mason?" asked the bot.

"It's called a Ric Flair," he explained. "Very handy against people you really don't like."

"I see, sir. I'll make a men'al note to find out who this hero was, sir. Was 'e on Mars, sir?"

"If only," laughed Mason.

We walked on, following both the ebb and flow of the traffic and the directions given by my personal comms unit. It was leading us towards Precinct 6 in the business district eight kilometers from city hall. Here, according to Argo, we'd find his contact.

"How's that pistol feel?" asked Mason at an intersection.

"Like a brick on my hip," I replied. "But I'm happier for it being there. Look at that guy."

Ahead, leaning against the doorway of a closed laundrette, was a man with folded arms who wore the expected long coat but sported a bald scalp, various scars on his ashen face and an expression of fixed concentration on those who walked by. He stood out and that was exactly his intention.

"Where's the real tracker?" I asked. Mason looked around discreetly.

"There," he said. "On your two, just examining the comms unit store."

The rain continued to fall, reducing visibility to a few feet. Everyone seemed to shrink, to bunch their shoulders and dip their heads as it fell on their backs. It made us stand out, walking as we had done since our first days on the parade ground. There was no point trying to blend in. As a spook had once pointed out to me, military or former military had a uniform of their own and you couldn't take it off. Even if you tried, you just looked like a soldier trying not to look like a soldier.

"He's moving," said Mason. "Nothing hostile just yet."

"But they used a decoy. That's not conventional."

"But it fits with Special Forces SOP."

"True."

On we walked, stopping only to investigate a coffee shop and give some attention to the cakes on display there. It gave us a chance to spot our tail again, this time on our side of the street, walking slowly behind and avoiding the oncoming people traffic.

"They'll change their man in the next thirty minutes," I said. "We'll grab a coffee then and sit for a while inside."

"I'd agree with that," said Mason. "I could do with some cake. I didn't notice anyone at the orbital platform or the customs gate."

"Neither did I but that doesn't mean there wasn't one."

We waited. The rain beat down and gave the pavement a glossy sheen, reflecting some of the pedestrians back at us. It was soothing in a strange way, kind of like white noise, drowning out the chatter and clamor of a hectic part of the city. People walked by, looking pretty much the same as us though slightly smaller. Some stopped to examine the cakes, others just walked on, heads down, probably wondering why they got themselves born on the wettest planet under Earth Government rule.

"Let's eat."

We went inside and Thor, ducking down a little, was able to join us. I noticed then that the shops all had tiled flooring with stainless steel grating to drain off the rainfall brought in by the customers.

"My shout," said Mason. "What are you having?"

"Double espresso; I feel sluggish."

He went to the counter and Thor stood idle, looking back out through the entrance. People looked at him but didn't dwell too long on his intimidating frame. Thankfully there were several servant bots on the streets and his newly constructed chassis helped him to blend in with them, though his outfit perhaps offset that.

"Are you expectin' trouble, sir?" he asked as I took a seat near the back. There was a marked fire exit through the kitchen, a possible escape route.

"You should always expect it," I said. "Then you won't be shocked when it happens."

"But we've never been 'ere before, sir. Who knows us?"

"That's what we're here to find out."

Mason returned with a tray straining with cake and coffee. I took my cup, drained it in one go and tucked into a slice of something gooey and chocolate coated.

"A recipe known only on Sargon," he explained, spooning a piece into his mouth while absent-mindedly scratching his chest. "Tastes a bit like sticky toffee pudding."

"It's moist enough, like this bloody planet. Seems apt."

We ate and watched the door. People moved past the windows which hadn't steamed up at all and given the nature of Sargon I guessed that the glass was specially made for that purpose. We could see through it just fine and when the first slice was gone and we started on some small squares of something both bitter and sweet, we saw the decoy stroll by.

"This isn't about us," said Mason. "We've just caught their eye."

"They're paranoid?" He nodded. "Still? After all this time?"

"Argo's contact was on to them. Maybe it stirred the hornet's nest."

"We're speculating again."

"What else should we do?"

"Carry on and improvise. I hate making micro-plans; you know that the first thing to go when the fighting starts is the plan."

"You're expecting a fight?"

"You're the one who insisted on these." I patted my hip.

He finished his cake and drank some of his coffee. I had respect for Mason for many reasons but near to the top of that list was his love for straight-up coffee with far too much sugar. Unlike Baz who drank fancy things with so much science in them that they had to be sponsored by CHERICA-AUTO. I was suddenly and very sharply reminded of the bitter taste of Angel's preferred drink, lemon tea.

We waited some more. The pungent aroma of freshly ground coffee was more than pleasant given that the last couple of days had given me only new carpet and hot metal scents to dine on. I scraped the crumbs from my plate with my fork and considered ordering more when a figure came walking into the cafe, shaking off the rain from his hood and looking around. He was gaunt with a head of unkempt brown hair and a mouth whose corners turned downwards in a kind of permanent grimace. His eyes were deep blue but reduced almost to pinpoints on an ocean of white and I could already see the snaking tendrils of scar tissue from the base of his skull creeping around his neck. He wore a long, battered coat and gloves of the same black synthetic leather and his boots made a creaking sound as he came towards us.

"That isn't a soldier," said Mason. "Looks more like a cop."

"Still," I replied, parting the buttons of my coat to give me an easy pull on the pistol. "You can never be sure."

The man stopped a couple of meters from our table and nodded once.

"Eldritch," he said with a faint tinge of the local accent. "I was told you were coming."

"...told that we were coming to *you*, not the other way around," I replied.

"True. But Sargon isn't the kind of city it appears to be. When a luxury ship docks at Theta and two soldier-types get off, Sargon PD tends to take notice. Especially given our mutual... interests."

I stood up and the man took a step forward, his hand outstretched and trembling slightly.

"My name is Malcolm," he said.

"Carter. And this is Mason and our... *friend*, Thor."

Eldritch greeted them both in the same way before gesturing to the empty seat at our table. I agreed and he sat down, taking out a small pill bottle from his pocket, shaking out a couple of pink discs.

"It says to take with food," he said. "How's the cake today?"

"Nice," said Mason.

"I'll order a slice then. I try not to drink coffee, but old habits die hard, they say."

A waitress came over, addressed him by name and went off to fill his request.

"How long were you in?" I asked. Eldritch looked sideways at me. "I saw the scar."

"25 under, 6 over."

"A lifer then?"

"Something like that."

Mason gave me a distrustful look and I shook my head, warding off further inquiry.

"I had a friend," I said. "Managed 5 before the law came in."

Eldritch gave me a long look, must have seen that I wasn't trying to offend him and changed his opinion of me.

"I was a detective for the program," he explained. "A damn good one. When the law came in and I was 'expelled' they offered me work at Sargon PD. I act as a freelancer, sometimes solving cold cases when it's quiet, that sort of thing."

"Do you enjoy it?"

"I miss home," he said. "I assume your friend does too."

"He did. Sadly, he took his own life."

Eldritch gave me a slow nod and shook the bottle.

"I take these four times a day. Sometimes I forget and the images begin to surface again. They blend with the day, like falling asleep but not."

"They weren't available to him."

"I'm sorry."

"Thank you."

His order came and he thanked the waitress. Then, sipping at the coffee he examined the cake.

"Looks nice today," he said. "Cheryl must be at the oven."

He took a bite and chewed on it. Then another, washing it down with more coffee. "Your company has gone, by the way."

"You were aware of them?" asked Mason.

"Yeah. They've been showing up for a couple of days now, ever since I got a break on where they're holding up."

"They?"

"I assume they're here for the same reason you are – to find that missing squad. Argo warned me you were coming, of course. No need for the cloak and dagger stuff now."

"How did you get involved?" I asked.

"They haven't been idle here on Sargon," he began. "The first time I heard of them was when one of the local crime syndicates began whining to our inside men that a rival faction was stealing their arms business but that they couldn't figure out who they were. Sargon PD handed the case to me and I've been chewing away at it for a while. Then, out of the blue, this Navy Captain contacts me about the reports I've submitted to JAG. You see, I had a gut feeling for a long time that they were former soldiers, the kind that have contacts for moving this sort of gear. So, of course, I start with the Judge Advocates office to find out which of our boys and girls are MIA, which ones have a history, and which have the access. I guess I kicked up some dust."

"What did Argo say?"

"That I was to keep him informed and that these suspects were implicated in other more serious crimes, the kind he couldn't tell me about. I'm not sure how he made the leap, but he seems to think that these are the people he's looking for. Then I got a message last night warning me that you were coming. So, I kept my eye on the ports and saw you dock. Now here we are and already you've picked up a tail. I don't know who this new element could be, but I've no doubt that we'll find out soon, right?"

Malcolm Eldritch was the kind of man who spoke as if he didn't really care if you were listening or not. He ate his cake, sipped his coffee and told you what you wanted to hear but already his eyes had become glassy and distant, like he was someplace else, which he was. He was home, the place he'd been for 25 years before Earth Government banned the use of all total-immersion systems and thrown 'lifers' out into the big wide world. The fact that he'd lasted this long was a testament to his willpower; he'd been living another life, a better life, for most of his own, one with a wife and children, a career and it would all have been perfect, man-made without suffering and sorrow. Now he'd had the plug pulled – the scarring on the back of his neck a vivid reminder of that, and his world was now bleak and wet and painful. The pills would keep his fractured mind together like superglue but for some, living this life was no life at all and they made other arrangements.

"How far did you get with your investigation?" I asked.

"Not very," he replied. "I have a few leads, some better than others. I was hoping that you'd be able to help."

"In what way?"

"I'm restricted by Sargon laws, even as a freelancer. Maybe if I were to give you the directions you'd be able to... achieve your objectives yourself."

"In return for some cooperation?" I asked. He shook his head.

"I don't give a shit either way. It closes a case, that's all. Argo said you had a keen interest in finding this rogue element, right?"

"It's a long story."

"They always are. They're always about people over missions, personal sacrifices over the bigger picture. Let me guess – a friend of yours needs your help, right?" I nodded. "Nothing new."

"No I guess it's not," I said. "Does that make it less important?" Eldritch shrugged.

"What does any of it matter?" he said. "Do you want me to help you for some kind of moral reason?"

"I never asked for your help."

"Argo did."

"I don't work for Argo."

"Are you sure?" He grinned and that lopsided smile faintly reminded me of the Captain. Were all scars basically the same? Did they inflict the same kinds of damage that Eldritch and Argo suffered

107

from? A cold, heartless view on living?

"No," I replied. "But I get it."

"Do you?"

"Yeah. You had a good life, I can see that. Things in a total-immersion environment were what you craved and you got it, every credit you paid for. For 25 years you lived a life the rest of us only dream about and when your time was up you found yourself facing reality and it sucked. I don't blame you for being bitter."

"Yeah, I'm bitter."

"But here we are. Right now. Here. This guy-" I pointed to Mason. "His chest was caved in and now it's made of metal. Me? I have an artificial spine because I was betrayed by a co-worker. We aren't married. We have no kids. We've got this and this is all we have. A friend is in trouble. We want to help her.

"Her?"

"Angel. She's locked up facing charges of treason and only this team has the answers we need. Now I tell you this-" Here I leaned forward, putting my face in his as I'd done for my friend so many years ago before he blew his own brains out. "You have a chance to help her. You can take it or you can walk away. It doesn't bother me which because either way I'm going to find these guys and drag them back to Earth Gov. It'll be easier if someone who knows what he's doing helps me."

Eldritch grinned. I knew it was a grin because even the dead parts of his face managed to crease along with the others. I saw his pain, there was no doubt about that, but as a wise man had once said, be careful with others – they're fighting a harder battle than you.

"Okay," he said. "I believe you."

"Believe me?"

"Yeah. Most people say they knew a lifer once. I actually believe you did."

13

Eldritch didn't waste time. We left the cafe and saw that our tails had gone – for now. He hailed a cab and, thanks to Thor's reduced size, we were all able to get in although the vehicle did sink considerably. According to the Freelancer's instruction, we were heading to Fall Street.

"Are you carrying?" he asked as the taxi lurched into the air.

"Yeah," said Mason.

"They don't let me own a gun," he said. "Don't let the PD catch you with it. Sargon Police are a little nervous around firearms and if they think you have one they'll call in the Shock Squad."

"The what?" I asked.

"Security bots. Very fast, very deadly. They'll drill you full of holes without a word. They'll even clean up the mess you leave too."

"Why the aggression?"

"Sargon has a long history of wanting to break from Earth Government and go it alone. Every so often we get a run of terrorism and the PD, not the Military, have to take the brunt of it. Last year 26 cops were murdered by Sicos."

"Who?"

"Sargon Independence Cadre. Not very original but effective at ruining the day for millions of people just trying to scratch out a living. They're our mutual interest's primary customers, or so I'm led to believe."

"Have they been here long?" asked Mason.

"I haven't been able to figure that out. Gun running has always been a problem here; Sargon is the home of Python Munitions and they have many warehouses beyond the city limits. It's not uncommon for them to get hit and report a lot of missing stock to the PD who promptly go about doing nothing."

"I get the impression you aren't a huge fan of local law enforcement."

"I'm not. They're a bunch of lazy ass-holes who like nothing better than to catch traffic offenders but show up late to break-ins and murders. A couple of guys got a visit from the Shock Squad because they were caught carrying gym bags into an all-hours gym. I mean, it might have taken most of the Investigation Squad days to work out what they were doing there I guess. Two guys. Big bags. A gym. The clues were there, I guess the answer just eluded them."

The taxi cruised along the lanes, its windows drenched in rainfall but the wipers cleared them long enough for me to see the city. It glistened in the darkness, neon lights twinkling in the wet making the streets below appear liquid, flowing like a stream but one that ran in many directions, this way and that. There was a beauty to it that overlooked the constant downpour and made it neo-noir like it had fallen straight out of a movie.

The cab descended to a stop on Fall Street and Eldritch was the first to get out. The rain hammered down on us as I pulled up my hood, my hair soaked already.

"This way," he said and we followed him down the empty street lined with imitation silver birch trees set in the stonework of the pavement. The buildings on either side loomed tall over us. They looked like apartment blocks. A few lights shone in the windows. Most were in darkness.

"Where are we going?" I asked.

"To the first breadcrumb," he replied. "Over there is an apartment rented under the alias of Fred Bolg. We're going to check it out."

"You haven't done that yet?" said Mason.

"No. Remember – this was a dull case until Argo called me. I had this place in the file, but I hadn't had any reason to follow it until now.

Things are going to have to move faster than a normal investigation would allow, especially given the appearance of those two outside the cafe."

"Because someone else is on the trail too?" I asked. Eldritch nodded.

"I doubt they have the contacts to alert them to Argo's snooping so that means someone else has warned them about other parties on the hunt."

We crossed the street as he did, noting that there was hardly a sound beyond the hum of speeders far overhead. I made sure my coat was unfastened and that the pistol was loose in the holster.

"Our friend was their pilot."

"And she's been arrested because of what they've been up to?"

"Yes."

"Maybe someone is looking to tie up loose ends?"

"That would be my first assumption," said Mason.

"Mine too."

Outside of a brown stone building perhaps 20 stories high, Eldritch stopped and mounted the concrete steps leading up to the door. He peered at the windows, maybe halfway up.

"Floor 9, apartment 12. Fred Bolg is a made-up name, he doesn't exist but the rent payments tie it to a company that sells underfloor heating to factories. Specifically munitions factories."

"Seems a bit of a slip up on their part," I said.

"People are lazy. They don't expect anyone to dig beyond a surface investigation and so they cut corners. What's a bank account for an apartment rent to someone investigating massive arms dealing?"

"I guess I expected more from them."

"It's like any profession – there are good ones and there are bad ones. If we're lucky then they'll be bad at what they do."

He opened the front door with a shove and we were soon inside, dripping onto the hardwood floor where the water ran into another gutter. Thor remained standing there in his trench coat and hat, not saying much.

"You okay to guard the door while we check it out?" I asked him.

"Of course, sir," he replied. I looked at him.

"Are you alright?"

"Yes, sir. Well sir, maybe not, sir." He leaned forward to speak lower. "I'm thinkin' about me little Jimmy, sir."

"He's safe with Jo and Baz," I said. "You need to focus on what we're doing here, buddy. This is important too – Angel needs you."

"Aye sir," he said. "It's just a little distractin' sir, that's all."

"I understand. Hold the door – don't let anyone in, okay?"

"Gotcha, sir."

I turned back to Eldritch who was staring at the bot with a puzzled look on his face. Moisture glistened on his pale skin. He looked deathly in the dim light.

"I'll let one of you go first," he said. "You look like you know what you're doing."

Mason and I drew our weapons and primed them, flicking on the flashlights mounted under the barrels. The hallway was in complete darkness with only the lamplight spilling in through a window in the front door. We shook off the long coats and hung them up on pegs fixed to the wall above another drainage gutter. Then we moved, taking slow steps along the hall, Mason opposite me with Eldritch behind.

We cleared the corner and saw the elevator up ahead. A stairwell was on the right and another to the left. We took the right hand one, sweeping the way above us with the plasma pistols using familiar drills. It took longer than our nerves wanted but that kind of work required stealth. Step, stop, listen, step again. Sweep, step, stop listen.

We reached the ninth floor and Mason pushed open the double glass doors while I dashed under his elbow, weapon raised. Nothing. The lights were faulty, and they flickered along the entire length of the hall, making my eyes struggle to keep focused. The place stunk of damp and the walls were a mottled yellow, faded and black in places where moisture was seeping in.

Eldritch silently pointed ahead and we moved, keeping one eye behind us as we went. There was no sound at all from any of the other rooms, no music, no loud obnoxious game shows, nothing. It was both deeply unusual and very disturbing.

Room 12 was on our left. We approached and Mason continued to the very end of the hall, clearing it before coming back. Then we stood on either side and looked at Eldritch who produced a codebreaker unit. He went to work on the lock, mashing the buttons with efficient skill. There was a click and the door opened.

He stepped aside and I looked at Mason, counting silently. On three we went in, me left, him right. The first thing that hit us was the smell – all too familiar. The next was the sudden noise that made my guts knot up and my heart thump itself out through my chest.

"AND ALL THE WAY FROM SARGON 8 IS MISS AMBER JETSON!!"

The viewscreen on the wall jolted into life the moment we entered, triggering an automatic activation routine no doubt set by the occupant. The lights came on and a coffee machine fired up. We both dropped to below window height and hugged the wall, facing back with our weapons aimed at the door. Eldritch was already working the panel, turning everything off.

"This is why I hate sneaking around," snarled Mason. "The world will know we're here now."

We waited. If something was going to happen it would happen immediately. Eldritch dropped behind the kitchen counter and waited too. I had to give him credit – he was savvy enough to follow our lead at every turn. I wouldn't have been happy in his shoes, unarmed, relying on two strangers to protect me.

My legs began to stiffen in the crouch and I shifted weight, never taking my eyes off the door. Silence followed. No hurried footsteps up the stairs, nothing.

"Anything at your end, Thor?" I asked. The comms unit crackled as the bot replied.

"Nothin' sir though I did just hear that racket meself."

We stood up and I let out a sigh. "Mason - watch the door while we check the rooms and find the corpse."

The smell was terrific, tearing away at the inside of my nose like sandpaper. Eldritch had opened the coffee machine and was holding up the filter; it was packed with mold. He shrugged and began opening the cupboards and drawers in sequence, disturbing nothing but cataloguing everything with his comms unit which snapped pictures of whatever he looked at.

Pistol raised; I went from room to room. The apartment was old and if it hadn't been for the overpowering scent of death, I knew that it would have reeked of poverty instead. The rooms were barely furnished and what little there was looked cheap and battered and faded with age. The bedroom smelled of sweat and urine and the sheets, yellowed in places, looked like they hadn't been changed for a long time. Dirty clothes were strewn all over the floor and half-eaten takeaway cartons were on every surface. There was an en-suite bathroom which I peered into, finding more than I wanted to see. Narc injectors, empty foil packets, and a sex aid.

I continued looking around the apartment until I found what I guessed was once Fred Bolg in the bathtub off the hallway with both arms opened at the wrists. He was bloated into a purple-blue sack of necrotic flesh, his features barely discernible.

"We're clear here, Mason," I said. "We've got one in the tub. Apparent suicide."

"Don't touch anything," called Eldritch. "I'll get to it in a minute or two."

He worked the apartment with amazing speed, leaving nothing unopened or overturned. The interesting part was how he was able to return everything to exactly where it had been; he made it look like he hadn't even been there.

He wasn't bothered by the sight of the corpse. When he got to the bathroom I followed him inside and he stood for a moment looking down.

"We won't know who it is without a lab report," he said. "I've found no ID, no paperwork, nothing so far to say this man even existed."

"Suicide?" I asked.

Eldritch crouched and peered at the cadaver. It took him several long minutes of staring to reach his conclusion.

"I can't be 100% sure, but I think it's murder," he said. Then he pointed to the wounds. "The person who lives here is left-handed. Things about the apartment have been left on the opposite side to where right-handed people would leave them – coffee cups, control units, that sort of thing. And if you look," He lifted the right arm into the air causing flakes of dried blood to fall off. "There's a tan line around the spot his comms unit would be."

"A tan line? Here?"

"He's either not from here or he took a vacation recently. He's left-handed and the cuts have been done from behind, with a right hand, the way someone would do if-" He positioned himself at the head of the tub, behind the body. "He was stood here, cutting an unconscious man. Plus, the arterial sprays are all wrong. If he'd cut himself, I'd expect the blood to be more over there than here."

"You've seen a few suicides before?" I asked.

"Yes. A lab report should confirm my suspicions though. Looks like he's been dead for over a week. I'm not sure that tells us anything without knowing who he is."

We both looked at the man in the tub and fell silent. Eldritch was no stranger to a corpse and his interest seemed totally detached like he was looking at a set of dinosaur bones or an interesting piece of art. If there was any depth of feeling to the man then I guess it hadn't got the memo.

"I'll have to call a team in to sweep the place," he said. "It'll take a couple of hours."

"We should vanish then."

115

"For now. I have something you can check out though, maybe more your kind of thing."

"What's that?"

"A munitions depot that got raided last week. It's sealed off as a crime scene but maybe you and your friend will find something else there I missed."

I looked at my comms. Eldritch had already sent me copies of his photos and the location of the warehouse.

"Okay," I said. "Let's meet up when you're done."

We looked again at the body. Eldritch tilted his head to one side and sighed.

"I think this was a loose end that just got tied."

"That's what bothers me."

Eldritch called in his team while Mason and I returned downstairs. Thor was waiting by the door, staring out into the darkness beyond the glass. It was still raining.

"Anything?" I asked, putting my coat on.

"Not a peep, sir," he replied. "What now?"

"We're going to search a warehouse Eldritch says was raided last week, possibly by those we're looking for."

"And do you expect to find anything?" asked Mason.

"It gets us out of the way for a bit," I replied, throwing up my hood before opening the door. "I think he-"

The first shot barely missed my face and scorched a white line across the left-hand side of my hood. As I dropped, another tore into the door frame and sent smouldering splinters of shattered metal in all directions.

"Break left!" roared Mason who was through and leaping from the concrete steps into cover behind a stone wall. I rolled sideways, getting to my feet behind the hallway entrance. My coat was fastened, and I tore at the magnetic clamps, releasing the pistol.

"Two, sir!" said Thor. "Plasma rifles on maximum yield."

116

"Where?"

The bot was behind me, his arm collapsing in on itself as a dozen overlapping plates slid back revealing a single tube with a large bore. It began to hum and his vision slit changed to a deep red glow.

"Get behind me, sir!" he cried. "My little friend here needs to say hello!"

I grabbed onto his shoulder and pulled myself quickly around him, my pistol up as he advanced through the doorway. I heard weapons fire, both Mason's and our attackers, and a bolt of energy struck Thor in the chest, rocking him backward.

"It's just... a... scratch," he said. "Nofink to worry 'bout, sir."

Then, without warning, the arm cannon fired and a parked speeder exploded in a ball of blue balefire, sending shrapnel in all directions.

"Cor!," he cried. "I wasn't expectin' that, sir! Me shooter makes a big bang."

"It's absolutely fine!" I shouted. "I'm out of here though."

And with that, I leaped down from cover behind the wall parallel to Mason and looked out. To the left of the burning wreck that now gave us plenty of light, I saw one target crouched in the doorway of the opposite apartment block. A second was to the right, further down, moving along the road to change position. Both were now focussing on Thor who continued down the steps and onto the street.

"I'm firing!" cried Mason and several jade bolts leaped from his weapon to my left, smashing into brickwork just above the figure crouching there. He moved, returned fire with the rifle and sprinted to another parked speeder.

"I've got 'im!" said Thor but just as he was about to fire, a round slammed into his shoulder, setting the trench coat alight and knocking the trilby from the top of his head. It threw his aim and the cannon fired a blast of energy into the road, throwing molten stone fragments into the air.

I fired a burst in response but in the pouring rain the shots faltered and dropped, causing burns to his cover and not much more. From where I was, I could do nothing and I suspected that another of those direct hits would finish the bot for good.

"Going left!" I shouted to Mason, throwing myself over the wall. In a roadie-run I dashed forward, reaching a parked speeder and then turning sharply towards a low wall. Thor fired again and the night lit up causing the rain to sparkle like falling glass. I reached cover just as a plasma bolt smashed into the spot I'd come from.

"I'm in position," I said.

"Moving!" replied Mason. He would go right, sticking to our practiced SOP. There was plenty of cover on his side. As I looked over the top of the brickwork, I heard a roar of agony from the bot.

"Don't worry!" he shouted. "It's just a flesh wound!"

I saw my chance. I stood up, pistol raised and sighted my target. Then I pulled the trigger repeatedly, sending a salvo of fire in his direction. Two of the shots found their mark, knocking him off his feet as a shield generator bore the brunt of their force. As he went down, Thor's cannon followed him, and a burst of brilliant blue light took his spot. When it cleared, all that was left was a scorched patch and plenty of rubble.

"Take him alive!" I cried.

"Already on it!" replied Mason who was sprinting across open ground with Thor flanking to the left. I ran to join them as the second man's rifle barked. Mason slid sideways, falling to the road but the bot was fast and one robotic arm clamped around the barrel of the weapon and tore it from his hands. Then I was on him, throwing my entire body weight onto his. I grabbed his wrists and locked them behind his back as we fell to the floor. My knuckles ground against the pavement.

"I've got 'im, sir!" said Thor. I rolled off just as he lifted the man off his feet, his cannon now a hand again, and pulled him tight to his chest. In the light from the wreck of the fire I could see his face, battle-scarred and furious. He was wearing the usual boots and long coat but underneath there was a spider's web of intersecting armor plates that crackled with energy. He had a pistol on his belt and a slim blade on his hip. He clearly saw no point in struggling against his captor and so he simply hung there, staring right at me.

"Take him inside," I said to Thor. "We'll look around."

"No problem, boss," said the bot and stomped off towards the apartment building. Eldritch met him at the door and called out to me.

"Don't hang around. Shock Squad will be on its way. No one will have missed that."

Mason and I looked up and down the street, still gripping our pistols as the rain came ever on. Thor's cannon had done a good job of vaporizing the soldier and a thorough search only confirmed that.

"Where did he pull that one from?" asked Mason, referring to Thor.

"I don't want to know," I replied, touching the smouldering pavement where the first one had bought the farm. "But maybe he needs to dial it back in future; there's literally nothing left to see."

"Do you think they're part of the bodyguard?"

"Highly likely. Or part of one sent to hunt them down."

"Let's go check out the prisoner then, he'll know. Let's see if he'll talk."

14

Eldritch hadn't been kidding about the 'methods' of the Sargon PD which extended no further than was necessary. We'd taken our new friend up a floor, found an empty apartment, and broke in. Then, once we'd sedated him with meds from our trauma packs, we sat down and waited for the PD to sweep the crime scene. Meanwhile, Mason and I watched from the front window as the Shock Squad arrived in force and secured the street.

"They're different," I said, observing the strange multi-legged bots that scuttled up and down, bristling with light arms and flashing beacons. "Like spiders."

"Very deadly spiders," said Mason. "They're not taking any chances."

"Guess they don't think to look under their noses for us."

"We didn't leave them much," he pointed out. "Two vaporized targets and some vehicle damage. What else do they have to go on?"

They'd arrived on one of those multi-turbine crafts, leaping from the doors like ants fleeing a nest and immediately began searching for targets. We saw Eldritch speaking to a uniform in charge and their posture changed to a less aggressive stance, securing the street and making automated patrols.

"I wonder if they'll believe his story about the suspects fleeing the scene," I said.

"Probably. They don't look like the kinds of people who want to fill in masses of paperwork. Easier to deal with an open-and-shut case of suicide I reckon."

"Eldritch said it was murder."

"I believe him but we don't want the PD to believe him. They'll interfere with our investigation."

"True enough."

I looked at Thor and the prisoner. They stood in the far corner of the room, away from any windows. The man was limp in the bot's arms, his mouth drooling saliva.

"As soon as they're gone we'll make a start."

"If he's who we think he is, how far are you willing to go?" he asked. I shrugged.

"I've never liked the idea of torture," I said. "But here we are and unless he starts singing like a canary what choice do we have?"

A couple of hours passed, and we had to dose him again before he came around fully. Then, as the Sargon PD packed up their things and began to leave, we heard footsteps in the hall and a knock on the door.

"It's me, open up."

Mason covered the door with his weapon while I opened it. Eldritch saw the pistol and shook his head.

"If the Shock Squad were coming for you they wouldn't bother with a ruse, they'd just tear through the walls and neutralize you in a heartbeat. Can I come in, please?"

I stepped aside and the Freelancer entered, letting out a deep sigh. Then, searching his pockets for the bottle, he took another pill along with what looked like a plastic cup of cold coffee.

"Someone makes you a drink, you take it. Who knows where the next one is coming from?" he said. "How's our suspect?"

I closed the door behind him and jerked my head in the direction of the bot. Eldritch went over, frisked him but came up with nothing more than a small ration stick, half eaten.

"Only a soldier would eat that shit," said Mason.

The detective pulled back the collar of the man's coat, revealing a strange device buried into the flesh of his neck. It looked like a disc of copper about three centimetres in diameter with several silver

121

filaments coming off its edges and into his skin. The only marking on its surface was a strange symbol, etched into the metal in the shape of two overlapping triangles overlaid with a single horizontal line. Eldritch took a picture of it and shook his head.

"It's obviously an implant," he said. "But not like anything I've ever seen before."

"Nor I," said Mason. "Or that symbol. Is that a product logo or what?"

Eldritch worked his comms unit and continued to shake his head.

"I've got nothing on the database," he said. "No products match that emblem."

"Maybe it's his unit," I offered. "Or something more personal."

"Wake him up and ask him," said Eldritch. I nodded at Mason who looked at his own comms.

"The last injection should be wearing off soon."

He raised his arm and slapped the man hard across the face, causing him to groan but little else. He repeated the process and the man's eyes began to open. They were red and sleepy but still cold, tinged with malice.

"What the-"

Mason administered one more slap and the man was definitely awake.

"Fuck you!" he cried, shaking the fog from his head. "It's in your best interests to let me go. Now."

"Not from where I'm standing," I said. "Talk."

He looked from me to Mason to Eldritch and snorted a laugh. Thor tightened his grip and the man winced.

"You're soldiers. So am I. We know the score. Either start the torture and let's play the game or let me go. Either way, I'm telling you nothing tonight. The way I see it, time is on my side."

"What makes you think that?"

"You'll find out."

I had little patience for interrogation, but the logic was sound – he knew that he could hold out for a certain amount of time, perhaps enough for the rest of his team to find him or maybe there was a backup plan involving that implant. Too many variables there and I wasn't comfortable with any of them.

"Sir?" asked Thor.

"What is it?"

"I've studied a bit of this kind of fing," he said. "Would you like me to give him a bit of... persuasion? To talk, I mean."

For a split second the arrogant expression on the soldier faltered. I looked at Mason who shrugged.

"Go for it," I said. "Just remember that we need him talking, okay?"

"Understood, sir," said the bot. "I know how to make this little birdy sing. Just you-"

It happened far too fast for any of us to stop it and if it hadn't been for the horror of it I'd have laughed my ass off. The soldier had been about to say something but no sooner had his lips parted to speak than the words became a scream of agony as his left arm was torn from its socket. The rest of him swung to one side, suspended only by his remaining arm which snapped so loudly that we all heard it.

"Holy shit!" cried Eldritch who turned and vomited where he stood.

"Erm..." began Thor who tried to reattach the limb by pushing the two parts back together, unsuccessfully. "I fink I applied a little too much torque."

"You think?" I cried. "Put him down!"

Thor promptly dropped the soldier who was still wailing in both terror and mind-blowing agony. He slammed onto the floor with a wet slap and landed on the hole where his shoulder had once been. In a purely animalistic reaction, he used his only remaining arm to grab at Mason but Thor, quicker to react, grabbed him first, crushing his hand into pulp.

"Oh dear!" cried the bot, letting go of the mangled limb. "That won't make fings better!"

123

"We have to stop the bleeding!" I yelled over the cries of the soldier who now lay on his back on the verge of passing out. "We-"

It was too late. No sooner had Mason stuck him with meds from his pack than he let out one final breath, sighed and slumped in a pool of his own blood which was quickly spreading across the entire floor. Instinctively I stepped away but I couldn't stop staring at him, at the mess.

"What... the... hell?" cried Eldritch, wiping his mouth with the back of his hand. "Why did he do that?"

"I-"

"I'm dreadfully sorry, sirs," said the bot, his hands folded in front of him. "I thought I could make 'im spill 'is beans, so to speak."

"It looks like you did," said Mason who gestured to the pool of gore. "He's certainly spilling them now."

I looked at Thor who was still holding the bloody arm.

"You can put that down now," I told him. He let it fall. Then, taking the soldier's blade, I went over to him and pulled back the collar of his coat, exposing the implant. "It's a lead," I explained. "Possibly the only one we have left because I reckon his DNA won't be on record." Then I began cutting.

We left the apartment block as soon as it was safe to do so. Eldritch said he'd put in an anonymous call about the soldier and leave it at that.

"Just another strange murder for the PD to brush under the carpet," he said. "I don't think anyone will care once they realize he doesn't exist."

We were in a cab heading out into the southern industrial districts where the Freelancer explained that the raided munitions depot was located. The rain hadn't stopped and I wondered where it all drained off to, where they pumped it once it went into the sewers. Surely it had to go somewhere? I thought about that as we left the glittering skyscrapers and pulsing arterial veins of the roadways behind us,

124

swapping them for vistas of enormous heat exchanger stacks, sprawling manufacturing plants and decaying architecture from the planet's earliest colonizing. All looked bleak and grey, like the shattered remains of a stone colossus, left to rot on the battlefield in shadow and rain. The sky here looked yellowed, like it was suffering some kind of storm, but was, in fact, a result of the scorched ozone above the biggest power plants.

"It's a long-running battle," said Eldritch. "Even though the planet doles out constant rainfall, people don't want the pollution either. When rain begins melting your coat or scorching the pavement it's probably time to think about the nature of these facilities."

"Are they mostly power related?" I asked.

"Sort of. Those primary heat exchangers are involved in producing power for 75% of the city's needs. The rest have built around it, forming smaller industries off the back of this one. Engineering firms, primary and secondary manufacturing bases, that sort of thing. Then, on the fringes, you have the smaller guys like our friends in the munitions business."

The cab skirted around one of the great stacks and indicated that it was about to land. We got ready to climb out. I noticed that Thor had been silent the whole time.

"Come on big guy," I said. "Shit happens."

He didn't acknowledge the remark. Instead, he waited with us, then clambered out when the cab had come to a stop in a landing zone. Eldritch left a command to wait. The vehicle's engines cut out and the doors locked.

"The cab isn't authorized to take us any nearer," he said, adjusting his hood as the rain came down. "We'll have to walk the rest of the way."

We set off in eerie silence. The place seemed deserted and even though it was late most industrial centres ran night and day. It didn't help that visibility had been reduced to only a handful of meters in front of us, a combination of the pollution and the downpour. I tried to look all about us, aware now that the chances were good that we'd picked up another tail, but I could see very little.

"Grim," said Mason over the din of rain on thin metal roofs. "Reminds me of the Martian production facilities at Sigma 3 site. Just a bit wetter though."

"When most of your employees are automated I guess you don't need to spend your money on aesthetics," I replied. He nodded.

"I guess not."

We approached the warehouse from the south, crossing one street wide enough to take a couple of decent sized tanks side by side. Then, at a right, we headed along a narrow pedestrian zone, one of only a few concessions for the scant workforce who oversaw the activity there. After that, we could just see the building up ahead because the rain slanted in from the east and was partially blocked by a smaller heat exchanger.

"That's it," said Eldritch as we stopped in the shadows.

"So you think it was hit by the people we're looking for?" asked Mason.

"Yeah. Fits the evidence – and my gut which is rarely wrong."

"Take me through it," I asked.

"Well," he began, leaning back against the wall and folding his arms. A shelf of concrete above our heads offered us a moment or two of peace from the downpour. "It only began to fit together when Argo got in touch. Until that point, all we had were a string of robberies that went nowhere. They bordered on being perfect crimes. Not a scrap of evidence, no witnesses, no trace on the stock. This isn't cheap crap, boys, this is high-end munitions and they have labels and tags and tracking systems. Not one of them in over 16 crimes triggered any of the security measures."

"What time frame are we looking at?" asked Mason.

"They happened over a five-year period, Sargon calendar. Okay, thought the PD, they're new kids on the block, looking to make a name. Except that when we checked our sources in the Syndicate-"

126

"The what?" I asked.

"The Mob. The Firm. The Mafia here on Sargon. Every planet has one though this one is made up of a peculiar mix of natives and outworlders, specifically drug barons from Theseus IV. They've heard nothing about this 'new gang' and have heard even less about illegal arms deals."

"Legitimate sources?"

"Oh yeah," he laughed and shook the bottle of pills in his pocket so that I could hear them rattle. "Sargon PD has a good working relationship with the Syndicate." He looked at the building and shook his head. "So Argo comes along and informs me that *his* sources point to an MIA team who might be on Sargon, having arrived in the last 5 years."

"Did he say how he knew that?" asked Mason.

"Nope. He was very guarded with his information. Anyway, I put the pieces together and figure that they're the right guys for the job. They have the skills to pull off this kind of robbery and the resources to ship them off-world or sell them here as I told you before. Either way, stopping them would be a big deal otherwise there'll be war on the streets before the new year."

"So why are we here if they haven't left a single trace?" I asked. Eldritch smiled.

"Not got much else to do, have we? Besides, after tonight it's clear that their story is coming to an end and thankfully you were just in time to see it. My plan is to wait here for our tails to catch up with us and see what occurs."

"How did they find us so easily?" asked Mason. Eldritch shrugged.

"That's what I'd like to know. Maybe they already had tabs on me because I was on the case. Maybe they have eyes on the docking platform and saw you arrive. Take your pick."

I took out the implant from my pocket. Eldritch had sealed it in an evidence bag to catch the fluids that continued to leak from it. Now I could see the back of the thing I was no wiser; if the device was doing

127

anything we'd never know without a lab.

"Alice, my sister, sends me regular reports from Earth Gov's R&D departments. I think RUND still own the contract, right?" Mason nodded. "There's been nothing like this mentioned since Mars. Other than augmented body parts, the military has a strong dislike of anything that smacks of mind control or performance-enhancing neural interfaces. The moral argument and a history replete with bad examples, has always kept the mad scientists at bay, thankfully." I shook the bag. "So if this is our team, what is this and why do they have it? And who gave it to them?"

"We might have known that had your bot not-" Eldritch stopped and shook his head. "It doesn't matter I guess."

We waited and the rain continued to fall. Thor, standing further into the darkness to our left, said and did nothing. I felt sorry for the bot. He'd only wanted to help and yet, tragically, he'd done the polar opposite. If it were possible, I'd have sent him back to the ship but I didn't know then if I'd need that transmitter. Plus, the cannon would come in handy again if this went horribly wrong, another hunch I felt inside my gut.

I remembered then to fire off a message to Baz, asking for a sit-rep on the ship's repairs. Then we waited some more.

"What was the simulation protocol?" I asked Eldritch who had closed his eyes as he rested.

"The what?" he asked, then seemed to realise what I'd asked. "Existing cold cases for the most grievous Earth Gov. crimes over the last century."

"Any reason?"

"I wanted the training. At that time, just as the technology was limited to experimental phases, the earnings were high and the risk not-so-low. If I put in 5 years I'd come out with the certification."

"Did you plan on leaving to have a career?"

"Yeah, at first I did. Then, like the contracted developers intended all along, a female NPC was introduced to woo me and keep me under while they soaked up my wages from the Government."

"You fell in love?"

"No, they're smarter than that. The NPC was to open up my mind to the concept of love within the simulation. Then they dropped the big bomb."

"Which was?"

"Another user. Neither of us knew the other was real. She was an investigator too and we met on the same case, clearly a coincidence, right?"

"Right," I laughed.

"So we fell in love, just like they wanted and the next thing I know we're married and adopting kids. NPC kids. The years slipped by until the law was passed and we were forced to exit. The trials were deemed too dangerous to both the mind and the body, specifically the brain."

"Forced? How?"

Eldritch hesitated. He looked about to answer but brought himself up short.

"I'd rather not go any deeper," he said. "Sorry." I knew right then that he was holding on to the pill bottle in his pocket.

"Okay," I said and lapsed into silence. My comms unit buzzed. It was a text-only message from Baz. All was well and Jo was fitting the nebulus buffer now.

I looked up and saw something ahead, just beyond the next unit. I undid the fastenings of my coat, freeing the pistol.

"Looks like they found us," I said. Eldritch grinned.

"Can we keep one alive this time?"

15

They sent four this time. We hadn't been able to hear any transport fly them in because of the rainfall but no doubt, being skilled in these arts, they'd tabbed in on foot from a DZ further away; it's what we would've done.

The first one gave his position away because he wasn't trying to hide. He wore tactical clothing, all black and grey, overlaid with a combat chassis, the kind we used to see other PRT teams use for more covert ops. It offered some of the benefits of an exo-shell like speed, agility, increased carrying capacity, that sort of thing but lacked any real protection. It looked more like a full body medical brace up close but that didn't mean I was about to underestimate them.

"ZR-4 unit," whispered Mason. "Made by ULTRA COMP. Built-in shield generator and refractors. Our pistols won't do us much good."

"You see the two on the roof?"

"Of course I do," he snapped. "One's already inside I reckon."

"We're exposed out here. I say we bug out."

"We can't," he replied. "They're hunting us whether we like it or not."

"What do you suggest?"

Mason looked at Eldritch and nodded his head in the direction of the door behind us. The freelancer took out his hacking device and went to work on it. We continued to stare at the one who now walked up and down outside the building, the decoy.

"He's not carrying a peashooter either," I said. "What is that? It looks similar to one of those Thundercats, the 09 series maybe."

"It's got twin cells on the breach and another in the stock. The

130

barrel has been reinforced with SAGE filaments too."

"You can see all that from here?" He grinned.

"No. I read the Python Munitions brochure while you two were bonding. It's their latest unit. I never entertained it for us because three cells with two that are linked is a recipe for catastrophic failure in the field. If those popped we'd be going home in a jar."

"What's the damage output?"

"65 watts maybe. Put through the SAGE, I'd bump that up to nearly 100."

"We're in," said Eldritch who moved quickly into the darkness and went to work on the alarm system. He was good and I suspected that in spite of his time under, there was some kind of military background there.

We followed. Thor tread softly, taking up a position at the window with his arm cannon already activated. Mason and I continued to watch through the open door, grateful for the lack of ambient light.

"Plan?" I asked him.

"Ignore the decoy and take them piecemeal," he replied, taking off his coat. I did the same. "Forget the shields, they're useless to us now. They'll just ghost our position in this weather."

I drew my pistol and checked it over, making sure the cells were primed but as I did so I caught Eldritch doing the same – with the weapon we'd taken from the soldier earlier.

"I never saw you take that," I said.

"You weren't supposed to. Four against four is fair odds." Mason laughed.

"It's not fair to them. I hope you know what you're doing."

"I've done a bit," he smiled. "I'm no soldier but I can shoot reasonably straight. What's the plan?"

"Mason, take the east side of the building and come around, sweeping for the one we think is inside. I'll climb onto the roof and engage one of the two up there. The other will have relocated by now so I'll have to track him down."

"And us?" asked Eldritch.

"Mop up. Once Mason and I engage it'll go loud. Take the decoy and help either myself or Mason." I looked at the bot. "You got that, Thor?"

"Understood, sir," he replied.

"Okay. Stay sharp. We'll communicate through Thor."

"Good luck," said Eldritch. I smiled.

"You too."

Mason went right out of a different door while I ducked low and dashed out through the front, going left. Immediately the rain hit me, running down my neck and soaking me in only a few minutes. There was nothing I could do about that. I went wide, keeping deep in the shadows as I circled around the target building where I'd seen one of the shooters set up. He'd been pretty good at hiding his movements and maybe a civilian might not have seen him but we did. It gave me a small amount of hope that they didn't know who we were just yet.

I avoided another of those wide roads and chose instead to scale the adjacent building on the western side. On this planet, no building could escape the need for gutters and drain pipes and in spite of the anti-climbing measures, I was able to clamber up pretty quick.

At the top I paused, making sure I wasn't about to pull off the same mistake they had and announce my presence with a bull-horn. The rain battered me now, drenching me to the bone, running into my eyes like rivers from my brow. I blinked a couple of times to clear them, then waited.

"Eyes on tango," whispered Mason across the comms. "In the building, north side. Same gear."

"Decoy still in position," replied Eldritch.

I continued to wait. Then, as the wind suddenly picked up, I saw something move in the darkness on the roof across from me. I didn't move. Holding my breath, I turned my head very slowly so that the shape was in my peripheral vision where things were sharper. It was

132

my target, the first one, but the second was nowhere to be seen.

"Eyes on tango," I muttered. "Zero on the other."

"Don't engage until you've found him," said Mason.

"Everyone hold their positions," I said.

We waited. I was aware that my temperature was dropping. That would mean shivers, trembling, easily giving myself away. I scanned the rest of the rooftops very slowly, making no sudden movements, then pulled myself up onto the roof and lay prone, taking long, deep breaths.

"Decoy is moving," said Eldritch.

"Where?" asked Mason.

"He's crossing the street, heading this way."

"Has he spotted you?" I said.

"Negative. His weapon is low and he's just walking towards me."

"Don't react," said Mason. "Not yet."

"Thor – take him silently *only* if he enters the building."

"Aye, sir."

I looked again. Still no sign of the other guy. I was running out of time.

"He's stopped," said Eldritch.

"Hold," I said. "I see him."

From where I was I could just make out his position in the middle of the road. He looked idle, bored, just passing the time. His mouth was moving so I guessed he was talking to any one of his team. I scanned the roof again hoping for a response and I wasn't disappointed. The second guy suddenly rolled onto his back from a prone position overlooking the building Eldritch and Thor occupied and began searching his gear for something. When he found it, the glow from its screen faintly illuminated his features, or I should say *her* features. It was a woman and she was consulting a device.

"Woah!" cried Eldritch. "He's seen me!"

I looked and now the decoy was alive, his weapon up and storming directly into their position inside the building.

"She must have a tracker – engage now!"

I leaped to my feet and cleared the gap between my roof and the first soldier, landing hard and rolling in the water gathered there. Pistol up I ran towards him just as he tried to get up from where he lay. I fired a salvo of shot that hissed and spat in the rain. Only two found their target, enough to cause the shields to crackle but not much else.

"Engaging!" cried Eldritch and I heard his weapon discharge in controlled bursts.

"Tango down!" said Mason.

I closed the distance just as my target was aiming his weapon at me. The shot missed, passed me by on my right side and vanished into the night. I felt the heat of it pass my face.

I slid onto him, throwing my whole weight onto his frame and he found himself laid out on the roof with my bulk on top of him. I had moments to react because that chassis was capable of tearing me apart like I was made of paper. One hand clamped around his throat while the other held on to the barrel of his weapon before he could turn it on me.

Grabbing someone's airway has a predictable response – they try to tear your hands away rather than attack you; unless you're expecting it and I was gambling on him *not* expecting it. In this case, his free hand shot out and clamped around my wrist. A split second later and he'd tear my arm out of my shoulder in pretty much the same way Thor had done earlier. But his mistake was made. In doing so, he lost focus on the weapon I held at bay in the other. I dove sideways, releasing my grip on his throat and dragged the barrel of the gun down with me, pointing it directly back at its owner. Then a quick jerk sent his elbow into the ground, closing the finger that rested on the trigger, blowing out part of his skull and incinerating the brain matter within.

Something snapped in my wrist as the hand released and a flash of white-hot pain shot up my arm. I rolled off him, grabbing it and stifling a yell.

134

"Tango down," I snarled over the comms. "Heading for the next target."

In agony, I yanked the medpack from my belt and tore it open. Then, grabbing the pain meds, I stuck the needle into my arm and hit the injector twice. My vision cleared and the torment subsided into a dull ache, long enough for me to wrap it in an insta-cast bandage which hardened my wrist in place. I only hoped the break hadn't misaligned the bones.

I picked up the weapon he'd been using and slung it across my chest so that I could still use it in my right hand without having to take the weight of it. My fingers still worked and once I'd wrapped another bandage around the stock and my forearm the thing became solid in my grasp. I couldn't aim down the sights but I could still hip-fire and I thumbed it onto its three round burst setting.

"Sitrep?" asked Mason.

"Thor grabbed him," said Eldritch. "But he got a shot off. The bot doesn't look so good."

"Alive?" he asked.

"Yeah."

"Carter?"

"Wounded," I replied. "Got my wrist. Back me up, pal."

"On my way."

I tucked behind one of the air conditioning units and looked to where the woman had been. She was gone.

"No eyes on the tango," I said. "Holding my position."

"Where was he?" he asked.

"West rooftop, 200 meters from target building. Female. Armed with a rifle."

"I'll find her."

"I'll take the north," said Eldritch. "Converge on that position."

I felt my heart racing. I was a sitting duck but moving wasn't an option. I couldn't drop down a drain pipe in this state and there was nowhere else to run. The only comfort I had was that she hadn't shot me already.

"I'm going up," said Mason. "On your seven, Carter."

I looked. I saw him climbing the drain pipe across from me and halt just before the top, peering over.

"You're clear," I said. "I have full eyes-on."

He finished, laying low on the roof, one of the enemy rifles in his hands just like me. Then he raised himself into a crouch and moved towards a similar unit, taking cover behind it.

"Well?" he asked.

"I've got nothing," I said. "Moving to the north end. Stay frosty."

I got up and part of me expected to feel the impact of a shot. There was nothing. I hurried forward to the next unit, paused, then moved onto the next until I was close to the edge of the roof. For some strange reason, I noticed the sensation of cold rainwater trickling down my inner thigh and it caused me to shiver.

"I'm in position," said Eldritch. "Nothing yet."

"Keep an eye on her exits," said Mason. "She could have fled by now."

I stared and realized that the painkillers were kicking in, making me drowsy. My vision swam and I regretted hitting the dose twice.

"I'm losing combat effectiveness," I said. "I'm tapping out."

"Understood," said Mason and I was thankful that we'd had years of working together to bypass our pride. "Hold position and provide cover fire. I'm moving on."

I leaned back against the metal casing and sighed, dropping to one knee and aiming ahead of Mason. As he reached the edge he looked about, saw that the gap was narrow enough to the next roof, and leaped. As he did so, a flash of red lit up the area and a bolt streaked past him, barely missing.

"I'm under fire!" he roared as he rolled into cover. "Did anyone see it?"

"Eyes on tango!" I cried. "Engaging!"

I pointed in roughly the right direction and fired, sending a burst

136

towards the muzzle flash I'd seen. Then, throwing myself back behind the unit, I was just in time to see two more shots slam into where I'd just been kneeling. I fired again and again, keeping suppression on the target as Mason tracked her position.

"Engaging!" he cried and stood up, firing into the glowing spot I was hitting. She'd gone.

"Anything?" I asked.

"Eyes on!" cried Eldritch and I heard his pistol firing. "She's heading north-west, towards the heat exchanger."

"I'm following," said Mason.

I saw him running, hitting the next rooftop hard as he gained on her. Then he vanished out of sight.

"I see her," he said over the comms. "Firing."

More flashes. Some cursing.

"I'm on your three," said Eldritch. "I still see her."

"She's fast, I'll give her that."

The waiting was killing me so I got up and stumbled towards another drain pipe, cutting the bandage from the stock and letting the thing swing onto my back. Then, with excruciating pain, I made the long descent down to ground level.

"Firing!" said Mason again. "Missed."

"She's changing direction," said Eldritch. "Heading north now. I think there's a vehicle in the air."

"What?"

"A speeder. It's hovering. Must be their exfil."

"Last chance," he said. "Firing... That's a hit."

"She's down!"

"Where?"

"Over the edge. I'm nearly there... Oh shit. She's dead."

"Confirmed?"

"Rail spike through her neck almost severed her head from her shoulders. I'm pretty sure she's gone."

I found Thor holding the prisoner in his grasp, still in the shadows. In spite of the damage done to his secondary body, he was still operational and hadn't gone full psycho just yet. Held firmly in his arms was the decoy from before, a man of reasonable height, maybe two meters with a closely cropped head of bristling black hair, a pock-scarred face and a taut, toned body. He now bore a number of cuts, having had the combat chassis torn from his body without the proper protocols and they wept gently into his close-knit midnight colored combats.

"Good work," I said.

"Thankee, sir," Thor replied, appearing a little happier now. "He has one of them thingies, sir. On his neck, like."

"I guessed he would."

"Are you injured badly, sir?" he asked. I shook my head.

"Broken wrist. Hurts like hell but I'll live. What about you?"

"Just a scratch, sir. A bit of paintwork will-" He paused, blurted out a string of random phrases that made no sense, then stopped. "I think one of those shooters hit my processors, sir. I must've got meself that too-retts fingy."

"Hang in there. We'll get you patched up."

We waited and the soldier said nothing. Mason and Eldritch would check the corpses before coming back. I had time to sit for a moment. The guy watched me with a predator's interest.

"Name?" I asked him as I slumped against the wall. Nothing. "Rank? Serial number? Health insurance? Last dental appointment? Nothing?" Silence. "Have it your way. But Thor here, he has ways of making you talk."

The bot said nothing. I laughed to myself which was probably a result of the meds and closed my eyes just as the world began to fade out of focus.

16

The salts burned my nose the way battery acid might. Whether he planned it or not, the effect made me shake my head away, slamming the right side of my face against the wall. Mason laughed.

"What the hell?" I cried. "Why do that?"

"I couldn't help it, buddy. How's the arm?"

I looked at my wrist. It was twice its normal size.

"Good as new," I said. "Don't give up your day job and become a corpsman, right?"

I got to my feet and saw that I'd only been out for a few minutes. It was still raining and it was still dark but the air stank of ozone and scorched metal. The meds were wearing off and my arm began to ache.

"Has he said anything?" I asked. Mason shook his head.

"Either he's one of the team we're looking for or he's here for the same reasons we are – to hunt them down."

"Well I'm getting tired of this," I snapped, looking at the prisoner. "Either he talks or we waste him. I've spent enough of my time on these clowns. If he is some kind of elite team then I'm not impressed – they came apart too easy for my liking."

"Or maybe we're better than them," said Mason.

"The thought had crossed my mind." I walked towards our prisoner and grabbed his chin with my left hand, yanking his eyes towards mine. "Talk or die. It's that simple."

Nothing.

"Last chance."

Still nothing. Just that glazed stare, not quite looking at me, not quite *not* looking at me. Just... not there somehow.

"Thor."

"Yessir!"

"You have my permission to tear one of his legs off in the next six seconds. Understood?"

"Sir?"

"That one," I pointed to his left leg. "I want that one, preferably in one piece. Pull at his thigh so his hip dislocates first. The flesh will tear pretty good then."

"Understood sir," said the bot and clamped his third arm around the man's thigh just below his groin. His eyes flashed terror much the way the other soldier's had. "Now?"

"Countdown from six, okay?"

"Understood."

I continued to stare at him. Horror. Panic. Fear. They were like ice cubes in a tumbler, bouncing around in a cocktail of emotions he didn't want to be feeling. Without realizing it I'd stuffed my bad wrist into one of my pockets to try and relieve the pain and my fingers touched the plastic evidence bag that held the strange implant. The moment they made contact I felt a surge of terror grip me, loosening my bowels and making my head spin. I let go.

"Thor!" I cried. "Stop."

"Understood, sir."

I took the bag out of my pocket with some difficulty and held it up, making sure I didn't touch it directly.

"What is it?" asked Eldritch. "You look pale."

"I felt it," I said, looking at the soldier. "I felt what he was feeling."

"Where did you get that?" he suddenly cried in a deeply accented voice. Sirakosen maybe? One of the Commonwealth planets?

"Off one of the team you sent to kill us," said Mason.

"You had no right."

"I had every right," I said.

"Not you," he replied. "Him." He nodded towards Eldritch who shrugged.

"Nice to be loved."

"But your comrades seemed happy to nail the rest of us too. Seems a little unkind to me. I'd never even met them. No flowers. No lunch."

"He was digging too deep. He still is."

"I don't really care that much," I pointed out. The pain in my wrist was fast becoming unbearable. "And I don't care for elaborate interrogations either. I want to know if you're part of the team who body-guarded for General Bourmont during the Mars campaign or not."

"What does it matter to you?"

"It matters a lot. Believe me."

"Must be worth something?"

"It's worth that leg to you, pal. Decide now – I'm in a lot of pain and I'd like to deal with it."

He stared at me, looked at both Mason and Eldritch and figured that he liked his leg more than his reputation as an operative.

"Fair enough. Can the bot take his hand off my leg first?"

I gestured to Thor who paused for a moment, made some more random noise and then withdrew the arm. The soldier nodded his thanks.

"You're not after us for the guns, are you?" he said. "I can see that."

I looked at Eldritch who shrugged.

"I get paid by the hour," he said. "I don't really care. I'd like it to stop though just so I have something to put in my report to Sargon PD."

"You a freelancer?" asked the soldier. Eldritch nodded. "Figures."

"Why?"

"No Sargon pig would put the effort in that you've done over the last six months."

"I needed a break," said Eldritch. "I got one a day or so ago but you kinda messed up by coming after me. Made my job a lot simpler."

"Always a risk."

141

"Well this is nice," said Mason. "But can we get out of here before his friends show up?"

"Friends?" said the soldier. "You just killed the last of us. Shana and me, we were going to split Sargon for the Commonwealth before you arrived. They're all gone now. We took a big risk in coming after you, but it didn't pay off."

"Bummer for you," said Eldritch. "But at least I get my report done."

We left the industrial complex and returned to the cab, soaked and tired. It'd been a long day, or night, whichever way you looked at it and I needed to get my wrist seen to. Our prisoner came along willingly without Thor needing to restrain him. I guessed that for him only one option remained now – to fully comply in the hopes of winning our trust and negotiating some kind of release. I didn't tell him this, but if I got what I wanted then he could go sing in the local barbershop quartet for the rest of his life for all I cared. Right there and then he was my last hope for Angel, a bargaining chip to put down against Argo's ally, the former Chief of Staff Wash.

The cab took us to a run-down part of the city in the southern quarter. It took too long. My wrist was swollen and turning a nasty shade of purple and the second dose of pain relief I took didn't even touch it. The only plus was that the clothing we'd bought were self-drying and when the cab ride was over only my back retained a little dampness.

"I'll call a friend of mine," Eldritch had said when he told us we were going to his place. "She'll patch you up off the books. Here on Sargon, you have to jump through some serious hoops to get a medical permit."

The sorry looking apartment the freelancer dwelt in sat on the corner of 8th and Charleston like a beggar and our cab might well have been the cup that coins clanked into. I noticed that he made a point of avoiding referring to the place as 'home' – a statement that his real home was someplace else, somewhere lost to him now. He bent his sentences around that fact the way a plumber might redirect his pipes around an A/C unit.

"I got it cheap," he said as we made the climb to his floor – the elevator wasn't working. "I pay a year in advance. I think I might actually be the only person living here."

"You don't see the neighbors?" asked Mason.

"Nope. I keep odd hours and in this part of town borrowing a cup of sugar can get you killed or raped or both."

His door was scarred and dented in places, perhaps from a previous tenant with outstanding bills, but the lock worked fine and looked new. When he opened the door the place was precisely what you'd expect it to be – clean but very cluttered. Stacks of hard copy formed a kind of mini-Sargon City with high-rises and low apartment blocks made from unsolved cases and the occasional coffee-cup-pinnacle. The floor was polished hardwood and the walls were a pale green color between the many collages of crime scene photos, graphs, and maps that were pinned to it. For furniture, there was a handful of odd chairs and a battered leather recliner in one corner sat under a lamp equipped with footstool and a throw which I suspected was often slept in. Beside it was a stack of fiction books with a couple of titles I recognized. There was a bedroom to the right and a kitchen to the left. That completed my assessment of the freelancer's quarters and satisfied my understanding that this was a man who lived and loved his work.

"Sit where you can," he said. "Freya should be here soon. Coffee?"

"I'll take a cup," said the soldier who seemed to have forgotten he was a prisoner. It didn't help that in the cab we'd chewed over old Martian War stories like we were buddies or something. It was always hard to hate someone who wasn't *actively* trying to kill you, even if he had been trying to kill you an hour earlier.

"A cup of coffee deserves a name," said Eldritch without a break in his stride. He was good.

"Most people call me Mozzy. I got it on Mars. Real name is Pete Garth."

"Mozzy?" I asked.

"Yeah. Got bit during jungle training and had a bad reaction. Spent six weeks in the field hospital. When the team found out that I'd been bitten in the ass they started calling me Mozzy."

I saw Mason tapping that name into his comms unit but Mozzy didn't seem to notice. Eldritch vanished into the kitchen with a smile and I saw the pistol sticking out of his waistband.

"You plan on keeping that gun?" I called to him. He snorted a laugh.

"What gun?"

"Just don't go blowing out your brains, okay?"

"That's not my style."

I looked at Pete 'Mozzy' Garth and tried not to think about my wrist which was now reaching that level of pain that brings on tears and a stomach that can't settle.

"Was Shana special to you?" I asked. The question caught him off guard; he hadn't been expecting me to take that line.

"Yeah, I guess so."

"She was on your team?"

"On Mars? No. I met her after. Don't apologize for her death-"

"I wasn't going to," I cut in. "What's done is done. You're alive. You've got decisions to make."

"Doesn't look like I've got that many." His face changed slightly. He'd kept up the military facade for long enough and now he looked tired and spent, especially when Eldritch returned with cups of coffee and handed him one. It never changed. On a battlefield, you're trained to ignore the humanity of the enemy. They're targets to be eliminated, that's all. But after that, when the fighting stops, you remember that your enemy has a heartbeat and a brain and likes things like coffee and good food and laughing. Seeing Mozzy sat there in front of me reminded me of that fact although I don't think I'd ever forgotten it since training.

"What is it you want, anyway? Surely you didn't go to all this trouble over a black-op from way-back-when?"

"We did," said Mason. "Do you remember the mission?"

"Which one?" he laughed. "The General had us running all over for him. We were his personal bodyguards even though no one was trying to kill him. You guys had to go in after Noctis, right? Isaac's rescue plan?" I nodded. "After that, he'd finished with us. We got redeployed and eventually, when the war ended, we split."

"Until?" asked Mason. Mozzy let out a sigh and shook his head.

"First I want a deal."

"Okay," I said. "Understandable. What kind of deal?"

"The kind that lets me go." I shook my head.

"No can do," I said. "One of my team is locked up on charges of treason and-"

"The pilot," grinned Mozzy. "It's not hard to guess. She was the only weak link and Frankie warned Bourmont at the time. Lucky you, she was pretty hot back then."

"You want your brain to go for walk? Keep talking," I said with as much composure as I could find.

"Ah. She's *that* kind of friend."

"No," I bit back. "She's one of my team."

"Shana was one of mine. You killed her. I think your sympathy vote just got squashed."

I stared at him and he stared back. This was proving to be another express-train to nowhere.

"I hand you over to certain parties, maybe I get my friend back. It's that simple. Unless you have something more than that, a deal is out of the question."

"Certain parties?" he said.

"They have a keen interest in nailing Bourmont. They think my friend will help them with that. I think maybe you might be able to do better."

"Maybe."

Eldritch sat in his recliner, his feet up, appearing not to listen. Maybe he wasn't. It seemed like either option held little sway over him.

"Well?"

Mozzy chewed the whole thing over with deliberate ease, stringing out the process in the hopes of making us sweat or perhaps just get us irritable. It was working. Eventually, he spoke.

"Okay, here's my thinking on this. I know what you're after and I think I might know where to find it. If I were to give it to you, it could get your friend off and not have to involve me in any kind of long-term imprisonment. I have some... *resources* set aside. I could vanish from Sargon and never bother you again."

"You've gotten over Shana pretty quick," said Mason.

"Hard credits helped," he replied. "Well? Can we do something here or what?"

"Give me a taste," I said. "What can you offer?"

"You're not going to like it."

"Try us."

He clucked his tongue. The whole charade was boring the living crap out of me and I began to reconsider my stance on torture. My wrist was drawing most of my patience away and I shot a glare at Eldritch who was looking out of the window like a cat does, bored and impassive. Where was this Freya?

"The boss wasn't stupid," he said in the end.

"Boss?"

"Lieutenant Seb Marks, our CO."

"Right."

"He was used to this kind of secret-agent bullshit. He was old-school-Commando, saw action in Hong Kong during the civil war, stayed behind enemy lines for three years on Sanpo and even claims he was running guns to Al Holland's forces during Ang '68. When Bourmont approached us the first time, long before the fall of Mars

Prime, Seb said we should be recording the details of our ops and storing them on encrypted data blocks as insurance. We did and he sent them away."

"Where?"

"To a secure location only he knew – until he found himself bleeding out after a sale went south last year. Then he made the smart decision to confide in me."

Now a smug grin passed over his face as he sat back a little more and sipped his coffee.

"Nice try," I said. "But I'm not buying it."

"Really?" He smirked. "Risky way to proceed, pal."

"No, I don't think so."

Suddenly there was a chime from behind and Mozzy visibly jumped where he sat, confirming a suspicion I had. Eldritch got up out of his chair.

"Freya," he said.

"About time," I whispered under my breath. A large woman carrying a silver medical case bustled into the room, huffing and puffing with cheeks a rosy red color to offset her short, curly blonde hair.

"You could've told me the elevator was not..." she tried to say but her words were poor English with a thick, syrupy Morvo accent. "Vorking?"

"Adastma," replied Eldritch in her own tongue. "Sini est mogaza. Me amoras." He gestured to my wrist. "Sima cor duest mon ma ma."

"Ma ma?"

"Sini."

The woman shook her head and beads of sweat flew away. Then she came waddling over to me, clamping one pudgy fingered hand on my forearm and leaning in for a closer look.

"Poor poor man," she cooed. "Very sore. I see this. Very hurt, right?"

"Right," I said.

"Fix this. Fix good."

She opened the case and spent several minutes running strange pieces of flashing equipment over my wrist with no visible effect. Then, talking to herself in her unintelligible dialect, she took hold of my arm in both hands, holding the joint between them and smiled at me.

"Safa est mo," she grinned. "Da... Des... GA!"

There was a loud crack and I screamed in pain as she yanked my hand almost entirely off the end of my arm. Then, with deft skill, she released me and wrapped a new insta-cast around the joint which felt lighter and even more flexible than my own had been. I could actually use the wrist with little or no pain.

"What did you do?" I cried, rubbing the spot. She was already gathering up her tools and packing them back into the case.

"Bodo fa," she laughed. "You sissy. You not break. Girly-girl. I fix silly man."

"Bada fee," said Eldritch as she bustled away again towards the door. "Moto fete hist."

"Moto. Bon amas, Malcolm," she said, kissing his cheek. "Afat ben."

"Afat."

I looked at Mason who'd taken a sudden interest in the toe of his boot. Mozzy was chuckling to himself. When the door was shut, I cleared my throat.

"Can we get back to what really matters now?"

17

He was right. I didn't like it. Mozzy took us through the whole deal from start to finish only leaving out the precise locations involved and the people he knew he'd need once he was free from us. I didn't mind that; I wasn't here to bring justice to the galaxy – just to get what I needed to free Angel.

"So you have access to this place?" asked Mason as the dawn crept up behind the endless procession of rain clouds outside the window.

"Not directly," said Mozzy. "But I have the system, the planet and the precise location of the place and without it I promise you, you'll never find it."

"Of course you're not going to reveal that until you're guaranteed an escape, right?" He nodded. "And this underground fortress-"

"Vault. It's a *vault*. Heavily guarded and impossible to crack open with a few plasma pistols and a bot," he smirked. "But that's not my problem."

"Maybe we just hand you over to Argo and let him deal with it."

"It's on a Commonwealth planet in a Commonwealth system controlled by a warlord the likes of which you've never met before. I doubt he'd have the balls or the jurisdiction to act."

"That narrows it down," Mason pointed out.

"Sure. Maybe you figure it out. But the exact location? This place is a secured vault for some of the galaxy's major criminal elements. In there you've got gold, precious jewels, hard copy documents and some of the most damaging Intel on Earth Gov. you've never seen. Do you think they leave the lights on?" He shook his head. "You need me. All I ask is that you let me go when our business is concluded."

"How can we trust you?" I asked.

"I'm a criminal, okay, I get that. But once we served together on Mars. That shit doesn't go away. You can trust me. Semper-fucking-fi."

"And everything we need to take Bourmont down is in that vault?" I asked. Another nod. I looked at Mason. "Well?"

"He's got a point," he said. "We give him to Argo and he talks, then what? He and Angel go down together. But if we have some hard evidence, maybe a little extra dirt on top, maybe we stand a chance of getting her off."

"And me!" he cried. "I'm not going down as a traitor, no way. We were only doing our job. That scum-bag Bourmont is the traitor."

I thought it over. I was tired and my wrist, though improved, was still aching. I needed rest and, more importantly, I wanted a way forward.

"So we take you with us," I said. "We get you off-world. You'll take us to this planet? Tell us where the vault is? Then what?"

"You seem reasonable," he said. "I heard about the *Aurelius*. Was it you?" I nodded. "Thought so. Maybe you're the good guys in all this, I don't know. I reckon I can trust you to drop me off once you've got what you need."

"Where?"

"Anywhere. I'm done. My team is gone and I don't have the strength to start over again. Just find me a planet with a non-extradition clause and I'll vanish, maybe become a farmer or something."

"Are you okay with that?" I asked, looking at Eldritch. He shrugged.

"Sure. On the condition that he reveals the location of his stash and contacts so I can close up his operation. Then I'll happily forget I ever met him."

"Sounds fair," said Mozzy. Then, getting up, he smiled. "Now for the next problem."

150

"Which is?"

"They're coming for me. We have about ten minutes."

I should have realized earlier that our time on Sargon had gone much too well. The tails that had picked us up after we'd landed had indeed been with a third party, someone with their own interests in Bourmont's former Ops team. Now they were coming and why? Mozzy explained as we got ready to leave.

"The discs are empathic links, kind of like a group sensory experience thing. We'd never seen anything like them before but they were cheap and we didn't ask many questions."

"Always a good idea," grumbled Mason.

"They made us fight better, closer, like we were all thinking the same thing."

"And?"

"And we never realized they could be used against us – until now. I just felt an unknown presence link in. It knows where I am and I don't have a clue who or what it is."

"But you know it's coming?"

"I feel it anticipating the attack. It's close. We've been holding off assaults for years now but the last one was the worst. They'd hired Death Squad units out of the Commonwealth, you know? Those synthetic-killer types that are swell at parties. 'Like, hi, what do you do? Oh, synthetic-killer-gun-for-hire? Sounds cool.' Those types."

"Can you pull it out?" I asked. "Preferably *before* they find us?"

"No. Not without surgery."

Eldritch waited by the door, ready to go. I shook my head.

"You've done more than enough, Malcolm," I said. "This isn't your fight."

"Maybe I want it to be," he replied.

"We're going to make a run for the shuttle back to our ship. There's no point risking your life for this. Call in the shock squad and wait for them to arrive once we've gone. I'll be in touch as soon as we reach our ship."

"Are you sure?" he asked.

"I'm sure," I replied, smiling. I held out my hand. "You've been a massive help. But this is our work now, this is what we do."

"What, make carnage?" he laughed and we shook.

"Kind of. I'd like to give your name to my sister, have you on the books. There have been many times when a damn good investigator would have turned a mission in a better direction. Would you be willing to work for us now and again?"

"It'd be a pleasure," he grinned but behind that smile, the bitter pain still lingered. It might never leave him, but maybe that was his edge. "Take care, Carter. And you, Mason."

"Time to run," I said. "Goodbye, Malcolm."

"Goodbye."

And with that, we descended to the ground floor, checked the front exit, and sped out into the dawn light.

The shuttle pad was too far to walk so we risked a cab. Traffic was light and although my instincts screamed at me to avoid being fish in the proverbial barrel, we had little choice. No sooner had we sat down than I gave the order for Thor to activate his arm cannon and both Mason and I drew our pistols. The rifle's we'd taken before were too obvious to carry in the streets and so we'd left them behind.

"Guess you don't have a spare for me then?" said Mozzy. Mason shook his head.

"You know the drill. When we get out just keep moving towards the platform. We have to get on that shuttle without being stopped by either them or the PD."

I tapped my comms once we were clear of Eldritch's apartment and called up Baz.

"Aye," he said, coming online. "What's up?"

"Sitrep," I barked. He visibly stiffened.

"The buffer is working and the ship is ready to fly. What's going on?"

"We're coming in hot with a VIP," I explained. "Looks like we're going to have to fight our way to the shuttle. I want the ship fired up and ready to leave. Get on with authorizing our departure with the station coordinator."

"ETA?"

"Thirty minutes, maybe more."

"Understood."

I signed off, confident that he'd get things ready for us. My stomach tried to knot itself up but I held it back, forcing reserves of adrenaline into my system.

"If they've been tracking us then they know where we're going," said Mason. "If they can't stop us then they'll try to take him out."

"I know."

Taking off his shield generator, Mason leaned over and fastened it onto Mozzy's belt. I did the same, doubling the efficacy of the devices.

"Gee, does this mean we're kind of married, fellas?" he laughed but the sound was empty and hollow; he was as nervous as we were.

"Sirs," said Thor. "I 'ave a problem, sirs." The bot was looking at his arm cannon, still in its collapsed form but not quite a hand either. There were impact burns around the elbow servos where a stray shot had struck it.

"It won't activate for me, sirs," he said.

Mason leaned over, trying to force the plates apart with his bare hands but none would give.

"It was working before," I said.

"I'm experiencing a couple of system failures, sir. I fink me brain is takin' a nap or somefink."

"Detach it," said Mason. "Give it to me."

"I'll try, Mr. Mason." The plates whined and screeched as they slid across each other until the entire unit dropped into his arms.

"What are you going to do with that?" I asked. He cracked open the

153

connection port and began yanking wires out, splicing some and re-routing others back inside. I kept an eye on the streets as the cab slowed for upcoming traffic but, thankfully, didn't stop.

"Have you got a C3 interface node?" he asked the bot.

"Aye, sir. Give me a mo." There was more clattering of parts and a fraction of his chest plates parted, revealing a small square of plastic. Mason took it and connected it to the exposed wires.

"A 556-22B regulator conduit?"

"Yessir, but that will make my long-distance comms useless, sir,"

"We won't be needing them," he replied. Thor complied and with the final piece he reattached all the connections and turned the cannon over in his arms. Holding it like a long tube, he was now able to fire the weapon from his hip and already it was thrumming itself into life. He handed his pistol to Mozzy.

"You even think about stabbing us in the back and I'll vaporize you with this," he said. The former soldier nodded.

"I'm starting to like you guys," he grinned. "Makes me think I joined the wrong team."

"You did," I snapped seeing movement on the rain-slicked pavements to our left. Three figures moving against the flow of people traffic, heading straight towards us. "Get ready."

We were maybe four clicks from the landing pad and between us and the shuttle was the entire commercial district of the city which, even at this early morning hour, was thronged with civilians. I felt a tightness in my throat as the cab ground to a halt in a long line of stationary vehicles. So much for Sargon traffic reports.

"Eyes on three tangos," I said, getting out of my seat and crouching by the door.

"Three more on my side," said Mozzy. "What do we do?"

"Go left," said Mason. "Let me out first, then follow."

I held the door handle and looked. The three coming towards us were wrapped in long black coats, hoods down revealing heads with tightly cropped hair and ventilator masks covering the lower halves of

154

their faces. Pairs of cold onyx orbs flashed in the neon from their eye sockets as they bore down on our position. *Death Squad.*

"Well that's not good," I said. Mason saw the same thing.

"It's always a bright day when synthetic killers show up," he said with dry mirth. "Someone really does want us dead."

"Go loud," I said, throwing open the door and knocking a passer-by to the ground as I did so. Mason leaped from the cab, the cannon charged and I followed, heading for the stone front of the nearest store.

"GET DOWN!" he roared as people began screaming. Then the cannon fired and the world came tumbling down around us.

18

I threw myself into cover just as the burst of automatic laser fire tore into the brickwork beside me. Dust and shards flew past me and another barrage slammed into the window behind, shattering it into a million pieces. Suddenly the world became a whirling cacophony of screams and cries, of stuttering weapon fire and the great booming of Mason's cannon. My focus was now sharp and alert and time began to slow, second by bloody second as years of combat training kicked in.

I dropped low and swung out, pistol already aimed and fired at the nearest target. His entire form staggered under the volley but a crackling shield generator bore the blast. He already had his Dingo SLG raised but the shots had thrown his aim and the burst ripped open a space above me. I felt a handful of sizzling stones drop onto my head, one managing to draw blood from my scalp.

"Tango down!" cried Mason as one of the three vanished in an explosion of bright blue plasma taking half an idling cab with it. The second responded with shots of his own, slamming into Mason's position behind a speeder but failing to find its target.

"Three more on our six!" said Mozzy who began firing straight away. "This isn't going good, guys!"

Thor was striding along the traffic, seemingly unable to draw any of their fire until he was on top of them. The three who'd approached on the right hadn't paid him any attention until his fist came slamming down on them, turning one into pulp. Then the carnage really began. Caring nothing for the civilian population, they opened fire indiscriminately, cutting a bloody swathe through anyone or anything between them and us. Dozens fell.

Mason managed to drop the next with a well-aimed blast but in doing so he brought the storefront they were standing down on top of them and two bystanders. I saw the horror spread across his face but we had no time to count the cost, that would come later.

"Secure that, soldier!" I roared over the gunfire now coming from the rear. "Tangos on our six!"

He shook himself, turned and moved into a stronger position, thumbing the improvised controls of the cannon. Across from him, Thor had killed another but was now taking a lot of laser damage from the third who deftly avoided his swinging arm. Part of the bot's face was missing and one of his legs dragged behind him.

I slammed my pistol into its holster and ran for the corpses barely visible under the rubble. Clearing away some of the debris I found both of the Dingos plus a couple of magazines. I slung them, checking the life signs of the civilians beneath. Dead. A man and a woman. *Just targets*, I told myself. *Collateral damage.*

"Man down!" cried Mason and I turned, seeing Thor grappling with the last attacker on the opposite sidewalk but dropping now to his knees. The synthetic had his hands on his neck, tearing away the conduit and servo arms. I brought up both Dingos, thumbed the cell recharge and sped towards him. He turned just in time to see both guns open up, filling the space between us with shards of red light until his face vanished in a splatter of cooling fluids.

The bot collapsed where he was, his mechanics finally giving out. His damaged head slammed onto the stone and gave a ghastly electronic screech.

"Don't go dying on me!" I bellowed over the rising wail of police sirens now close to our position. "Eject your CPU you stupid pile of junk!"

I pushed hard against the bot's shoulders, turning it over onto its back with no small effort. As I did so, his chest cavity collapsed inwards, exposing a glowing square of translucent metal that pulsed with power. From its center a tube perhaps the size of my forearm slid

157

out and I took it, stuffing it into my belt. It was almost too hot to touch.

I rammed the cube back inside, jamming open the cavity to ensure that the self-destruct mechanism would activate. Then, speeding back to Mason, I shouted into his ear.

"FIRE IN THE HOLE!"

We ducked and ran, pulling back from where we'd been until we were clear of the explosion that came hot on our heels. By now the street was empty and only the idling cabs and the windows of several stores bore the brunt of the explosion, sending concussive ripples out in all directions. It gave us breathing space, enough time to run some of the way towards the landing pad before our pursuers caught up.

"Mozzy, take the left," I said, tossing him one of the Dingos and a fresh clip. "Mason, go down the middle and take cover by the column."

I looked up. Three bulging craft were now hovering overhead like buzzing insects fat with blood. They were lit up in blue and white and red and belly-mounted laser cannons began stitching the ground with fire as they disgorged their cargo.

"Shock Squad!" cried Mozzy. "We're screwed, man!"

"Hold positions!" I shouted over the bullhorn, telling everyone to stand still and drop weapons. Suffice it to say, we didn't comply.

On came the Death Squad, now strengthened by four more identical attackers who didn't even pause in their stride for the Sargon PD or the spider-like robots who were now forming battle lines in the street. Six turned to face us while twelve more began moving along, directly towards the faceless enemy.

I opened fire first. One of the spiders dropped straight away, another managed to get off a couple of shots before I was able to take off its head. Mason destroyed two more and Mozzy, after smashing the one nearest to him with a volley found himself swinging the butt of the gun like a club to ward off the last. Clearly, they'd been programmed to take us alive at any cost. Arms fitted with restraint clamps came spiraling towards him from all directions until he could pull back far enough to blast it to pieces.

"Fall back!" I shouted. Mason covered me as I sped past him, taking up a position maybe six cars back. Mozzy followed, stopping shorter and shouting the retreat to Mason who did the same. We managed to peel back twice more, now almost within sight of the landing pad, until more robots were dropped in behind us.

"On our twelve!" I roared, emptying my clip into three of the bots. Then I felt a shot cut through the air beside me, burning a hole through the collar of my coat. Behind us five of the Death Squad had managed to overcome the robots and were now advancing on us.

"Mason, cover our six," I said. "Mozzy, with me."

Together the former soldier and I strode out of cover and advanced, firing as we went, smashing apart another six of the spiders until we were forced back into cover. It worked; the landing pad entrance was just up ahead and we'd gained some serious ground.

"Mason, pull back!" I cried. "We've got you."

We turned and began firing in controlled bursts as he ran towards us, head down. Fire followed him, blasting through the tail of his coat as he went but he made it to an empty cab and set his cannon upon its hood.

"I'm nearly out," said Mozzy. I looked at my own cells. One more mag left. I handed it to him.

"Make it count," I said. Then, looking ahead, I saw another PD craft settle in the middle of the road. This time it opened its rear compartment and several bulky looking exo-shells emerged, rifles in hand. My heart sank. Mozzy let out a string of expletives.

"What do we do now?" asked Mason as he let off two more blasts.

"Hell if I know," I said. Then, like a call from heaven itself, my comms unit came to life.

"Carter! Run for the landing pad. Don't stop!" It was Eldritch and when I looked up I saw him in the doorway, gesturing for me to come. "I called in a few favors."

159

"You're a bloody miracle in human flesh!" I laughed. Then, to the others. "PULL BACK!"

We ditched the spent weapons and ran like the devil was on our heels, which some might argue, he was. We passed the hulking exo-shells who ignored us and began to open fire on the last of the Death Squad. I turned back just in time to see them advance, unafraid of the heavy armor coming towards them, bent only on their mission which was now about to get off-world. We made it inside, blinded by the bright interior where Malcolm Eldritch stood, flanked by two uniforms carrying scatter lasers.

"Thanks for shooting up our streets," he smirked. "Now get the hell off Sargon." I was about to say something but he waved me away. "It's been a hell of a day, right?"

"You're telling me. Goodbye again, Malcolm."

"Goodbye, Carter. I hope your friend makes it out okay." Then, to Mozzy, he said. "Well?"

He handed him a cube and the disc I'd taken from one of the soldiers. "That's everything I know, my word on that."

"It'll make you a hunted man," said Eldritch. Mozzy shrugged.

"No one will be seeing me again, I can promise you that. Thanks, Cop."

Eldritch tipped his head, then gestured for us to move along. We did so and, looking back, I saw him smiling like a man who'd found a sliver of excitement in a world he'd thought was all too dull.

19

In the shuttle, the stench of ozone and hot metal followed us all the way to Theta. It'd been unsettling to go from the center of a warzone straight into civilian life. The passengers around us suspected we'd been involved but were either too intimidated or simply uninterested to ask us about it. We took our seats along with everyone else and as the craft lifted off from Sargon, I stole a look out of the window.

"Good riddance," muttered Mozzy under his breath.

I looked at Mason who remained silent, staring at nothing in particular and occasionally rubbing at his chest. I didn't say anything. That would come later.

Once we were docked with the station, we disembarked in a long line where security waved us through the barriers, no questions asked. That made us officially free and I'd been tense all the way there wondering if Eldritch could pull strings that long. Evidently, he could.

Baz and Jo met us outside the *Hikane*. The ship was thrumming with life and ready to sail and I felt a wave of fatigue wash over me. We'd been awake for too long, done too much and eaten nothing since the cafe. We were drained.

"Where's Thor?" asked Jo. I waved the tube at her. "What the hell happened?"

"Let's be underway first," I said. "Then we'll fill you in."

"Who are you?" asked Baz, looking at Mozzy.

"Our guest," I replied. "He tried to kill us but he's okay."

Puzzled beyond belief, Baz shook his head and followed us onto the ship. In less than ten minutes I was in my room, under a shower and already beginning to drift off with long blinks of my eyes. Another

161

ten minutes and I was gone.

It was Jo who woke me four hours later with a tray of coffee and some toast and little Jimmy at her side. It was the nicest way to be woken up and I said as much as I invited them both into my room.

"Sleep well?" she asked as I sat on the edge of the bed, sipping at the cup. It had to be the best coffee I'd had in a long time.

"Well enough," I smiled. "What's happening?"

"We've just received a coded message from Argo and another from Angel's defense-"

"Aleksei Rokossovsky?"

"The same. You say it like it isn't a mouthful."

"It's not when you've heard it so many times," I laughed. "He'll be looking for a sitrep."

"And Argo?" I shrugged.

"It seems like everyone has an interest in this thing. Speaking of which, what's Mozzy doing now?"

"Sleeping I guess. He's being closely monitored and Baz says he hasn't left his room since he went in."

"Good."

"Who is he, Carter?"

"Right now? Angel's best hope of freedom. He knows the location of a data vault where evidence of Bourmont's treason was hidden away. We get that and we clear Angel's name."

"That sounds simpler than it probably is."

"I've no doubt about that but right now we're out of options. He was on the team, Jo. If we hand him over the chances are that he'll go down with her. This way we might be able to help them both."

"I hope so."

I looked at Jimmy who hadn't stopped staring at me since he'd come in.

"How's Thor?" I asked.

"He's fine though a little shook up if that's-" She stopped herself.

162

"Obviously it's possible, right?" I nodded. "His systems appear fine though now he's back in his original frame. He's already begun constructing another to replace that one – and yes, I'm keeping a close eye on both of them." She smiled and turned to the little bot. "Come on, buddy. Let's get back to work and let Carter enjoy his breakfast."

"Okay, ma'am," he chirped. "Top of the mornin' to ya, Mr. Carter, sir."

"Good morning to you too, Jimmy."

When they'd gone I settled back on the bed and tried to unpack the last few days whilst I munched at the toast. It wasn't easy. There were too many fingers in too many pies and right now I'd had enough of food metaphors. It felt like the old days of 'go over there and shoot that' had long gone and I was now some Spook or Operator, deeply involved in plans and schemes I didn't have a clue about. I was glad that Mozzy and his team had ineptly come right at us; I'd needed the simplicity of combat to clear my head and if his bargaining chip proved legal tender, I'd be happy to play his game until I got what I wanted. Facing an all-out assault on a fortress seemed infinitely more preferable to any further breadcrumb-chasing.

I finished eating, put on some clothes and made my way to the bridge. Baz was there, sat with his feet up watching some video on his comms unit. I went and sat in the weapon control seat and turned to face him.

"Anything I need to know?" I asked. He shook his head.

"Not a thing," he replied without taking his eyes off what he was watching. "Getting the buffer was a cake-walk."

"Have you seen Mason?"

"Still in bed I guess. What happened down there?"

I filled him in, probably in more detail than was necessary but at that moment I felt I had to get it off my chest. It also helped to put things in perspective. I included the part where Mason's stray shot had killed two civilians and as I told the story Baz visibly winced.

"Poor guy," he said. "That's not going to go away any time soon."

163

"I don't expect it to, nor should it, but bear it in mind when you speak to him, okay?"

"Sure, no problem. We've all been there, right?"

"Sadly, that's true."

We chewed over some less important stuff like the shopping he'd done on the station and his time spent playing games with Jimmy. He couldn't get over how childlike and real the bot was and, though disturbing by its implications, he actually enjoyed having him around.

"What are you going to do with him when we go home?" he asked. It was a good question.

"Keep him hidden for now," I said. "Jo is going to investigate the whole thing, find out just what Jack managed to create when he started messing with Thor's CPU. There's a basic degree of AI to most bots but he goes beyond anything directly man-made. Even those Death Squad synthetics aren't capable of independent thought like Thor. If the wrong people find out I dread to think what might happen to them both."

"You actually give a shit now, Carter?" he laughed. I kicked his shin with the toe of my boot and he yelped.

"Don't spread it around. One day I might even start giving a shit about you."

"You couldn't live without me," he grinned. "I'm the MVP of the team."

"If you say so, man. If you say so."

I turned back to the consoles and began playing with them, trying to remember how to bring up the external comms. The layouts had a flavor of the systems on the *Helios* but I began to wonder if that was more of a hindrance than a help. I got there eventually and called up Aleksei's message first. It was a simple call-back. Argo had left a message on a secure network.

"As usual you've managed to poke the hornet's nest on Sargon. If you aren't lying in a pool of your own blood, which I severely doubt you are, return this communication as soon as possible. We must meet."

"He's got such a way with words," snorted Baz.

"He must read a lot. So many big phrases. Sometimes I find myself wishing I had a thesaurus."

He'd left intercept coordinates embedded in the message and I read them aloud to him.

"You want to meet him again?" he asked.

"What choice do I have?" I replied. "If we're going to hit this data vault then we're looking at some serious planning time and a shop for hardware."

"Sounds like my kind of Op."

"Yeah, sounds just like something Argo will pat us on the back for doing."

"What do you mean?"

"It's a data vault. That's dirt on a whole lot of people and if Mozzy is telling the truth then it involves a number of Earth Gov. personnel. Do you think Argo won't want some of that?"

"Hmm," he said. "Possibly."

"Well I can almost guarantee it and I intend to milk it for all I can."

"Make him foot the bill?"

"In a manner of speaking." I checked the console. "How long until we intercept?"

"Six hours," he said, scanning his own screen. "They didn't pick up much pace since we parted from them. Engines must still be struggling because they're bound for Indigo-Six."

"The Commonwealth shipyard?"

"The very same."

"He must be desperate."

I turned back to the console and brought up the secure channel for Aleksei. He answered the call after the third ring.

"Carter," he said, appearing on the display sat behind his desk. Did he ever go home? There was a pause as the comms-lag kicked in over such a long distance. "I'm glad you returned my call."

"I guess you're looking for an update?"

"Yes, that's part of the reason I called."

"The other?" I said, feeling my throat constrict.

"There's been an... *incident* involving Angel."

"Is she okay?" I blurted out. The lag was suddenly infuriating.

"Yes, yes – she's fine. I cannot say the same for those who attacked her but-"

"What?" I cried.

"There have been several attempts on her life and the Warden has only recently seen fit to inform me of them. I've had her transferred to a more secure wing but I don't know how long that will hold them back. I suspect it may have been an internal plot."

"By who? Bourmont?"

"Who?" he replied and I realized that my mouth was moving faster than my brain. "Perhaps you should fill me in on what you've discovered so far."

So I did, spending a lot of time thrashing out just what Argo had told us and how it had led us to Sargon City. Aleksei listened intently, making notes on a tablet at his right hand. I offered to forward the recording to him but he shook his head.

"Although I'm grateful for your candor, it would be wise to respect Argo's need for secrecy."

"Do you think he's right? I mean, the whole scheme to move his own people into positions of power?"

"I'll admit that it makes me nervous; having a government with strong military leanings is dangerous at best. But I take his point and this unknown fleet troubles me too, confirming what you've told me. Argo is a good man, his father's son."

"You know them both?" I asked, a little taken back.

"Of course," he chuckled. "I defended Admiral Argo at the Battle Of Mars inquiry led by a witch-hunt of a JAG investigation. I got to know them both and have a long-standing respect for the family."

"Can I trust him?"

166

"If you're in line with his interests? Yes, I'd say you could."

"And if I wasn't?" He shrugged, barely moving the soft material of his expensive suit.

"My advice is to try your hardest not to be." We shared a laugh together and I saw him consult his wrist. "I'm afraid I have another appointment. Please let me know how your second meeting with the Captain goes before you decide to act. Time is moving quickly even though you've only been gone a couple of days. I believe Bourmont will attempt to tie up loose ends as quickly as possible."

"Seeing Death Squads again after so long makes me agree with you."

"That is very troubling, I'll admit. Synthetic killers from some dark corner of the Commonwealth are expensive and to throw them away in that manner tells us much about our opponent. He's desperate."

"That's the impression I got."

He nodded and reached to end the call.

"Take care, Carter."

"Likewise. If you get a chance, pass on our regards to Angel."

"Will do."

And with that, the image snapped into darkness and I sat back, letting out a long, low whistle.

"That went well," said Baz with evident sarcasm. "I especially liked the bit about trusting Argo. Kind of makes me feel like the proverbial gap between a rock and that hard place people keep talking about."

"We spend so much time there that we should buy a house or something."

"I hear the prices are pretty cheap too."

I left the bridge and made my way to the crew quarters, stopping first at Mason's room. I pressed the chime but after a minute or two I got no answer. When I consulted the display next to the door it told me that the room was unoccupied and had been for the last hour or so. There was a good chance he was at the gym so I moved on to Mozzy's

167

room a few doors along. Before pressing the chime I checked to see if he was still inside and hadn't slipped past Baz's careful watch. He hadn't.

"Mozzy?" I called after receiving no answer from the chime. "You awake buddy?" Nothing. I pressed again, harder this time as if that would make any bloody difference. Still no response.

"Baz, can you work out the life-sign scanner and tell me if this guy is still alive or what?" I said into the comms.

"Yeah, can do. I figured it out earlier. Give me a sec."

I waited in silence. The hum of the engines was soothing but still the dominating noise on any space-faring vessel, including expensive pleasure yachts.

"Shit – get in there!" cried Baz. "They're through the floor."

I tapped in my override code, miss-spelled it and tried again. The door slid open and the coppery stench of blood filled my nostrils. There, on the bed, lay Mozzy – a knife in one hand and the other pressed loosely against a gaping wound in his neck. Beside him was the implanted disc sat in a drying pool of gore that had soaked into the bed sheets and turned brown.

"Holy shit!" I said, rushing to his side. "Get a medpack down here!" I called over the comms. "He's bleeding out."

Suddenly a warning siren blared across the ship and the lights dimmed. The day had just gotten worse.

"Carter! I've got two ships approaching on attack vectors. Fast moving F-Class vessels. ETA six minutes."

The ship began to pulse with crimson light and an audio warning wailed down every hallway and deck across the craft.

ALL HANDS – INCOMING ATTACK.

ALL HANDS – INCOMING ATTACK.

ALL HANDS...

20

Mason reached Mozzy's room with the medpack in seconds. He tore open the seals and began the emergency treatment we'd all been trained in. I helped administer the life-saving drugs that would stop the bleeding and help with blood re-gen and he applied the dressings once he was sure the idiot hadn't nicked an artery. Above our heads, the siren continued to wail and the verbal warning repeated itself over and over again.

"Is he stable?" I asked.

"I think so. It's the best we can do for now. We're going to have to leave him here and head to the bridge."

Just then Jimmy appeared in the open doorway behind us and coughed to get our attention.

"Miss Jo said I might be able to help," he said over the racket.

"Stay here and watch Mozzy," I instructed. "If he stops breathing or tries to get up, let me know immediately, okay?"

"Okay, sir."

The little robot walked over to the bed and stood staring down at the ashen-faced man. Then he seemed to freeze in position, barely moving an inch.

"Let's go," said Mason and out we went into the chaos.

Suited in the new armor, we made it to the bridge and found Baz eager to put on his own. We relieved him and I took the command chair while Mason took his place at the guns.

"They're almost on us," I said. "They have to be Death Squad. Probably followed us from Sargon. Someone is paying a lot of money to have synthetic hunters come this far after us."

"I'm just glad they're only running subroutines and not thinking for themselves yet."

"It's only a matter of time before whoever builds them figures that out. Jack did."

"I really don't want to go there right now," he said. I looked at the screen.

"Here we go."

"Their weapons are hot," said Mason. "They're getting ready to make a firing run."

I glanced at the engine status. They were almost in the red, burning at maximum thrust and it was clear that Baz had tried to outrun them. Even though we were sailing in a luxury craft it was clear that our pursuers had anticipated a chase and got themselves some swift vessels. The only plus to that was the speed versus firepower equation – more in the engines, less to shoot.

"Fusion reactors are maxed out," I said. "We should bring her around and make a stand."

"Sounds good to me," he replied. "Use the Anderson-pattern flightpath and put them in front of our guns. Let's see what we can do before they try and board us."

"Inputting it now, if I remember it rightly."

My fingers flew across the console, recalling the delicate high-speed manoeuvre made famous by Mark Anderson during the Lunar conflict. It was used so often because it offered very few counter-manoeuvres and only a truly skilled pilot could avoid the fatal last-minute showdown with a broadside.

"That's it," said Mason, glued to his screen. "We're coming about."

"One of them is shifting, attempting to break off," I said. "Engaging in three... two..."

"Got 'em!" he cried. "Multiple hits on the first vessel. Damage to forward shields. Hull breach on their upper decks. One forward lancer is down, another badly damaged."

171

"What about the other?"

"Nothing. He managed to break away in time."

I looked. Behind that red blip was a skilled pilot or an expensive AI control unit because the ship had now shifted to our port side and was bearing down on us. The craft we'd hit broke away and put some space between us.

"Incoming!" said Mason. The ship rocked as we took a barrage of fire and impact icons flashed across my console.

"Damage report," I said over the comms.

"We took a beating, Carter," said Jo. "Port shields have failed and we've got hull damage on the lower decks. Port broadside is offline and there are fires on decks three through eight. Automated systems are tackling the blazes and the shields will be back up in two minutes."

I took the ship downwards, banking hard to starboard to protect our weakened side from the enemy ship now turning to make another pass. I plotted a flight plan, one that would close the gap between the *Hikane* and the damaged craft and set us on it.

"You're thinking about destroying the other ship?" asked Mason. I nodded. "Good call."

"If it's Death Squad then they won't try to stop us. They'll use the destruction of the other ship to their advantage."

"But?"

"But at the last minute, I want you to change the firing pattern to target them as they come about. Use the forward plasma lances to cripple the wounded ship instead."

"It might work."

The engines fired and the *Hikane* sped towards its target with the other vessel on our tail. If I was right then they'd bank hard to port and bring their full broadside to bear on us as we made our pass. That was the moment when we'd strike, offering them our full weight of shot in a direction they wouldn't expect. I just had to hope that the other vessel was more crippled than it appeared.

"Thirty-six seconds," said Mason. "Firing pattern A is locked. Firing pattern B is ready to go on your mark."

"Understood," I said. Then, watching the delicate movements of the red markers on my screen, I judged the timing as best I could. I wasn't an AI control unit but sometimes the human element was the best kind of advantage.

"Okay, hold on," I said, sweat collecting on my brow. "Here we go. On my mark..." I waited. One wrong move... "MARK!"

The ship rocked again as we exchanged fire in the blink of an eye. More damage icons raged across my console but as I still had a chair beneath me I guessed that we hadn't been turned into space debris just yet.

"Report!" I cried.

"Engines are offline!" yelled Jo over the sirens behind her. "We're dead in the water. Direct hit. Shields failing."

I looked at the display in panic but was relieved to find that one blip had vanished and the other had come to a halt just beyond our prow. The crippled ship was gone and the other listed where it was, navigation controls lost and judging from the exhaust plumes venting from its rear, the core was about to blow.

"They're launching boarding pods, dozens of them. They're heading this way."

"Shit," I said, getting up. "Jo, is Thor with you?"

"Yeah, he's here."

"Prepare to repel boarders. A lot of them."

"This should be fun," said Baz. "They'd better not ruin the décor."

The modified escape pods were the bane of any craft that found itself under attack by Death Squad ships. Synthetic killers didn't really go in for self-preservation so whenever they found their vessels crippled beyond use they were more than happy to launch themselves directly at their targets in the hope of latching on to the hull and boarding. Most would die in space, blasted to dust by lancers and low-yield missile launchers, but some would always find a way through and burn great holes in the sides of the ship, opening crude entrances into vital areas. As our shields were down and subsequently our weapons and engines, every one of those pods had a clear run towards us.

"It's going to get busy," said Mason, handing me my rifle. "They'll try and sabotage the ship, maybe even take it over. They'll know that they can do little against these suits."

"Kind of like whack-a-mole then?" asked Baz. "See one, hit one."

"Yeah, perfect analogy," I groaned. "Look, just kill them and kill them completely – even injured they'll try to wreak as much havoc as they can. I've sealed Jimmy and Mozzy in their room. Now that he's removed the implant maybe it won't lead them right to him."

"They're here for him?" asked Baz.

"And us; they'll expect him to have talked so they won't risk leaving us alive too. I want you on their deck, guarding those hallways. Mason, hold the upper decks and most importantly the bridge."

"And you?"

"I'm going to have to manually seal the hull breaches myself, killing as I go. Thor should be able to protect the engine decks by himself but if he gets in trouble then I want you to back him up. The bridge is useless without the engines anyway."

"And me?" said Baz.

"Protect Mozzy at all costs. If he dies, then Angel dies with him."

I slammed in a fresh magazine of anti-boarding rounds and checked that my combat rig was loaded with as many as I could carry. Then, activating the full helmet, I saw my vision vanish behind overlapping plates to be replaced with a high-definition HUD.

"Good luck," I said before heading for the nearest breach. My stomach rolled inside the suit and I strained to suppress the fear welling up the way it always did before an engagement.

There was a surreal feeling to stomping along carpeted corridors in full exo-shell armor. I followed my HUD to the nearest breach on deck four. Before leaving the bridge, I'd locked down the entire ship and door control was one of the few systems that ran on emergency power. They would only open for us now and the boarding party would have to either hack or cut their way through them if they wanted to complete their mission.

As I rounded a corner a stitch of laser blasts skimmed across my chest plate and refracted into the wall. I didn't stop moving. I'd already raised my weapon and I fired off two bursts, killing the nearest target and wounding the other so that it fell back behind a smouldering doorway. The entrance had been made using breaching charges and most of the arch and surrounding wall were fused into a molten mass of plastic and metal.

I stepped through, sweeping my rifle left and right. The wounded figure on the floor wore an environment suit with SINKO plating, a kind of metallic weave that would stop most rounds but not the kind loaded into my weapon. This wasn't my first engagement with synthetic boarding parties and like most machines, they fell into predictable patterns very easily. I blasted the crippled synthetic skull open, splattering white liquid onto the wall behind it. Then, approaching the next corridor, I saw two more emerge from the gaping wound in my ship. No hesitation, no fear, they raised their weapons and fired at the same time I did. The one on the left found a hole the size of my fist open up in its chest cavity, the other lost its head from the shoulders upwards.

"Sealing the first breach," I said into the comms, approaching the sizzling mass of metal that looked like a kind of mouth into another dimension. The pod on the other side was barely functional and air hissed out into space where it hadn't properly sealed.

I popped the control panel located a little further down from the opening, keyed in the correct codes and felt a shudder run beneath my feet. Magna-locks in my armor clamped onto the deck as the hull plating separated from the ship. The bodies of the Death Squad and the pod they'd come in were sucked out into space along with an ugly painting in a gold frame that was torn off its fixings by the vacuum. I pressed the green icon on the display and a replacement panel slid into place, overlapped the hole and fired self-guiding rivets into the skin of the ship. It was a temporary fix, one that cast my mind back to the space above a frozen planet not-too-long-ago. I shook it off and made my way to the next breach.

The annoying aspect of a boarding pod was its ability to override the automatic hull repair systems which under normal circumstances would've ejected the invader by itself, pretty much the way I was doing. Designers of these things installed nano-mites to burrow into the hull before the cutting torches opened it up, finding the sensor nodes before the ship could register the breach and neutralize them. As this effectively made the bridge controls useless, a manual override had to be performed at the site of the boarding pod. Safety specs wouldn't let anyone just open up their own ship from the bridge, instead, they expected you to risk being sucked out yourself. I guess they figured that if you were that set on destroying yourself you should do it in person.

"How many per pod?" asked Baz.

"There were four in this one," I replied, sweeping the next room. There was another breach on this same deck. "But don't count on that for all of them."

"Contact!" cried Mason. "Tango down. I've got three more, possibly four."

I moved along, sweeping each corridor with ominously sealed doors on either side. The lights were low but my HUD compensated and a spinning alert light seemed to be the only thing moving.

"Jo – talk to me," I said, turning a corner. The next breach was a few meters up ahead.

"I'm working as hard as I can I-" An explosion over the comms. Gunfire. I heard Jo stifle a scream.

"Contact!" called Thor. "Who wants a little syn'fetic-flambet?" The burst of his flame-thrower sounded like ripping cloth. "Cam' on ya barstards!" he bellowed. "'Ave some o' that!"

I quickened my pace, following the line of my display to the next left turn. Already plumes of smoke were billowing out into the corridor. I yanked a WP grenade from my hip, twisted the activator and hurled it around the corner. A few seconds later and a brilliant flash of white light made my HUD dim. I followed it in, rifle humming with life. Nothing. Three bodies lay slumped against the wall near the breach, their suits glowing with smouldering fire. One stood by the control panel; hands frozen on the icons. It looked inactive but I fired anyway, blowing off the top of its skull, toppling it to the ground.

I checked the panel. It'd been trying to access the main system, but the grenade had fried its circuits mid-way. It'd bypassed the lock-down somehow and was about to enter the mainframe.

"Be advised, units are attempting to hack our systems," I said. "Stop them at all costs."

"Understood," said Baz.

"I see that," said Mason. "Just found one. It's neutralized."

Again I ran through the protocol and left before the panel had finished riveting itself in place. I also stomped on the head of the hacker, turning the mech-flesh and quantum brain units into mulch. I was taking no chances.

"Moving on," I reported. "Jo – are you okay?"

"Still here," she said. "They've regrouped beyond the outer decks. Thor held them off."

The next breach was below me and I hurried to the stairwell. I was in that focused place where all other thoughts and worries had been pushed out in favor of the immediate mission. I didn't always like being there but I was thankful for it now. Thinking would come later when the mind and the conscience would put you on trial for everything you were doing now.

On the next deck, they'd managed to push deeper, already working the control panels that now gave them access to the rooms on that level. As there was nothing vital to the ship down there it wasn't much to worry about for the time being. I guessed that they were systematically hunting for Mozzy now that his locator was deactivated.

With no small amount of satisfaction, I carved my way through them; six were in the corridor just adjacent to the stairs and three more were moving between rooms. All of them met with the business-end of my rifle. I sealed the first breach I found and saw that the control panel had been used recently. I moved on. Three more guarded the next pod and died for their troubles. As I was changing magazines, two rounded the corner and opened up. Shots bounced off my helmet and one of them even hurled a grenade at me. My HUD identified it as an HE bomb and plotted its course in a heartbeat. Mind and exo-shell worked effortlessly together; my hand shot out and batted the rolling ball back towards its sender. The explosive tore the synthetic apart, splattering a mural of early Earth colonials painted into the bulkhead with white gore.

I kept up the pace and managed to clear the deck before Baz reported his first assault.

"Here we go!" he said with a certain unnerving amount of glee. "Contact!"

The last pod vanished into space, sucking out more bodies just before the tear was sealed. Already my HUD was calculating a course down to the next deck which was two above engineering. Before the rivets had even fired I was gone, sprinting back to the stairwell and checking the ammo counter in the corner of my display.

"They've opened the doors!" cried Baz. "Moving to protect Mozzy now."

"How many?"

"A lot!" he bellowed over his own gunfire. "They're swarming my position. GRENADE!"

An explosion ran down the comms line and made me wince. I reached the stairwell and stopped momentarily, considering running to back him up. I decided against it.

"Mason, help Baz!" I said. "I've got to get these breaches sealed."

"I'm already moving," he replied. "But now we know they're hacking our systems they'll head for the bridge next."

"Do what you can but if it looks like they're heading there, all of you fall back to secure it. Understood?"

"Understood. Stand by."

I swore under my breath but carried on moving down. With only Thor to protect Jo and the engines, I had to make the difficult call on which was more important to our survival. In a cold, detached mind, Mozzy's death was secondary to keeping the ship in the air. If they were able to take over the *Hikane*, we were screwed anyway.

Just then I felt the ship rock beneath me and the armor warned me that it was compensating for the turbulence. There was a low rumble, then a sudden shock as something big impacted the hull.

"What now?" I said. "More ships?"

"We're blind," said Mason. "It could be. Keep going, Carter. Clear those decks."

I moved downwards, feeling my stomach knot. If another Death Squad craft had caught up with us then we were doomed. It wasn't like we could negotiate with them. They'd complete their mission and destroy the ship with us inside it.

I reached the lower deck and came under fire immediately. I blew apart two of them and took the arm off another. It tried to continue its task, but another two rounds took off its head at the neck.

I heard an explosion up ahead and my HUD flashed a warning light – incoming targets that were not Death Squad. The scanners had detected armored units emerging from the hull that could only mean that there was now another boarding craft attached to us.

I moved into cover at the intersection and dropped to one knee, changing magazines. Three shapes marked by green dots were moving rapidly towards me. I took a deep breath and waited.

"MARINES MARINES MARINES" blared down the corridor towards me. "Stand down!"

I stood up and lowered my weapon. Around the corner three heavily armored figures moved into view and I sighed with relief. They crossed the deck with effortless grace in FARGO exo-shells, weapons raised, and they secured the intersection with the skill of practiced ship-boarders.

"Carter?" said the nearest. I nodded. "Henderson. We're from the *Pearl*. What's your situation?"

"Multiple boarding pods have allowed synths to gain access to most of the ship. They're primarily targeting our bridge, engineering and living quarters. We have a high-value asset currently being protected there."

"Understood." He spoke into his own secure comms for a moment before turning back to me. "I've sent teams six and three to engineering and team four to the bridge. Let's move."

I led the way to the stairwell and up to the living deck with the Marines in tow. There we encountered heavy fighting and the corridors were scorched black with gunfire and the burning bodies of dead synths.

"MOVE MOVE MOVE," ordered Henderson and with well-disciplined strikes the Marines swept through each hallway and room, slaughtering as they went with cool precision. I made my way to Mozzy's room, killing two more who'd sheltered in an open doorway as Mason laid down heavy fire.

"Friendly coming in," I called.

"About time," said Baz. "That was hairy."

"We've just had our asses saved," I replied. "I guess God loves TRIDENT."

"Did I hear right?" asked Mason. "They're from the *Pearl*?" I nodded. "Hell, that's impeccable timing."

"How's our asset?"

"Alive but shook up. Mozzy regained consciousness and tried to join in but Jimmy sat him down. He's strong for such a little guy."

"Good. We'll wait for the Marines to do their job and then stand down." I spoke into my comms. "Jo – status?"

"Alive. Barely," she replied. "Thor nearly torched the Marines but they managed to identify themselves quickly enough for him to stop."

I relaxed a little and looked about. The place was a mess. The air was thick with smoke and the stench of burning plastic and it seemed that the décor of the ship had taken the brunt of the attack. On her maiden voyage, we'd nearly written her off already.

"She doesn't look as pretty now," said Baz. "Shame."

Mason scowled down at the carpet.

"That synthetic blood will be a bitch to get out of the shag-pile."

21

The *Pearl* came alongside us and attached multiple tow cables to the *Hikane* before setting off at low speed. She hadn't finished her own repairs since last we'd met but it seemed that the important work had been completed enough for them to be able to come to our aid.

"When you'd reported your intention to intercept the fleet we monitored the space lanes for your approach," said Captain Sole as he arrived on our bridge flanked by a squad of Henderson's Marines. "Captain Argo seemed to know already that you'd be pursued."

"We're predictable like that," I laughed. "We don't play well with others." Sole smiled and looked about him.

"Nice ship," he said. "Shame about the attack. Is this...?"

"No, it's not what we normally sail in. It was a kind of last-minute thing." He nodded.

"Lot of money here."

"Yes."

He dismissed the Marines and they left, taking up guarding positions outside the door. Then he sat at the weapon's console, now blank, and leaned back, straightening his uniform.

"The *Pearl* is almost ship-shape again. I've been able to spare a small engineering team to assist your Chief with repairs and a medic to tend to your *guest*. It seems that you took a beating from the Death Squad ships."

"It certainly feels like it," I said. "They know how to throw a punch."

"This is my first time encountering them directly. I've heard about them, of course, and my Marines are no strangers to their kind, but to

182

actually be able to take one apart is quite a treat."

"Henderson made quite a mess of them," I grinned.

"They're some of the best men and women in the Corps. It took a lot of favor-pulling to get his team on my ship. I gave them orders to bag a couple intact so we could see how these clockwork-men tick."

"Because...?" He opened both of his arms in a 'what can I say?' kind of gesture.

"They're a menace. No one has been able to find out where they're made or how they work. Earth hasn't been able to recreate anything like them and with so many civilian casualties put to their name they'd never lift the production ban anyway. To submit my findings would make some waves in the scientific community."

"Glad we could be of assistance."

He smirked and flattened out another crease in his jacket.

"Artificial intelligence is a kind of hobby of mine. I still find it incredible that in all this time, with all these advances in space travel and automated robotics, we've been unable to unlock the secret of being self-aware. Whoever created these synthetic killers must be on the verge of discovering it. To operate solely on subroutines so far from their maker requires more than just ones and zeroes?"

"I wouldn't know," I said with rising fear. "That's not my field of expertise."

Sole nodded and looked down at his feet. Then, looking me directly in the eye, he spoke.

"I hear rumors. Whispers. A few words here and there."

I felt that cold terror creeping up my spine like a spider scaling its web. Had Henderson said something about Thor? Had one of them noticed something in Jimmy?

"I see your team and a close involvement with Captain Argo. I have little pieces of what I feel is a much larger puzzle." I slowly nodded, eternally grateful that he was no longer talking about robots and AI. "I think I understand what he might be trying to do. Am I sailing close to the mark, Carter."

"It depends," I said. "If you were, what would your feelings be on that?"

"Honestly? I'd want to be involved."

"That's not my call to make."

"I understand that. But to me, it seems that wherever you and your team go, things happen on a large scale. You might only see yourselves as bit-players in Captain Argo's plans, but already you've brought home a prize worthy of an Admiral and caught the attention of very dangerous enemies."

"I'd have preferred not to," I smiled. "But shouldn't you be having this conversation with him and not me?"

"I will, in due course. I've known the Captain a long time and I feel a strong sense of loyalty to him, especially after our recent engagement. But you aren't Navy, you aren't tainted by our biases. Answer me this one question." I tilted my head. "Do you trust him?"

I thought about that for a moment. We hadn't really been given a choice in trusting him from the moment we'd first met him. But if you could measure something like that in real terms then I guess, like most people, his actions told me more than his words did. He'd saved us from the D122, involved us with Wash' plans when he could have told us to go away and sent (or allowed) the *Pearl* to come to our rescue.

"Yes," I said. "I do."

"Then that is all I need to know," he said and got to his feet, straightening his uniform tunic. "We will continue to tow you towards Indigo-Six where we will rendezvous with the rest of the fleet. We don't expect any more of those Death Squad ships to try again, especially once we re-join."

"Thank you, Captain." He nodded.

"Our ledgers are balanced, Carter. My debt to you is paid in full I think." I laughed and showed him to the door. The Marines snapped to attention.

"Oh, that reminds me – Corporal Henderson asked me to inquire

184

about your armor."

"Yes?"

"He says he's never seen anything like it before and he considers himself an expert on exo-shells. He would appreciate a conversation about it at your next convenience."

"They're prototypes. I'll have Mason invite him over when he's off duty to explain further," I said.

"Much obliged. Thank you again."

And with that the Captain left the bridge and the ship, returning to the *Pearl*. With his words weighing heavily on my mind I went down to engineering to make sure Jo had taken the break I'd ordered her to have. She hadn't. She was directing the team sent over from the *Pearl* and when I saw her she turned, looked at me with dark eyes thick with fatigue and shrugged.

"I need to know-" she began but I simply took the data tablet from her hands, set it down on the bench and took her arm in mine, leading her to the door. "But Carter, I really have to-"

I said nothing and she didn't resist. I led her to the stairs, up to the living quarters and to her room, opening the door as she stifled a yawn. As I went in I saw that her cases were still sealed and nothing had been put away. The workaholic hadn't even bothered to unpack but had gone straight to engineering once she'd boarded.

"Well?" I asked, gesturing to the pile of cases.

"I was busy," she said with a flush of red on her cheeks. "I haven't had time."

"Jo – I know that you love your work and that right now you want your hands on your ship rather than some strangers. But I need you operating at 100% efficiency and you can't do that when you're dead on your feet."

"Tell me this," she snapped, turning on me. "Would YOU be taking a nap right now if you needed to?"

"No," I replied. "But Mason would make me. He's a good friend like that."

185

I pushed her gently towards the bed, saw a t-shirt and some shorts discarded on the pillows and handed them to her.

"Change," I said. She shook her head.

"I'm covered in sweat and oil. I need to shower first."

"I'll wait."

I turned my back and heard her slip out of her overalls. Then she padded over to the shower cubicle and turned on the water. I waited, feeling a little uncomfortable at being so close to her. To pass the time I stared at a painting on the wall, some kind of representation of a war I'd never heard of. Why had the team in charge of the décor chosen so much military-themed art for the ship? I gazed into the smears of topaz and ochre and silt and wondered what kind of soldier had fought there and why. No answers came.

"I'm done," she said and I turned. She stood there in a towel, her hair wet and dripping onto pale shoulders that looked young and smooth and the scent of coconut shampoo followed her to the bed. She sat on the corner and put her head in her hands.

"I'm so tired, Carter," she whispered through her fingers. "I'm dead on my feet."

"Get some rest then," I said. "8 hours. No less. That's an order."

I handed her the bedclothes and turned away, letting her change. Then I threw back the cover and she got in, rolling on to her side away from me. As I tucked her in her eyes were already closing on a gentle frown and I brushed the damp hair from her cheeks. In another moment she was softly snoring. I watched her for a minute, looked at the cases and sighed. Then I began to unpack for her.

We arrived at Indigo-Six the following day, ship time, and found the security of the entire fleet reassuring. The station was in high orbit above a planet hostile to human life but one that was rich in precious metals. This allowed the structure to expand on a massive scale, allowing for a dockyard to be built capable of servicing a great many ships both Commonwealth and Earth Government.

The *Pearl* contacted the dockyard and released the *Hikane* into the hands of tow-ships that came speeding from the station like a swarm of worker-ants. With almost no noticeable shift in the ship's balance, we were pulled into a vacant dry-dock and attached to the mainframe along with all the other members of the fleet. Then, with practiced politeness, we were asked to disembark whilst repairs were carried out.

"What do we do now?" asked Mason as we found ourselves standing on the passenger platform surrounded by people-traffic of all shapes and sizes. The scale of the station was awe-inspiring. Snaking walkways wide enough to take a tank vanished in all directions. Shops, service portals, traders of all stripes and workers looking for a ride off gave the place a hectic, 24/7 feel. Vid-screens blared irritating advertisements for Commonwealth services that appeared quirky and faintly propaganda-esque compared to what we were used to on the other side of the border. The air stunk of sweat and humankind, all squashed into neat lanes that funnelled you towards a dozen eateries or bars, forcing you to part with a lot of credits for not much return.

"Argo wants us at conference room B on level six at 1500 hours," I said. "That leaves us with time to kill I guess."

Thor and Jimmy had been left on the ship with orders to monitor repairs but stay reasonably out of sight. The last thing I wanted in this frontier station was to draw attention to strangely behaving AI bots or a wounded prisoner locked in his room.

"I need a few things," said Mason. "I might have a look around."

"I'll tag along," said Baz. "It's my first time in the Commonwealth apart from work."

"Stay out of trouble then," I warned him. "They don't take kindly to 'Earthys' poking noses into their business."

The two of them melted into the crowd heading clockwise along the walkway. That left Jo and I with our hands in our pockets watching people come and go.

"Do you want to grab a coffee?" she asked with some hesitation.

"Sure," I replied though I found the word cold on my lips. I felt a kind of funk come over me, maybe an effect at once again having stopped moving towards Angel's rescue. Delays were starting to irritate me in much the same way that strangers working on Jo's engines must have felt to her.

We set off anticlockwise, against the traffic in most places and it seemed like I was noticing for the first time how at home she was on a station like this. Whereas the formal meal with Captain Sole had given her obvious discomfort, this down-to-earth installation made her swagger with hands casually in her pockets. It sent me reeling back to my youth, to days playing with Alice in the streets of military bases or on dilapidated service stations. I guessed then that history still managed to divide people like that, the haves and the have-nots.

"If I gave you the choice," I said, mustering up some good humor. "Would you rather be here or in a Captain's mess?"

She snorted derision and laughed. It made her face look soft and playful.

"Give me a stinking mass of common people any day of the week," she replied. "You can keep your rich elite."

"I didn't realize they were mine," I joked.

"Come on – don't tell me you and Alice didn't have it easy growing up?"

"Quite the opposite," I pointed out, avoiding a line of on-coming bots trailing after a mobile trader like ducklings. "One of the reasons Alice and I signed up just before the Martian war was to escape the poverty. Earth was in a deep depression until the conflict began and our parents were struggling to make ends meet."

"And after?"

"We formed TRIDENT with what money we saved up. There was nothing to spend it on during the campaign and with Alice being high-up in the logistics Corps and myself in Armored Infantry, we managed to save up a lot of cash. Until recently surplus credits haven't exactly been rolling in."

"The *Aurelius* has changed that, right?"

"For all of us, don't forget," I winked, reminding her subtly that her share of the prize money wasn't unsubstantial either. She tilted her head in acknowledgment just as we found a coffee shop with exterior seating.

"My shout," she said, gesturing with her comms unit. "I owe you one."

"What's the occasion?"

"You unpacked for me. I had the shock of my life when I woke up and found everything had been put away, even my smalls."

"I'm sorry if I-" She held up a hand as we joined the queue and I noticed her cheeks flush a little pink.

"I've known you long enough to see the gesture for what it was. Thank you."

I nodded and we both stared into the glass display where rows of cakes were stacked on three tiers, mouth-watering in the soft lighting. Layered sponge, chocolate fudge, sticky-toffee pie, lashings of whipped cream and fruit compote. Combined with the aroma of freshly ground coffee, I felt my stomach growl with need.

"Look at that one!" said Jo, pointing to a slab of marble cake topped with fresh cream. "I've got to have it. What about you?" I pointed to the salted caramel slice on its own on the middle tier.

"That one please," I said. We waited. The seating outside the cafe offered us a sectioned-off place to sit and watch people come and go and once we'd placed our order we took seats on the furthest edge, right in the heart of the traffic but apart from it at the same time. On the table was a small floating disc with our order number on it and Jo gave it a spin in mid-air. Now that she was sat opposite me and not with her hands inside the workings of the ship I could see that her hazel eyes, deep and thoughtful, had the effect of dragging your attention to her face the way a tow rope might pull a ship into dock. Her hair, far from untidy, was carefully gathered into a bun where a few strands were allowed shore-leave to visit her temples, stroking

189

her cheeks as they went. They gave her both a young but wise expression, a kind of balanced character that made talking to her very easy. Combined with a smile that showed a row of not-quite-perfect teeth, I felt like I was having coffee with an old friend, someone who knew my heart even before I did. I felt a little ashamed that I hadn't noticed any of this before.

"How's the nebulus buffer?" I asked. She grinned.

"Fine now. I still can't believe they put that thing in our beautiful ship. I mean, what kind of cowboy does that, even to meet a deadline? Are you going to get in touch with them when we get back?"

"What, and complain? I'll forward that to Alice, she enjoys that kind of thing," I said. She shook her head.

"It might put them off doing it to some other schmuck next time."

"Are you calling me a schmuck?"

"Yeah, I guess I am." She winked and saw the waiter coming with our order. "Brace yourself – cake incoming!"

We waited until he'd put the plates and the cups down before talking again. Jo, with a spoon to her lips, let out a strangely erotic groan as she tasted her dessert.

"Oh my," she said. "It's divine!"

"Mine is superb," I said and I meant it. The next thing I knew her spoon was coming across the table towards me and, more importantly, my cake. I deftly struck it aside with my own and the clash of cutlery made the couple next to us turn around.

"Woah!" she cried. "I'm paying so I get to taste."

"This isn't a sharing portion," I pointed out. "If you wanted it you should have ordered it."

She struck again and we met, this time overturning the salt shaker on the other side. We broke up into a fit of laughter as the duel of spoons continued. In the end, I went on the offensive, allowing her to slip past my guard and thus enable me to plough my spoon into her cake and scoop out a very large piece. I stuffed it into my mouth at the same time as she did, giggling and spitting crumbs everywhere.

"Mutually-assured-destruction," she said, wiping caramel sauce from her cheeks where she'd smeared it. "Bravo, sir. Bravo."

"You forget that I'm an expert in war."

"I never forget that," she laughed, struggling to bring her humor under control. "How could I? You keep blowing up my ship."

"*Your* ship?"

"Our ship then, if you prefer. As it's me that keeps fixing her then maybe it's more of a 70/30 split of ownership."

"Really?" She nodded and sipped at her coffee. "Last time I heard it was TRIDENT's coffers paying for this field trip."

"A small matter of the frozen planet? Ahem?"

"You helped, sure. I'll grant you that."

"Helped?" she chuckled and the sound was sweet to hear. "I was *instrumental*."

"If you say so. I felt that it was more of a team effort, and when I say 'team' I mean me."

She licked her spoon and looked straight at me like I was the only person in the world. For a moment I enjoyed the feeling I was getting and all the wrong signals I was happy to receive. But when I looked away and saw the crowds of people coming and going, of normal life carrying on and on in an endless stream of insignificant events, I forced those emotions back into a corner and took a deep breath. Gone was the lover after a sliver of freedom and back in his rightful place was the soldier simply *between wars*.

"You never told me how you got into this kind of work," I said.

"You ever read my file?"

"I leave that kind of thing to Alice," I lied; I'd read all their files and made background checks on those in what I considered to be my 'core team'. It wasn't suspicion, just common sense. I suddenly realized that Angel's file hadn't prepared me for any of this though. If Argo was to be believed, even the name on it wasn't her true one.

"Well," she said, scraping the last of the sauce from her plate. "I didn't really get a choice." I cocked an eyebrow. "Yeah, I was one of the unlucky ones who was 'asked' if I would like to get involved in more... *masculine* trades, so to speak."

"Not that whole quota fiasco?" I asked. She nodded.

"Not enough women in male-dominated subjects. Answer – *invite* more women to get involved. My family were on the breadline, I was an only child and we needed the money. If I went to college and studied astroengineering right through to my HGD, maybe even university level, they'd receive food coupons while I learned. Not really much of a choice, right?"

"No."

"So I did, of course. I can't say that I enjoyed it. A girl like me who didn't really fit in side by side with some of the best engineers in the business, trying to compete with them day in and day out. It was hard, I can tell you that. There were times when a project had to be in the following day and the only way I could meet the target was to work through the night. I'll confess – the guys managed it better than I did. They were machines themselves while I was flagging. I wanted to go home and curl up under a duvet with a cup of tea."

"But you survived?"

"Yeah, just. Turns out I had a knack for it, as you can tell. I had to fight from the ground up for every single merit but by the end, I finished top in my class for the final year before heading to University on the lunar base. Zero-G repair work, suited and booted, all kinds of crap you'd encounter on a space-faring vessel."

"Then what?"

"Then..." She trailed off and looked away into the crowds just like I'd done a moment or two earlier. *I get to do that, not you,* I thought to myself. "Jo?" I asked, very gently. She turned back.

"It's nothing," she replied and sipped her coffee. Silence and a subtle shift in mood between us. Walls, I thought. They go up so easily.

"I could eat that cake again," she grinned but it was half-hearted and she barely made eye-contact with me.

"I know about the addiction," I said very softly. "We both did when we hired you."

She looked up then and I could see the pain behind those eyes, welling up like tears yet she was not crying, not showing any visible emotion that might make her look weak. No doubt she'd had to bury her feelings in that environment just to survive. Some days I felt like everyone was a veteran of war, a conflict that left plenty of scars. Some you could see, others not so much.

"It wasn't my finest hour," she laughed. "But I got through it, still am getting through it I mean."

"I know."

"Can I ask you something?" she said. The place suddenly seemed to go quiet for her, for no reason whatsoever and I found I was leaning on the table now, closer than before. I could almost smell the scent of coffee on her breath.

"Sure."

"Can you ever switch it off?"

My expression turned to something a little more confused and I found myself asking her to repeat the question.

"I mean, *being* Carter. Can you?"

"Maybe it's the calories talking, Jo, but I'm-"

"I think you understand," she cut in. "There was someone there before, someone knocking spoons with me who grinned like he was a boy again but when I tried to talk to him he vanished." I felt my throat constrict and my stomach tie itself in knots.

"What are you getting at?" I managed to say.

"I understand okay? Mars was bad and ever since then you've been all about the work and the business and whatever else you're supposed to be doing. But now and again that young man shows up, he was there next to my bed when he thought I was dying from the crash. He was there last night, unpacking my clothes because he saw I needed help."

"But he's not there the rest of the time, right?" I finished. She nodded and that beautiful face broke into a smile that I thought should blind everyone around us.

"So you've met him before?" she said. I nodded. "I thought so. He's sweet."

"He's..." I stopped, felt a surge of panic run down my spine, and I wanted to shut the whole thing down. Angel had done this not too long ago and the reaction had been the same, perhaps not as intensely as this one but the assault was the same. "I can't do what I do when I need to do it and be that man; it's just not possible."

"Why?" she asked.

"You don't just wake up one day, kill a dozen people and then go home and put your feet up. Because when you strip away all the nice PR work and the brochures, TRIDENT is nothing more than killers for hire."

"That bothers you?"

"No, it doesn't. What bothers me is the fact that it *doesn't* bother me. Not anymore. I actually think we provide an important service, we fulfil a need, a necessary evil to keep the bad guys at bay. But it comes at a price."

"Your soul?"

"No," I said, looking away, willing myself to stop speaking. "My heart."

Jo said nothing. She was looking away as well and I guessed that it'd been too much, that she was probably regretting asking the question now. Seeing men weak is off-putting, especially when those men are tasked with getting you home off dangerous missions. That's why we never show it, never let you see the demons lurking in the shadows. Because if your protectors are weak, where does that leave you?

I got up to go, clearing my throat and downing the last of the coffee. Jo stood up too and we stepped out from behind the table, inches apart.

"We should find the others," I said. "Otherwise Baz will have

194

blown our budget on-"

I hadn't seen it coming. Never in a million lifetimes had I anticipated it or planned it. But the next thing I knew I felt her lips pressed against mine, one hand on my cheek and the other on my arm, pulling me into her. I didn't break away, I did quite the opposite. I put my hands on her hips and returned the embrace. She tasted sweet and heady, like taking a deep breath of air before a plunge into ice-cold water. Her skin on mine was soft and scented and as my mind melted into the moment I felt something snap inside me, something I was aware of but couldn't quite figure out until much later, much later. When it was too late to do anything about it.

She pulled back an inch from my face, lowered her own and held her eyes closed. Our breaths came in short gasps, foreheads touching.

"Wow," she whispered. I grinned.

"Where did that come from?"

"Somewhere very hot."

"People are looking."

"Screw them," she laughed. Then, pulling back with flushed cheeks she looked directly at me. "I've wanted to do that since the medibay."

"It was that skin-tight thermal suit, right?" We both laughed.

"It was your *heart*. I saw it. You showed it to me."

I said nothing. She smiled, touched my cheek again, and let go. Standing there before me, brilliantly beautiful in a way I'd never even noticed before, this woman had blind-sided me the way so many of those closest to me had done and would continue to do in the years that followed.

22

The conference room left a lot to be desired. It looked grubby in spite of the bullet-proof glass which swung around in one great arc, overlooking the entire sprawling shopping mall below. The furniture was aged and faded where artificial lights had bleached the color from them. Deep armchairs flanked a reasonably round table of artificial wood the color of burned lumber but there was room enough for the five of us and Argo's contingent of Marines and officers. Mozzy had been carefully escorted from the ship to the conference room, his medic in tow, and he looked pale and tired but alive at least.

"Take a seat," said the Captain as his Marines, dressed as plainly as possible, took positions at either door. His two Lieutenants flanked him as well as the mysterious-looking Intelligence officer who'd been strangely absent until now. As a pleasant surprise, Captain Sole had been invited also and he sat to Argo's left just as anti-surveillance devices were posted around the room. We were seated, Mason on my right as we faced the Captain, Baz to my left with Jo and Mozzy on either side. As I caught her eye I could swear that my lips felt a faint echo of that kiss that now threatened to distract me from what needed to be done.

"Not ideal," said Argo, gesturing with a sweep of his hand. "But things being what they are, a necessary evil." I nodded. "I considered refreshments but I feel that time is passing rapidly now. With the threat of Death Squad units, perhaps the time for niceties has gone."

"Why the diversion here?" I asked. "The Commonwealth I mean."

"I have my reasons, one of which is to refresh old acquaintances with former shipmates who can tell me the 'lay of the land' so to

196

speak. If I'm right then the enemy fleet will first move against the Commonwealth before any direct action is taken against Earth Government itself."

"Why?" asked Baz.

"To prevent an alliance of sorts. Without full Commonwealth support, Earth Gov. will be forced to stand alone. I'd very much like to prevent that possibility. Commonwealth shipyards boast some of the best and most powerful craft. If we let that fall into enemy hands we might find ourselves at war with familiar ships."

"I assume you've read my brief?" I asked. He nodded.

"Tempted as I am to arrest this man-" Here he tilted his head towards Mozzy. "I'm willing to hear you out. Be warned though, should this be a ploy to buy your freedom with false coin, I'll see you spaced from my own decks. Are we clear."

The former soldier nodded as if shaken from behind. He looked frail and tired, unable to put up any kind of smart-ass defense this time. Argo seemed to notice that too.

"Start from the beginning," I said to Mozzy. "The whole plan this time, and the location."

Clearing his throat, which now sounded wet and phlegmy, he began to croak out his plan.

"Corano runs most of the planet's Opho production," he said and coughed. "He was once a member of the Bala Tribe, the drug-runners who were smashed back in '008 as part of a Spec Ops 'war on drugs' in the Colony worlds. Back then he only dealt in the small stuff, coke, heroin, the old-school Earth narcotics that were sometimes cultured on those colonies found to have the best conditions. The tribe was almost wiped out but the action managed to disband the survivors and scatter them into outlying systems. Corano made it to Remus IV, the only planet in the Alpha-Four system with working atmosphere recyclers.

"For fifty years or so he worked his way up the political ladder which to Remus IV colonials was nothing more than a local

197

Governance. Here he dropped off the radar for Spec Ops and was presumed dead along with his other cronies in the Bala Tribe. Time passed. Soon he'd risen to the top seat, High Governor of the colony which by now was the size of a small city. Out of there came rumors of Opho shipments, reasonably small scale to begin with, but still enough to make some of the Commonwealth dealers a little edgy."

"Opho?" asked Baz.

"Ophomius Lo Phina," said the Intelligence officer. "A potent narcotic that brings euphoric pleasure with very little risk of long-term addiction."

"I didn't think that was possible," he replied. He gave a wry grin.

"In this case, it is. But the price for this momentary high is brain cell corruption and major organ failure in 46% of cases. It also renders the user either catatonic or, in some cases, extremely violent."

"It's like playing Russian roulette with a broken plasma pistol and overcharged cells," said Mason. "It's not a matter of *when* it kills you, just how much damage it does to the rest of the world when it does."

"Ah," he said and fell silent. Mozzy continued.

"Soon we got wind of other competitors vanishing off the face of the Commonwealth. Corano simply had them 'taken care of' using his own people or those he'd managed to implant into other colonies. By his 94th birthday, Opho production was the sole export of Remus IV and at a reasonable 34 credits per gram, the cash started rolling in. The planet's reputation grew under this trade and any kind of political competition was quickly put down. He's been in that seat ever since and no one has ever managed to take him down."

"What do his people have to say?" asked Mason.

"Nothing," grinned Mozzy. "They're starving in the streets. The entire city is in ruins because he controls all imported goods and forbids any kind of independent enterprise. He claims that it's in their own best interests and that lining up at the food dispensaries shapes their character. The streets are filled with refuse and anything that can be taken apart and weighed in as scrap has long since been torn up.

The entire place is a dump."

"And there's no risk of a rebellion, an uprising?" I asked.

"Corano is quick to put them down but they rarely ever get started. During the day an average Remus IV colonist takes a hit of Opho cut with pain meds and zones out for most of the time. Then, when the temperature drops and the ice forms, he or she might wander down to the breadline to collect rations, only to die in the cold. They can't think straight and if both partners in the family are taking the drug then they're pretty much doomed."

"Unemployment?"

"Most work for Corano in his production plants, others doing tasks like repairing the power generators or maintaining the atmosphere recyclers. He pays them in Opho."

"Sounds like somewhere I could retire," laughed Baz.

"Okay," said Argo. "What about the vault."

"Corano has built his empire on the drug but he maintains it through blackmail. Toppling his competition was easy; he struck hard and fast at the heads of the opposing Cartels. But Commonwealth leaders have 20/20 vision and so turning blind eyes to his activities was not even on the table. Instead, he opened up another line of business – buying and selling information. He bought anything he could on anyone he might need to have leverage over at a criminal price, forgive the pun. People knew that if they had a photo or a recording or a feed he'd buy, then they'd be making a lot of credits for almost no work. It also meant that if they needed his help in using that data, he'd send one of his best 'advisors' to help them out. He ranked you on the quality of your product and how useful it would be to him. When we started feeding him data blocks on Bourmont's schemes during the Martian War, he let the credits fall into our pockets until they threatened to burst."

"But they're not kept online?" asked the Intelligence officer, now leaning forward on his elbows with rapt attention.

"No-way. If someone stole or destroyed it most of his power over the Commonwealth leaders would be gone. Earth Gov. would make a move on him in a heartbeat and pulverize the planet into dust. So he keeps them in solid-state, only *one* copy mind you, buried deep in his vault on Remus IV."

"And how do you know this?" asked Argo.

"It's his sales pitch," grinned Mozzy. "He says that 'his best-kept secret is his worst kept secret'. If you manage to win him over with what you've got he shows you around the facility, takes you deep into the planet to see the warehouses of data he has, the sheer volume of dirt he's got on people or that he's holding on behalf of other people even more evil than himself."

"So it's a fortress-vault then?" said Mason.

"Well he's not going to let anyone just walk in and steal from him, is he? We're talking about a structure so vast and so well-built that to penetrate it with orbital strikes would be pointless. There's so much plascrete and steel in the thing that you'd need a million tanks firing a million bunker-busting rockets to get in. He staffs the surface installation with civilians, human shields."

"Describe it in depth," I said.

"On the surface, it's just a normal looking factory where clothes and, of course, Opho is manufactured and processed for distribution. Nothing more than a few stories high, no bigger than a normal office block in width and length. But beneath that lies the real fortress. If you manage to penetrate the shield-"

"Shield?" I said.

"Yeah. Stops direct hits to the entrance and keeps out lancer fire from orbital strikes. If you get past that, the vault doors are three meters thick and take a massive amount of machinery to open. Then it's down into the heart of the beast; twenty-six levels to the power room, another thirteen to the vault itself surrounded by meters of plascrete shielding, impenetrable to the hardest drills. Each level has a timed door, resistant to explosives or chemical devices."

"And you're telling me that we should hit this place, rob him blind and hope he doesn't come after us?" asked Baz. Mozzy laughed.

"If you manage to hit the vault, then by that time his full response force would already be fighting you for every inch of his facility."

"I thought they were all off their heads on Opho?" I asked.

"Not his automated forces which he can call upon in six minutes from the moment the alarm first goes off. We're talking drone units, armored divisions, specialist infantry, AI tanks, the whole caboodle. From the moment you trigger that alarm the entire planetary defense force will be gunning for you."

"Sounds delightful," smirked Argo with that slanted crease in his face. "And you believe that this information will make us release you?"

"Not that information," said Mozzy. "The information in that vault. And the fact that I'm willing to go with anyone who wishes to attempt it." We all looked at him, stunned. "Don't look so surprised, I'm not doing it for you or that pilot-bird. I'm doing it for me. Plus I have the shield codes. You'll need them."

"How did you get those?" asked the Intelligence officer.

"I think it's the reason they've sent the Death Squad after me – after all of us in the squad. Jonesy managed to hack the defense grid while we were on the tour and steal a copy of the encoder key. He gave us all a data file with it in. Given how hard he's come after us I reckon he's not been able to scramble them yet or install a new key."

"That would explain how someone has been able to pay for them," said Sole. "Someone like Corano could pay for that out of his back pocket."

"So we can rule out Bourmont tying up loose ends then," said Argo. "And you stole these codes because...?" Mozzy shifted uncomfortably in his chair.

"Maybe we might have had a plan to hit the vault ourselves. Some of that data would've fetched a good price and now that I'm the only person left I'd see it as honoring my squad by helping to pull it off."

"What kind of plan?" I asked.

"One that only lacked firepower," he said. "We didn't want to attempt it until we could buy enough arms to hold off the planetary defenses long enough to secure the vault and steal the data."

"That would need a lot of firepower," said Mason, scribbling on a tablet by his hand.

"I know," he replied. I stared at him and saw that Argo was doing the same.

"Detail the plan for me," I said. "From the top."

"Do we have a deal first?"

"It depends," said Argo.

"On what?"

"On whether or not I think we can achieve it – and by 'we' I mean Carter and his team."

He gave me a lopsided smirk and I felt the urge to punch him again. Sure, he'd support a plan to assault a fortress and get myself killed as long as he got a share of the data loot. Maybe I should've tried to be less shocked by that; it was becoming a pattern.

"Here's the pitch," he began and I sat back. I wasn't liking the feeling I was getting already. "The shield codes must be inputted into the central terminal inside the production facility on ground level. This done, the outer defenses will shut down, allowing for orbital deployment of equipment and personnel."

"Drop pods?" asked Mason.

"That was our original plan. There's no way you're sneaking a small army in through the front door. Two people might be able to get in at first, secure the building and input the codes. Then, call in the pods."

"Onto the building itself?" I asked.

"Our plan was to blow a hole in the ceiling and call them in with precision laser targeting, drop them within a few meters of the vault entrance which is inside the factory."

"Then what?"

"Then start fighting," he laughed. "They'll be sending their preliminary attack force at you six minutes from the moment you trigger the alarm. Drones, bots, you name it. Divide the force into a defense pattern while the others get to work on cutting through the vault door."

"What's it made from?" asked Mason.

"We guessed an alloy of molanium and triton-steel. You'd need high-end plasma cutters mounted on robotic CNC units. Set those babies up and hold off the attackers until you're through."

"Then what?" I asked.

"Once in you'll have to split your force again, one group to head for the security center to shut off the automated defenses, the other to begin cutting through the first door that leads to the stairwell down. Let's understand each other here – there are no elevators, no direct shafts downwards. The place was designed in such a way that in order to reach the bottom floor you would have to use every single stairwell and cross every single floor."

"Okay, what internal defenses are there?"

"So your first team heads for the security center and begins cutting open the door there. Inside they'll find human personnel in armor. Once they're defeated, all the internal defenses can be switched off from there, allowing full access to the lower levels. If you don't you'll be facing plasma turrets and drone squads on every level."

"Is door control there?" asked Mason.

"We suspected that but didn't plan for it. We expected to cut through every door once the alarm was tripped. It's likely that the whole facility will go into lock-down at that point."

"So this gets done," said Baz. "What's waiting at the vault?"

"The last door – same as the first. Robotic cutters will have to be set up and left to do their thing. Meanwhile, your team up top will be holding off most of Corano's forces at this point. Expect *massive* resistance; you're stealing his entire empire out from under him, he won't let you do that without a fight."

"Lastly?"

"If we'd managed to get that far, our plan had been to hack the library terminal in the vault and bag as much of the best data as possible. Then, manually carry it up to ground level to exfil using drop-ships. The only hitch to that is the suspicion that Corano will deploy anti-air units the moment he comes under attack, knowing full well that in order to physically steal the data you'd have to fly it off-world. He'd rather see it destroyed than taken from him."

"That it?" I asked. Mozzy nodded, exhausted from the telling. I turned to Mason. "What do you think?"

"We need a map of the place," he said. "But if we can put a team together and get the gear, it's possible."

Argo looked at us both and seemed to survey the whole idea the way a man might weigh a slab of gold in front of him with his greedy eyes. Then he slowly nodded.

"I believe we will need more hands-on Intel on this location," he said and turned to his Intelligence officer. "Thoughts?"

The man gazed impassively into the table, cogs whirring inside his mind. Then he spoke.

"In return for our aid, perhaps a fine selection of materials from the vault would help our cause? That's before you destroy the rest of course." He grinned. "Perhaps we could arrange a tour of the facility ourselves. How enticing does the intelligence need to be in order to grab the attention of this Corano?" Mozzy shrugged.

"We offered him ten data blocks on a General in Earth Government, career destroying stuff."

"I'm sure we can better that," grinned the Intelligence officer and I believed him.

"We'll be in touch," said Argo looking directly at me.

23

We left the conference room and Argo's team and went in search of somewhere we could get a drink. We were told that there was a quiet bar somewhere on the far side of the station and after dismissing his medic, Mozzy and the four of us made our way over there.

"Well?" I asked Mason as we walked, not missing the fact that Jo was walking beside me. It felt good.

"Suicide," he replied. "But hey, it's what we're good at."

"Is it possible?"

"I think anything is possible if you have enough guns."

The bar was something straight out of the Colonial days, all neon signs in science fiction writing with silver paneled walls, slick lino floor planks, and bright red plastic seating. Posters lined the aisles with recruitment cartoons, calling on Earth citizens to 'brave the stars and build better worlds', worlds like Remus IV I wondered. The place was empty save for two men at the far end nursing metal cups of alcohol and what looked like military rations on their plates.

We took a booth that looked directly at the entrance and sat down, glancing at the menu.

"Colony stew," said Baz. "Space rations. Anti-gravity chips. Mac and cheese re-heat. Galactic steaks. Sounds yummy."

"I like the sound of the hyperspace doughnuts," said Mason. "Comes with ice cream and space-sauce."

"I didn't think places like this still existed," I said. Jo smiled.

"Must be popular with the kids birthday parties or something."

"Do you ever feel that the Commonwealth is a little behind the times?" asked Baz.

205

"They'll catch up," said Mozzy. "I don't know about you guys but I'm having the space-steaks; I'm famished here."

We ordered drinks while he put in for his meal with extra space-fries. When they came, he inspected the strange looking meat and poked it a couple of times with his fork.

"Probably human flesh," said Mason. "I don't see any cows around here, do you?"

He pushed the plate back and nibbled at the fries. At least they looked like fries though none of us had seen any potatoes either. I drank some of my beer which tasted okay and checked we were out of earshot of the two at the bar.

"Well?" I asked. "Thoughts, people."

"I'm up for it," said Baz. "Sounds like a cakewalk."

"You would say that," said Mason. "But I'm only sold on the plan if we can find the hardware." I turned to Mozzy.

"Well? You're the arms dealer. Anyone around here got the stuff we need at the right price?"

He shrugged and picked at the side-salad. He looked disappointed. I would be too.

"Maybe," he said. "It would mean a trip to the Badlands."

"Where's that cliché?" asked Mason.

"Alpha-Six," he replied. "A lot of our stock came from there. I might be able to get you an audience. After that, the rest is up to you. Credits speak volumes out there."

"We can manage credits," I said. "It's time we don't have a lot of."

"It's on the way to Remus IV though I don't think towing a lot of Earth Gov. Navy with you will help."

"They won't be coming," I pointed out. "Argo will have to keep his hands clean. We'll be on our own for this one."

"Don't underestimate Corano. I wouldn't be surprised if he had a fleet of his own."

"We'll check that out when we get there," said Mason. "One step at a time."

"Is there anything you want to tell us now that we're not with Argo?" I asked.

"What do you mean?"

"Anything you might have left out for fear of getting arrested? It's important, Mozzy. I need to know that we've got a chance of pulling this off and I feel like you're holding back here."

He looked at me, weighing up his options. I stared him out until he looked back at his meal.

"I'm just a grunt," he said in the end. "What would I know?"

"Don't give me that," I replied. "You were Bourmont's bodyguard. Intelligence was part of your act."

"You sure you want to know?"

"I am."

"Corano isn't his real name. The Bala Tribe were part of a failed colony attempt of the outer rim. They went rogue just as the mission got underway and took their ships and made for the Commonwealth. They were pursued and then vanished into thin air. Nobody knows why the fleet pursuing them turned back. After that, they became a real thorn in Earth's side."

"And this matters because?"

"Because Corano was once a Navy Captain. His real name is *David Argo*."

"Plot twist!" cried Baz, laughing. "You expect us to believe that?"

"He's Admiral Argo's brother. Do you think that the brass at Spec Ops gave two shits about the Navy when they told us that? It's in the files. The Admiral moved heaven and earth to go after his brother and bring him back. Halfway there he turned around and to this day nobody knows why. He faced a court martial and got off on a technicality."

"And Captain Argo, his son, doesn't realize this?" asked Mason.

"Do you want to tell him 'cause I don't!" he said. "At the mention of Corano, he didn't even blink. He's in the dark as much as the rest of Earth Gov. is. I bet that in that data horde you'll find the real reason

207

that fleet turned back and let David Argo run. What you do with it is up to you I guess."

I rubbed my eyes and tried to process it all. The beer was good and we had a couple more, still thrashing out the beginnings of a plan until I could see that Mozzy needed to lie down. If he was going to join us on the mission he'd have to regain some of his old strength first.

"How about we rent some rooms here?" I said. "Repairs won't be completed until tomorrow. Just use the credits you've been given and we'll meet up tomorrow for breakfast."

"What about me?" asked Mozzy. "You're not going to leave me alone and unarmed are you? Don't forget I have the codes. You can't do this-"

"Shut up," said Mason. "You talk too much. I can't see Death Squad showing up here with Navy ships and hundreds of Marines wandering about, can you?"

"But-"

"Take a room near mine and I'll keep an eye on you, that's the best I'm offering. We aren't sharing, pal. Not happening."

"There's a hotel near the dock," I said. "Let's go there."

We headed over there, glad to find it more modern and recently refurbished compared to the rest of the station. Clearly, money made regular stays there. I ordered my room first, took my coded key-card and began to leave.

"Stay sharp and unless anything changes, meet down here for breakfast," I said before heading towards the elevator. "Keep your comms units on you at all times."

"Will do," said Baz. "I might do some more shopping first."

"Alice will love you," I said. "She'll enjoy taking it out of your wages."

"What can I say? I've got to look good for the company image, right?"

"Turn around and look at Mason," I laughed. He did so, noting that

208

his arms were folded across his chest and his forearms looked like knotted tree roots. His shoulders and traps bulged from under his shirt and, towering above us all with a head of cropped hair and mutton-chop sideburns, he scowled at Baz, no doubt as ashamed of his shopping habits as I was. "That's the company image right there. You should be more like that though you won't find it for sale here, pal. See you later."

I went up to my room and flopped on the bed, staring up at the ceiling. It could've been a room on the *Hikane*. The décor was almost the same, similar walls, slightly cheaper carpet underfoot, same style of furniture. The air wasn't as fresh though and I had a feeling that the recycling units hadn't been serviced in a while. There was a balcony through double-glass doors and it led onto a platform suspended above the precinct below but surrounded in glass like a bubble.

I thought about the last few hours and wondered if I'd get a headache trying to process it all. I'd have to speak to Aleksei, fill him in before we committed to the assault but I wanted to put that off until we had more options. Time was running out and once it did we'd be out here on our own, no doubt having to explain why we weren't on the retreat and why attending court to testify against our friend wouldn't be possible.

That led me to thoughts of Jo. What had happened? Why had I been able to keep Angel's prying at bay but let Jo slip straight on in past all my guards? What made her different and was this really the time to have to work all that out? I'd never been one who could be led by his groin and I'd never understood why men so often were, especially when it was obvious that the end result would be disastrous. Mason had drawn a line with Lorna – this far and no further. He'd tried to love her and when it was going south he'd walked away, just like that. So why was I stuck thinking about my engineer in her coveralls, sweat glistening on her brow as she repaired the ship?

I continued to lie there for at least an hour, thinking just that as I heard a gentle knock on the door. Without getting up and answering it I knew it was Jo and my heart decided to skip a few of those beats I needed. I mentally checked my feelings, mastered a bit of control, and made for the door.

"Hey," she said when it slid open. "Tell me to go away if you want but I've got a bottle of vodka and what I was promised was authentic Commonwealth Bara Cake by a strange looking man in-"

"I could sack you for bribing your boss," I said flatly. "Cake and vodka?"

"Yes," she said, her voice hoarse with emotion. "I thought it might get me a pay rise."

"I'll be the judge of that," I grinned. "Come in."

She was in a pair of baggy shorts and a loose tee and her hair fell in gentle waves to her shoulders like she was fresh from the shower and ready for bed. I realized then that she'd gone back for her overnight bag and kicked myself for not doing the same. She wore no shoes and she stood with one delicate foot on top of the other as if balancing on a wire. She walked past me and I caught the scent of a mild perfume on her skin. Closing the door behind me, I turned on the lamps and switched off the bright overhead lighting. She grabbed a couple of pillows from the cupboards and threw them on the floor, sitting cross-legged against the wall. I went and sat opposite her, setting two glasses between us.

"Bara cake?" I asked as she opened the cardboard box and handed me one of the round balls of dough. "What's in it?"

"I didn't ask." We bit into them and cream squirted out of the other side and down our fingers. They tasted spicy, like cinnamon but more pungent, richer, and topped with a sweetness I couldn't put my finger on. We laughed and began wiping our hands with napkins from the box.

"What do you think?" she asked. I nodded my approval.

"Delicious," I said. "Better than my caramel slice from before."

"Right?" she laughed. "I overheard someone talking about them

210

when I went for the vodka so I knew I had to get us one."

"Thank you," I said. "I mean it."

She licked her fingers clean and sat back as I poured us both a generous amount of vodka. Again I was struck with how comfortable she made me feel even when we weren't speaking. It felt okay not to say anything and I didn't find myself straining for words.

"Cheers," she said and we clinked glasses.

"You're a vodka drinker?" I asked. She nodded.

"It's always been cheap," she said. "When I was in college most of us drank it neat so we could get drunk quicker and with less of an impact on our tiny bank accounts."

"Classy."

"You bet. Guys there sometimes distilled it themselves but our tutors cottoned on pretty quick. If anyone was caught with the equipment it was instant dismissal from the course."

"Was it good stuff?"

"Larry made a batch that could strip paint," she laughed. "Ran up dozens of bottles before he got rumbled. Got away with it though."

"How?"

"Turns out he was supplying our fusion-reactor tutor who used it to dull the pain from his cancer. The college brushed it under the proverbial carpet."

"Wow," I said. "Sounds like you had a wild time."

"Yeah, laugh a minute," she groaned and emptied her glass, pouring us both another. "Maybe I should've got two bottles."

I leaned over and pulled open the fridge beneath the desk. A light came on inside the little box and we counted at least three half-bottles on the top shelf.

"Cheers!" she beamed and we clinked again. "What should we drink to?"

"How about a suicidal-assault on a heavily-defended, highly-criminal data vault?"

"I was thinking maybe something more serious?" she giggled. "But

211

okay, here's to that." We drained the glasses and I poured another round. "I'm coming with you."

"Like hell," I replied. "No chance."

"Because we...?"

"Yes," I said and felt the weight of that sit in my gut. *Because we kissed.* "And because you're not combat-trained."

"And you're qualified in level IV plasma-cutting tech, right? You know how to operate the robotic units and avoid blowing yourself up cutting through triton-steel?"

"Stop talking dirty," I grinned.

"I'm getting aroused, I'll admit. But I'm being serious – none of you can do that. You need me down there doing the tech-stuff."

I thought about it as we drank, this time sipping at what was pretty good vodka given that the drink never really had a strong taste unless it was from Sweden on Earth. Somehow they'd managed to capitalize on that flavor in spite of galactic expansion.

"You'd have to be in armor," I said. She nodded.

"Already thought about that. If Mason can get me a FARGO Technician suit, maybe one of the S6 models, its controls will be similar to the ones I trained in for zero-g repair work. Heavy armor but without compromising my motor functions."

"Can we put cards on the table?" I asked. She nodded but first gestured that we should move on to the next round. We did and she poured another. My head was starting to swim already.

"Shoot," she said.

"You'd be a distraction, one that I can't afford."

"Yes," she replied. "I would be. I won't say I'm sorry for kissing you. I won't say that I'm not aware that Angel was already on your mind." I looked at her and sighed. "Maybe an evil part of me wanted to get in first, you know? Beat her to it. That's horrible, isn't it?"

"No," I said softly. "I get it. I'm not sure I'm worth fighting over but-"

"Please don't," she cut in. "You're sliding back into the soldier

212

again, Carter. Selfless. Doing the whole 'I'm no good' routine but meanwhile seeing the very best in everyone around you. That's not fair to me and it's not fair to you."

"Okay," I said and put my hand on her knee. She was warm to touch and the feeling of something other than metal, of armor or the hull of a ship, suddenly felt alien to my fingers. Had it been so long?

"Answer me this," she said. "Would you only be distracted by me or are you actually distracted by your entire team?"

"I don't understand."

"So if Mason or Baz gets hurt would you feel any less care for them than if it were me?" I stared at her, suddenly realizing what she was saying. "What about Thor? You brought his CPU back while under fire and he's just a robot! And Jimmy? Mozzy?"

"I hear you," I managed to say.

"I hope so. Because if you try to shelter us, if you try to wrap us in a protective film then TRIDENT's days are numbered."

"What's your answer then?"

"Let us do what we need to do," she said. "And understand that some of us might not make it back and it won't be your fault."

Silence fell between us. She was right, it was the same theme Mason had spoken to me about not-so-long ago. The team's strongest link, our friendship, was also contradictorily its weakest.

"In that thread of an idea," I said. "We have to realize the ugly truth of this entire mission."

"Which is?"

"What if we succeed? What if the mission goes to plan and we get into the data vault and find that there's nothing there to help Angel? What if, in the end, she still faces execution after all we've done?"

She shrugged with such care that it felt like an embrace, a kind of understanding *I don't know but we'll get through it together* kind of unspoken gesture. She raised her glass, her eyes sparkling in the light where tears were welling. I nodded and we drank.

Just then my comms unit chimed and as I poured another round

Mason's name appeared on the display.

"Go," I said.

"Channel 62. Hurry because you've only missed the first few minutes." Then he hung up. Jo shot me a quizzical look. I got up and found the remote for the screen opposite the bed and turned it on. Then I started laughing.

"What is it?" she asked.

"Possibly one of the greatest movies of all time," I said. "A.P.E.X."

"Isn't that like hundreds of years old?"

"Yeah," I replied. "Fancy watching it with me?"

"Only if you order room service. That cake was nice but it was no meal."

I passed her the plastic-coated menu and wrote a text-message to Mason.

EVEN IN THE DEPTHS OF SPACE, THEY HAVE GOOD TASTE.

I pressed SEND and drank a little more vodka, watching the movie as Jo paced up and down, scanning the menu. Then came the reply.

MAKE SURE YOU EDUCATE JO ON THE MERITS OF CLASSIC CINEMA. ENJOY YOUR EVENING, PAL.

How the hell had he known? He must have seen her heading to my room, it was the only explanation. I thought about it as she made her choice, pointing to the menu.

"Wanna share?" she asked, looking up at me with those fathomless eyes framed in golden hair.

"Mmmm," I said and leaned into her, meeting her kiss as it rose up to greet me. She closed her eyes and wrapped her arms around my waist. When we broke she chuckled to herself.

"I meant the food but that will do for starters."

So we watched the film curled up on the bed with empty plates and full stomachs and already making efforts with our second bottle. As it ended she sat up and looked at me with a wild grin.

"That was frickin' awesome!" she said. "It was so bad it was brilliant!"

"It lacks nothing," I laughed. "Great cast, awesome script."

"That guy with the lisp – hilarious!"

"What about the ending?"

"A classic. Didn't see that coming."

She poured the last of the bottle into our glasses and passed one to me. By now we'd reached that pleasantly-drunk phase where the world seemed rosy and bright and our lives nothing but a fairy-tale. If I was to avoid a hangover tomorrow I'd have to rein it in from this point on.

Jo turned off the screen and the room was plunged into silence. Then, deftly straddling my thighs, she looked down and grinned.

"I want so badly to do this," she said, squirming a little and causing the obvious reaction in me. I shook my head.

"But we're not going to, Jo." She smiled and one of her tears fell from her eyes and landed on my cheek.

"No, we're not."

We kissed and held each other in that place for what felt like forever. Then we pulled back and she rested her forehead on mine, openly crying now.

"This has been the best night of my life," she sobbed. "I mean that, I really do. But I want this to be special, not here, not now, not before a mission that might take all this away from us."

"It's a risk we have to take," I said in a voice I found was hoarse and choked with emotion. "We're not cheap. This isn't cheap."

"But it would cheapen it, right? Turn it into something worthless." I nodded a little and she managed to laugh. "I want to stay the night. Here. In your arms. I want to feel safe for one more night before..."

"And tomorrow?"

"Tomorrow we go back to work," she said. "Tomorrow we begin our plan to save Angel, one of our own. We've had this and I feel lucky and blessed but after tonight we-"

"We focus on the job," I finished for her. "Until it's done."

"Until it's done."

She kissed me again and then, reaching for the light, she threw us both into darkness. As I lifted the covers off the bed she climbed in beside me and fitted into my arms like she'd been made for that space. Her last words, whispered into the poorly recycled air sounded like *I love you.*

24

Jo slipped away to her own room around 6.30 the following morning and I lay there, staring up at the ceiling smiling. I allowed myself that because the moment I got out of bed it would all go away, back into that place I kept those feelings, back where I'd put them at the end of the Martian war after-

I shook my head of that line of thought and sighed. No going back, I'd told myself all those years ago. No digging that memory back up. Only Mason knew about it and I planned to keep it that way. The Mars conflict had taken a lot from me but I wouldn't let it continue to make withdrawals on my life.

My comms unit chimed and I lifted my arm to look at it. A single message from Mason.

GOT A SEC? BALCONY OUTSIDE OUR ROOMS.

I got up, threw on my trousers and boots and walked out into the corridor feeling a little ropey. The air inside the room was hot and so I felt better walking bare-chested to the balcony a little further down where I found Mason looking out over the other floors below. He was in his gym vest and the service tattoo on his arm stood out in the painfully bright lighting from above. I stood next to him, matching his stance by resting my forearms on the rail. We both looked down.

"We good?" he asked without turning his head.

"We good," I replied.

"I was worried for a moment that maybe you'd lost focus on what we're doing here."

217

"I haven't lost it but it sure feels sharper now." He nodded slowly in the corner of my eye.

"She's a good kid," he said. "And God knows that after... you know, Mars, you deserve something like her."

"Are we having a big-brother kind of chat here?" I asked. He smiled.

"Yeah, we are. Now shut up and let me finish."

"Okay."

"When I asked for help with Lorna, you gave it, no questions asked. I respected that. Even though the outcome wasn't what I'd have liked, we got the job done and the chips fell where they did. I don't regret it. Now here we are, out in the ass-end of nowhere on behalf of a teammate this time, one I thought maybe you had an interest in."

"I'm not sure that I did now, not really," I admitted.

"So where does Jo come into this?" I shrugged.

"She made the first move yesterday, kind of blind-sided me. I didn't know she felt like that and I'm not used to-" I felt my skin heat up. "You know. This kind of attention. Then she came to my room last night and we had a fantastic evening together. Nothing else happened by the way. Just want to make that clear, right?"

"I might have lost some respect for you if it had," he said. I went on.

"Now I'm left thinking all the same things I've thought for years. Is it just the environment? Is it just the rush of danger? What will happen in a year? Two years?"

"Do you like Jo?" The question came out of left-field and I felt my heart stagger under its bluntness.

"Yes," I said. "If you'd have asked me three days ago I'd have wondered what that question even meant. But now, after last night, I see her for who she really is and I can't believe I never noticed her before."

"Maybe you did. Maybe you never let yourself know it."

"That's a bit deep, Mason," I laughed. He slammed his fist into my shoulder and I shuddered under the blow.

"You know you've cursed us, right?" he said.

"Why?"

"You didn't sleep with her. I bet you made all kinds of 'after-action' promises. In any movie that means one or both of you is going to die, you know that, right?"

"That's dark comedy even for you."

"Got to keep it that way," he said, turning serious once more. "This isn't going to be a walk in the park, brother. We're going to have to plan and plan some more on this one. We're going to need every single piece of hardware and every scrap of training we can muster to pull this off."

"I hear you," I nodded. "It's been playing on my mind since Mozzy came up with the crazy scheme. It's a heist of epic proportions."

"Biggest bank-job the Commonwealth has ever seen."

We looked down some more and watched people checking in and out of the hotel. The place was busy and we noticed a couple of Argo's Marines leaving with women in tow and not the kind that sail on Navy vessels either.

"If we're having a big-brother talk," I said. "What about Sargon."

"What about it?"

"You know full-well what."

"You get their names yet?"

"Eldritch sent them to me last night. I didn't see the need to spoil your evening with them."

"So spoil my morning instead."

"Anne Harrow and Marcus Block. They didn't know each other, just happened to be leaving the store when they heard the gunfire."

He nodded very slowly and repeated their names to himself, no doubt memorizing them. I said nothing.

"Unfortunate," he murmured, rubbing his hands together slowly. I waited. Then he spoke. "Wrong place, wrong time. I didn't intend to kill them. I can live with that." I nodded.

"Now would be a good time to tell you to keep your hands off my sister," I said. He didn't turn to look at me but I could see his grin.

"Might be too late for that," he said. Then, pushing himself off the rail, he began walking back to his room.

"What the hell is that supposed to mean?" I called after him but he was gone. I went back to my room even more confused than I had been before. A message had just arrived telling me that the *Hikane* was ready to sail. *After breakfast*, I thought and left.

When we returned to dry-dock and to the *Hikane*, we found Argo's Intelligence officer waiting for us, seated on a pile of crates like it was the most normal thing in the world. He was dressed in civilian clothes but still managed to appear shifty; his implanted eye flashed back and forth and his beard was still unruly. He saw us and grinned.

"It's all been arranged," he said, standing up. Out of his pocket, he drew a data block. "Don't examine it, don't open it and don't even think of copying it." He passed it to me. "Contained within is the bait that even Corano couldn't resist if he tried. It's bought two of you a guided tour of the facility in three days from now. The rest is up to you."

"So we give this to him, no questions asked?" I said.

"He'll pay you for it, very handsomely I might add. It will go into an account that has already been arranged so don't worry about handling dirty credits; it will go towards furthering Earth Government's aims and objectives elsewhere blah blah blah."

"Blah blah blah?" I mimicked.

"Yes. It means that you don't need to concern yourself with the minor details. When, or should I say *if* you manage to succeed, I would very much appreciate that data block back – intact."

"So that's it?" asked Mason. "Argo just sails home and leaves us to it?"

"Well it's not like we can divert the entire fleet to assist you now, is it? How would that look back on the desk of the Lord Admiral himself?" He sniggered and began to walk away. "But as they say, help often comes unlooked for. Good luck, gentlemen. Until next time."

We watched him go and turned our attention back to the ship which was now open to us, the barriers having been pulled back to allow access. Baz, loaded down with shopping bags, shuffled up the ramp and kicked open the door.

"Home sweet home," he said, then openly and very loudly, swore. "Holy shit!"

I followed him in and there, standing in the corridor with grinning faces, were Grant, Fara and Sam Columbine.

"Long time no see," I said and stepped forward to shake their hands. "Has it only been a few months?"

"Maybe more," laughed Fara. "Feels like a lifetime." The two veterans of Perseus IV looked pleased to see us but maybe not as pleased as I was. Since Golan IV I hadn't really thought about them and when they'd hitched a ride home aboard the *Agamemnon* I'd expected them to vanish into the past. I guess that with so much that had happened to us since then I'd begun to feel that more time had passed than actually had. For them, they were still riding the train back home.

"Mr. Columbine," I smiled. "I hope you haven't drawn all over this ship while you were waiting."

"No sir," he grinned, still looking boyish and charming. "But I heard about Angel and demanded that we get a chance to help her out. Plus it's been a hell of a boring trip so far. Being almost killed by ship-to-ship action turned out to be quite frustrating."

"I can imagine," I said. "So you want in on this crazy scheme?" I asked the three of them. They nodded.

"Our suits and gear are already loaded," said Grant. "Ready to sail when you are."

"How much is it going to cost us?" asked Baz.

"Oh a few credits," grinned Fara. "And a ride home of course."

221

"Looks like we have a team," Mason said to me. "Now we just need some gear."

25

The first stage of the assault was to gather Intel. That would mean making sure we met with Corano and, if things went well, go on the tour of the facility. From there we could build a layout of the place and make the necessary alterations to our plan. It would mean going in without tech, without weapons and having to rely on our memories to map the place out when we returned to the ship. That wasn't my strongest skill and I said as much to Mason.

"What about taking Columbine?" I suggested. "He's an artist. Surely memorising what things look like is one of his specialities?"

"I'll talk to him," he said as we sat on the bridge, our journey to Remus IV underway. "Did you speak to Aleksei?"

"I did," I replied. "He's worried about using evidence acquired in such a heavy-handed way."

"If it comes from Argo's creepy intelligence officer it'll carry enough authority."

"I told him that. It didn't seem to make him any more confident though."

I looked at the readouts and saw that we'd make the appointment on time. It was eating into our remaining days and I wondered if at the end of it all we'd have enough time to make it back to Titan 5 to keep our absence a secret. The information would travel much faster than we could but, I supposed, as long as Aleksei got what he needed, then our punishment would seem light compared to dodging the executioner's block.

"I made contact with Mozzy's dealer. Right after we finish at Remus IV we need to waste no time heading there. I've flashed our credits her way and-"

"Her?"

"Yeah. Madam Sill, arms-dealer extraordinaire," he said. "Has a reputation in these parts for holding a lot of stock."

"The kind we need?"

"And then some. Plenty of legal and illegal items mind you so keep your head down when we go shopping. The way we've gone about this it's going to take some serious legal muscle to keep us from facing criminal charges if we ever get caught."

"Let's not get caught then," I said. I let out a sigh and sat back in my chair, spinning once on the mechanism. "Corano."

"Yeah?"

"David Argo. Doesn't that sound a little weird to you?"

"Sure," said Mason. "But why would he lie about it?"

"Do you think Mr. Beard knew?"

"Who?"

"Intelligence." He nodded.

"Do you think Captain Argo knows that Mr. Beard knows that he knows?"

"Exactly. Let me hit you with this hypothetical scenario."

"Shoot."

"Coffee first?"

"Sure."

I got up and went over to the machine, tapping in our orders and waited for them to dispense. "Imagine that Corano – aka Argo number three is there at the vault when we hit it. We take him prisoner, take him off the planet with us. Then what?"

"Other than an absolutely ridiculous series of chance events occurring, say this did happen. So what? Why take him back at all? Why not simply shoot him there and then and do Remus IV a favour?"

"He could stand trial."

"Why do you care? What good will that do the world? I'm all for

224

making a difference but what possible good would that serve other than to cause a rift between Papa Argo and his beloved son? Do we need Argo on our side or not?"

"Good point."

"You know how I feel about loose ends," he went on as I passed him his cup. "We tie them or they come loose again. Don't forget that chances are he was the one who dispatched Death Squad units to kill Mozzy and his team and, subsequently, us. If I see him in combat I'm going to end him, it's that simple."

I nodded and sat back down. He was right to a point but some part of me looked beyond our immediate concerns and saw a fraction of the bigger picture. Why had Admiral Argo turned back after chasing him for so long? Why hadn't anyone done anything to end Corano's reign of bloodshed on Remus IV? Opho was deadly yet Earth Gov. didn't seem to give a shit. Lots of questions. No answers.

"You'd better get into civilian clothes," I said, still thinking. "We're a couple of hours away and we'll be in scanner range in half that. Did Baz manage to stow all the gear in the hold like I asked him to?"

"Yeah. I'll go see to Columbine as well. I'm sure he'll love this kind of mission."

"Tell him if he wants a ride home he'd better do a good job. We're counting on him."

Remus IV appeared on the screen like a frozen ball of white on a tableau of black. It reminded me of a jewellers cloth, displaying some obscure diamond from a forgotten mine in the depths of Sinavon. Part of the city radiated heat whilst the other seemed subject to the sub-zero temperatures Mozzy had told us about. Looking at it on the viewer I felt a shudder of memory, remembering where we'd been only a month or so earlier.

"We're good to go," said Mason over the comms as we docked with the orbital platform stationed above the planet. "See you in a few."

"Be safe, man," I replied and felt my guts churn. I wanted to be down there overseeing the operation but I had to step aside for this one. Columbine was the right man for the job and Mason had an eye for the needs of a fighting force. They were the two best men for the job and I had to accept that. All I could do was make sure that the platform didn't try to scan beyond the recognised limits of intergalactic law and discover our exo-shells in the hold.

The bridge was empty. Baz, Fara and Grant were running simulation drills with Mozzy, trying to coax him back into shape. A few years on Sargon had softened the fighter and he needed to remember what his former training had given him. Baz knew his drills and I was happy that he was willing to oversee that task for me.

Behind me, the door slid open with a gentle hiss and I turned around. Jo stood there, overalls around her waist and a smile on her lips. She carried a bottle in her hand and a couple of glasses.

"Thought you might need a break," she said. "You've been sat there since we left Indigo-Six."

"I snatched a few hours between shifts," I replied. "But yeah, I'd be happy to have a drink."

She poured two generous measures and sat down in the weapon's seat, handing me one. We clinked and drank.

"You do realise you're an enabler to my drinking habit," I said with a smile.

"I know you," she grinned. "You wouldn't have had a drop since that night in the hotel and now we're here, waiting for Mason and Columbine to do their thing, you're feeling left out. You wanted to be down there, right?" I nodded. "But you can't. You're a good leader who knows the strengths of his team and your own weaknesses. Right now you just need help sitting back, relaxing, and letting your team get the job done. Am I somewhere near the mark?"

"Will you marry me?" I laughed. She raised her glass.

"So relax, Carter. Talk to me."

"About what?"

"You weren't always like this," she said. "What makes a man fight the Martian war, then go into private response work and continue fighting without obvious PTSD?"

"I can't help it," I said. "I love lost causes."

"I'm being serious."

"I know," I smiled. "And I'm grateful for that." I drained my glass and offered it to her. She poured again. "But if you're looking for a sob-story about how I wanted to fight evil in the world and be the hero then I'm going to have to disappoint you."

"Why?"

"Because it's very simple, really. Before Mars, I didn't know what I wanted to do. We were poor, we had nothing and no hope of breaking free of that. Mum and Dad did their best but life was what it was, there was no changing it. My big sister decided she'd go into admin, working for a local chain-store when the Martians decided that independence was something they could pull off. Within days of Kumar's assassination, Alice had signed up and headed straight into the logistics corps."

"Did that bother you?" she asked.

"Not at first. Dad and I both read the feeds, we knew the war was coming and we saw that with the poor number of recruits available they'd offer some kind of welfare eventually. Better to sign up the moment it did before the best spots were taken and the drafts were made. Meanwhile, talks continued and Alice found herself writing home with tales of boredom and inactivity."

"But...?"

"But things escalated if you know your history. Pretty soon more ships were being built, more soldiers recruited and Dad saw that the time had come. I signed up. After that everyone was doing it to escape the poverty and with the promise of welfare Dad had seen coming it was a no-brainer."

"So you went," she said. "Is that where you met Mason?"

"Yeah. I passed out of basic and applied for Armoured Infantry, the division most likely to be issued with exo-shells and thus the one with the best chances of surviving. The rest, as they say, is history."

"That it?"

I tilted my head and said nothing, emptying my glass. She hadn't touched her second.

"It's raw, isn't it?" she asked. I nodded. "Not just Mars."

"No."

"Does it help to talk to me about it or does that just make it worse?"

"I don't know yet. A woman who comes with vodka is already at an advantage."

She got up and came closer, running her hands over my cheek as she sat down on the floor and looked up at me. She refilled my glass.

"I'm an engineer," she said.

"I noticed."

"I fix things. I have a leaning towards fixing things, it's what I do. Right now I want to fix you but that's wrong, that's not what you need. On the other hand, I might not have fought in the wars that you've fought but I've been through shit I don't know how to process. We all have. Baz. Mozzy. Mason. Angel. But with you and me, I think we have something I want to get my hands on, to work at, to see if we can bring something out of all this bloodshed and mayhem. I can't do that on my own, Carter. I need your help."

I looked at her, sat there, staring up at me with those eyes that wouldn't let me go, wouldn't let me wriggle out of her embrace. Mason had been right – if no one ever made the first move I'd just stay where I was, going from one conflict to another, never really *moving on* deep down.

"Why?" I said, finding my throat tight and constricted.

"I don't know," she replied. "I really don't know. But here we are, about to go to war against a drug lord and all I can think about is us. Go figure."

I offered my glass and we clinked again. She shook her head and drained hers, pouring us both another.

"Our relationship is doomed if every time we meet we drink like this," I laughed.

"It seems like the only way to bring our walls down," she said. "Mine are ten metres high and made from triton-steel. What about yours?"

"Something similar."

I got out of my chair and sat on the floor beside her, leaning against the console for support. Jo tucked herself under my arm and rested her head against my chest. I could smell the engine grease in her hair and the strong odour of ground metal. It made me smile.

"I think I'm falling for you," I whispered into her ear. She put her hand on my knee and squeezed.

"I fell for you long ago," she replied. "I just hoped we'd meet each other on the way down."

26

"We're on."

Mason and Columbine walked up the ramp, those words echoing in my ears as the *Hikane's* engines thrummed into life, authorised now to leave the platform when we were ready. Baz gave the order and the ship pulled away, plotting a course at high speed for Madam Sill's floating warehouse in Alpha-Six.

"Get to the conference room," I said. "Start drawing."

When we were underway I gathered everyone into the biggest room on the ship that we hadn't yet had a chance to use and waited for Columbine to finish sketching out the map. I was glad to find Mozzy well again, looking like his normal self and wearing combat fatigues bought at Indigo-Six. Thor joined us but Jimmy remained in secret for now in the engine room.

"How are you doing?" I asked the bot when he stomped into the room.

"Bloody marvellous, sir," he bellowed. "Cheers for pullin' me off that street, sir. Haven' 'ad a chance to fank you until now."

"Don't mention it," I replied. "I'm just glad we all made it off there."

"I'm workin' on me next project, sir. Ready for the heist. I guess we're puttin' the gang back together for one more job, right?"

"Something like that, Thor."

I turned to Mozzy who was watching Columbine work. The two had hit it off straight away, having shared a few friends in the PRT circles.

"How is it looking?" I asked, leaning over his shoulder.

"Nearly done," said Columbine. "Just a few more details I need to pin down.

Mason came over and pulled me to one side out of earshot of the others.

"What is it?" I asked.

"It's him," he said.

"What? Argo?"

"The same. You can't mistake the family resemblance, pal. Nice guy really. Not what you'd expect from a criminal Kingpin."

"I'm glad you like him," I said with words soaked in sarcasm. "How about the facility?"

"Ever cracked a nut?"

"Yes."

"Well imagine if the nut was made of triton-steel and protected by a planet full of machines and enhanced soldiers and your nutcracker was made of play-dough."

"Nice illustration," I said. "Do we stand a chance?"

"We're going to need bigger guns."

"I'm ready," said Columbine and I called for everyone to take a seat, noticing Jo sat near Thor, looking at me and smiling. I went to the front of the room before the display wall and brought up the images made by Sam. They were good, I had to admit. He'd remembered nearly everything about the layout.

"Before I begin, it's worth going over the events of the last few weeks for you all. Even if you don't benefit, I think it'll help me put the pieces into a coherent picture." There were a few sniggers, but as I began debriefing them all, their faces turned very serious. The truth was, the whole mess was *very* serious and by the time I'd finished, they were all keen to get started.

"Thanks for your patience." I called up Sam's images once more. "So, here's what we're looking at," I said, gesturing to the first building, the factory that acted as cover for the vault. "The plan is still in its early stages, but the first part of the assault is this. Two people

231

will infiltrate the city and move towards the target building. Once inside, they must locate and neutralise the shield generator that will allow us to launch equipment pods and personnel from low orbit."

"We saw the control panel," said Mason.

"Okay," I nodded. "Once this happens, the rest of the force including our engineer will deploy. Exo-shells and other defence equipment will also be launched for the two infiltrators. We expect that by this time the first wave of Corano's security will have arrived. A force headed by Mason will keep them off us while we begin cutting our way into the vault." I pointed to the map at intervals, building up a mental picture of what this would look like.

"Who will be left on the ship?" asked Grant.

"We can't afford to leave anyone on board," I replied. "We're going to need everyone down on the planet. This is the weakest part of the plan; we're going to be relying on a remote terminal to pilot the *Hikane* from the ground. Both Baz and myself will have access to the FARGO drives and one of us will monitor the ship and coordinate the pod launchers from within the vault.

"Once we've penetrated down into the first levels, the force will split. Grant and I will continue to cover Jo as she begins cutting while Fara and Columbine will move towards Security and disable the internal defences."

"From what we saw it's a pretty heavily defended room but the doors looked like thermite would take them out," said Sam.

"Good. While that's going on, Mason, Mozzy and Thor will be topside, holding back the attacking force. Baz – you'll be on standby to help whoever needs backup as the mission progresses, okay?"

"Got it," he said.

"We're going to drill straight down," said Jo. "Create a shaft through every floor right down to the vault. From there we can fit a fast-line rig to pull each bag of data up to the ground floor."

"What did the inside of the vault look like?" I asked. "How much physical data are we talking?"

"Honestly?" said Sam. "More than we could carry. It's wall to wall in there, maybe the size of a football field. Not just data either, gold, silver, molanium ingots. It looks like it's not just a vault for data but for Corano's entire wealth, or a fair part of it."

"So how do we pinpoint what we're looking for?" asked Baz.

"We'll need a data sniffer," said Mason. "One that can plug into the storage mainframe inside the vault and locate what we need. That will take time."

"So we get what we're looking for and then what?" chipped in Fara. "Bag the rest and bug out?"

"We get what Argo needs and we destroy the rest," I said. "We're not risking our lives more than we have to."

"And the metal?"

"It's dirty," I said. "But if we've got time, bag some of the molanium and the gold. It can be left above ground for the colonists to use. Maybe it'll do some good if it survives what comes next."

"Which is?"

"Thermo-nuke charges," said Mason. "Planted at intervals to destroy the data. We arm them, go topside and fly out."

"What's our exfil?" asked Grant.

"The data will be collected by a drone piloted by either Baz or myself which will be able to move fast enough to avoid anti-air defences. It'll grab the loot and head straight back to the *Hikane*. Our own escape will be a little trickier."

"I don't like the sound of that," said Grant.

"Mason?" I said. He nodded.

"Anyone ever ridden the lightning before?" Columbine began laughing and shaking his head whilst Grant and Fara gave each other a knowing look.

"You can't be serious," said Mozzy.

"Very. If we bring the *Hikane* in there's a good chance it'll be shot down. We can't call a drop-ship either because that too risks being blown out of the sky. We need something fast, something that can outrun anti-air. Banshee launchers are our best chance off the planet."

"And risk being spaced instead of blown up?" said Fara.

"Once in orbit the Hikane will fly in and scoop us up. Each launcher can be retro-fitted to the pods. They drop the gear, we shoot straight back up. Simple."

"But that will leave the last pair vulnerable," said Baz. "Those things take two people at a time. Those left until last will have to hold off the entire force until-"

"I'll be there," said Thor, speaking for the first time. "I'll hold the buggers off whilst you escape. Least I can do for ya."

"What, and leave you behind?" said Baz. "No way, buddy. We don't leave *any* of the team behind."

"We won't be," I said. "We'll clone his CPU. Thor on the planet won't be the Thor on the ship. When the last pair exfil, Thor will self-destruct using another thermo-nuke inside his frame. That'll bring the facility down on top of itself, destroying any direct evidence that links us to the attack."

"You're happy with that?" asked Baz, looking at the bot.

"No," he replied. "But if we're gonna save Angel then I fink it's a risk worf takin', sir."

"So the real Thor will be on the ship, right?" asked Columbine. I shook my head.

"A cloned CPU cannot co-exist with its copy on the same neural network; both would try to destroy the other, like a virus attacking a computer. By doing this, the original Thor would have to be taken offline." *Along with Jimmy*, I thought to myself. What I didn't mention was that there was no real way of making sure they were entirely off the network, it'd never been done before. Most systems continued to remain linked even in shut-down mode. The risks to Thor and Jimmy were high but Mason and I had discussed this with him first. He wanted a chance to try and I couldn't stop him, not if I was willing to recognise him as a teammate only a few days earlier. We were all risking something on this trip, most of us either death or capture.

"Can I say something?" asked Columbine. I nodded. "Your plan sucks, but I'm in."

"I agree, pal. But it's all we've got. Any other questions?" Heads shook. "Okay. We're 12 hours from Madam Sill's. I want combat prep and suit acclimatisation by zero-eight-thirty. Grant and Fara pull loading duty with Thor. Mozzy, Baz and Jo, oversee the adaptation of the FARGO drives into the suits. Mason, you're with me on weapon detail. Good luck, folks. Dismissed."

It felt like the clocks were turning faster than they should have been. It was like rolling downhill in a go-kart, out of control, heading straight for the bottom. It was too late to get off now. We had to ride it down and wait for the impact.

No sooner had the work been carried out than I saw the floating fortress of Madam Sill's on the viewscreen with over twenty weapon platforms training lancer cannons directly at us. Built into the fixed orbit of an abandoned battle cruiser, the entire facility glistened in the darkness with a myriad of lights and exhaust plumes. Spires and salvaged pieces of other ships had been grafted onto the hull, expanding the monstrosity like cancerous growths. Situated over a desert planet, the famous Emporium reminded me how far from our path we'd come and how deep into the rabbit hole we'd gone.

"Welcome to Madam Sill's weapon and armour emporium," sung the artificial voice over the comms. "You have thirty seconds to identify yourselves before our state-of-the-art defence matrix becomes active."

"Mark Nando," said Mason. "We have an appointment with Madam."

"Nando?" I said to him. He grinned.

"Welcome, Mr. Nando. Please enter through docking arm 4 and follow directions to landing platform Theta. Enjoy your visit to Madam Sill's Emporium."

With our hearts in our throats, we guided our ship into the belly of the cruiser and watched the doors seal shut behind us. Internal lighting blinked into life, forming a long tunnel of winking white globes set into the wall on all sides. As we ambled through, platforms armed with plasma cannons trained on us like waiting dogs, ears pricked and staring at us until we passed them by.

"Very welcoming," said Mason. "As a customer, I feel we're getting the 5-star treatment."

"You think?" I laughed. The collision alarms continued to flash long after I'd muted them. This passageway had originally been designed to allow access to the massive engine drivers deep in the heart of the cruiser, not as a means to dock a ship. We barely fit inside the pipe and only the FARGO drives stopped us from scraping the paintwork all the way down.

When we reached the vast open space where the drivers would have been, we found a brightly lit array of docking arms spread out on all sides topped with many more automated turrets that swung back and forth. Above each was a stencilled number and the *Hikane* slid alongside the massive number four.

"Baz, you have the bridge," I said, getting up out of the chair. "Mason and I will go. Any requests?"

"Ask her if she's got any Coke," he grinned. "I'm gasping here."

"Sure."

We stepped out onto the docking arm and felt the artificial gravity drives weigh us down a little too much. Mason gave me a knowing look and adjusted his stance.

"Not very trusting," I said. "Where would we run to anyway?"

"Can you feel that?" He asked, sniffing. I nodded.

"She's reduced the O2 in the air by a fraction. This'll be fun."

"Don't get too excited, you're liable to pass out buddy."

We waited. Beyond us, maybe 300 metres down the arm, two massive steel doors began to part and two security bots came stomping towards us, weapons raised. Between them in a long flowing dress of black and red silk topped by long waves of silver hair, was Madam Sill.

"It can't be," said Mason. I looked harder at the woman striding with confident steps towards me.

"What do you mean?" I asked. He didn't reply. In a moment they were upon us and standing at a safe distance away from where we stood. The two bots trained their cycling autocannons at us and growled.

"Madam Sill?" said Mason. "Is that what you're calling yourself now? Very exotic." The woman looked gracefully aged with high cheekbones, thin lips and what had to be the darkest ebony coloured eyes I'd ever seen on a woman from Tokyo's elite class. She bore a wicked smile for Mason who she obviously knew and as she put her hands on her hips she blew him a playful kiss.

"I had a feeling it was you on the comms," she said, her native accent just beginning to show around the edges of her words. "It's a small universe, isn't it?"

"Getting smaller by the hour," he replied. Then, gesturing to me, he said, "This is Carter, an old friend from the Martian days. Carter, this is Madam Sill, formerly known as Princess Himari of Akishino of the Imperial royal family."

Madam Sill smiled warmly at me and tilted her head in a gentle bow.

"A pleasure. Now that we're acquainted perhaps I will make my home a little more inviting." She lifted her arm as if the move was a choreographed performance and pressed a delicate nail onto a control button on her wrist. I winced as the gravity was altered and the air suddenly became oxygen rich. My head swam a little.

"A security consideration," she explained. "You understand of course." We nodded. "Tea?"

She turned on heels I'd only just noticed and began striding back down the arm. The security bots didn't follow. Instead, they waited for

Mason and me to follow then, rotating on their waist axis with grinding metal, they watched us go. I had a feeling they were going to stay there, watching the ship instead of us.

"So you survived?" asked Madam Sill as she led us through the doors that closed behind us.

"Just," replied Mason. We continued on, the structure of the corridor shifting from bare industrial to a more pleasant functional décor. The bare conduits were now hidden behind painted sheets and the floor turned from grid plates to coated decking. The change was not so much subtle but obliging, like the nod of the head from Sill earlier; a concession to politeness and good manners.

"I managed to escape the madness before Prime fell," she said. "Sometimes turning a profit at the expense of a planet's independence gets stuck in one's throat."

"I thought you'd remained neutral?" he laughed.

"I had. But when the war tilted in favour of Earth and the body count had reached many zeroes I felt it was time to move on."

"You mean when it looked like an investigation might be launched into certain outside bodies involving themselves in under-the-counter arms deals?"

"That too. My father would not have appreciated the reputation of the Imperial family being mentioned in criminal proceedings when the soldiers finally came home."

"What does he think about it now?"

"Not much. He is dead. My sister, Mako, now sits on the proverbial throne. That is no longer any of my concern, however."

We turned left into a narrower hallway lit with softer lamps and carpeted with intricately designed patterns on a red and black background, similar to the dress Madam Sill wore. Then two wooden doors swung open on their own, allowing access to her personal chambers. They were richly furnished with deep leather couches, drapes of expensive silk and hand-painted images of Japanese history and culture suspended on grav hooks. The air was thick with scent, of

238

burning oils that made my lungs tingle and filled my mind with thoughts of history and age and honour.

"Please, take a seat," she said and pressed her wrist control once more. A gong chimed somewhere far off and in moments a young woman in a tightly-fitting smock of black silk hurried in bearing a tray. It bore a kettle and three cups made of fired clay and painted in purple enamel with silver filigree designs. The woman set the tray down on a low table beside three couches and retreated back the way she came. We sat and Mason leaned over to pour the tea.

"You remembered," said Sill with a wry grin. Watching Mason pour tea was priceless. I'd seen that man storm the trenches on Mars, take down a gigantic mutated rat and single-handedly engage an exo-shell in mortal combat and here he was, his enormous hands delicately tipping the spout of a tiny kettle so that a small stream of hot tea would fill an even smaller cup for a Princess of Japan. Why had I not thought to record it?

"It remains one of the fondest memories of my time during the war," he said. "Shore leave spent in Tokyo with this same pot and this same cup."

"You only wanted me for my guns," she grinned, enjoying the banter. I was still stunned that this was actually happening before my eyes.

"Your guns. Your grenades. Your tungsten-tipped 25.4mm caseless rounds."

"Stop it," she laughed. "You're making me blush."

"When I pulled my trigger, I thought of you." She covered her mouth with her hand and even I found myself smiling. Was this what passed for Mason's charm with the ladies? Discussing the finer points of munitions?

"Is that why you're here now?" She took the cup from his hands, bowed again, and sat back in her chair, crossing her long, slender legs at the knee. Mason passed me the next cup and I held it under my lips, breathing in the rich scent of chamomile.

239

"Yes, though had I known that 'Madam Sill' was, in fact, a Princess, I'd have come sooner."

She blew gently at the cup and sipped. I found myself doing the same, relaxing into the flavour as much as the cushions of the couch. The entire room seemed designed to break down a person's defences the way a masseuse would work knots out of tired shoulders. I found my eyes heavy and my legs turning to mush and I could imagine myself accepting any price for anything this exotic Princess wanted to sell me.

"What's the occasion or dare I not ask the liberators of the Hades-class vessel *Aurelius*?"

"Still got the connections then?" he grinned.

"As you say, the universe is smaller than you think," she said and sipped again. "TRIDENT is doing very well I hear and pretending that your actions were somehow 'secret' isn't fooling anyone. That kind of prestige isn't just bought off a shelf. When it comes, the wise person rules it like wind in a turbine, managing, manipulating, making it work for them. Your sister," Here she turned to look at me with those pitch-black irises. "Is a *very* wise woman."

I nodded but said nothing. This elaborate game was between Mason and Sill and I refused to get involved. I could already hear Alice cautioning me to step back and let them do their dance.

"Very wise and very... *wealthy*," said Mason.

"Hmm."

"But now that I know who Madam Sill really is," he said. "It seems only courteous to offer information as well as credits."

"Facts as well as guns?" she chuckled softly. "You have hidden depths, Mason. But what do you think I need to know that I don't know already?"

He gestured to his comms unit and she gave a slight nod, a permission almost unsaid. He tapped at the display and activated the holographic projector. An image hovered over his wrist and I saw her eyes begin to sparkle, like stars inside two black holes.

"Confirmed recordings of an unknown fleet," he explained as the image rotated around what Argo had believed had been their command ship. "Have any of your connections informed you of *this*?"

She shook her head once and I saw the muscles in her jaw tighten for a moment.

"Our friends believe that they're a serious threat, an unknown and very dangerous threat. One that's heading this way."

"The Commonwealth?" she asked and some of that cold, professional exterior slid away. Her accent began to seep into her words, no longer restrained.

"We think so."

Madam Sill, or perhaps now Princess Himari of Akishino as she truly was, set her teacup down on the table, sat back and steepled her fingers in front of her, resting her lips on the structure. Her eyebrows knotted in concentration and concern.

"I would have to see it for myself," she said.

"I have the recording ready now. You'll understand that I have had to-"

"Yes, yes," she snapped, waving away his warning with a flick of her wrist. "We can drop the pretence now. You've brought ill tidings to my door, Mason, and though I'm grateful I do not wish to openly admit that my intelligence network has failed me."

"What will you do?" he asked.

"Do? What can I do? This vessel is a derelict, a floating hulk, it's not capable of moving and to transfer my merchandise would take years and would prove very dangerous to my operation. And where would I go? I'm not some travelling saleswoman, dragging my cart behind me as I-" She'd raised her tone with every word, reaching almost fever-pitch as she realised what she was saying. Mason and I remained silent. My cup was now empty and I caught his eye, gesturing. He poured the last of the pot into each of the three cups and the tension eased a little. Traditions had that effect.

"How long?" she sighed.

"We don't know. Our contacts believe that this was simply a scouting party, an advance force testing the waters, so to speak. The main assault could be right behind it or years away. We just don't know."

"And why don't we know? Who the hell are they?"

"All unknown," he replied softly. "I'm sorry."

She nodded and sipped her tea, staring down into the table as if boring holes into it. Then she managed a smile as if reaching a conclusion that settled her nerves.

"I will think of something," she said. "I always do."

"If there's anything-" She waved one slender hand and stopped him in his words.

"We did very good business together, Mason. A lot of it would have cost us both dearly had the truth come out. But that was a long time ago and we've both grown since then. TRIDENT is doing very well and I'm happy for you, but being caught helping a known illegal-arms dealer move her merchandise would destroy us both. I would not allow that.

"But as we all know the real powers for change in the universe are cold hard cash and big guns. This, I believe, is where we can help each other."

She stood up, smoothed out the creases in her dress and smiled.

"So shall we do business, gentlemen?"

Madam Sill led us out of her chambers through another door and into a warmly lit hallway. At the far end, two soldiers in combat-chassis stood to attention, rifles by their sides and they turned at the sight of Madam Sill and opened the doors behind them. We passed between them onto an open gantry and stopped mid-way along.

"Gentlemen," she said, gesturing with a sweep of her arm over the side of the rail. "Take whatever your ship can carry and your need requires. Let's call it 'friend-rates', shall we?"

I looked across and felt my chest tighten. Vanishing into shadow far across the length and breadth of the ship, row after row after bloody row of shelving and racking, the armoury of Madam Sill stretched into infinity or something approximate to it. No wonder she couldn't consider moving premises. Like images of the terracotta army found hundreds of years ago, the uniform lines of weapons, arms and munitions stood waiting for the most skilled practitioners of war to come and buy them, in this case, at a knock-down price.

"I will leave you to your work, gentlemen," she smiled. "Come and see me when you've finished and we will share one more cup before we part."

Mason turned to Sill and bowed, arms at his side. I saw tears welling in her eyes as she stood and returned the gesture.

"Thank-you, Princess," he whispered.

Then she was gone in a flurry of dress folds and a mobile staircase slid into fixtures in the gantry. We began to descend.

"Hidden depths," I said to him as I followed him down. "So many hidden-"

"Shut up," he said. "It's time to shop."

27

At the bottom of the stairs, two loader bots rolled towards us on rubber wheels dragging multi-levelled racks behind them. A human worker dressed in perfectly clean and pressed overalls joined them, smiled politely at us and held up a tablet with stylus.

"Shall we begin?" he said in almost perfect English.

"Yes," said Mason. "Let's start with orbital drop pods and Banshee launchers."

The man began scratching at the screen, smiling the way a waiter might take a drinks order.

"This way please."

We followed him down the aisles, passing through row after row of racked weapons arranged in meticulous order with intent and purpose. I tried not to look too hard, it was distracting enough already.

"This next aisle," he said and turned a corner. More loader bots passed by, taking items off shelves and lifting them onto their own racks behind them. "Any particular make or model?"

"Let's look at a few," said Mason. "I was thinking FARGO or RosCO."

"Good choices both," grinned the man. "We have 26 units of the FARGO 'Banshee' and 34 units of RosCO 'V115'. I personally would lean towards the RosCO as they quite recently modified the launcher system to overcome a lag in the activation circuits. A delay of 3.4 seconds was recorded during FARGO inspection testing when compared to the RosCO at 1.2 seconds."

"Okay. We'll take six units of the RosCO V115."

"Excellent. Might I ask if you're considering retrofitting them to drop pods?"

"You read my mind," laughed Mason.

"If you were to deploy using drop pods then I would expect the need for a rapid exfil as well. Simple logic. We have twelve units of the V115 already compatible with RosCO X3 drop pods. Perhaps I could interest you in six of those units instead?"

"That will do nicely," said Mason. The man scribbled away on his stylus and one of the loader bots began moving down the aisle, selected the appropriate rack and began lifting enormous wooden crates onto his own shelving.

"What else can I help you with?" he smiled.

"A 654 rapid supply drone with a balanced payload/speed ratio."

"Anti-air?" he asked. Mason nodded. "Please step aboard one of our loaders; the item in question is much further away."

We did so, only now noticing the cages suspended at the front of the bots. Once we were all onboard, the loaders gained speed and began moving rapidly through the aisles, blurring the shelves as we sped past. Within seconds we were slowing down in a much larger open space with fewer racks. Here drone craft were on display, already assembled whilst some remained in their original packing crates.

"Here we are," said the man, leaping down. "The 654 series are this way. Please follow me."

We did. The volume of stock was unbearably large and it began to feel overwhelming. I focussed in on the direction we were going, noting that there were a great many pieces of equipment that had never seen the light of day, let alone a battlefield.

"Is that the Thunderbird 34?" I asked, pointing to a sleek midnight-blue coloured rocket with narrow wings and a sharp nose. It bristled with armaments.

"Indeed. Only six were made and we own five of them – we sold one last week."

"Must be expensive," I said. He cleared his throat.

"More than you realise."

We continued on, arriving at a less elegant craft raised on a display platform with a fat belly and large engine ports.

"The Ottoman 654. An equal balance of payload-to-speed, the fastest drone for the maximum possible weight distribution. Fitted with anti-air shielding and afterburner exhaust porting for a twelve-second boost into orbit."

"How much can it carry?" asked Mason.

"Three metric tonnes." He nodded his approval.

"We'll take two units."

"Excellent."

Again the loaders lifted two of the packed drone crates onto their backs and the man gestured that we should climb aboard again.

"Exo-shells," said Mason before he had a chance to ask.

"Any particular make or model?"

"Let's browse."

We shot off again and I felt the beginnings of nausea. The journey took longer this time and we turned right at an intersection, joining the rapidly moving lines of loaders coming and going. When we came to a stop I had that momentary feeling that we'd stumbled onto a staging ground for an army ready to deploy. Row after row of stationary exo-shells was lined up in deployment fashion, all empty of course but bearing a faint reminder of massive troop movements during some of our larger campaigns. We climbed down and one suit, in particular, grabbed our attention.

"Everybody does that," said the man with a grin on his face. "Quite magnificent, isn't it?"

"I thought it was a myth," said Mason, walking towards it. "They've never been seen on a battlefield and most assumed they were just a silly designers idea."

"I assure you, this one is not. The FARGO T-105 'War Suit'. Four units were recorded as having been manufactured and this is one of them. The other three are suspected to have been lost in transit but no true report has ever been submitted to FARGO."

Standing at over three times the height of a man, the T-105 was a Titan of battle, bearing multiple weapon platforms on two solid legs each the width of my body. Shoulder mounted rocket launchers looked down on us while multi-barrelled cannons and plasma lancers took the place of arms. From behind the pilot could continue to wear his or her own exo-shell inside the body of thing and in the event of catastrophic failure, eject and continue fighting.

"It's beautiful," said Mason, running his fingers over the two-inch thick armour plating.

"Indeed," said the man. "But so is the price."

"We'll take it," he said and my heart dropped. There was Alice again, her head in her hands, looking at the invoice.

"Do you want to find a prize on the way home to pay for it?" I said.

"I'd pay for this out of my own bank if I thought I needed to," he laughed.

"Done," said the man. "This unit will need to be walked onto your ship," he explained. "I'm sure that a man of your skill will have no problem dealing with that."

"You're right," nodded Mason. "Onto the next items."

I face-palmed before taking one last look at the monster and tried not to hear that voice inside my head screaming at me, asking why I'd let him buy it.

By the time we'd finished we had everything we needed which was a miracle in itself. Even the thermo-nukes had been in Madam Sill's cache. As the last of the loaders vanished in the direction of the *Hikane*, we made our way back towards the gantry.

"It's been a pleasure, gentlemen," said the worker, heading in another direction, possibly to consider retiring on the fat commission that we'd just made for him.

"Likewise," said Mason and I knew he meant it. I looked up and saw Madam Sill leaning on the rail, smiling down at us.

"Find what you were looking for?" she asked.

"Pretty much."

"Come," she said. "Tea is ready."

We returned to her personal chambers, exhausted like kids worn out in a sweet shop. The tea tray had returned and there was a small buffet of sandwiches laid out on another table between the couches along with a vast amount of cake.

"Please, help yourselves. You've just parted with a lot of credits, a vulgar amount of credits and I feel that this paltry fayre is quite insulting in comparison. I can remember what you like, Mason. Still eating too much cake?" He gave a broad grin and nodded.

"It's wonderful," I said. "But to say you have quite a collection would be just as vulgar."

"But accurate. As you've just taken one of my show-pieces it has diminished somewhat. Perhaps I should have hidden it away." She laughed then and the sound was pleasant on what I believed could be a very callous woman when she needed to be. "But I'm afraid you've made me a very nervous woman."

"In what way?" asked Mason.

"A data sniffer. Cutting equipment. Heavy defensive weaponry and static ordinance. Rapid exfil. Nothing says grand-theft like that kind of shopping list."

We said nothing. Over the corner of a ham sandwich on white bread, she looked at Mason and waited, biting off a small piece and chewing on it with some thought. Time passed.

"Corano," I said in the end. "Remus IV."

She stopped chewing and her cheeks took on a tint of pink. She put the sandwich down and cleared her throat.

"Why?" she managed to say.

"He has something we need."

"Such as?"

"You know exactly what he deals in," I replied. "And because you know I suspect that he has something you might need too. Something

248

he's taken from you."

"Taken?" she snorted. "Taken? You mean something he has *on* me, information that would put me on a prison asteroid for the rest of my life and see my bank accounts emptied into his own. If that's what you're referring to then yes, he does have something I want."

"Which would also mean that the kind of force we will be going up against is probably taken directly from your own stores, right?" She nodded, looking directly at me. Gone was the confident Matriarch of War and in her place was now the frightened Princess from Tokyo.

"I could check my receipts if he were a paying customer. Instead, he simply tells me what he wants and I deliver. It's that simple."

"Do we stand a chance?" I asked. She tried to smile, but she shook her head.

"No," she said flatly. "You'll be annihilated."

"Even with our charm and wit?" said Mason. She stifled a giggle behind her tears and reached for her tea.

"Damn you twice you bastard," she said to him. "I was pleased to see you at first and now I feel like I'm saying goodbye for the last time. Are you absolutely sure you must go through with this?"

"We are," I said. "It's one of our own."

"We'll do it," said Mason with a firmness that seemed to shake her. "We'll get what we need and we'll level the place. We'll bury his empire under radioactive rubble so deep he'll have to dig up half the planet just to find the melted mass we'll leave for him. His hold over you will come to an end one way or another. I promise."

Madam Sill stared at him and a single tear escaped down her cheek. She put her thin-fingered hand gracefully on his knee and patted it twice.

"I'm very grateful that the universe continues to shrink for us, Mason. I truly am."

We returned to the *Hikane* in time to see the first of the items being lifted into the rear of the ship. Baz and Grant were overseeing the process from the gantry and when they saw us down below they waved.

"Got everything?" called Baz.

"Yeah. Even some Coke." He shot me a 'thumbs-up' and returned to watching. Mason was climbing into his exo-shell, the prototype that we'd brought with us. Thankfully it turned out to be compatible with the T-105 and as he stomped back down the arm towards his new toy I smiled.

"Penny for your thoughts?" said Jo, appearing beside me. I turned. She looked beautiful even in the artificial light coming from above, dressed in plain combat fatigues and a vest. My eyes passed over her ink, following the thin black lines that snaked up her arms and wrapped themselves around her soft neck, vanishing behind wavy locks of golden hair. I leaned towards her, kissing those lips that had become so familiar to me now. She giggled as she pulled back and wrapped her arms around me.

"You should go shopping for guns more often," she said. "It makes you glow."

"That'll be the fear of seeing Alice's face when she gets the bill. Imminent death always warms my skin."

She kissed me then, held it for longer than usual and broke away. She was holding back her emotion, I could see it in her eyes.

"It's going to be okay," I said. "Try not to think about it if you can. Switch it off."

"I'm trying," she said though the words came out a little broken. "It kind of hit me when I saw how much equipment was coming on board. This is a big deal, isn't it? Not just some one-day Op." I shook my head.

"I wish it was. But everything we needed was here and we've got it. Not many soldiers can say they started a mission with 100% of their requested gear, can they?"

"I guess not."

"Speaking of which..." I let her go as one of the loader bots came onto the docking arm bearing the exo-shell I'd picked out for Jo. I waved at it to unload it onto the deck and it did so, service station and all. We walked over to it and she whistled with admiration.

"You did one better than the FARGO suit," she said and ran her fingers over the enhanced armour plating. "Does it stick in your throat to see your woman in CHERICA-AUTO?"

"She's not wearing it yet," I grinned.

"You're going to just stand there and watch me undress?"

"I most certainly am, honey."

With a sassy smirk on her lips, she stepped up onto the platform and began powering up the suit from the control panel. I watched as her brow furrowed in concentration while she began to remember her old training in zero-g repair suits. I said nothing.

"Why CHERICA-AUTO?" she asked without turning to look at me.

"The guy said that the CA-443 was far superior to the FARGO equivalent. He has it on good authority that only this suit can match motor controls with human neural impulses within blah-blah-something-de-do."

"At three-times the cost I'd expect it to," she said. "This puppy is high-end gear. I'll be the envy of my class, maybe even the entire school." She suddenly clapped both her hands together. "Got it!"

The rear portion of the suit parted as power thrummed through the chunky-looking exo-shell. It lacked much of the elegance and style of other combat suits; CHERICA-AUTO were often criticised for having a lack of aesthetics on all their products, but a technician's suit wasn't meant to be anything more (or less) than a tool. Bearing twice the armour value of front-line suits, these things were built with protecting the occupant as its top priority, followed by providing an independent power source and a range of tools. The HUD on these suits bore almost no resemblance to anything I might have used in the past and instead offered Jo scanners, schematic overlays and automated directional hints as she worked. No one could argue that a high-spec exo-shell like this didn't deliver value for money.

She slid out of her boots, looked around and let her fatigues drop to the floor. In her underwear, she climbed inside, activated the internal power generator and vanished as the rear plates slid back over her body. I gave her a moment or two, then saw something moving in the shadow beyond the large steel doors.

"Oh shit," I muttered to myself. Jo in her suit turned sideways and looked.

"What the hell is that?" she cried over the external speaker.

"It's a boy who just had a visit from Santa. You'd better watch out."

Baz and Grant came running down the stairs from the gantry and stood beside me as the shape took form. Beneath us, the deck plates rumbled with each footstep it made. When it stopped before the doors to allow them to open wider, it raised one weapon platform and began spinning the barrels. I felt my insides turn to jelly.

"STEP ASIDE, BITCHES!" boomed a voice from the monster. "DADDY'S GOT A NEW TOY."

Flanked by the security bots who now seemed tiny compared to the T-105, Mason made his way towards us, testing the motor controls as he went like a giant waking up to stretch out stiff limbs. When he reached the loading bay of the *Hikane* he stopped and ejected from the back. It was quite high up and he dropped to his feet a little clumsily.

"Anyone else want a go?" he said, opening his helmet.

"I'd love-" said Baz but Mason laughed.

"No chance. I was kidding. It's mine, no one gets to play with her."

Jo stepped down from the service platform and began moving up and down, getting used to her own suit. Then, looking up at the T-105, she laughed.

"What's so funny?" I asked with a smile.

She said nothing. Then we all stepped back as the rear compartment closed without anyone inside and the machine took a step backwards.

"Hey!" cried Mason. "Who the hell is doing that?"

Laughing over the external speaker, she began to walk the War Suit up and down the platform remotely. Mason didn't look impressed.

"Here, you can have her back," she said and the machine opened up again. Dropping her HUD, I saw her face appear inside the suit and she was still laughing.

"Don't worry – the suit has to be empty for the remote access to work. I won't pick on you, I promise."

"It's good to know though," he said, returning her smile. "Might help us out down there."

I looked at the queue of loaders still coming with more gear and then, looking at my comms unit and the time, I felt my insides tighten.

"Let's get things stowed away," I said. "We need to be moving. The one thing Madam Sill can't sell us is time."

Jo and Mason nodded, turning serious along with me. As fun as that was, it was time to go to work.

28

Remus IV hadn't changed since we'd last been there. No new orbital defences, no armada of attack-ships in high orbit, nothing to indicate that our last visit had aroused suspicion. We gave the same hand-shake to the docking platform we used before and were told to stand-to whilst our bona fides were checked.

"Are you ready?" asked Mason over the comms. I turned to look at Baz who stood near the emergency hatch and he nodded through the blacked-out visor of the stealth suit.

"Good to go," I replied.

I felt the ship begin to turn as we prepared to dock. We'd only have a few seconds of confusion whilst she 'accidentally' collided with the ramp and discharged our shield dampeners at the same time. It happened, it wasn't too overt a stunt, but it would snatch vital seconds of scanner delay from the platform itself.

"We're cleared," said Mason. "Docking in two minutes."

Baz and I moved towards the hatch and took positions on either side. He gripped the release handle and paused. Waiting sucked. I felt my nerves make the most of the inactivity and begin organising a rock concert in the pit of my stomach.

"Sixty seconds," said Mason. Baz nodded once and yanked the handle back. The seals popped.

"Go left out of here and kick off, don't wait," I said. Another nod.

"Thirty seconds."

"Now," I said. Baz pulled the handle towards him and the hatch swung open revealing the infinite black of space. There, just coming into view, was the shuttle leaving the docking arm.

"Go," I said and out he went. I was right behind him and together we planted our feet onto the side of the ship, bent our knees and with as much force as we could manage, kicked ourselves free into space. We flew like silent arrows, arms tight by our sides, legs locked in place. The shuttle was about to pass us and the intercept couldn't have been timed better. Baz made contact first and his hands clamped onto the smooth metal like the suckers of a leech. I hit the vessel a metre further down from him and felt my arms almost pulled out of their sockets by the clamping mechanism of the suit.

"In position," he said over the comms.

"In position," I confirmed. "Moving to the escape hatch."

My HUD marked the path around the hull of the craft and using one hand at a time I moved across its surface. Before us on the starboard side was the opening we were looking for.

"How long?" I asked.

"Three minutes until we reach low orbit," he said. "Two more and we'll be cooking."

I grabbed hold of the handles protruding from the hatch and deactivated the clamps in my gauntlets. Using my feet to keep hold of the shuttle, I unfastened the alarm suppressor from my rig and began wiring it into one of the control panels exposed near the hinges. Baz took up a position opposite me and watched.

"Want a countdown?" he asked.

"No," I replied. "Stay quiet."

"Okay."

I worked like a man possessed, sucking down panic as I felt time slipping through my fingers like sand. One wire here, another there, bypass that one, make sure the green one lights up my board. I took a deep breath and tried to ignore the planet looming up ahead.

"Got it!" I cried and snatched the suppressor back, throwing it into space. "Let's go."

I slid the handle back and Baz lifted it open, throwing himself inside. I quickly followed and drew it shut behind us.

255

"How long?" I asked.

"You did it in one-thirty-five. Not bad."

"It felt longer."

We waited inside the hatch, not needing to go any further into the ship. We were hitching a ride, that was all and the lower our profile the better.

"Planet-fall in ten," he said. "So. You and our engineer?"

"Shut up," I laughed. "I'm sorry I couldn't get you any 'mind-your-own-business implants when we went shopping. They were all out."

"Clearly they had designer outfits for that 'special person'."

"You should look in the mirror someday, see the guy who spent most of his time shopping for clothes."

"There's only one person in my life who deserves *this* amount of love. Me. I know how to treat myself right, show myself a good time."

"I bet you do," I said. "You'll go blind, pal if you keep that up."

"I practice safe sex."

"Safe sex for you is making sure you're not caught in the bathroom with a copy of 'Men and Machines' and some of Thor's servo-lube."

"I just read the articles."

"And the lube?"

"The flusher squeaks. Just doing some maintenance."

"That's a lot of maintenance for one toilet."

"Six minutes," he said. "It's a really squeaky handle."

"You should find that special person, mate. Someone who you can fight the mirror for in a morning or go shopping with, maybe do each other's nails."

"I did, remember, and she got murdered on *that* ship. We had a future together. Long walks on the beach. Afternoon tea. We were going to grow old together, you know?"

"She was already three times your age."

"So she had a head start, who cared? Age is just a number."

"It can be a big number or it can be a small number."

256

"I guess I'll never fall in love now," he groaned. "I'll have to return to my former career."

"And what was that?"

"I was known in these parts as 'Stert Golery – intergalactic pornstar and purveyor of small women'." I snorted out a laugh. "What?"

"Really?"

"I specialised in midget-porn in zero-g. It was quite tricky to pull off – no pun intended."

"How long?"

"Three minutes. I suspect you don't believe me."

"You're right," I said. "I don't."

The shuttle began its landing procedure as predicted and when it was less than thirty metres from the ground Baz and I leapt from the open hatch and dropped the rest of the way onto compacted snow and ice. Rolling forward with the momentum, we continued east from the pad, never looking back until we were able to fall behind a snowdrift and into cover.

"I don't hear anything," I said, noticing that the patterns on my suit had changed to a shifting blend of white and blue colour.

"Not exactly an international airport, is it?" he replied, gesturing to the lone platform, the shuttle and a small insulated hut.

"Big-M said that those visiting the target had their own shuttle. The rest of the planet travels economy."

"Big-M?" said Baz.

"His choice, not mine. Come on, let's go."

The HUD set a course for the target building and displayed a distance of ten kilometres to the north-east. The land around the city was a frozen waste where years of snow and ice had built up into treacherous slopes and violent drifts. It lacked the danger of our last encounter with the cold but the memory was still felt fresh as we sped along.

"How do people live on this rock?" asked Baz, barely panting.

257

"They don't for half of the day," I pointed out. "Most of the time they're off their faces on Opho."

"Must be good stuff."

"I don't want to find out."

We closed the distance quickly, meeting no resistance whatsoever. It was only the early hours of Remus IV's morning and even though the light level was pretty low there was a bit of activity here and there on the streets to the south-east. Lamps moved in the twilight and the far-off sounds of machinery could just be heard over the enhanced ears of the suit.

"Report," said Mason.

"Approaching the target building now," I said. "Five klicks out."

"Most of the population will be taking their first hit," he reminded me. "Now's the best time to strike."

"I hear you," I replied. "Moving as fast as we can."

We increased our pace as the land flattened out a little. Groundwork had begun there, it was obvious by the tracks, but it hadn't continued and the snow had filled in the holes left by machinery. It meant we could risk sprinting and I felt my chest groan at the increased exertion.

"Not far now," said Baz. "Three clicks."

"Keep moving. We'll stop just before the hill."

On we ran and no one noticed. We saw nobody until we were half a click out and saw the land rise sharply upwards to the plateau the factory had been built on. We slowed to a halt and, dropping to a crouch, gathered our breath.

"That was warm work," said Baz, his hands on his knees. "Shall I go up or you?"

"I'll go," I said. "Wait here."

I crawled up the slope, digging my fingers into the hard compacted snow for grip. It took a minute or two to reach the top and, peering over, I saw my first glimpse of the factory outside of Columbine's art. He'd been pretty accurate. The building was basic, nothing more than a factory with plain walls of concrete and triple-thick glass windows that had been misted over. Snow piled lazily where you'd expect it to and an asphalt road leading up to the door had been cleared recently.

"Impressive," I said. "I see two guards at the door, just goons by the looks of them."

"Just for show," said Mason. "The real deal is inside. Dispatch those two quickly and get in."

Baz came up to join me and together we stared into the storm that was beginning to whip up around our ears. Even though natural vision began to fail, the HUDs managed to keep the target building and the goons in sharp relief.

"Stealth?" asked Baz. I laughed.

"Be my guest," I said. "Wait until the tall one comes back around and starts talking to the other. I'll follow."

"They don't call me the 'Silent Killer' for nothing."

"Who the hell calls you that?"

"My mum."

He went over the top of the rise, crouching low but moving quickly. I detached my weapon from my belt and unfolded the stock, screwing in the barrel from a pouch before inserting the plasma cell. When the display hit green, I took aim and sighted the stationary guard. Baz was within a few metres of him, almost invisible in the stealth-suit and the storm. He drew his knife as the other approached from around the corner.

"Tangos in sight," he whispered.

"Go for it buddy," I said and eased my finger on to the trigger. "Ready when you are."

As the walking guard made his approach, Baz leapt out from where he crouched and plunged the knife into his throat. At the same time, my weapon discharged in utter silence, cut a swathe through the falling snow and burned a hole the size of my fist through the chest of the static guard. Both dropped to the floor at almost the same time.

"Tango down," said Baz.

"Tango down," I repeated. "Move to the door."

Dragging his victim with him, Baz made his way to the other side and waited. I sprinted to him across the open land, noticing that there were no turrets outside and no obvious security other than the two goons.

"Nice," he said as I got there.

"Likewise. Rig the door."

He got to work setting thermite charges on the hinges and the lock whilst I covered him on one knee. The man I'd shot was steaming from the entry wound and I could see down into his body, noticing what remained of his ribs was made of molanium.

"Ready," said Baz, stepping back. "Clear."

"Clear. Do it."

With his own weapon now drawn and the detonator in his free hand, he nodded once and turned his head away, mashing the button three times. The doors exploded inward in a brilliant flash of white light and we followed it in, firing the moment our HUD sighted the real defenders.

"Tango down," said Baz calmly.

"Tango down," I responded as one man in a combat-chassis dropped. Another took his place in the confusion and got the same treatment. Dust and ice chips flooded the open factory, causing the workers to stumble to the ground in blindness and begin screaming. This helped clear the civilians from the enemy and one by one our HUDs changed their outlines from blue to red.

"Moving!" cried Baz, dodging incoming fire and heading left into the corner of the factory floor. I was already moving right, aiming upwards at targets on the gantry who fired down indiscriminately. I saw two unarmed workers killed where they cowered and two more shot as they ran for the door.

"That's another down," I said. "Moving up. Cover my flank."

"Roger. Moving up too. Another tango down. Watch your three, by the vending machine."

260

"Got that. Nice one. Tango down," I said. I was fluid now, my body and my training working together like precision machinery. Gone were exterior thoughts, gone was fear and anticipation. We were engaged now and nothing else mattered.

"Move quickly," said Mason in my ears. "The alarm will have been raised by now."

"We're on it," snapped Baz. "That's two more gone."

I fired a burst into an overturned table covered in what I presumed was Opho product. Something groaned on the other side and the arm of the last defender flew upwards, still holding part of his weapon. The rest was gone in a smouldering mess of superheated plasma.

"Clear?" called Baz.

"Clear mate," I replied. "Moving to locate the generator. Standby."

I slung my weapon and drew out the scanning module, assembling it quickly from three other parts. Then, activating the power node, I began to move in a pattern, up and down the overturned tables, past pallets of product compressed into dark yellow bricks. I caught the gasp of a civilian and I kicked at her leg, urging her to run.

"Get them out of here," I said to Baz. "Quick as you can."

"I'm on it."

Sweat collected beneath my helmet as the scanner yielded nothing. I swept it over the place Mason and Columbine said it was but I got nothing back.

"The clock is ticking," I heard him say over the comms. "Where the hell is it, Carter?"

"I've got nothing on this thing," I replied. "No signals, no visible electronics, nada, zip."

"Look at the spot we told you," he replied.

"I did!" I growled. "But I-"

I looked up from the display. There, embedded in the wall, was a control panel and it was clearly powered because I could see the glowing icons. It should have shown up on the scanner regardless of what it did, it was electronic. Why didn't it?

261

"Shit," I said. "The scanner doesn't work."

I looked at the panel. It displayed controls for the air conditioning units. "A/C on a frozen waste?" I looked closer. When I pressed an icon it changed the display and suddenly the overlay of the building itself appeared with a percentage gauge set at ninety-four. There were two other icons – ACTIVATE was shaded out but DEACTIVATE was lit up.

"Surely not?" I said aloud.

"Talk to me Carter, time is running out."

I pressed the icon and waited. A code-pad appeared on the screen and I tapped in the numbers Mozzy had given me moments before leaving. Something beneath my feet stopped rumbling and ground to a halt. The lights above us now brightened as if finally running on full power and I smiled.

"That's it!" cried Mason. "You found it! Now input the data cube Mozzy gave you so that it can't be reactivated."

I did. The panel went dim, then vanished altogether.

"We're in," I said. Then, looking out through the smouldering doorway I saw aircraft coming in to land just beyond the plateau. Even in the swirling maelstrom outside I could make out units disembarking into formation.

"Launch the pods," I said. "We've got company."

29

The first attack came quickly. Once the *Hikane* had broken free of the platform and begun taking out the planetary defences, all bets were off. Safely in orbit and free from attack for the time being, the first of the pods were launched and on the ground, the troopers of Corano began to realise that the proverbial excrement had hit the fan.

Baz and I ran to take positions by the doorway as the first units marched up the long sloping road towards us.

"Grunts," I said. "Get ready."

Without visible armour and carrying solid-shot rifles, the men and women began to slow as they looked upward, now seeing the opening we'd made in the factory. I sighted my weapon and waited.

"Let them fire first," I said. "Each second of hesitation gains us more time."

We watched. Hesitantly they were ordered by someone at the rear of the line to advance. They did, weapons raised, looking about for cover. There was none. It was a killing field.

"They look drunk," said Baz, checking his weapon for the third time. "Are they high?"

"Either that or were about to get that way," I replied. "You know the drill, they're targets, switch off that head of yours."

"Hard to do that when they look so scared."

"Yeah," I admitted. "I know."

We waited. Still they came on very slowly and I wondered how gravity hadn't pulled their sorry looking faces back down the slope.

"I'm inbound," said Mason. "ETA two and a half minutes."

"Here we go," said Baz and I saw that they'd found some courage

263

by following one of the grunts in charge. "I've got him in my sights."

"Take him. Maybe it'll spook the others."

Baz's weapon bucked in his grip and a shimmering line of blue light shot out from the barrel and down the slope. The man leading them was sent reeling backwards as his head vanished in a plume of steam and blue-flame. As his body fell the line of advancing troops stopped, looked up, and bolted back down the way they'd come.

"Good call," said Baz.

"Nice shot," I replied.

It bought us the remaining minutes we needed. Before the grunts could reform there was a tearing sound from above, like fabric being ripped apart in one long pull.

"Brace!" I cried and dropped to one knee, covering my head with my hands. Baz did the same as my HUD blinked out for a moment and the ceiling collapsed inwards. An explosion knocked us off our feet and we slammed into the arch of the doorway, head-first.

"Mother fu-" cried Baz but began coughing as his helmet-filter struggled to clear the debris from its vents. I felt a stab of pain in my shoulder where it'd connected with the stonework but I was able to get back on my feet.

"Report," said Mason and I turned to see the T-105 coming online having deployed with its own internal guidance system. He'd basically ridden the thing down as it was, without a drop pod.

"Area secure – for now," I said. "A small force at the southern entrance have withdrawn."

The morning light began to seep in through the hole in the ceiling that Mason had made and the dust rolled effortlessly off the massive shoulder launchers of the titanic machine as it readied itself for war.

"All units, launch immediately. Area secure," he said over the comms.

"We should move," said Baz and I agreed. "Pull back to the vault entrance."

"Go!" Together we leapt over the fallen debris and made for the corridor on the north-west side of the structure where the vault doors would be. As we got there, one of Mason's platforms opened fire, tearing apart most of the southern wall.

"Multiple confirmed kills," he said. "Armoured units are inbound. Get ready."

A drop-craft shot past overhead and as we saw it go the shoulder cannons on the T-105 tracked it automatically and fired. Streaks of vapour snaked after it, turning it into molten fragments in seconds.

"Thor's going to be pissed," said Baz.

"Why's that?"

"He won't be the biggest, baddest bot in town."

"Don't be so sure about that," I reminded him. Then that ripping sound could be heard again, not as loud perhaps but still enough to make my guts churn.

"Incoming!" said Baz and we both turned our backs to it. The ground shuddered with the impact and fresh clouds of dust blinded us again. When they'd cleared, three of the pods had landed almost perfectly vertical where the plascrete floor had refused to budge. All three opened up with mechanical precision, sliding outwards into the shape of a defensible position and revealing the cargo inside.

From one Grant and Fara emerged, spreading out towards the northern end of the building. In the other, Mozzy and Columbine leapt forward and secured the opposite corners of the factory. In the last were our exo-shells and two crates of equipment to take with us down into the vault.

"Suit up," said Mason. "Perimeter is secure for now."

We did so and we shed the stealth-suits, throwing them into the storage bins of the pods to be returned on our exfil. Then, climbing into our waiting armor, I felt the sudden calm of being wrapped in metal.

"We're good," said Baz, taking one of the racked AP40s from the pod and loading it with HE rounds. "Let's rock."

"Jo – you're clear to launch," I said. "Thor – whenever you're ready

265

pal."

"Inbound," replied both of them almost simultaneously.

I moved towards the vault and took up position, waiting for Jo to arrive with the plasma cutter. The doors looked impossibly thick from where I was standing and I stifled a sudden panic that we wouldn't even get past them, let alone the rest of the facility.

"Ready up," said Mason. "Here they come."

"Oh great," said Mozzy. "They've got mechanised units. What happened to those grunts?"

"Baz demoralised them. They've gone home to get high," said Grant.

"Stand to!" cried Mason. Ahead the ripping sound came and this time I didn't need to brace. As Jo landed near to my position, a much larger pod almost landed straight on top of the T-105 and broke open the plascrete floor like it was made of gingerbread.

"What the actual fu-"

"IT'S TIME TO ROB A BLOODY BANK, BOYS!" cried Thor so loud it registered on my suit as an offensive attack. What I'd initially thought was a pod was in fact now unfolding itself from the ball it'd come down to the planet in. When it rose onto unsteady feet, Thor's massive frame, grotesquely made from spare parts and pilfered armour plating, roared into life standing over a metre taller than the T-105 and at least two wider at the shoulders. Perhaps the effect might have had more of an impact had the head of the thing not been painted black with white eyeholes and the word SWAG not been stencilled on the bulging weapon holder hanging from its back.

"Oh shit," laughed Fara as the first shots came rattling through the walls. "Mason's been outdone by a bot!"

"Stand to!" he cried again. "Defensive positions. Incoming mechanised units. Carter – do what we came here to do."

Jo had emerged from her pod carrying the crates of equipment and together we began unpacking them at the mouth of the vault.

"Nervous?" I asked her.

"Shitting myself, Carter. Stay with me, please."

"I'm here, Jo. I'm not going anywhere."

We began to assemble the cutter, clamping the torch heads onto the rails that would move around the vault door as the cut penetrated. We'd managed to build it in two and a half minutes on the ship but that was without the horrifying orchestra of war playing in the background.

"Movement!" cried Grant as the comms continued to pour into our ears. "West side!"

"I see him," said Baz. "Firing!" The AP40 launched grenades at the rate of bullets and the distinctive thud-thud-thud shook the wall behind me.

"He's mush," said Fara.

"South-east, on your eleven, Mason," said Columbine. "Three more. Look out – they're-"

An explosion ripped through the entrance followed by a hail of fire which slammed into Jo's back, rocking her on her feet. She screamed and I stood up, returning fire.

"Stand back!" cried Mason. "Deploying foam."

Jets of the stuff I hadn't seen since Golan IV spurted from one of the T-105's weapon platforms and made a low wall in the space the rocket had made.

"You're fine, Jo. Keep working," I said as calmly as I could. She nodded and took a deep breath.

"This stuff works, right?" she said. "This armour. Didn't feel a thing."

"Without it, you'd have been vapour now," I managed to laugh. "Done?"

"Done. Let's fit it to the door."

Together we lifted the rails into place and the suit she wore kicked in, guiding her hands to precisely where they needed to be. A self-driving rivet gun rotated around onto her shoulder and she reached for it, slamming twenty-five milimetre heads deep into the plascrete around the door.

"Cutting now!" she said and activated the three blue jets that crackled with energy. In moments the metal was glowing beneath the rails and molten slag began dripping onto the floor.

"How long?" I asked.

"Six minutes," she replied. "I need to monitor its operation from here."

"Baz!" I called. "Form up on me. Covering fire."

"Aye boss. I'm coming."

We moved to flank Jo's position and, taking a foam dispenser from the nearest pod, I made two wide sections of cover with it and reinforced the exposed western wall.

"Handy shit," said Baz, kneeling behind one. "Shame we weren't fighting the undead again. They don't fight back as hard."

"That's true," I laughed. *Six minutes*, I thought. A lot can happen in six minutes.

Mozzy hadn't exaggerated and neither had the hint been when it was given by Madam Sill. From the moment we'd begun cutting, the strength of the attack trebled and the factory soon began to fall down around our ears. Withering amounts of fire came in from all directions as both human and automated units began to converge on our position.

From their higher vantage points, Thor and Mason returned devastating quantities of firepower but also exposed themselves to the worst of it. Aircraft made deadly bombing runs overhead, spitting down streams of laser fire whilst trying to avoid the T-105's AA guns or Thor's improvised rocket launchers.

On the ground, spider-tanks and armoured soldiers crawled up the sides of the plateau, trying desperately to establish a foothold but to no avail. The drop-pods had been loaded with every weapon imaginable and as one ran dry, another was picked up and put to devastating effect. All in six minutes.

"We're through!" cried Jo as the centre of the vault door slid hissing onto the other side and came to rest at an angle against the wall. "Help me dismantle the cutters."

I slung my weapon and went to work. Jo blew out the rivets with another tool from her back and I unfastened the rails, carefully placing the cutters back into the crates from which they'd come. Then, when she was almost finished, we moved on to stage three of the plan.

"Grant, Fara and Columbine, form up. Mason – we're ready pal. Going inside."

"Okay, the clock's still ticking pal," he said. "Work fast."

Grant and Fara stormed through the gap and into the corridor on the other side. I ushered Jo in next, followed by myself and Columbine. The chamber was filled with smoke and dust and my HUD automatically compensated.

"What do you see?" I asked.

"Door up ahead. Setting charges," said Fara. "Stand clear."

An explosion. More dust. Then gunfire that rattled inside the narrow confines of the corridor. It lasted less than thirty seconds before "All clear," came down the pipe.

"Move, move, move!" I said and together we pushed into the next hallway just as the map had indicated.

"Columbine, Fara, the security room,"

"Moving," she replied.

"I'm on it," said Columbine, rushing past me.

"Stay here," I said to Grant. "I'll get the cutters."

Jo's arm clamped on mine and yanked me back with some force. "You said-"

"I'll go," said Grant. "You cover her."

"Thanks."

She vanished back into the haze and I felt Jo's arm relax.

"It's okay," I said. "I'm right here." And it was okay – no one without military experience could be expected not to feel terror in that place, under those circumstances, man or woman. Sometimes specialists were needed from outside and in my years of experience they'd always shown courage and resolve far beyond anything they thought they were capable of. Right there and then Jo was demonstrating an almost inhuman amount of strength under fire and I felt my heart burn with pride.

"You do this for a living?" she tried to laugh.

"Sometimes. Other days we just play cards."

"Maybe you should consider retirement."

"I'd be bored."

Grant returned, dragging both crates behind her and turned to go back.

"More guns," she said, grinning through her clear visor. "I'll be pissed off if I don't get to fire one of those FARGO lance-rifles on this trip."

"They're worth more than your armour," I laughed as she went.

"I know!"

I heard shouting over the comms. When Grant returned with another crate I indicated for her to cover us while I switched to camera mode on my HUD. Dropping to one knee, she raised the lance-rifle to her shoulder and watched the corridor.

On Columbine's HUD, I saw him outside the security room, returning fire into the doorway which now hung from its hinges where thermite had only done half the job. On the other side, two exo-shell units had bunkered down behind mobile cover, those annoying molanium barricades sometimes used by low-level security forces. Fara was on the opposite side, priming grenades and throwing them into the room to good effect. I hoped they were thermite charges too because nothing else would do harm to those suits.

"Moving," said Columbine. "Fara, pull back on my word, we need to draw them out."

"Understood. Say the word."

I saw him break cover and retreat maybe five or six metres. Then he called to Fara who did the same. The exo-shells, thinking they had the advantage, began to follow. One looked badly damaged and was dragging a leg behind it. The other hadn't taken a scratch.

Again, the urge to micro-manage them over the comms was strong but I resisted. Instead, I switched to Baz who at that moment had chosen to check his comms unit for social updates, no doubt because of the lack of incoming fire coming in his direction.

"I don't pay you to tell your fucking public what you're doing right now!" I yelled over the comms. "Watch your corner!"

His weapon shot up and he returned to sweeping his area, saying nothing. I moved on. Mason's camera was a little disorientating as I suddenly found myself higher up, looking down. My breath caught in my throat as I saw hordes of units moving towards us, swarming the blasted land around the factory like ants. Thankfully they were holding back, kept at bay by the volume of firepower we were throwing their way. Already piles of smouldering wreckage from downed craft and smashed mechanised units were collecting about us.

"Man down!" came the chilling cry as I switched quickly back to my own HUD.

"Sound off," I said.

"It's Columbine. Direct hit. Suit immobilised."

I checked his life-signs at my end and saw that they'd plummeted to dangerous levels. Grant looked at me.

"Go!" I said and she sprinted away to support Fara. Jo turned to look at me. "Don't think about it," I said. "Think about that first cut." She nodded.

I heard the lance-rifle firing, a kind of hiss followed by a thump as the cyclic compensators kicked in. It fired again and an explosion ripped down the corridor towards us.

"Tango down," said Grant.

"The other is incapacitated," said Fara. "Moving to terminate." A single shot. "Tango down."

"Okay Jo – let's do this," I said and picked up one of the crates. We

271

moved into the hallway and towards the site of the first part of the shaft; we would cut directly through the floor, straight down. Once there I opened the crate and began passing her parts for the cutter as she assembled them.

"Carter," said Fara. "Sam needs medevac."

I flicked my eye over the life-sign indicator and cursed but there was nothing I could do.

"Understood. Stabilise him as best you can and move to control the security-"

"Grant here – unable to do that, Carter. The systems were fried in the assault. Nothing we can do here."

"So the internal defences are still active?"

"More than likely."

I passed Jo the final piece of the cutter which made up a kind of frame suspended a metre above the floor. Again the three heads began to rotate on the rail clockwise sending sparks of electric-blue flame downwards.

"How long?" I asked.

"90 seconds per floor," she replied.

Grant and Fara returned to our position dragging Sam Columbine behind them.

"Take him up to one of the pods and secure him," I said. "We'll just have to hope he holds on long enough."

They nodded and vanished back down the corridor the way we came. I checked my weapon and stood guard over Jo, wondering just what defences the place would throw at us.

"Poor Sam," she said. "Do you think he'll make it?"

"Let's hope so."

She nodded, her outline glowing in the light thrown from the cutters as they made their slow orbit. I waited for Grant and Fara to return and when they did I went back to overseeing what was happening up top.

By now the first wave of attacks had come to an end. Realising that they were facing a heavily-armed foe dug in on an elevated position, Corano's units withdrew to a safe distance to regroup. The moment they did, I ordered our team to re-arm and get ready for a fresh assault. Another pod was launched from the *Hikane* and with it came fresh munitions and some of the heavier weapons we'd been holding in reserve.

"Report," I called over the comms as the disc of floor Jo had cut through dropped down. Grant and Fara moved to follow the moment we'd taken apart the cutters.

"All good here," said Baz.

"Fine boss," said Mozzy.

"Still rockin', sir," said Thor.

"Systems at 55% efficiency. Still fighting though," added Mason.

I helped Jo partially break down the cutter and when the hole was clear, Fara leapt down and began firing. Grant followed and a bitter few minutes of combat ensued as mounted turrets trained on them and drone-bots moved to engage.

"How many?" I called.

"A lot," said Fara. "The system has called most of the units up to this level."

"Mason – can you spare Baz?"

"Take him. I'll let you know if I need him."

In moments Baz had arrived, loaded with grenades on his rig and a shorter carbine in his arms.

"You rang?" he joked, standing by the hole.

"Support those two," I said. He nodded, then jumped. In seconds he was returning fire and I looked back at the security room. "There has to be a way to access the core, right?" I said to Jo.

"I guess so," she replied. "Worth a try while we're stuck up here."

We moved to the room that now billowed smoke from fires raging on the consoles where thermite had landed. Jo, using her suit's internal schematic system, began scanning the wreckage and looking for an access point.

"I might have something," she said. "Move those panels there."

I did so, gripping them with the armoured gauntlets of my suit and tearing them out of their fixings like they were made from cardboard. Jo began pulling wires and conduits, separating them as she went.

"It all runs into here," she explained. "If I can just isolate the ones I need..."

I cycled through the cameras again, this time dwelling on Baz who was blasting apart one bot after another in the tight confines of the corridor below. There seemed to be no end to them and the debris was piling up around their feet.

"Hang on," said Jo. "I think this-"

The entire floor went dark and my HUD switched to night-vision in a heartbeat.

"Maybe not," she said. "Let's... try... this..."

"That's it!" cried Fara. "They've stopped."

"What about the turret?" I asked.

"That's still looking for us. Grant – take a shot with the zappy-gun, babe!"

Hiss. Thump.

"Turret is down," said Grant. "Can you do anything about them, Jo?"

"We need to start the cutters," I reminded them all. "We can handle a few turrets as long as the bots are deactivated."

Jo followed me back to the hole. She leapt down and I handed her the crates. In seconds the cutters were running again and as they burned away in the darkness, Fara approached me.

"What about seeing if we can open the doors from up there?" she suggested.

"No time," I replied. "And even if we could, it would mean running the length of each floor over and over again to move the data. This is the quickest way."

"Okay boss, just a suggestion."

274

"It was a good one," I said, smiling. "Thanks for bringing it to me."

"Carter?" called Mason.

"Yeah?"

"They're back – and this time they've brought friends."

The most intense part of the fighting now began. Baz returned to the surface just in time to face an onslaught of the best Corano could throw at us. Withdrawing all grunts to a safe distance, the next ground force consisted of enhanced humans; genetic freaks bristling with heavy weapons and armour supported by more spider-tanks and drones.

"What the hell has he been doing here?" cried Mason as both his weapon platforms glowed from the continual rain of fire being poured into their ranks. Shoulder cannons tracked drone after drone, blasting them out of the sky while Thor moved back and forth firing heavy-calibre burst-rounds into the sky and the infantry.

Mozzy was standing in a mountain of spent casings and discarded plasma cells, part of his shoulder plating blown off and his left leg damaged but still functioning. Baz hadn't yet taken a scratch but he'd long since abandoned the AP40 and was now behind an RR6 laser on a bipod, cutting through their ranks with sustained beams that threatened to detonate the cells inside it.

"HOLD THE LINE!" roared Mason as incoming fire tore at the plating of the T-105, removing one of the shoulder cannons which fell to the ground, almost landing on Mozzy's position.

"You'd fink we were stealin' the crown jewels or somefink the way they're comin' at us, sir," said Thor, flattening a squad who had managed to scale the side of the plateau with the flat of one giant hand. "Rude, it is. Very rude."

"Feel free to tell them that," said Baz. "I don't think they've quite got the message yet."

Beneath this carnage, we continued to cut through floor after floor, encountering only turrets and the occasional brave worker who attempted to stop us with small firearms. The time between cuts had decreased as we got quicker and quicker at dismantling, dropping and rebuilding between floors until, with only two left, one of the cutters exploded sending molten shards in all directions.

"Shit!" cried Jo. "Shit shit shit! We need the other crate."

"Where is it?" I asked.

"Back up top. The last thing I expected was a blowout."

"I'll go," said Fara. "I need to reload."

"Bring some back, okay?" said Grant. "I'm almost out too."

She nodded and, standing under the series of holes above her, fired her jet-pack and launched upwards in a risky manoeuvrer. My fear was unfounded however as she made a perfect landing on the top floor and vanished back up to the surface.

The other two cutters continued to rotate but their performance was obviously slower and far less efficient.

"Typical," snapped Jo. "Had to happen now, right? So close to the vault."

"Shit happens," said Grant. "Ask Baz's mum."

We all laughed then and the momentary humour eased the tension. I switched to Fara's HUD and saw she was on her way back already, dragging the crate behind her. When she reached the hole she lowered it over the edge and allowed it to fall in a perfect drop. I was ready at the bottom and I caught it effortlessly.

"Let's get this thing going," I said. I expected Fara to drop down too but suddenly there was firing directly above the hole and when I looked up she'd gone.

"Tango's in the perimeter!" she cried over the comms. "Baz — where the hell are you?"

"What's going on?" asked Grant. "What's happening?"

"Go!" I said and with that, she followed Fara's path up the shaft and vanished out of sight. More firing and I tried to shut it out from my mind. Jo was already unpacking the replacement cutter and I helped her fit it in place.

"Talk to me, Mason. What's the situation?" I called.

"Baz is down. Grant and Fara are holding back a squad that managed to get the drop on him. It's under control."

I looked at his vitals. He was in the amber levels.

"Does anyone have eyes on him?" I asked.

"He's alive," said Fara. "He's still fighting."

"What's his injury?"

"I LOST MY FUCKING LEG YOU PRICK!" screamed Baz over the comms, momentarily drowning out everyone else. "WHERE THE FUCK IS MY LEG???"

30

"Last one," said Jo as the glowing disc of floor dropped with a clang to the level below. "Then the vault."

We dismantled the cutters and prepared to drop. With my weapon raised I leapt down, followed by Jo but on this floor, no turret turned to aim at us. In fact, the entire décor was completely different and looked unfinished.

"Did we make a mistake?" she asked as we looked about us.

"I don't think so," I replied and walked a little further along, sweeping my weapon back and forth. The corridor was empty and there were no side doors, no other entrances or intersections to be seen. In utter darkness, the entire place looked deserted, like no one had ever been down there.

"Shall we carry on?" she asked.

"I guess so," I said and couldn't shake the strange feeling I was getting. Something felt wrong but I couldn't place it. "Let's get them going – I want to have a look around."

We assembled the cutters and set them off, aware now that the sounds of battle above had been reduced to distant thuds, like thunder somewhere far off. Only the constant feed from the comms kept us involved in what was going on.

As the blue light flickered up and down the corridor, Jo and I set off walking until we reached a dead end. Then, coming back on ourselves and passing the rig, we checked out the other side. There was a single door on the right and I tried the handle.

"Locked," I said. I raised my foot and kicked it in. The lock splintered apart and the door swung inwards. Somewhere far off a light came on. The chamber it illuminated was massive, perhaps a mirror size of the vault below, but the most startling thing was what it contained.

"Well that explains a whole lot," said Jo. "That's how he was able to do it."

"Yeah," I grinned. "I guess it's not expensive if you build the things yourself."

Wall to wall in every direction were birthing chambers for synthetic humanoids, the same ones that had been hunting us since Sargon City. There had to be thousands of them, all in the final stages of manufacture. Control units and programming centres ran the length of the production facility and several figures were already seated in the activation chairs. Corano had been the source all along, the mysterious producer of these artificial killers-for-hire and now here we were, about to blow the place to hell.

"I like a bargain," she said. "Two-for-one."

Behind us, we heard the floor drop with a sound similar to a gong being rung. Maybe it *was* a gong, signalling that phase four of the plan was about to begin.

We dropped into the vault, in awe of the sheer volume of data we found there. Even after the endless racks of Madam Sill's armoury I was stunned by the scope of Corano's operation, the effort that had to have gone into such a cache of information used to blackmail any and everyone he wished. It was hard not to feel a kind of moral superiority in destroying it once and for all.

"Wow," said Jo. "Who'd have thought so much was down here? And why the hell hasn't he used it to take over the galaxy or something?"

"I don't know," I said, unpacking the sniffer unit from the box. "That's a question that's going to give me sleepless nights. The synths. The data. The precious metals. None of this makes sense right now. Maybe it never will."

"Do you think it ties in with the fleet turning back from pursuing him all those years ago?" I shrugged.

"Right now I just don't know."

The unit went to work on a terminal nearby which it was designed to power independently and locate the data we needed. On Jo's HUD would be a location icon, telling us where to start.

"This way," she said and off we went down one of the long, dark aisles. Soon we were pulling tray after tray of data blocks, hard copy and tablets and stuffing them into bags we'd brought with us. These were then moved towards the shaft we'd made, ready to be zip-wired back to the surface.

"How's it going down there?" said Mason. "It's getting warm up here."

"Almost done," I said. "I'm going to start bringing up the bags shortly."

"I'll go," said Jo. "You get the rest of it and I'll assemble the zip-line.

"Okay," I replied. "Be careful."

Then she was gone, climbing up the holes one at a time using short bursts from her pack.

"Can you spare someone to watch Jo?" I asked.

"Grant here – I'm outside the vault door, I have eyes-on."

I sighed, feeling exhausted beyond anything I'd felt for a long time, maybe not since Mars. Alone in the vault, I felt the oppressive weight of all that data around me and as I dragged the last of the bags towards the shaft I saw one item flashing inside, highlighted by my HUD. Then I remembered – I'd programmed the sniffer to find the exact data block that mentioned Angel's involvement. That had to be it. I drew it out from the bag, not wanting to risk losing it and was about to stuff it into a compartment inside my armour when a thought compelled me to upload it and see. What if it wasn't what Aleksei could use? I had to be sure before we blew the place up that we got exactly what we needed to set her free.

I disconnected my audio feed from the network for a moment and played the data block directly into my HUD. It was a surveillance recording taken from somewhere onboard a ship, a conference room perhaps, and in view was a man in casual military fatigues and someone who I recognised immediately as Bourmont.

"I thought you said you were fine with all this, sir?" said the soldier, stood with his hands firmly behind his back as Bourmont paced up and down the room.

"I am, I am," said the General. "But you've yet to offer any assurance that the pilot will keep her mouth shut."

"That's her job, sir."

"Really? You don't think that half the bloody soldiers in this war are stone-cold patriots of Earth? Do you think that if they hear I'm about to hand vital details of the campaign over to the Martians that they'll understand the bigger picture?"

"Maybe if you weren't so underhanded you'd-"

"Don't bullshit me," he snapped back. "Are you that simple or did you study the subject in depth?"

More pacing. Bourmont came back into view and eyeballed the soldier.

"Angel. That right?"

"Yes sir," he replied.

"And you're sure she'll keep her mouth shut?"

"If you asked her directly you'd find that keeping her father alive is far more important than winning in Noctis."

"Her father?"

"He's a Martian, sir. Fighting for the other side. He just so happens to be stationed at Noctis. *Sir.*"

"You mean she knows?"

"She... *suspects*. She won't be any trouble. Sir. You have my word on that."

The image faded and the recording came to an end. For a moment I couldn't move.

She suspects.

That's what he'd said. Angel had had her suspicions about those missions all along but hadn't said anything. To spare her father. A Martian. I didn't really care where he came from but thousands of Earth Government soldiers, her brothers and sisters, had died in that failed assault. And she'd *suspected*?

I regained some composure and opened up the secure compartment in my armour, dropping the data block inside it. Then I remembered to reactivate my network audio and Jo was calling to me.

"Are you okay?" she asked. "I'm ready for the bags now."

"Yeah," I mumbled. "Be with you in a minute."

By now the fighting had reached the walls of the factory and if we didn't get off the planet soon we'd be overrun. As the bags were ferried to the mouth of the vault on the ground floor, Mason called in the drone.

"Two minutes," he told me. "Though maybe we don't have that long."

No sooner had he spoken than there was a deafening explosion that came from somewhere deep within the T-105. Mason found himself ejected backwards, slamming into Thor as the entire War Suit went up in flames. Mozzy ran to the western wall to avoid being crushed under the weapon platforms as they fell from the thing and crashed into the ground.

"Here we go," he cried as more mechanised units appeared in the openings in the wall. "End-game boys and girls!"

The thermo-nuke was armed and situated in the centre of the vault. I set the timer myself, giving us 10 minutes to be off the rock the moment the drone made it back to the ship. Then, after we'd used the zip-line to carry some of the wealth to the surface, I rode it straight back up and met Jo at the top.

"Ready to get out of here?" I asked.

"You're damn right I am," she said.

We came out into the middle of the firefight, seeing automated machines swarming at us from all directions. Gunfire poured into them but still they came, clambering over their fallen comrades with the cold regard of man-made automatons.

"Deploy the turrets!" cried Mason who began punching the big red buttons on each of the pods. Our last-stand pieces emerged from recesses in the structures and instantly began firing bursts of bright green plasma into the drones. Anyone standing near the pods did the same and soon the air was thick with more firepower than I'd ever seen in such a confined space.

I led Jo to one of the pods and helped her into the rig. Then, going back for Baz, I lifted him onto his one good leg and was glad to see that the wound was cauterised around the remaining armour and the suit's internal systems were maintaining his vitals.

"NO NO NO!" he cried. "You're not sending me back, not like this!"

"Sorry mate, that's the way it is."

"But my leg! I haven't found my-"

"'Ere it is, Mr Baz!" cried Thor, waving the thing still inside the casing of the exo-shell. "I'm sure they can-"

Something struck the giant bot and made him spin round. Suddenly Thor was beating it to death with Baz's own leg. I tried to say something but he spun back around, saw one of the enhanced freaks heading for Mason and beat him down too, following it to the ground with blow after blow. Baz was wailing now as what was once his beloved body part was now being used as a weapon of reasonably mass destruction. Thor felled three more freaks before he remembered just what it was in his hand and dropped it like it was alive. I guess it had been until that point.

"Oh my, I'm so sorry, Mr Baz," he tried to say but by then I'd stuffed him into the pod and activated the launch sequence. Later Baz

283

would claim that the last thing he saw was the leg falling into the gooey mess of a freak's intestines and it made him cry.

"How long on that drone?" I called to Mason as I watched Jo and Baz vanish out of the planet's atmosphere.

"Thirty seconds."

It came sweeping in, followed by a dozen rockets which screamed past, unable to lock-on. Its VTOL jets dropped it just outside the vault door and whilst the fire continued to pour in Grant and I slung the bags into the belly of the craft one after another.

"Faster!" cried Mason.

"I am!" I bellowed after him.

Shots bounced off my armour but I ignored them. Grant felt her shoulder buckle as a bolt of plasma hit it directly and her arm failed. With her only working limb, she dragged the last of the bags into the drone and lifted the ramp as I returned fire.

"Send it!" I cried and the jets burst into life, spun the drone around, and launched it almost directly up into the sky. All that remained were the stacks of metal we'd left for the colonists but most of those had taken fire as well.

"That's our song," said Mason. "Grant, Fara – into the pod. Get out of here."

Together they mounted the frame and I slammed it shut behind them, smashing the controls that launched it into the sky. I looked around. Two of the turrets were now inactive. Only Mozzy, Mason and I remained.

"Off you go buddy," I called to the former soldier. "You get the meat wagon I'm afraid."

"You guys are going last?" he called.

"That's the plan. Always has been," said Mason.

Mozzy ran for the pod where Columbine was still hanging by his suit. I closed the doors and hit the launch button.

"Get Sam into a medipod the moment you dock. Good luck, guys," he said and then was gone. Rockets were launched after them but none managed to get a lock-on.

"Carter – this is Jo. We're safe," she said. "Get your asses back-"

Silence. She didn't finish what she was saying and the comms had gone silent. I'd now moved to cover and was emptying one of the RR6 lasers into the doorway we'd come through at the start. Jo's clipped sentence distracted me from reloading and I ditched it, grabbing a massive rail cannon in both hands to cover Mason who was doing the same.

"Pull back to the pod," he said.

"You first," I called.

I looked at Thor who now bore a shield in one hand and a length of concrete-rebar in the other. He was smashing apart anything that came close to him.

"Will the other Thor remember this?" I asked him as he cried out after every kill. He said nothing, appearing to ignore me.

"Carter!" It was Jo, panic straining in her voice. "He didn't do it!"

"Do what?" I said.

"Clone his CPU. That's the only Thor down there. He didn't want to-"

"I wasn' gonna' do that to me poor little Jimmy," he said over the roar of the guns. "Wasn' gonna' take the risk, see."

"You idiot!" I bellowed at him. "There's no way we're leaving you behind you gigantic piece of shit! You should have known that!"

"I was hopin' you wouldn' find out, sirs," he said.

"Well that's that then," said Mason. "Game over, gentlemen. It's been a pleasure."

"You can still go, sirs," he tried to convince us but I think that even he realised his mistake then. He hadn't counted on our loyalty to him when he was considering his loyalty to Jimmy.

"It was going too well, I told you this," I said as the last of the turrets fell silent. "Stand down, guys. It's over."

I dropped the rail cannon and raised my arms over my head. Mason did the same. The firing gradually stopped.

"Sorry, mates," said Thor and his shield clanged to the ground, accidentally crushing three more drones. "I didn't fink that one through, did I?"

31

"What's going on down there?" cried Jo. "Why haven't you launched?"

We said nothing. I'd miss her, I thought to myself as the automated units backed away and flesh and blood soldiers came marching into the smouldering ruins of the factory. I'd lowered my arms when it was clear that they weren't going to destroy us right away and I took a slow step back to one of the empty crates and sat down. I was tired and, if I was honest, quite glad that the shooting had now stopped.

"This was your rule, right?" asked Mason, lowering his helmet. I did the same. "To be the last two on any mission?"

"Yeah, that sounds like something I'd say," I replied.

"You let Mozzy and Columbine get away, one of whom tried to kill us not so long ago, yet it's us two here now, about to die."

"Yep," I said. "That's about the size of it."

"You're a dick to best friends, you know that?"

"Blame him," I said and pointed to Thor. "He's the one who ruined the plan."

"He's right," said the 'bot, coming a few steps closer and making the ground shake. "It's all my fault, sirs."

"Can you at least do the last bit of the plan for us?" I asked. "Save us from potential torture and death?"

"What? The fingy inside me-"

"How about you just do it and keep quiet, okay?" snapped Mason. "I'd like my last few minutes to be filled with silence." He opened a compartment in his armour and took out a cigar. Lighting it he took a long pull and blew out a smoke ring.

"I could murder some ice cream right about now," I said. He nodded and flicked ash onto the floor.

"Rocky road," he said.

"I'd settle for chocolate. With a wafer and a flake." I sighed. "Look who's here."

"Who?" Mason gazed through the smoke. "Oh shit."

"Yeah. I thought that. At least we get to take him with us I suppose."

"I have to eject my CPU," whispered Thor. "To... you know? Make the boom-boom?"

"Great! He won't even be here at the end, he'll be inside a tube of blue goo. Thanks, Thor. Real nice of you, pal."

"Again, really sorry sirs. How long?"

"Give it five minutes," said Mason. "I sense a monologue coming on."

The soldiers snapped their weapons upwards as Thor's chest slid open and revealed the CPU ejection port. I stood, raised both my arms and edged towards him, slowly reaching to pull it out without taking my eyes off them.

"He bailed on us," I shouted to them. "I want to smash his brain before you kill us."

Corano came walking towards us, suited in an expensive looking custom exo-shell with the helmet down and a mane of silver hair framing what looked like Captain Argo's face minus the obvious scarring and lack of an eye. He stood a safe distance from the two of us, looked at the inactive Thor and grinned. It was straight, no lop-siding for him.

"Clearly," he said in that Argo family accent passed down from generation to generation. "You're not selling cookies door-to-door."

"We're collecting for the intergalactic Red Cross," I said, sitting back down. "Care to make a donation?"

"Looks like I already did. The drone, right?" I nodded. "What, two tonnes of my data?"

"More like three," said Mason. "Give or take a document here or there."

"And I guess the rest is about to go up in thermite-flames, right?"

"Not quite. More like radioactive flames. So to speak."

There was a rumble beneath our feet and dust spouted from the gaping maw of the vault like vomit.

"Scratch that. It just did," said Corano. "Well then. At least tell me what it was you wanted that you didn't feel you could just buy from me. That's what I do... *did*... I guess. Buy and SELL information. Surely all this equipment cost you a fair bit?"

I looked at Mason who was already looking at me. We were both thinking the same thing but I decided to take a more altruistic approach.

"This was an ethical plan," I said, realising that perhaps buying Angel's innocence hadn't even crossed our minds. "You know, blackmail and extortion doesn't sit well with heroes. Sort of."

"I see."

He looked around at the dead and dying, the wrecked equipment and levelled structure.

"You killed a few people. Seems a little *unethical* to me."

"They were bad guys," said Mason. "We checked."

"And that drop-pod? That was meant to be your escape, right?"

We both turned and looked at it, nodding.

"Yes. Well, if that idiot there had stuck to the plan and-" I stopped. "Well, you don't need the gritty details. Suffice it to say that all was going well until now."

"He's going to explode too, right? The robot?"

Again Mason and I looked at each other and shrugged.

"I guess so."

"Nuclear?" We nodded. "Noble."

"Stupid," I replied. "We weren't supposed to be here when it happened."

"Can you disarm it?" asked Corano. We shook our heads. "Can't or

289

won't?"

"He can't, I won't," I said. "Our options are limited."

"Hmm."

Silence. It was odd to have someone you've just robbed blind be so cordial but that was the problem with the Navy, once a Captain, always a Captain. He seemed to understand this and once he'd surveyed the carnage for himself he dismissed us both with a wave of his hand.

"Just go," he said in the end. "The damage is done. What can I say? You've filled the water with my blood and the sharks will start circling soon. I can no longer continue operations on this planet so I am now forced to leave." He turned to go and the soldiers did likewise, though with more haste now that they knew what was going to happen.

"Just like that?" I said. He nodded. "That's very kind of you if you don't mind me saying."

"They say you can take a Captain out of the Navy..." Here he looked at us with a cocked eyebrow and there was Argo again, looking back at us.

"Any messages for your brother or your nephew?" I asked.

"Did they have any for me?" he retorted.

"Your nephew doesn't know."

Corano shook his head slowly but smiled.

"We'll meet again, gentlemen. Be sure of that. Now get the hell off my planet."

We stepped into the pod, still expecting to be shot down in a hail of plasma fire, but when the thing actually launched with the three of us inside it we began to think that Corano was the likeable kind of villain.

"What the hell took you so long?" cried Jo as we emerged from the pod inside the loading bay of the *Hikane* and made for the bridge. She was still in her suit but it didn't stop her from throwing her arms

290

around me as we met. Kissing was impossible, of course, what with all that armour in the way.

"You wouldn't believe us if we told you," I said. "Let's get out of here before he changes his mind."

"Who?"

"Corano. Argo. Whoever he is now," said Mason.

On the bridge, we took our stations and Jo carried Thor's CPU back to the engine room to return him to his original frame. Baz had been sedated and both he and Columbine were in medipods. It looked like the artist might make it after all. Grant, Fara and Mozzy were extricating themselves from their damaged armour in the hold.

"Punching in a rendezvous course for the fleet," I said, tapping the controls. My eyes felt like they were filled with sand. "Maximum speed to the nearest gate. Any signs of pursuit?"

"None so far," said Mason. "Let's just-"

The alarm sirens began wailing and I lowered my face into my palm.

"Of course it was too good to be true," I said. "He knew he could chase us down the moment we left."

"That's what he meant – you can't take the Navy out of the Captain. He wants a victory on *his* terms, not ours."

"That sucks. You know we're not so good at this flying thing, right?"

"I've noticed. How many?" I asked. Mason consulted the display.

"Four Corsairs, six Corvettes. Outgunned, outnumbered."

I sighed. At least I could stay seated while we died this time; my legs were killing me.

"Okay, maximum speed out of here and activate the distress beacons. We'll run until they catch us and decide what to do then."

291

32

We managed twenty-six minutes before the lead vessel, identified as the *Wandering Star*, came to within weapon-range. They fired a burst of lancers which reduced our aft shields to less than 34% and launched several rockets to finish the job.

"Fire countermeasures," I said. "Then we'll turn and fight."

The rockets veered off and detonated on our starboard side at a safe distance. Then, as our engines decelerated, I banked to port and down, sweeping back and under the *Wandering Star*.

"Weapons firing," said Mason. "Multiple hits on their port and aft shields. Plasma-battery got through and smashed their inter-stellar comms relay. Lucky hit."

"More of the same, if you please," I said. I looked at the scanner. The other ships were closing now, seconds from joining the fight. I tapped my comms and hailed the *Wandering Star*.

"Well met, Captain Argo," I said. No response.

"Maybe he-" I raised my hand for silence as a message came through.

"Likewise, Carter. The *Hikane* is a damn fine vessel. I've never seen so deft a strike before. I'll enjoy taking her as a prize."

"See what you think of this one then," I replied and signed off. Then, scrolling through a narrow list of manoeuvrers, I selected one of his own from some forgotten battle before the Martian War.

"Did you get that?" I asked Mason. He nodded. "Alter the firing pattern and reverse the broadside, aft to fore."

The ship came back around and the joining vessels opened fire but the shots went wide. Being this close to their Captain's ship they didn't want to risk blowing us both up in the engagement.

"Six seconds," I said. "Five... four..."

"Locked on."

"Here we go..."

The *Hikane* rumbled as multiple hits were scored on our forward and starboard shields but my plan had worked; recognising his own tactical manoeuvrer Argo had altered his own firing pattern to match. But he hadn't expected the change in order and although he'd managed to hit us, the altered broadside had devastated his underbelly and was now venting plasma in his wake.

My comms chimed as we drew away, just beyond the range of the other ships.

"Go ahead, Jo," I said.

"The shields won't take another hit like that," she said. "Generators two and five are fried and the others are struggling to compensate."

"Understood," I said. Then another message came through and I grinned.

"Not bad, Carter. Not bad at all. Using my own tactics against me. I can still remember defeating the *Invincible* with that one back during the War. You appear to be giving me a history lesson."

"Perhaps you'd like another?" I asked.

"I'm afraid not," he replied. "You've nicely crippled my ship and so I am forced to withdraw. I've enjoyed this brief engagement but now it's time to end this. I'm willing to accept your surrender, should you offer it. You have ten minutes to decide."

He signed off and I looked at Mason who was smiling.

"It's not often that grunts get to kick the crap out of the Navy, is it?" he said.

"No, I guess not."

I looked at the scanner and saw the other ships moving to surround us. Corano, or Argo, was right – surrender or complete destruction were the only options left.

"What do you think?" I asked him.

"We're outside of Earth Gov. jurisdiction. If we surrender we're putting ourselves in his hands with no hope of fair treatment. The chances of them ransoming us back to TRIDENT are slim. We'd vanish into some prison and die a horrible death, eventually, or he'll just kill us outright. Either way, the outlook is grim."

"We fight then?"

"If they cripple the engines and board then it might not be a fight to the death. Self-destruct is the only sure way to deny them us and the data."

"Well, that sucks," I smiled. "And all of this will be for nothing because ten minutes isn't long enough for me to sift through the data and burst-send it to Mr. Beard on the *Agamemnon*."

"Game over, I guess."

We sat there for a moment or two in silence, staring at the display. I felt my heart sink and I thought of Jo, of her and Jimmy being captured. It wasn't a nice place to visit.

There was a chime from the console and I heard Mason tapping at the controls.

"What happened?" he suddenly cried and I looked up from the floor I'd been staring at.

"What?"

"One of the ships just vanished off the scanner," he said. "They're moving... Wait... That's another gone."

"What's happening?" I cried. "Switch to an external feed!"

Space appeared before us, and far away a battle was raging beyond our sight. I zoomed in as far as it could go and saw in the blink of an eye the *Pearl* bearing straight down on the Corvettes, all gun-ports blazing.

"Move to engage!" I said, tapping the NavCom. "We might just survive this day after all!"

The *Pearl* and her sister ship the *Achilles* had been able to pass through our scanners and cause a devastating amount of damage on

Corano's ships before they could even register it. In the first minute of the battle, three of the Corsairs were destroyed with all hands and two of the Corvettes were crippled. As the remaining ships began to withdraw, two more were destroyed by a withering amount of lancer fire from the *Achilles* and Corano's own ship, the *Wandering Star*, was now dead in the water.

We powered down once the battle had ended and waited for both ships to return. Eventually, Corano's entire force was destroyed and the crippled ships were taken by Marine contingents.

I looked at Mason who looked at me. There were no words. Once again, either by good luck or good fortune or by a power some people believe guided the lives of mankind, we'd been snatched out from the jaws of death and allowed to live. It was a sobering moment when we saw both titanic ships coming towards us, gun-ports wide open and the scars of recent battle damage marking their hulls like warpaint.

"Carter?" said a familiar voice over the comms. "Damage report."

"Shields took a beating but we're still in the air. We've got two seriously wounded, one of which needs treatment for an amputated leg," I said. "You've gone and messed up our ledger again. I'm in the red, Captain."

"Was your mission a success?" he asked.

"It was."

"Then perhaps the score will be even once again. We'll escort you back to the fleet and send our medical team to deal with the wounded."

"What about Corano?" I asked. "On the *Wandering Star*?"

"My Marines report that he was not aboard that ship."

"But I spoke to him," I cried. "He was piloting it!"

"The bridge was empty," said Sole. "Unless he somehow escaped us, I don't believe he was ever there to begin with."

I looked at Mason who scratched his chest without thinking. Had Corano been speaking remotely? Observing the battle from Remus IV somehow? Was that even possible? We were too far away for the level of technology required to remote-pilot such a ship. Or had he escaped somehow? I was tired and weary and I wanted to sleep. Answers to those questions would have to wait.

When our wounded had been taken on board the *Achilles* to be treated and we were safely on our way to rendezvous with the fleet, Mason and I sat on the bridge, exhausted.

"You should get some rest," he said to me. "It's been a long day."

"Likewise. The medic says that Baz was lucky – the cauterisation sealed his arteries and prevented bleed-out. They'll be able to graft an artificial leg once they've done surgery on the area."

"Alice won't be happy."

"I don't think Baz will be happy. It'll harm his image."

"Death would have harmed it more."

"True enough. Sam has lost a lot of blood but his suit managed to keep him alive long enough for the medics to work on repairing the damage. They're pretty sure he'll live but he won't be fighting again any time soon."

"That's good news. I really thought we'd lost him when they pulled him out of the vault."

"So did I."

Behind me, the door opened and Mason, seeing who it was, stood up. "I'm going to get my head down," he said. "I'll leave you to it."

"Wait," said Jo, stepping onto the bridge barefoot. "Have a drink with us, please."

He nodded and she placed three glasses on my console and poured. Then, raising them, we clinked and drank. I dimmed the lights a little and turned the viewscreen onto the stars before us.

"How's Thor?" asked Mason, leaning against the rail.

"He's with Jimmy," she replied, pouring him another. "I think he's feeling pretty guilty about the whole thing."

"So he should," I cried. "We nearly bought the farm, the land and the barn full of cows because of him. He's got some making up to do once we're home."

"He's..." She searched for the words. "He's like a teenager, trying to figure out where he fits in the 'gang'. Take it easy on him, guys."

We nodded. It made sense but most teenagers don't almost get you killed every time you did stuff together.

"So what happens now?" she asked. "Do we just sprint home or what?"

"We'll have to enjoy the pleasure of Captain Argo's company a little while longer," I said. "He'll want a full briefing on what happened now that it's open knowledge that his Uncle is actually alive and going under the name of Corano."

"And Angel?"

"The Intelligence officer aboard his ship should handle all that. You'd better speak to Aleksei and warn him," said Mason, pointing at me with his glass which he emptied again in one long gulp. I hadn't seen him drink that hard for a long time. Jo poured him another.

"Sit down before you fall down," I laughed and he did, dragging a chair over for Jo and one for himself. We sat around the main console and the drink flowed.

"To Columbine," I said and raised my glass. "And to Baz' leg – perhaps the most useful part of him I've ever seen."

"Here here!" said Mason. We clinked again and drank.

"How can you laugh about it?" cried Jo but with a guilty grin on her face. "The poor guy just-"

"But did you see Thor use it?" said Mason, warming to the subject of reliving the battle. "He took out two with one swing! Magnificent."

"Poor Baz," she said and began giggling to herself. "It was a pretty good weapon to be fair."

We laughed it out, feeling the tension drain away. When we began to give a blow-by-blow account of the entire battle, Jo went into full swing, gesturing wildly with her hands as she explained her part, how amazed she was with Grant and Fara just getting on with it and how the rounds had felt slamming into her armour. Mason and I chipped in too, filling in gaps we both had until the entire thing was out there, not in the shadows where monsters hid, but in the light where the pain and the trauma wouldn't get a chance to fester.

The bottle was soon empty and I pulled another from one of the storage lockers on the bridge. It was then that I remembered the data cube I'd taken from the vault, the one of Bourmont and the soldier. I saw my armour still standing near the door where I'd left it and Jo was looking at me.

"What's wrong?" she asked, seeing my expression.

"It's nothing," I lied. Then I shook my head. "I'm sorry, it's not *nothing*. It's something I-"

Walking towards the suit I thought it over again and decided that, just like we'd dragged the battle into the light, this too had to be brought out from the dark where it would rot quicker and with much more far-reaching consequences. I popped open the storage compartment and took out the cube.

"What's that?" asked Mason.

"The data-sniffer found it," I explained. "It relates directly to Angel."

"Shouldn't it be with the rest? Unless..." He stopped. "Play it."

I went over to the console and fitted it into the slot. Then, locking the bridge door, I played the recording, sitting back down with my glass. We watched. Nothing had changed since I'd last seen it, no fresh insights or misunderstandings. It was there in plain sight.

The recording stopped and the bridge fell silent.

"Holy shit," whispered Jo. "She-"

"She knew," said Mason. "She knew what Bourmont was going to do and she did nothing."

I let the thought sink in like it had done with me back in the vault. A few moments passed.

"I feel sick," said Jo. "How could-"

"We need to be careful," I said softly. "None of us here is guilt-free. Maybe Corano had a point – we didn't *need* to go to war with

298

him to get that data, there were other ways, but a lot of people died today because of us. And Sargon?" I looked at Mason who agreed with a slow nod. "And what about just recently? We watched a whole space-station filled with women and children vaporized because of our actions. Maybe we didn't directly kill them but without us, it wouldn't have happened, would it?"

"Good point," said Jo. "I've got my own demons too I guess."

"And we're talking about her *Father*. How far would you go to protect family? I know that if it were Alice or you or any of this team, I'd do a lot more killing to get you back."

"She couldn't have known beforehand what the full extent of the defeat at Noctis would have meant, not completely," said Mason. "Thousands upon thousands of soldiers died in that battle. She's had to live with that all her life since then."

I had a sudden thought and I began working the console, searching the history files for the casualty lists on both sides. It took a while but, in the end,, I found it.

"There," I said. "Not only has she lived with their deaths, but it was all for nothing. Her father died anyway."

"Poor girl," said Jo.

We sat back down and lapsed into silence, lost in our own thoughts. Then Mason spoke.

"Now what?" he asked. "What do we do with that?" He indicated the data cube. I shrugged.

"There was enough in the vault without it to set her free. This would, in fact, do the opposite. It would condemn her."

"You knew that, didn't you?" said Jo. "When you programmed the sniffer to look for data. It pulled out that cube because you'd set it to find anything that would convict her as well as set her free." I nodded. "Why?"

"I suspected something was wrong," I said. "She didn't try and defend herself when she was arrested, there was no attempt to prove her innocence. She went quietly, like someone loaded down with guilt

299

and who *wanted* to be punished."

"What are you going to do?" asked Mason.

"Don't you think she's been punished enough?" I said. "If I hand this over I'm basically saying that we're somehow morally superior to her. We've just done illegal arms deals with Madam Sill for fuck's sake! If we start cleaning house where do we stop? We'll all be inside by the end of the year."

"So what? We just forget about it?" asked Jo.

"No," I said. "I don't have the answer just yet. Maybe I won't until I see her face to face. Maybe I-" I shook my head. "Maybe I just need to see that guilt for myself just to make sure..." I trailed off but Jo's hand fell on my knee and she smiled.

"You'll know what to do," she said. "You always have done – when the time is right."

"I don't envy you," said Mason, getting to his feet a little unsteadily. "But as you say, I've got two fresh reasons to be grateful for merciful friends. None of us has a clean ledger. But I don't think I'd be able to get past that much blood. She has my pity either way. Goodnight, folks."

And with that he unlocked the bridge and left, heading for his room no doubt. That left Jo and me alone.

"He's a good man," she said, getting up out of her seat. "Scooch over." I did, making room for her to curl up beside me on the chair. I reclined a little and she snuggled up under my arm, resting her head on my chest.

"I can't believe you knew all that while the fighting was raging around you," she said. "How did you feel?"

"Stunned," I said. "But I carried on. There's time for thinking when the battle is over, not during it."

"I think I'll pass on any more of those," she laughed. "I've never been so scared and yet so alive in all my life. I'll stick to looking after the engines." She looked up and at me and grinned. "And you of course."

33

We made the rendezvous in good time and thanks to speedy repairs we were able to dock directly with the *Agamemnon* and walk safely onto her decks. Captain Argo met us there along with his book-ends and Mr. Beard.

"Do you even have a name?" I asked him as he saw the first of the data bags being off-loaded.

"Smith," he grinned. I shook my head.

"I'll stick with Mr. Beard." At this, he let out a bark of laughter and walked away like a man who knew he was about to count a hell of a lot of money.

"Carter," cried Argo. "I can honestly say I'm glad to see you on this occasion." That lop-sided grin, that scarred face. "So I hear you met the infamous Uncle?"

"He's better looking than you," I said. "But not as charming." He laughed too. It seemed that no matter how insulting I was people still laughed. I guessed that the data meant a lot more to him than the barbs of one of his minions.

"Will you join us for some supper?" he offered. I shook my head.

"Our business is done here," I said. "You have the data you asked for and now you have a bonus Uncle to send Christmas cards to. I think me and my crew have earned a swift return home, don't you?"

"Indeed," he said. "Indeed. I have one small request though, a personal one this time."

Suddenly he looked very sheepish and he wrung his hands nervously before him as he looked up and down the docking arm for listeners. His two lieutenants appeared to be looking the other way.

"Go on," I said.

"It recently came to my attention that... after a... *friendship* developed a little too much with one of my crew, said person might have illegitimately sired a-"

"Get to the point," I said. "It's been a really long couple of weeks and I'd like to be on my way, Captain."

"Of course," he said and flushed pink at the cheeks in spite of his scarred complexion. "This is-"

A young man dragging a case behind him appeared on the arm, ushered in like a performer from the stage wings. He was dressed in plain fatigues and had a haircut to match Mason's and he looked just as awkward as Argo did.

"This is Steven Riggs. Nice boy. Could do with a little experience and thinks that TRIDENT INC. is the kind of place he-"

When they were stood side-by-side I realised what he was saying. My jaw involuntarily dropped for an instant as I saw the same features I'd noticed in two other family members – but under a different name.

"Riggs?" I said. "You've got to be kidding me."

"I just thought-"

I shook my head. I didn't have the strength to argue and if, as I suspected, he was unfortunate to be the bastard-child of Captain Argo, maybe taking him away from his Father would be doing him a favour. No doubt Argo's wife and family back on Earth would prefer me to do that too.

"Paperwork," I snapped, holding out my hand. One of the stone-faced lieutenants marched towards me and passed me a sealed envelope. Hard copy. No traces. "Grant and Fara have also decided to apply for TRIDENT. Must be my lucky day. So many new-starters."

"Marvellous!" said Argo, retreating a few steps. I noticed that Riggs hadn't even looked at his father before walking past me to board the *Hikane*. "Then I bid you a safe journey. Angel will be free by the time you reach Titan 5, make no mistake."

"It won't be me making a mistake if she isn't," I said. I turned to go but stopped. Looking back, Argo was still smiling. "It was a big vault, Captain. A very big vault."

"I'm sure it was," he said but his words faltered a little on his lips.

"Bear that in mind from now on," I said with a smirk. "A *very* big vault."

The smile vanished. We understood each other. As the door sealed shut behind me I gave the order for us to depart. Steven Riggs was standing in the corridor looking lost when I caught up with him. He was hopelessly young, barely eighteen years old and I noticed a slight tremble in his hand when we shook.

"Thank you, sir," he said. "For the opportunity I mean."

"I said exactly that when I was recruited into the army," I said. "Then they shipped me off to Mars to put down a war of independence. Most of my friends were killed and those that survived were broken men and women. I barely made it out alive with that man," I pointed to Mason who stood with his arms folded at the top of the stairs. "We've just come back from a mission to save someone who is responsible for a hell of a lot of deaths by her inactions. Before that, we helped blow up a station full of women and children and before *that* we butchered a planet full of undead-civilians."

Riggs had gone pale and beneath our boots I felt the ship lurch out of the docking bay and into the cold void of space.

"Now come with me and let's say hello to the rest of the crew."

We walked down the corridors until we came to Baz's quarters. When the door opened, the injured man was just coming round from the pain meds. The timing couldn't be better.

"Baz – you're awake," I said and stood beside him. "How do you feel?"

"Awful," he groaned. "Who's he?"

"That's Riggs, he'll be joining us on the ride home. What did they tell you on the *Achilles*?"

"They said that the graft had been successful." He looked down at

303

the sheets covering him. "I can't feel anything though. Is that normal?"

Mason tutted and shook his head. I put my hand on Baz's shoulder and tried to look sympathetic.

"I've got some bad news, mate," I said. "Your body rejected the synthetic limb."

"What?" he cried. "How? They said-"

"It's true, pal," said Mason. "I'm sorry."

"This can't be happening," moaned Baz. "What will I do without my leg?"

"Don't worry," I soothed and patted him on the shoulder. "Thor stepped in. He knows all about robotic limbs and such. I hope you're happy with what he's come up with."

"You're shitting me!" he said. "Don't let him come near me!"

"It's a little too late for that," said Mason. "I think he's done a bloody good job if I'm honest."

"Show me!"

"Don't rush things, Baz. You need time to-"

The poor lad yanked off the sheet covering his leg and began screaming. Meanwhile, Mason and I tried not to laugh as he looked down on the chewed-up piece of wood taken from a table and fastened to the stump of his missing limb. Thor had done a good job of carving eyes and a nose into the bark and he'd even shod the end with a bit of an old tin can.

"Good as new, mate!" I said. "You'll be running around in no time."

Riggs looked at me, his face a picture of stunned confusion.

"Welcome to TRIDENT."

EPILOGUE

Alice hadn't exaggerated. The retreat was located deep in the western hills on Titan 5's less-industrial landmass that hadn't yet been given a name. Maybe nobody wanted to spoil the place with a name. Maybe no one wanted to claim direct ownership of it. I didn't understand that until the shuttle arrived and dropped us three clicks from the site. The pilot informed us that we'd have to walk the rest of the way.

"Orders from the boss," he said as we gathered our things. "Part of the experience."

Then he'd dusted off and we watched it go. When the air was quiet again, it finally hit us.

"Earth," I said. "It's like Earth."

"More specifically, England," said Mason. "Good choice, Alice," he said aloud. "Good choice."

The land was rich and green and filled with endless swathes of pine and birch that stretched off into the distance on a carpet of lush grassland. The sky was a crystal blue and the sun, now cresting the horizon, gave a comfortable warmth to the air which was thick with the scents of the forest I'd known from my youth. Bees danced between wildflowers and the hum of insects came and went in our ears.

I took a deep breath, shouldered my bag and took Jo's hand in my own. Thor and Jimmy were right behind us and Mason helped Baz as he got used to the genuine synthetic leg he now wore and not the one we'd made for him.

"Let's go," I said and began to walk.

As we reached the knot of low-rise buildings at the end of a marked path, we saw two figures waiting for us by a wooden gate in the fence. One was Alice who we hadn't seen since returning. The other was Angel.

"Welcome!" said my sister as she slid the latch open and let us in. She was in a summer dress of bright colours and her hair, normally styled for business, was free on her shoulders and made her look like a little girl again. "You made it!"

We hugged and I felt hot tears pricking my eyes. For the first time in a great many years, it actually felt like I'd come home. She buried her face in my shoulder and I felt her sob.

"You do it every time," she whispered. "Every time you come home it's like I nearly lost you."

"You nearly did," I said. "I love you, sis."

"I love you too, you big oaf!"

We broke away and she moved to embrace the others in turn. I looked at Angel who stood aside, waiting. Her hair was still the same shocking purple I'd last seen as she'd been carried away yet now it had grown in length and was tied back in a low pony. She wore loose pants and a shirt and yet on her feet were the same boots she always wore. She avoided looking directly at me until I was stood before her and then I noticed how red her eyes were.

"Carter," she said, her hands by her side. "Good to see you."

"Likewise," I replied. Then I moved in and wrapped my arms around her and she let go. The tears flowed onto my chest as her arms wrapped themselves tightly around me. When she reigned herself back in I put my arm around her shoulder and we walked away towards a glistening lake I could see just beyond the fence.

We sat by the water's edge and watched the waves gently lap the stony shore at our feet. We said nothing at first and she avoided looking at me again. I was okay with that. I sat side-on to her and began throwing stones into the water, watching them skitter across the reflection of the sky. I had a sudden desire to never leave that place ever again, never set foot inside an exo-shell or pick up a weapon.

306

That wasn't going to be a feeling I could entertain for too long.

"You suspected," she said eventually. I nodded. "Why?"

"I saw your face. You were resigned to it the moment they said your name at the platform. Like it was something you'd been waiting for all along."

"It was," she whispered and threw a stone herself. "I knew after the first mission I flew that Bourmont was handing information over to the Martians. It was obvious. When one of the team approached me afterwards I told him I was fine with it, that I had my own reasons. He wanted to know what they were so I told him."

"Your Father." She nodded.

"He wouldn't leave when the war started. He didn't agree with the whole thing but he felt that he had a duty to Mars to stay and fight. He didn't even mind when I told him I was joining up myself but on Earth's side. He said he was proud of me and that he hoped I did well for myself, maybe even go up the ladder."

"But?"

"But nothing. I sat back and flew those missions until I knew that the biggest one was about to happen. Noctis Labyrinthus. I still had a way of communicating with my Dad and when I found out that he'd be deployed to defend the mines I was glad – I knew that Bourmont's information would save him if the Martians knew about the attack. I just didn't-" She broke away and stifled a sob. "I didn't think that he'd be on the front-lines when the fighting started."

"And he died anyway," I said.

"Along with thousands of my comrades," she said. "Thousands, Carter. They butchered Earth forces and buried them under tonnes of rock and sand. And I did nothing. I weighed their lives against one. My dad. And in the end, I still lost it all."

"What happened when you realised that?" I asked.

"Do you want the truth?" she said, turning for the first time to look at me. I nodded. She took a moment to compose herself, then lifted both hands to her head and moved her fingers to the edges of her scalp. In a moment she was lifting back her hair in one piece, exposing plates of molanium covering places where her skull should have been. I felt my stomach clench in momentary revulsion.

"I blew my brains out," she said and returned her scalp back into place. When it was fitted, you couldn't see a single hair out of place. "But the pistol miss-fired. The round entered my head and blew off the top part of my skull and a lot of brain tissue that, ironically, turns out I didn't need. A medic found me and I was rushed into surgery. A few days later and I woke up to find that I'd been given top-market implants by an anonymous benefactor."

"Your Dad." She nodded.

"It was in his will. He'd made a lot of money in Martian mining before the war, that's how he'd bought his commission. In his will he'd added a clause that would cover any of my medical bills through third-party channels, keeping the whole thing a big secret. Ironic, right? I tried to save him, failed and managed to kill him anyway, so I try to kill myself and he saves me. No implant in the world will help me get my head around that."

I nodded and we returned to that silence again, knowing that we still hadn't moved forward. There was something left unsaid or undone or...

"I'm resigning," she said flatly. I nodded again.

"You know you won't be able to work in this trade again, don't you?" I said, trying to sound helpful and not threatening. "Even though you were found *not guilty* it'll stick. No one will hire you with that kind of suspicion hanging over you."

"I can't carry on like this," she said. "I can't bear to see your face every day knowing what I did."

"I don't excuse it, Angel, none of us do, but we *understand* it. You made a bad call, I'll give you that one. You have to bear the burden of those who died but so do all of us who do the kind of work we do. War, fighting, it's not clean and simple, it isn't a set of instructions you follow and get perfect results every time. People die. Some days the right people die and some days the wrong people die. Behind us is a team who knows deep down what that means and not one of them stands in judgement on you – only yourself."

She looked at me then and I could see in her eyes that the last thing she wanted to do was go. She wanted something from me that maybe I could never give her. Absolution? Forgiveness? I didn't know. Instead, I reached into my pocket and handed her the data cube.

"What's this?" she asked.

"The only proof that you were involved," I said.

"But I-"

"Aleksei got what he needed to get you off the charges. I dug this one out myself. I guess it means we're all involved in what you did now. I could be executed as a traitor just for holding it."

I stood up and helped her onto her feet. She stared at the cube and then at me.

"You have a choice here," I said. "You can keep that and know that with it you could send us all to the block. There's enough there to convict you, me, Baz, Mason and the others. I'm giving that power to you.

"Or you can take it, the last piece of that guilt-pie you're feasting on and hurl it into that lake along with all the pain and suffering you're putting on yourself. Then we can go back up the hill and go forward from here together. The choice is yours."

She held the block in both hands and sniffed some of the tears back. Then, nodding to herself as if reaching a conclusion she knew was the right one, she began to crush the thing between her palms until it was nothing more than a handful of fragments. Turning, she hurled the rest into the water and let out a pain-soaked scream that followed it all the way down into the deep.

I began to make my way back up the hill to where the others were waiting.

"Is she going to be okay?" asked Mason. I shrugged.

"Probably about as much as the rest of us are." Mason slapped me hard on the back and laughed.

"Alice brought cake," he said. "And ice cream."

Printed in Great Britain
by Amazon